INSUFFICIENT MATING MATERIAL!

"*Insufficient Mating Material* is an outstanding sequel to *Forced Mate*! Cherry skillfully combines mystery, romance, and humor with a fast-paced science fiction adventure. I couldn't put it down!"
—Jean Cooper, Fallen Angel Reviews

"Rowena Cherry is one of the best subgenre writers due to her skill at placing the heroic characters in impossible scenarios."
—Harriet Klausner, *Affaire de Coeur*

"For those...who...enjoyed *Forced Mate*, the long-awaited story about Jason is finally here, and what a story it is!"
—Kathy Boswell, The Best Reviews, Vice President of Reviewers International Organization

"The rare sequel that betters the original! Djetthro-Jason's story is awesome. Worth waiting for."
—Brenda Clark, MystiqueBooks.com

"A powerful romance laced with devastating... secrets, treachery and a sizzling passion hot enough to singe your fingers as you turn the pages.
—Romance Junkies

"What a fantastic read! A book full of possibilities, humor, intrigue and action. I loved it!"
—Les Stroud, aka "Survivorman"

MORE RAVES FOR ROWENA CHERRY!

"I really like Cherry's writing; it is...fast moving, with active imagery, and it challenges the reader."
—Jean Cooper, Fallen Angel Reviews

FORCED MATE

"A fantastically original page-turner!"
—Susan Grant, *New York Times* bestselling author of *The Scarlet Empress*

"An intriguing story that has lingered in my memory."
—Kathleen Nance, bestselling author of *Day of Fire*

"Wow! What a book!"
—Kathy Boswell, The Best Reviews

"*Forced Mate* is a terrific science fiction tale."
—Harriet Klausner, Simegen.com

"*Forced Mate* absolutely ROCKS!"
—Brenda Thatcher, EscapeToRomance

"You will laugh until it hurts."
—Diane Tugman, The Romance Studio

"This is fantasy on a mega-scale."
—Celia Merenyi, A Romance Review

"*Forced Mate* is one of the best science fiction romances I've read all year."
—Nicole Hulst, romancejunkies.com

"Highly recommended. *Forced Mate* is something any fan of futuristic romance will enjoy."
—Shelina Emery, MyShelf.com

A TRICKY EXPERIMENT

"Maybe, sweetheart, we should have sex to prove to you that you can and will enjoy it."

"I enjoyed it once. I am very happy with my memories. I don't need you or your experiment to prove anything," she said stiffly.

"Once?" He raised an eyebrow. His lips twitched. Too late, Martia-Djulia realized that she had just contradicted one of her earlier statements.

"The Aim of the Experiment is to discover whether or not we are sexually compatible," Djetth said loftily. She suspected that he was amusing himself by parodying a formal checklist. "Method: to have mind-blowing recreational sex using positions and techniques that mitigate or avoid unfortunate consequences. Expected result..."

"What unfortunate consequences?"

"Insects in your hair?" he teased. "Sand in your baby box. A baby. Infection. Injury. Legal consummation of a Mating we might not want."

His gaze flickered. Martia-Djulia had the impression that his list was deliberately ordered.

"Injury to whom?" she asked, ignoring the glossed-over "baby."

"I've wondered why you haven't blasted me backward onto my butt since our Mating Day. I've certainly deserved it."

"Yes, you have!" she agreed heatedly.

Other *Love Spell* books by Rowena Cherry:

FORCED MATE

INSUFFICIENT MATING MATERIAL

ROWENA CHERRY

LOVE SPELL

NEW YORK CITY

LOVE SPELL®

February 2007

Published by

Dorchester Publishing Co., Inc.
200 Madison Avenue
New York, NY 10016

ISBN 0-505-52711-1

Printed in the United States of America.

ACKNOWLEDGMENTS

I would like to acknowledge the winner of the Bioluminescent tattoo contest—Brenda Clark—who correctly guessed what secret symbol Djetth kept hidden.

I would like to thank the following for their help with verisimilitude:

Survival consulting—Les Stroud, aka Survivorman
Rock music consulting—Geoff Nicholls of Black Sabbath
Gym scene advice—C. J. Hollenbach
Atmosphere/plant life research—Jen Lassiter
Tarot reading—Christine D'Allaird (and others who prefer to remain anonymous)
Psychic research—Debbora Wiles (and others who prefer to remain anonymous)
Dynamics of a plane crash on water—pilot and author Susan Grant

I would also like to thank Scott Merrill (www.skippy.net) for allowing me the license to use his copyrighted photographs of Stonehenge, used in pre-promotions.

Finally, I would like to thank my editor, Alicia Condon, for believing in me—twice!

Dear Reader,

What Royal Family doesn't have a Family Tree?

In 1995, I painted myself into a corner by publishing Who (officially) has sex with Whom; who fathered whom—as far as the Royal Family was prepared to divulge—and when.

Did you notice that I left myself a loophole? My Royal characters don't necessarily tell the truth, and there isn't a free press in the Tigron Empire.

Not knowing the rules that considerate authors follow, I also set in stone a mistake or two. If I could turn back time, perhaps I wouldn't give all members of the Royal Family names beginning with Dj-, the Royal Prefix, with a silent D.

At least, when they have six or seven names (like European Royals), they don't have to use their Djinn name! Tarrat-Arragon won't use Djustin or Djohn (or both) until he becomes Emperor. Djarrhett (pronounced Jarret) can be 'Rhett.

There's a simplified Family Tree at the back of this book, and every time I thought you might like to be reminded that it's there, I put an asterisk by words such as "Genealogy," "Who's Who," or "Family Tree."

For those who would like a more comprehensive overview, an interactive Djinn Family Tree is up on my Web site: www.rowenacherry.com/familytree.

Just don't expect to see which alien died of the mumps.

—Rowena Cherry

Part One

Insult and Injury

EARTH DATE EQUIVALENT: JUNE 30, 1994

CHAPTER ONE

Tigron Empire of the Djinn
ARK IMPERIAL, Operating Theater

Damn them! Prince Djetthro-Jason eyed the masked males and the unpleasant array of implements they were preparing to use on him.

I haven't told them everything, and I'm not about to. No way am I going to invite anyone to take a laser to my privates. Ahhh, Fewmet!

The "battlefield analgesia" was wearing off. During the duel that he'd begun as Commander Jason and ended—defeated—as Prince Djetthro-Jason, he'd felt almost no pain despite the damage Tarrant-Arragon had inflicted.

Now, his massively bruised thigh throbbed heavily, his neck muscles ached, and his jaw . . . it hurt even to think about his jaw. Perhaps worse—but less so by the moment—was the damage to his alpha-male machismo as he lay strapped down, stark naked, in his enemy's operating theater, preparing his mind for surgery without anesthetic. Also for "the fate worse than death" which was to come.

If Tarrant-Arragon had observed Great Djinn tradition, the duel they'd fought less than an hour ago ought to have been to the death.

Why hadn't Tarrant-Arragon killed him then and there? To the victor went the Empire, the *Ark Imperial*, and gods-Right to any female he wanted . . . and they both wanted the same female.

Damn it! Even if he *wanted to stop, I should've fought on after he'd crippled my leg and shattered my bloody jaw. Why didn't I? What's left for me?*

What indeed?

I'll be the Djinn equivalent of a broken thoroughbred stallion put out to stud. It's fairly obvious why Tarrant-Arragon made an excuse not to finish me off.

The Great Djinn were nearly extinct. In twenty years' time, Tarrant-Arragon's and Djinni-vera's children would need true-Djinn mates, all entitled to the silent D- prefix to their royal Djinn names. That's why!

When the "fate worse than death" had been spelled out, it had been sheer bravado to mumble that he *wanted* to marry Princess Martia-Djulia.

Maybe I do. Maybe I don't.

It hurt how much he still wanted Djinni-vera, who'd been the last Djinn virgin in all the Communicating Worlds, and betrothed to be his, until Tarrant-Arragon abducted her by force and took her virginity.

What consolation would it be to have Tarrant-Arragon's sexy, fashionista bitch of a sister in his power and in his bed instead?

Djetth winced at the savagery of his thoughts about Martia-Djulia. Shards of pain shot along his broken jawline.

"Well, Djetthro-*Jason*, are you ready to be carved up for your new identity and your new life as my little sister's glorified love slave?"

From somewhere out of Djetth's line of sight, Tarrant-Arragon taunted him, stressing the part of Djetth's real name that he'd used until his cover as "Commander Jason" was blown and he was overpowered and arrested.

Djetth did not turn his head. The pain in his face and head was intolerable enough without moving.

"Ahhh, I do believe that Our Imperial surgeons are ready to do away with that distinctive jagged scar on your cheek," Tarrant-Arragon crooned. "And screw together your jaw."

What else might they do while he was under the laser and the knife? While his face was open, might they carve out a sensory gland or two? Implant a tracking device? Use his broken jaw as an excuse to weld a mask over his head?

Prince Djetthro-Jason would be a latter-day "Man in the Iron Mask" if they realized how closely he resembled Crown Prince Tarrant-Arragon. Which he would, without his scars, his colorful contact lenses and his long, blond-dyed hair.

Djetth glanced at the treacherous, turncoat 'Rhett, who'd been his bloody useless "second" at the duel, and who was still hanging around.

What for? Damn him. 'Rhett was too much the intergalactic statesman for his own—or anyone else's—good.

If the patient lost consciousness, Tarrant-Arragon could decide that the chances for galactic peace would be better if Djetthro-Jason were neutered . . . one way or another. Given the secrets 'Rhett knew, 'Rhett might agree.

"No—" Djetth groaned with the unexpected agony of trying to speak. He wanted to refuse anesthetic again. How he wished there was somebody present whom he could trust!

A door swished open.

"Does he have to be in such pain?" The cause of all the trouble spoke from the doorway. She sounded on edge, as if she felt his pain telepathically.

Djinni-vera! No longer *his* Djinni. By conquest, by the

irrevocable exchange of vows, and finally by her own choice, she was Tarrant-Arragon's.

By All the Lechers of Antiquity, how he loved her! At that moment. For coming. Mentally Djetth qualified his thoughts. Djinni-vera might not love him now, but she was honorable to the core. Tarrant-Arragon wouldn't dare do anything dastardly in front of her.

As she glided to his surgical table, Djetth looked at her wildly, helplessly, with mute appeal, hoping that she would read his mind and aid him this one last time.

Djinni-vera's amethyst eyes widened as if she had Heard him and understood. Her gaze averted, she reached out and dropped a gauzy white cloth of some sort over his monstrously inappropriate erection.

To others, her action might have looked like public modesty on her part. Djetth assumed that Djinni had read the part of his mind that was worrying about the striking tattoo that only showed up in the dark or when he was suitably excited.

Thank you! he thought. *Please help me. Stay.*

She nodded, and took his fettered hand with her undamaged left. "You've been macho about this too long, J-J. Why won't you let them put you to sleep?"

"Careful, my love," Tarrant-Arragon said, moving possessively to her side. "You can never call him J-J again. Nor may you use any of his other damned traitor's aliases. Not J-J, not Commander Jason. Traitors cannot be seen to survive their attempts on my life. Commander Jason is officially dead, and everyone—including Martia-Djulia—must believe it. From this day forward, he's Prince Djetthro-Jason."

"What a mouthful . . ." Djinni began; then her changing expression told him that she must have read a thought-pun he couldn't resist. "Djetth!"

She frowned sternly.

"I know you Great Djinn males can't help thinking of

sex all the time. But it's not helpful, Djetth. As long as you have your saturniid gland, you're dangerous."

Not dangerous to you, kid. You won't ovulate while you're pregnant, and probably not for a while after that, he thought back at her.

Her mouth twisted in a wry smile.

"You'd be safer if you let them remove it."

Some aspects of Royal Djinn maleness one would rather die than surrender, he rejoined, hoping she would not read his darker thoughts.

"Martia-Djulia would be better off if you couldn't have the rut-rage again, too. . . ." As she spoke, Djinni tossed her head as if shaking off a bothersome fly.

Djetth wondered if Djinni had unexpectedly Channeled someone else's reasoning. Djinni couldn't possibly know how savagely Martia-Djulia liked to be served in bed.

"I saw Palace footage of you having the rut-rage with Martia-Djulia." The little mind-reader's voice rose in protest at the thought he hadn't meant her to sense.

You saw? You saw what, exactly? His thought question was a ploy to distract her from thinking about the rut-rage, but no sooner had he asked than he dreaded how detailed her reply might be.

"What you might expect, given that the camera was behind a mirrored ceiling, and you were on top," she retorted, keeping his tattoo a secret. "Tarrant-Arragon fast-forwarded you, because you went at it so long."

"Not that long," Tarrant-Arragon murmured maliciously, probably to remind them that he was listening to Djinni's half of the conversation.

"Long enough," Djinni said. "Djetth, you might already be a father."

"Granted, that is remotely possible," Tarrant-Arragon sneered while appearing to examine a wicked-looking lancet. "Let's hope you weren't *that* thorough, Djetthro-Jason, or your firstborn would have to be—and remain—a bastard. Unfortunately, my slack-wit of a sister can't keep a secret. If Martia-Djulia thinks Commander Jason got her pregnant, the rumor will be all over Court before we get home, and before she hears that her lover is dead."

Djetth felt an inexplicable distress at the idea that he could never claim this theoretically possible child as his own.

"Shall we begin?" Tarrant-Arragon's too perceptive eyes ranged over Djetth's body, lingering for an instant on the cloth covering his penis. Not for the first time in his life, Djetth thanked the Great Originator that Tarrant-Arragon had lost the power to read minds.

"I am staying with him," Djinni announced, gripping his hand tightly.

Djetth was careful not to wrap his fingers around hers or to respond to Djinni's comforting touch in any discernible way. Touching the Heir Apparent's Mate was yet another act of high treason punishable by death.

"Very well, my love. You may stay as long as you keep your gaze on his face." Tarrant-Arragon's lips curled into a sneer. He had certainly noticed the hand-holding.

"Djetthro-Jason, I'll ask you for the last time: Have you declared every identifying mark on your body that my sister might recognize? Every scar . . . ?"

"Yes!" Djetth snarled back, one eye on Djinni to see whether her face betrayed his lie.

Head turned, distracted by Djinni and the explosion of pain in his face from speaking aloud, Djetth forgot that his neck was exposed where 'Rhett could reach it.

He felt the cold, numbing touch of 'Rhett's fingers on his most vital acupressure point, strove to turn his head, and couldn't.

'Rhett is using Djinncraft to put me to sleep! Damn 'Rhett and his secret agendas!

The growing paralysis had not yet reached Djetth's eyes. As his vision dimmed, his desperate gaze met the cool green, inscrutable eyes of his bastard cousin and half-brother, 'Rhett.

He'd be lucky to wake up with a new face, a new and dangerous identity. If he woke up.

CHAPTER TWO

ARK IMPERIAL, Imperial Suite

Ohhh, Jason. You're so big! Ohhh. So healthy! Ohhh! Martia-Djulia's softly sighed grunts came more often and more forcefully in response to her lover's faster, and increasingly savage, thrusts.

Sex-flushed and well and truly tumbled, Martia-Djulia moved her face restlessly from side to side. A glossy, dampened strand of her silvery hair caught in her open-smiling mouth unnoticed.

Martia-Djulia braced her pale, beautifully cared-for hands on Commander Jason's tanned, broad shoulders, as if she wanted to push him back down her body, to stop him from driving quite so hard and so deeply into her.

He kept it up.

"What am I not seeing?" Tarrant-Arragon mused, thoughtfully tapping his pursed lips with two fingers. "There must be something remarkable about this particular sex marathon."

He rewound the retrieved back-up fragment of footage,

and frowned as he prepared to play it in the slowest of slow motion.

It was only a fragment. Possibly it was not the *right* fragment. It was the merest chance that it had not been deleted.

Now, Martia-Djulia arched her back, fully extended, her arms still above her head but relaxing away from the bed-headwall.

From what Tarrant-Arragon could observe—since Commander Jason was busy with Martia-Djulia's abundant, corset-enhanced cleavage, and his long blond hair was in the way—Martia-Djulia's cheeks, neck and chest looked flushed, her bliss-shuttered, blue eyes sparkled, and there was a sly smile on her love-swollen lips.

Ahhh, yes. This was the beginning. Unnoticed by Jason, she must have just reached for the secret panel on the wall and had started the surveillance recording.

This was a few heartbeats after Martia-Djulia had decided that she wanted this long-lasting male in her bed forever.

It was quite a damning moment.

Martia-Djulia would be mortified if anyone saw it and realized that—at that moment—she had intended to use blackmail to force Commander Jason to become her Mate.

"Tarrant-Arragon! What are you watching?" demanded his own dear little Mate in her native Earthling English. She was standing in the bedroom doorway, where she should have been taking an overdue and much-needed nap, given her pregnancy.

"Surveillance footage," he said.

"Of a sex marathon?" Djinni queried. It was too late to switch programs. Djinni's half-Djinn senses were as good if not better than any Great Djinn's.

"Martia-Djulia and Djetth," he admitted. "Do you want to watch it with me?"

Tarrant-Arragon deliberately ended on a hopeful note. Djinni was not too far along for leisurely, consensual lovemaking.

If she were in the mood, he had no objection to playing the voyeur, although—in truth—the large, naked male on top was not a natural object of interest for a royal blue-blooded Great Djinn. Nor was his excessively curvy sister.

"Is that the footage you showed me shortly after you'd tricked me into saying the Imperial Mating vows, and all the Communicating Worlds thought you were busy deflowering me?" Her voice vibrated with indignation.

Tarrant-Arragon grinned impenitently.

"At that time, my love, you were too upset to enjoy being ravished repeatedly. You'd only just discovered my true and terrible identity. I hoped some mild pornography would divert you. I admit that I miscalculated. How was I to know that you'd recognize the male in bed with my sister as your jilted fiancé?"

Djinni tossed her unusual, red-brown hair.

"You told me that you'd destroyed all that footage at Martia-Djulia's request," she accused him. Her memory was flawless. "I distinctly remember you complaining more than once that you couldn't retrieve any trace of J-J, or Djetth as we now call him."

"I honestly thought I had, my love."

She raised a skeptical eyebrow, the way all Djinn did.

"Do you remember . . . ahhh, you wouldn't because you fell asleep exhausted from crying after the Saurian Dragon unfairly cursed you for daring to be seduced by me."

Djinni had come near enough to be grabbed and scooped into his lap. He did so, and held her close, with his interlocked hands cradling her belly where his heir grew a fraction of a finger-joint every day.

"While you slept that day, I caught Martia-Djulia in

my office attempting to erase the footage. She had already made an incompetent start. What Martia-Djulia didn't know is that whenever someone who doesn't know my personal code tries to erase anything on my systems, it backs up to a new file here, on the *Ark Imperial*."

"Only if the *Ark Imperial* is in range, I suppose?"

"Of course," he agreed.

If only he had known then what he knew now, he wouldn't have been so quick to enter his code to stop whatever damage his wayward sister had initiated. By doing so, he'd halted the automatic back-up.

However, the fragment had been preserved, and it had not occurred to him to bother looking for it until Djinni blurted out a very odd non sequitur as they were preparing to operate on Djetth.

"Why are you looking at it now?" his aggressively suspicious little mate demanded.

The percentages were not in his favor if he were to lie to his mind-reading mate, especially since he had recently vowed never to lie to her again.

"My curiosity was fired by something you said to Djetth, my love."

She blushed adorably. Pale sheet lightning flickered in the deep violet of her telltale eyes. Djinni was afraid he'd discover a secret from the footage.

Tarrant-Arragon spoke so many languages fluently that it had not until now registered as significant that Djinni had always conversed in English with Djetth.

He filed that thought for later, and reported what had piqued his interest in the operating theater.

"You told him, 'I saw footage of you having the rut-rage . . .' Then you made a mysterious, ungrammatical leap to 'what you might expect, given that the camera was behind the mirrored ceiling, and that you were on top. Tarrant-Arragon fast-forwarded you. . . .' "

The Tiger Princes of Tarrant-Arragon's generation

had lost the power to read minds, but he could tell when Djinni was about to be economical with the truth. She squirmed on his lap.

"Is there any doubt in your mind, little love, that Djetth was having the rut-rage?"

He could have asked her whether she'd read Djetth's mind, and whether there was any doubt in Djetth's mind. He could have asked what Djetth was afraid might be exposed on the footage.

There were many skills Tarrant-Arragon lacked; finesse was not one of them.

"Noooo," Djinni said slowly, probably truthfully. "I do think Djetth had the rut-rage, but it must have been mild, or he wouldn't have left Martia-Djulia's bed after only two days. He wouldn't have tried to rescue me from you, even if he was convinced that rescuing me was the right and honorable thing to do. His encounter with Martia-Djulia left him very confused, frustrated and angry, you know."

The same thoughts had occurred to Tarrant-Arragon.

"I've heard you make disparaging comments about your sister before," Djinni added as if thinking aloud. "Maybe her fertility pheromones are dormant, in a sort of Sleeping Beauty mode. Maybe . . ." Djinni yawned and patted his cheek with her good hand. "I think I'll go back to bed."

Her ungrammatical jump to camera angles and Djetth's sexually dominant position had been skirted. However, the fragment and its mystery could wait.

Tarrant-Arragon got up and followed Djinni to the bedroom. He had a grammatical ambiguity of his own to put to her.

"My love, shall I join with you?"

CHAPTER THREE

ARK IMPERIAL, Recovery Room

'Rhett had half expected to hear stealthy footsteps. He did not open his heavy-lidded eyes, or uncross his ankles under the morgue-like hospital bed. He gave no sign that he had not nodded off in the pull-out, segmented chair-bed at Djetth's bedside.

He flared his nostrils slightly, and breathed in the approaching cocktail of stale Old Spice men's grooming products, lungs recovering slowly from half a human lifetime of tobacco use, and the nervous tang of an Englishman off his world and not quite at ease among gods and aliens.

What was Grievous doing here?

If Tarrant-Arragon had sent his "Earthways Advisor" to quietly smother Djetth while he was unconscious, Grievous would be the one to die.

Keeping his arms folded, 'Rhett slipped his right hand inside the front opening of the white Saurian Ambassador's uniform that he wore night and day. He curled his fingers around the hidden handle of a surgical knife that he'd palmed during the organized chaos of Djetth's operations.

"You got yours, then!" Grievous muttered vindictively from the open doorway.

'Rhett sat very still in his chair. So far, it would seem, Grievous hadn't noticed that Djetth was not alone.

"Serves you right. You bloody, dirty-fighting bastard, I hope it hurts."

'Rhett understood Grievous's outrage. Djetth had not fought the duel with Tarrant-Arragon according to Anglo-American notions of good sportsmanship.

"As if Princess Djinni-vera didn't have enough to contend with . . . and I dare say I don't know the half of it!"

Grievous was right. He didn't know the whole story. Few did.

Because he had been a failed assassin's escort, 'Rhett knew how Djinni's long-preserved, fertile fragrance had been smuggled into the Imperial Palace on a sterile decoy's body in order to rut-enrage, disgrace and destroy Tarrant-Arragon.

The plot had misfired because Tarrant-Arragon's greatest enemy, the Saurian Dragon, hadn't known that the Occasion of State was to be Tarrant-Arragon's formal Mating, or that the Mate-to-be-Taken would be Djinni-vera herself.

Consequently, when Tarrant-Arragon sniffed a maddening whiff of fertile-female pheromones, he assumed that the source was Djinni.

It was Djinni who was carried off to the Imperial bed to bear the violence of His High-and-Mightiness's sudden, rut-raged lust. Since Imperial, allegedly virgin brides were traditionally treated to rough and semi-public sex, there was no scandal. Everyone thoroughly approved of Tarrant-Arragon's depraved behavior.

Ironically, the malicious assassin had planted a small

dose of Djinni's ovulation pheromones on Tarrant-Arragon's sister, the Princess Martia-Djulia.

No one had foreseen that Djetth would be in the Tigron Imperial star space, let alone at the Virgins' Ball, or that the assassin's unauthorized subplot would set Djetth's hormones to raging.

It was quite possible that Djetth had made love to Djinni-vera's scent on Martia-Djulia's generous body. Luckily, Martia-Djulia had been willing!

"My boss wants you out of the way," Grievous continued, moving to the foot of Djetth's bed.

'Rhett opened his eyes a slit, to be absolutely sure that Grievous was doing nothing more deadly than standing at a distance from Djetth's bed and muttering.

Grievous had something behind his back.

'Rhett balanced the small, sharp knife in his hand. In Tigron gravity aboard the *Ark Imperial*, a hardworking, human jugular vein was a big enough target.

Then he saw what Grievous held.

Djetth was aware of a threat.

He could hear a gruff voice like the rumbling of distant thunder. Sounds were muffled, like falling snow. There was cottony stuff over his ears.

His eyes wouldn't open, but he knew someone was in his room.

Drifting in and out of consciousness made him all too vulnerable, damn it. Even when he was half awake, he couldn't force his limbs to move. The pain was tolerable. It was no worse than a full-body hangover. That was the drugs. Fewmet, he was as helpless as a baby.

He heard a closer sound, a sharply indrawn breath. Slack-damn, he couldn't see, couldn't turn his head.

Oh, shit, there were two of them.

"Prince Djarrhett! Didn't see you, Sir. Sorry to disturb you."

Neck bones clicked. The surprised one must have turned his head.

"You may call me 'Rhett. I've no plans to use my rank to save a world—or a life—without bloodshed tonight."

So 'Rhett was there. Double-talking bastard! So, he had no plans to *not* shed blood? Whose blood *was* he planning to shed tonight? What was he up to? Fratricide, perhaps?

Someone with human body odor was too damned close to his bloody bed. And the insensitive bastard was bending closer.

"Those aren't nail clippers on that cord around his neck, are they, Sir?"

Grievous! Only Tarrant-Arragon's right-hand man went around calling Princes and title-stealing impostors "Sir." What was Grievous up to?

"They're wire cutters, Grievous. I imagine there is a limit to how advanced medicine can be. Djetth's broken jaw is not only braced by the half-mask, but wired shut. If he had to vomit, the wires would have to be cut immediately, or he'd die."

Bloody hellfire!

"That's bad, Sir."

Too damned right.

"Giving Djetth the means to get himself chunk-blowing drunk could also be fatal."

Good of you to say so, 'Rhett. That's exactly the sort of thing I want my enemies and future in-laws to know. Perhaps you'd like to point out that an involuntary mouthful or two of wine could choke me while I'm in this helpless state? Grievous might not have thought of that. Slackness damn you, 'Rhett!

"He'll have what you'd call a 'glass jaw' for quite a while," 'Rhett continued unconcernedly. "The rigid half-mask will give him some protection for the next month or so. Nevertheless, he'll have to swear off fistfights, and give up getting wall-banging drunk. He can't afford to get his jaw broken again."

"So, you're saying he has a drinking problem, Sir? I dare say he's not happy with his life."

No shit, Grievous!

"I guess not," 'Rhett agreed.

Psycho-bloody-analyze me, do! Djetth's brain flick-flacked unpleasantly. If he'd been drunk but not incapable, at this point he'd chug down two long glasses of the nearest alien equivalent of orange juice to counter the imminent mind-somersaults.

How the Carnality had the topic turned to boozing, any—? Djetth felt his brain take a dive. *Wheeee!*

No way to stop himself from cartwheeling back into unconsciousness. No wayyyyyy. . . .

"What were you planning to do with whatever you've got behind your back, Grievous?" 'Rhett asked in a deceptively sweet, Tarrant-Arragonian tone of voice.

He twirled his nasty little knife through his long, flexible fingers, as though it were a ballpoint-pen-sized baton.

"I thought I'd crack open a bottle." Grievous held up a swan's-neck-shaped bottle as if it were a large silver passport at a corrupt checkpoint.

Still seated, 'Rhett held out his hand for the bottle. He'd decided that Grievous would drink whatever was in it, but there was no advantage in being uncivilized.

"Gotcha, Sir." Grievous left the foot of Djetth's bed and handed over the bottle. "I dare say that might not have been such a good idea if he doesn't hold his drink well."

'Rhett inclined his head, and deftly sliced the top off Grievous's bottle with his very sharp surgical knife, releasing a pungent fragrance that reminded him of sweet fennel seed and heavy-duty antifreeze.

"I remember the time you came to visit me with a bottle of wine, Grievous. You hoped to loosen my tongue, as I recall. You'd arrested me, thinking I was Princess Djinni-vera's troublemaking fiancé."

They exchanged conspiratorial smiles.

"And you, Sir, were willing to be tortured or put to death in his place rather than let on that you weren't him." Grievous jerked his head, indicating the sleeping Djetth. "I never figured out what possessed you to be so noble."

'Rhett never revealed information without a very good reason to do so. He thought he had one. Djetth could use a sympathizer in his enemy's camp, and the Englishman had potential, if only because of the English fondness for underdogs, dark horses, and noble men.

"He *is* my big brother." Having lobbed an informational bombshell, 'Rhett ducked for cover, and reached for a stack of paper receptacles. "Did you think to bring Djetth a flexible drinking straw, Grievous? No? Then we'll drink it. Pull out a pallet."

'Rhett nodded to one of the pull-out drawers, and swiveled his own segmented chair to face away from Djetth's bed.

"His *brother*, Sir?"

Unhurriedly 'Rhett poured the acid green wine into one of the paper bowls left for the patient's use. Without rising from his seat, he passed the first bowl to Grievous, who took it and sat down.

"Your Great Djinn relationships confuse me," Grievous grumbled. "Not so many days ago, you told us you're Princess Djinni-vera's brother—"

"I apologize if I misspoke, Grievous. To be strictly accurate, Djetth and I are *half*-brothers. He and I had the same mother. We are also cousins because Djetth's father and mine were half-brothers."

'Rhett poured a bowl for himself before continuing. "Djinni-vera and I had the same father but different mothers, so Djinni is my half-sister. Her mother, as I think you know, was an Englishwoman."

In referring to his and Djinni's father, 'Rhett used the past tense misleadingly. If Djinni hadn't told anyone that their rogue Djinn father was alive, let alone that he wore the Dragon headmask of Tarrant-Arragon's greatest enemy, then the Saurian Dragon's son wasn't about to do so.

"Your very good health, Grievous." 'Rhett set the bottle down at his feet, then raised his paper bowl to his lips and tilted it. The opacity of the paper and the shape of the bowl made it impossible for Grievous to tell whether or not he'd drunk any.

Grievous took the first sip, then another. Almost immediately, the man's personal, nervous aroma mellowed.

"Incestuous lot, you Great Djinn," he remarked, glaring suspiciously over his bent shoulder at Djetth. "So, he was all fired up to marry his half-brother's half-sister."

"Oh, absolutely," 'Rhett agreed cordially in a very upper-crust English drawl, as he swirled his wine in its full paper bowl.

"My dear fellow, you must bear a couple of facts in mind. We Djinn are almost extinct. Great Djinn males are highly sexed. Moreover, our exiled ancestors were granted conditional sanctuary on Earth. The condition was that we don't interbreed with Earthwomen."

"I see. That explains the little miss's mother." Grievous's sarcasm was heavy.

It was also entirely justified.

"Your own Anglo-American taboos are relatively recent, Grievous. Think of the Egyptian pharaohs. They practised sister-marriage, even though they weren't on the edge of extinction."

'Rhett bent from the waist and set his full bowl on the floor at his feet beside the silver bottle.

"My half-Earthling half-sister was the last virgin of the

Imperial blood line. Virginity is more important to Royalty than it is to commoners. It was inevitable that Djetth, being the oldest, would claim her . . . in the sense of an early, formal, legally binding betrothal. He was betrothed to her since she was eighteen months old."

'Rhett threw out carefully chosen information like shark bait. He was fishing . . . for a friend for Djetth.

From Grievous's body language, 'Rhett could tell that the man was reluctantly drawn in by a side of Djetth's story he hadn't heard before.

"Djetth was honorably waiting for Djinni to reach legal Mating age—not always synonymous with marriageable age—when Tarrant-Arragon sneaked through the exclusion zone around Earth and bagged her before her birthday. Can you imagine how Djetth must have felt to lose her and everything that went with her, after waiting nearly sixteen years for her?"

"Well, when you put it like that . . ." Grievous stood, as if agitated. "Sixteen years. That's quite a time."

Still standing, Grievous brought the paper bowl to his mouth and tossed back the wine as if it were a shot of vodka.

"I lost my wife to another man," he said gruffly, glaring into his emptied wine bowl. "I half killed the bastard when I found out. Ruined my military career. Well, he was my commanding officer. In prison, it helped to have a 'hard' handle. That's when I began to call myself Grievous, after my crime. See, I did the bastard Grievous Bodily Harm."

"Have another," 'Rhett said gently. He took up the bottle by its long neck and reached over to refill Grievous's empty bowl. "Sit back down."

In thoughtful silence, they each stared at Djetth, whose regular breathing was interspersed with dreaming grunts of discomfort.

"It's all over, then?" Grievous turned a statement of the obvious into a question.

"Is it?"

'Rhett had doubts of his own.

Surgery was over. The patient had survived. As for the rivalry between Prince Tarrant-Arragon and Prince Djetthro-Jason, that might be far from over.

"He won't thank you." Grievous glanced again at the unconscious Djetth.

"No," 'Rhett agreed wryly. "He's not one for gracious speeches, even if he could speak. Did you have any specific reason in mind?"

"Castration for a kick-off. Poor bastard."

Grievous had not been in the operating theater. Being human, he apparently didn't understand the difference between the sensory neutering of a Great Djinn and the crude removal of bollocks. It was Djetth's capacity to have the rut-rage that would have been quietly "fixed," if Djinni-vera hadn't interfered.

'Rhett rested his elbows on his knees and steepled his fingers.

"You didn't think Tarrant-Arragon would Mate his lonely younger sister to a physical eunuch, did you, Grievous? That would be a dirty trick."

"Then, what the Dickens—?"

"Let me explain about the rut-rage, and Djinn male anatomy. The truly dangerous organ isn't the penis or the testicles. It's a moth-shaped gland in the sinus area."

'Rhett stroked the sides of his nose with his index fingers to indicate where his would be, if he still had it.

"A fully functioning Great Djinn male can smell an ovulating Djinn female from the equivalent of fifty Earth miles away, if the wind is in the right direction."

'Rhett smiled at Grievous's expression.

"Legend has it that a male falls irrevocably and permanently in love at first scent with the first ovulating female he smells."

"Before he sees her?"

"Exactly. Sight unseen. It is a fatal flaw in our Djinn evolution. Another is that Great Djinn alpha-males do not share Mates. They don't accept substitutes. They fight to the death to have and hold the first Princess they smell. That's why Tarrant-Arragon's sisters were sequestered—presumably—at the Island School for Princesses from menarche until marriage."

"Wait a minute, though. Crown Prince Tarrant-Arragon and Prince Djetthro-Jason didn't smell the same girl," Grievous interjected. "Why did they fight over Djinni-vera?"

The human caught on fast, too fast.

"Confusing, isn't it?" 'Rhett agreed.

"Confusing?"

Djetth struggled towards consciousness like a deep sea diver with the bends coming on, circling up towards a dappled circle of blue-white light.

'Rhett, you slack-damn sensory eunuch, you have no idea what confusion is.

". . . if you ask me, Great Djinn males are worse than rutting rogue elephants," Grievous was opining.

No one is damned well asking you to compare Great Djinn males with elephants, you ignorant human. Besides, bull elephants don't rut. They go into musk and run amok. It is not the cows who leak stinking pheromones when they're in season. The bulls do.

"Grievous, you're absolutely correct. Not perhaps—ah—diplomatic, but correct. The rut-rage is why the Great Djinn are close to extinction, and why the Tiger Djinn's enemies—"

'Rhett, you're such a mellow bastard. Did your boyhood mumps destroy your penile bone along with your saturniid gland? The way you run your slack-damn mouth off, I'm surprised I'm still alive.

"Meaning you Saurians?"

"We Saurians," 'Rhett agreed.

So, 'Rhett, are you now usurping the Royal Pronoun? Or does "We" include me? Though you threw me to the Tigers, do you still think of me as one of the greatest of the undercover Saurian Knights?

"The Saurian Organization is like a combination of your N.A.T.O., U.N., the Freemasons, the International Red Cross, and Amnesty International, with a few James Bond types on the side. We think of ourselves as the good guys."

Djetth could not identify the papery sound that followed this virtuous-'Rhett pronouncement.

"I dare say you do. So do we, Sir. To the Good Guys!"

That sounded like a toast. Someone who'd never really listened to himself drink went ahead and slurped, swallowed and exhaled.

"The Good Guys!"

Presumably, 'Rhett drank, too. "*Good choice,*" he complimented Grievous. "It reminds me of Pernod."

What does Pernod have to do with anything? It's a French export. What I'd give for a drop of it right now. And why the blue blazes is 'Rhett implying that we grew up on Earth?

"I never saw the famous film of your brother"—Grievous's neck bones crackled—"making out like a dog with the Princess Martia-Djulia."

Not accurate. Another ignorant comparison. No dog could get stuck in for the long haul like I did with Martia-Djulia.

Djetth remembered the longest lasting docking session of his life. There was a lot to remember, if he put his mind to it, and he would.

Though the lower half of his face was frozen, he felt smiling tingles around his lower eyelids and where his bleached-blond sideburns had been before he was shaved for surgery.

". . . there in the Imperial Portrait Gallery. . . . For the life of me, I can't think what possessed you to interfere, Sir. Anyone could see that the Princess Martia-Djulia didn't want a gallant rescuer. She liked being manhandled."

Grievous's inadequate remarks intruded on Djetth's pleasurable musings.

Djinnhandled! I djinnhandled her. And she didn't just like it. She loved it. Of course, she didn't know I was a Djinn.

Djetth mentally corrected the man without rancor this time. He wanted to get well and have at Martia-Djulia again. It seemed that Grievous approved of his doing it. Why fight?

"You should have seen the excitement on her face when he swept her up in his arms and carried her off, Sir. Won't she be thrilled to have him put it to her again!"

I hope so, Grievous. I'm quite looking forward to nailing her again.

Grievous's distinctive neck bones popped trapped gas buildup again as if he were cocking his head, like a puzzled wirehaired terrier. "What beats me is why Martia-Djulia isn't to be let in on the secret that Prince Djetthro-Jason is the old Commander Jason with a perfect new face and his real name. At least, I get the impression she's not going to be told."

Damnation! She isn't? Was I warned of this? That'll make her a bit less of a soft furrow to plough. I'll have to start from scratch. Not that it took me long to breach her defenses last time. . . .

Without warning, Djetth's mind took a roller coaster ride, and he felt himself careen into a purple haze. This time, he took thoughts of Martia-Djulia with him.

"It looks bad that she's not to be told, doesn't it, Sir?"

'Rhett took a deep breath, and considered what to say.

"I can't explain it, Grievous. I don't know Martia-Djulia except by reputation. I've heard that she's a bit superficial, an airhead, only interested in fashion and beauty treatments. Maybe she's a thoughtless gossip. Maybe she has a temper and blurts out secrets that should be kept. Maybe Tarrant-Arragon can't risk his father or Great-uncle Django-Ra reading her mind."

'Rhett stopped musing aloud. He had probably hit on the answer.

"You mean to say, Sir, that the older Great Djinn may have sneaky powers that inbreeding has eliminated in the younger ones? I don't know about that. It seems to me, there's a lot goes on in the Empire that the Emperor doesn't know about. Of course, Tarrant-Arragon mind-shields."

'Rhett wondered whether Grievous knew too much. Perhaps not. The greater the god-Prince, the greater his arrogance. It would not occur to any of the older Tiger Princes that Grievous's mind might be worth reading.

'Rhett imagined the six-foot-short human from the Emperor's point of view. Beneath his notice! The god-Emperor Djerrold Vulcan wouldn't lower himself to confide in a lesser being. Why, he'd think, should his son and heir?

"The Emperor doesn't even know where his Empress Tarragonia-Marietta is," Grievous was saying. "I don't suppose Tarrant-Arragon's likely to tell him Prince Djetthro-Jason's history."

"He'll notice the old name."

The old name was trouble enough. There had once been a line of Emperors named Djetthro-Djason. Somewhere along that line, a set of Rings of Imperial authority had been lost.

The Emperor was known to be vindictive and vengeful. To those who lived on any of the Communicating

Worlds, he might appear to be a figurehead, but on Tigron, Djerrold Vulcan had his Rings and his Right.

If the Emperor knew that Djetthro-Jason had tried to kill Tarrant-Arragon, Djetth wouldn't be safe in the Palace. The Emperor was quite capable of trying to incinerate the groom on his Mating Day.

Part Two

The Underdog and the Ogress

EARTH DATE EQUIVALENT: AUGUST 30, 1994

Chapter Four

Tigron Imperial Palace
Two Imperatrix menstrual cycles later

Never in all Great Djinn history had any Imperial Princess had such a Mating Ceremony on such short notice, and to a mate freely chosen by the Princess!

Princess Martia-Djulia savored her unique happiness. The second-best part was that she was going to get away with it. By taking an alien and a commoner like Commander Jason to mate, she poked a defiant finger in the eye of Imperial tradition.

"You're glowing," her tall, grimly magnificent brother commented as he joined her on the raised throne-stage and offered her the support of his bent arm for the slow, gyring descent of the stage into the Throne Room below the Imperial suite.

"I've a lot to glow about," Martia-Djulia retorted. She could have made a barbed remark about how Tarrant-Arragon had tricked his own cold, pale bride into saying the irrevocable Imperial Mating Vows, but she didn't.

After all, Tarrant-Arragon had hunted down Commander Jason, and brought him back to her.

Her thoughts returned to Jason, who shared her taste for subversion and mischief-making. He was the Mate who would change her sad, lonely life; her boring, bottled-up life. He was her rescuer, her lover, her private hero, the warrior who made her feel young and beautiful, and who awed the Fewmet out of her insolent, uncontrollable sons.

He was the only male in all the forty-two gestates of her life who had ever given her an orgasm.

Martia-Djulia took a deep, happy breath as the last notes of the Fanfare Royal drifted up from the balconies of the Throne Room. The Crown Prince's throne-stage—its stark, craggy contours pleasingly draped for the occasion in her favorite colors of dusk-sky mauve and midnight-purple—descended silently, like one of her brother's deliberately placed chess pieces, only fortress-sized.

"I can hardly believe it," she whispered to herself as she nodded graciously to the crowd below. "I'm about to be Mated to the only male who has the physical strength to pick me up and sweep me off my feet, and the desire to do so."

Tarrant-Arragon lifted an eyebrow at her.

Under the layers of his black open robe and high-necked State-Occasion uniform, complete with black sash and rope upon elaborately knotted and looped rope of cloth-of-silver across his chest and forearms, she felt him flex his hard arm muscles.

"My dearest sister, you couldn't expect me to have 'the desire to do so'?"

Once, she'd hoped that her dark, dangerous, unattainable brother might have the desire, and he knew it. She'd had a foolish crush on Tarrant-Arragon until the blond, scarred Commander Jason came swaggering into her life.

"Oh, when I think of Jason's passion—" she said, ignoring Tarrant-Arragon's innuendo. "When I think of how violently he knocked the ceremonial headmask off an interfering Saurian Ambassador, and of the wicked, sexual insults he threw . . ."

"You liked that, didn't you?" Tarrant-Arragon teased. "But I hope you don't expect your new Mate to pick you up, attack Saurian Ambassadors, and hurl sexual insults in front of our distinguished guests."

Martia-Djulia took in the carefully orchestrated tableau from her place on the stepped stage, waiting for Jason to make an entrance through one of the Throne Room's soaring central portals.

What would he be thinking? Would he remember how they had met at a Virgins' Ball in this very Throne Room? Would he mentally undress her with his strange, dark-nebula eyes and notice that she looked better than he remembered?

Surely, even a fashion hawk like Jason would approve of her sense of style. For her second Mating, she could hardly usurp the pallor of a Royal Virgin bride. She had chosen the subtle, shifting colors of a fast-frozen sea, glittering with the palest, most precious gemstones aligned in all the right places for the most flattering effect.

"They all came back!" Martia-Djulia breathed, gazing out at the heads of state, ambassadors, military leaders, and subject royalty who had been hastily recalled, some before they had returned home after her brother's nuptials.

"Of course," Tarrant-Arragon murmured. "On occasions like this, no matter how lofty the ceiling, it is never high enough, is it?"

The pentagonal Throne Room shimmered with the warmth rising from the thronged guests. Massed body heat made the vast room a battleground of assorted perfumes and less intentional odors that only Djinn nostrils might identify.

Suddenly, Martia-Djulia was conscious of emerging mature notes from her own signature perfume.

"Tarrant-Arragon," she whispered anxiously. "Did I overdo the Queen of the Night?"

"You seem to have put it absolutely everywhere," he drawled, and grinned, confirming that his Djinn-sharp olfactory senses were as embarrassingly acute as those of a sea-predator.

"I'll let Jason lick it off," Martia-Djulia quipped, brazening out her secret embarrassment.

"If he's got any Djinn in him, he might find that joy a little overpowering," Tarrant-Arragon said.

Martia-Djulia felt a vague, fleeting apprehension. Was there a certain enigmatic tone in her brother's voice? Something wasn't right. Tarrant-Arragon had once threatened to kill Commander Jason if her lover turned out to be of rogue Djinn lineage.

Why was Jason late?

Her anxious gaze searched the double avenues of ground-lighted, living trees which flanked the four grand entrances.

"Ah. The so delightful Henquist and Thor-quentin." Tarrant-Arragon jerked his head to indicate the upper level balcony where Martia-Djulia's two tall sons leaned negligently on the elaborately carved stone balustrade. "They look pleased."

She smiled hopefully at her usually sullen, sulky sons, until she realized that Tarrant-Arragon was being ironic.

"They're resentful that the one debauchery they thoroughly enjoyed at your Mating festivities—the Virgins' Ball—has not been held before mine." Martia-Djulia paused for emphasis. "I had no wish for virginal competition on the happiest day of my life."

She looked around.

"Where's Djinni-vera? I don't see her."

Tarrant-Arragon's face softened. "She's too far along

in her pregnancy to risk gravitational changes. I've left her safe on the *Ark Imperial*."

Martia-Djulia nodded. "You're wise to keep her away from our peculiar Great-uncle Django-Ra. Look at him. At his age!"

Prince Django-Ra sprawled on the parapet of the tiger pit, like the indiscriminate stud he'd once been. His ancient, disproportionately long legs were spread wide; he rested his elbow on one thigh, and gently stroked himself with the tiny, brush-like toy he always carried. His other leg was straight, and the long fingers of his beringed hand splayed wide, high on that thigh.

Great-uncle Django's silver hair, as usual, was in a wild crest. He looked like a predatory wading bird from the abandoned Island School for Princesses.

Sometimes Martia-Djulia wondered with a kind of detached horror whether she might resemble her sadistic great-uncle if she were ever to lose weight and let her hair fly loose.

Django's red-rimmed, pale blue-gray gaze followed her. An inscrutable smile formed on his lips.

She had the strong, strange impression that Django knew what she was thinking, and he also knew something she did not know. It was as if he were gloating that she wouldn't like his nasty secret at all, if she were to be told.

Martia-Djulia shuddered.

"Nervous?" Tarrant-Arragon asked mockingly.

Before she could retort, a loud fanfare made further conversation impossible. The pentagonal room vibrated with the thunder of massed war drums. Colored plumes of scented smoke surged up and tumbled from the Imperial throne-space, reminiscent of an ultraviolet-tinted, pyroclastic cloud. The Emperor's throne-stage thrust up through the smoke like a coldly gleaming ice-volcano rising out of a swirling fog.

Her father, The Emperor Djerrold Vulcan V, appeared to stroll on the pinkish-purple vapor trails, high above his guests. Martia-Djulia tried to imprint on her memory every detail of this splendid, dramatic illusion.

"Dear friends, welcome back," the Emperor began with his customary affable menace. "You are now here to witness the exchange of vows between my younger daughter and her new Mate. Since the Princess Martia-Djulia is a widow, and a mother, and since this is her second Mating, there will—obviously—be no display of proofs of virginity."

He pointed his Fire-Stone-Ringed forefinger around the room, his guests shrank in their seats, and he smiled tigerishly.

"There will come a point when my dear daughter will ask anyone who objects to her choice of mate to speak out. Anyone who dares to do so will be incinerated."

Star-blue lightning sizzled and flashed from the Emperor's finger. Regrettably, her father had flatly refused to even try to color-coordinate his laser ring's fire for this one occasion.

"Out of consideration for your fellow guests' nostrils," Djerrold Vulcan V continued pleasantly, "I advise against any interference. Proceed!"

High above, another fanfare blared from long, deep-noted instruments. The massive central doors at the far end of the Imperial throne room opened.

"I kept my promise . . ." Tarrant-Arragon said quietly, "to bring back Jason, if he agreed to come, or to find you a mate *like* your Commander Jason."

She wasn't paying attention, though it was an odd thing to say. Unseen, a massed male choir roared out the Mating Anthem . . . usually heard only once in a generation at the Mating of an Emperor or the Emperor's male heir.

This, too, was her due. She'd been promised that her Mating would be as splendid as the one she had organized for her big brother. And so it was. Only prettier.

"Here he comes!" Martia-Djulia whispered, trembling.

A tall, broad-shouldered silhouette limped from the darkness beyond the doorway.

His beloved, scarred face was a shadowed, distant blur . . . but something wasn't right. Had Tarrant-Arragon tortured and starved Commander Jason into agreeing to Mate with her?

"What is wrong with him?" she hissed accusingly. Time stretched out. A sense of creeping horror chilled her vitals. "You promised not to force him."

Her thoughts raced back to three Imperatrix cycles ago.

She vividly remembered what they'd agreed, just before Tarrant-Arragon left to exact terrible revenge on the unknown villains who'd tried to assassinate him on his honeymoon.

I want him to be happy, she'd protested when Tarrant-Arragon had caught her trying to erase compromising footage of Jason on top of her. Jason's happiness hadn't been on her mind when she'd triggered the surveillance systems.

Do you think he'd be happy with me if I force him to be my Mate? she'd asked her brother, who had no scruples when it came to mate appropriation.

No, Tarrant-Arragon had bluntly told her, dashing any lingering hope that she could blackmail Jason into returning to her bed permanently.

At the Virgins' Ball, Commander Jason had made it clear that he'd rather be searching the rim worlds for his errant mate-to-be, but he was on duty. Since he had to be at the Ball, he'd been in the mood for a revenge dock in any bay that would accommodate him.

Martia-Djulia had only wanted illicit excitement—until Jason gave her so much, she wanted him to do it for the rest of her life.

"Did you force him? Did you torture him?" Martia-Djulia demanded urgently.

"Not really," her appalling brother replied.

Something *was* wrong. Martia-Djulia's heart thumped. She clasped nervous hands to her glittering breast, and glared in an effort to get a better look at her promised Mate. At this distance, across the Throne Room, it was hard to tell . . . Closer he came. Closer.

Her senses heightened. With a great effort of will, her eyesight sharpened. She almost felt the dark holes in her eyes widen. She could now see that he wasn't in the silver and green dress uniform of an An'Koori Star Forces Commander. He wore dark blue and joy-bright gold.

"Your Majesty, Your Imperial Highnesses, my Lords and Ladies, Ambassadors and Knights, Gentlemales—Prince Djetthro-Jason Djinnmagister!" the herald announced.

"No! Nooooooo!" Martia-Djulia howled.

Royal protocol be damned. Be damned to Court etiquette. She could not take this in silent dignity. It was as if a charging bull Hunnox had gored her in the chest.

It wasn't Jason!

As he limped closer, her horror and indignation sharpened. Oh, cruel trick! This strange suitor was *bald*! He was gaunt. Worst of all, he had a horrible, villainous, thin streak of facial hair forming a distorted, elongated frame around his mouth.

What was he hiding? Obviously he was diseased and impotent. Why else would Tarrant-Arragon permit another Djinn Prince to live?

Even so, even if he were impotent, to Mate with a Djinn Prince—an equal, or worse—would be terrifying. And then, there was his disease. Was it communicable?

"Oh, slurrid!" A half-lifetime's worth of tamped-down feelings erupted inside her. Overwhelming and violent was her sense of outrage, of betrayal, of humiliation.

So they thought she'd accept any substitute, did they? "Weighty matrons should be grateful." Was someone thinking that, or had someone dared to say it?

Never, never in her life had she felt such rage.

Without thinking what she was doing or why, she raised her hands, palms flatted and outwards, in the universal "Fend Off" gesture. She pushed the air, as if shoving an invisible attacker in the chest.

"Haaaah!" she screamed.

Something happened. Something unexpected. A heartbeat after her "Fend Off" and scream, Prince Djetthro-Jason crumpled forward and was lifted off his feet and thrown backwards. He must have flown at least two tiger lengths before landing on his bastard rump.

Guests and courtiers gasped, like the harsh, chattering swirl of wind and dry leaves before a storm.

Martia-Djulia was as confused as everyone else. Had she done that? She'd had no idea that she had such power in her. Or that her rage had such force when she let it go.

The only comparable experience had been the time she'd watched a hunt as a child. The desperate prey—a little desert peccarian—had taken refuge under her pavilion. For no reason that she could articulate then or since, Martia-Djulia had thrown back her head and let out a "Hwooooyyyy!"

Oh, the astonishment to discover that her voice had the carrying power and authority to turn aside an unnatural pack of hunting tigers. Oh, the angry glances of the huntsmen! Her Imperial Highness, the hunt saboteur!

Then, as now, no one seemed to know what to do, and so the Court had chased off after the Palace tigers . . . in the wrong direction.

Martia-Djulia attempted to look unimpressed with herself, as if she blasted impostors to the ground with monotonous regularity.

"Whoa!" commented the would-be usurper of her affections, sitting where he had fallen, his long legs spread, with a rueful, lopsided grin on his fascinatingly sinister, barbarian face. "Was that Djinncraft?"

Djinncraft! How interesting that he should think she

was capable of Djinncraft! No Tiger Djinn Prince at the Palace had ever deigned to notice any trace of talent or giftedness in her.

Curious, Martia-Djulia stalked towards him with all the dignity of her long-time status as senior Princess in the Imperial family.

Her purposeful advance was pure bluff. Martia-Djulia had no idea how she had knocked him over and absolutely no confidence that she could ever do it again.

The Imperial Tiger Princes knew that she was near-sighted. They would infer that she was moving in for a closer look at the proffered male, this unknown Prince Djetthro-Jason. Presumably, no one had told Prince Djetthro-Jason that she couldn't see very far. He might think she was moving in to follow up on her psychic attack.

He drew in his long legs and crossed them across his crotch, all the while continuing to watch her warily. At least, she thought he did.

As she came closer, he raised a hand. She might have imagined he meant to shade his eyes, as if dazzled by her beauty—although not even the most ingratiating courtier had ever, ever pretended to be in danger of being blinded by her—but his hand stopped short, shielding instead his nostrils, or his jaw, or his disturbingly sexy little beard. Perhaps he was afraid she'd pluck it.

What should One do? All the Communicating Worlds were watching. What now?

Say something cruel, her evil djinnious prompted.

"By the Malevolency of the Eften-folk, you are the most unattractive impostor I have ever seen." She shrilled the first insult that came to mind.

"That is my loss, Princess," he said grimly. He spoke quietly through clenched teeth, hardly moving his lips, like a voice-throwing entertainer.

As she stared, he held up his hand. Did he expect her to kiss it? Was he so feeble that he needed help to stand?

"On the other hand, I've never seen you look so lovely," he said. "What would you call that particular shade you're wearing? Amazonite, perhaps?" He named a rare alien crystal of the palest milky blue. "It really does bring out the color of your eyes."

Her eyes might be bad, but there was nothing whatsoever wrong with her Djinn-sharp hearing. His voice sounded familiar. Had he just implied that he had met her before? Who was this Prince Djetthro-Jason? If he *was* a "Prince."

His name was Djetthro-*Jason*.

Hope sparked. His voice did something to the pit of her belly. Of course, he was a Djinn, so he might be expected to have a deep voice, even if he was a bald, animal-bearded, scrawny Djinn.

She glared into his face, hoping to see Commander Jason's dark-void eyes streaked across with meteoric sparks of green and blue.

His eyes were all wrong. His eyes were gray as volcano smoke reflected on water. He had no briefly beloved, ragged scars on his cheek. No trace of blond hair. He never could have blond hair; his raunchy little beard was as dark as her brother's hair. No, he was not the Jason she loved.

Her faint, rekindled hope died a bitter death.

People were restless and murmuring, now. Her Djinn senses brought her myriad perceptions. She ignored them. Her eyes stung with swirling misery.

She became aware that Tarrant-Arragon had left her side and joined other serious-looking males. No doubt they were plotting to "save face." Prince Djetthro-Jason had mentioned Djinncraft. It came in many forms, some subtle. Would they use mind control to force her to take this inadequate mate?

"Princess, if you truly do not wish to Mate with me today"—Djetthro-Jason's voice was soft, urgent—"perhaps it would be better if you were to withdraw?"

Martia-Djulia looked blankly at him.

"Quick. Run away," he urged through oddly stiff lips. His words contradicted the body language of his outstretched hand. "It wouldn't be too egregious a breach of protocol for you to leave the throne room before the Emperor, would it?"

She hesitated, not understanding his motives.

"I will marry you if you stay," he warned.

All her life, males had made decisions for her. *Mate young before you give someone the rut-rage. Take this hero as your Mate. He's honorable.* He wasn't. *Mate with that stranger. Run away or I'll Mate with you.* She was sick of it.

"Take his hand," she thought she heard her father's voice purr in her head.

"He's tall enough, and big enough, and your Jason is dead. What's the difference?" another male's voice reasoned.

Jason is dead?

Oh, crowning cruelty that no one had told her. She could not bear it. Apparently it was impossible to defy them all. She obeyed the minority voice.

She ran.

Crazy like a fox, to tell Martia-Djulia to run. Djetth would have grinned, but that would give his game away. Surrounded as he was by enemies, he judged it wiser to stay down.

The great doors had been shut after he'd entered. Martia-Djulia could have run into an impassible barrier. She could have been brought back by force.

Had he assumed she would be? Had he thought he'd nothing to lose by acting the Nice Guy?

Just in time, Tarrant-Arragon had raised his closed fist, as if holding up a candle or triumphal sword, uncurled four fingers, then made a fist again. It was the Star Forces

"Open-and-Shut" signal to the four teams of door openers. Tarrant-Arragon had actively let his sister leave.

Ah, well. Public Mating was for the birds. He'd prefer to hook up in a more *human* manner.

One thought led to another. It was pretty bloody funny, really. Here he'd been, all but frog-marched up the aisle for the alien equivalent of a shotgun wedding, and it was the bride who turned tail!

Nice bit of tail, too.

Absently Djetth rubbed his thigh, which hadn't healed properly in what would have been six weeks in Earth time. However, both his leg and his jaw had healed rather better than he let on.

Six bloody weeks of sucking thin sludge through a straw! No wonder he was malnourished. Quantities of the alien equivalents of Tequila and Pernod probably hadn't aided bone regeneration either.

Of course, his penile bone didn't need regenerating. There was nothing wrong with his royal scepter. Never had been. Inside his extra-high-rise trunk briefs, he was in great shape, but Martia-Djulia wasn't to know that.

No one could blame Martia-Djulia for balking at the wreckage Tarrant-Arragon had made of him, least of all Tarrant-Arragon himself.

Hopefully, Tarrant-Arragon wouldn't blame *him*.

They might be deadly rivals, but Tarrant-Arragon was fair-minded. He could hardly execute the newly incarnated Prince Djetthro-Jason because Martia-Djulia had run away and left him at the proverbial altar.

Djetth checked what His Efficiency, Tarrant-Arragon, was up to. The Emperor, the Emperor's elderly uncle Prince Django-Ra—who pretended to be gay, but wasn't—and 'Rhett had gone into a huddle. They reminded Djetth of American football's Pro-Bowl: a lot of "players" who weren't used to being on the same team having to figure out what to do next.

As long as the Tiger Princes stood where they were, protocol pinned the guests. Heads of state might stand to stretch their legs and chat, but they could not leave.

Tarrant-Arragon had turned slightly away from the Emperor and Django, and was firing off low-voiced orders—presumably—into his forearm communicator.

Djetth guessed what the orders would be. Propaganda would need a quote to explain why the broadcast of the Royal Mating had been interrupted. Someone would have to find and comfort Martia-Djulia. Not a Prince. Djinn males by long tradition never ran after anyone. The kitchens would have to be told to bring forward the banquet. There's nothing like rich, prompt and plentiful food and drink to mollify disappointed wedding—or Mating—guests.

He sighed. As for his own fate, if he got lucky—not literally—this would not be the end. Since he wasn't going to get to Mate with the Princess anytime soon, it'd be nice to go back to Earth. Perhaps they could be exiled together, and he'd woo Martia-Djulia his way, out of everyone's way.

Slim chance! For that to be possible, Tarrant-Arragon and the Saurian Dragon would have to set aside seventy years' worth of assorted differences.

Djetth might have let his thoughts drift to what he'd do with Martia-Djulia, and what he could or couldn't tell her if they were permanently marooned on Earth, when he noticed a Djinn-tall male whose white robes and stylized Dinosaur headmask identified him as a Saurian Ambassador.

Until he'd blown his cover and been captured, Djetth had been a high-ranking, undercover Saurian Knight with his own private army. He knew all the ambassadors, all the Saurians' dinosaur and dragon code names and stylized contact suits and frilled, horned or crested headmasks. He did not recognize this headmask.

Greeting by brief greeting with other V.I.P. guests, this

Ambassador was working his way ever closer to the Princes, and all the time the Ambassador's heavily masked head was cocked, as if he were discreetly eavesdropping.

Djetth relaxed his shoulders, half closed his eyes, cradled his neck in one hand, and gingerly eased his head back, like an athlete with whiplash. He focused his Djinn-acute hearing on what the Tiger Princes were saying.

". . . not a wise Mating." Djetth hadn't heard Django speak before. The old bastard's voice was like purred evil. What his Mating had to do with Django-Ra was anyone's guess. "Martia-Djulia may encourage his pretensions to your throne."

"Do you think he has pretensions?" That was Tarrant-Arragon. Dangerous. Deceptively soft-spoken, understated arrogance. A lawyer to the core, never giving a direct answer. Never showing his cards. "If he has, would the Communicating Worlds encourage *Martia-Djulia*?"

Until he overheard Tarrant-Arragon pronounce Martia-Djulia's name with such scorn, Djetth had never considered her as—what? The Imperial equivalent of a Presidential candidate's liability wife? The feminine baggage that makes a candidate unelectable?

"—true," 'Rhett was saying. "The Saurian Dragon would probably prefer Djinni-vera as the next Emperor's consort."

Du-uh! Djetth thought. *No "probably" about it.* Apparently, 'Rhett had neglected to tell Tarrant-Arragon that the Saurian Dragon was Djinni's father.

"Bah! Females are only good for three things. Why should our enemies care whom the future Emperor impregnates?"

Three things? Djetth had been studying the mysterious Ambassador in the unknown headmask, but curiosity made him glance quickly at Django. What had made the old bugger too flustered to remember that gay guys shouldn't have that many good uses for females?

"Merely the existence of another, weaker Prince

might unite those who would like to overthrow the Tiger Princes of Tigron. The Saurian Dragon might support this unknown Djetthro-Jason, if he were to challenge your power. Tarrant-Arragon, you should kill Djetthro-Jason."

I guess I won't pretend to like you, either, Great-uncle Django!

"The Saurian Dragon has no influence over the Imperial Succession." Tarrant-Arragon retorted. "We're no democracy. The firstborn male rules. Besides, do you think Prince Djetthro-Jason is likely to be anyone's reliable puppet?"

Out of the corner of his eye, Djetth noticed that all four males turned their heads and glared at him—which meant they did not notice the Saurian Ambassador's proximity until he had penetrated their circle.

Djetth watched as the Emperor acknowledged the official enemy at his side. His Imperial Majesty bowed slightly to the masked, white-robed Saurian Ambassador.

"We are surprised that Our daughter did not accept the substitution, Ambassador," Djerrold Vulcan said, using the haughty Imperial pronoun. His admission of surprise would be the nearest he'd come to an apology for the fiasco. "We thought she was more desperate."

"Prince Djetthro-Jason was a substitute?" the Ambassador questioned.

The Emperor blinked slowly as if surprised at himself for revealing more than perhaps he'd intended, and inclined his head in silent acknowledgment.

"Willful daughters have a most unfortunate tendency to fall in love with the most unsuitable males," the Saurian Ambassador said urbanely. No one seemed to notice the irony Djetth detected in his voice. "It's a problem we encounter all over the galaxies."

Particularly when the willful daughter in question is Djinni-vera, and she marries the Saurian Dragon's great-

est enemy instead of the tame Prince to whom her father betrothed her, Djetth thought cynically. He'd figured out who the masked Saurian "Ambassador" was. There were some very big brass balls in the Palace that day, and not all of them were Tarrant-Arragon's.

"Martia-Djulia's Mating with Prince Djetthro-Jason is hardly strategic," the Emperor blustered. "If she will not take him, it is not 'a problem.' "

"No?" the Ambassador said, sounding very much like Tarrant-Arragon at his most dangerous. "The Princess Martia-Djulia is a powerful full-Djinn." He'd changed tack. "My compliments, Your Majesty."

Tarrant-Arragon glanced sharply at the Saurian for the first time. So did 'Rhett, Djetth noticed. Django's attention had drifted. He seemed to be sniffing something that looked like a Scottish thistle, only white.

"Ahhh," continued the Ambassador. "What became of the unsuitable suitor? The one for whom Prince Djetthro-Jason was substituted, apparently without Martia-Djulia's knowledge or consent?"

"He's dead," Tarrant-Arragon said baldly.

"Is he indeed?" A pause, while the Ambassador's masked eyes might have flickered from one Prince to another. "How did you find Prince Djetthro-Jason?"

The Emperor did not answer. No doubt he didn't know, Djetth inferred.

Tarrant-Arragon raised an eyebrow, as if the question were an impertinence. It would have been, if anyone other than that particular masked male had asked it.

"How did you induce him to be willing to Mate with the Princess Martia-Djulia?" the disguised and incognito Saurian Dragon probed again.

"I proposed it to him as a matter of life and death," Tarrant-Arragon drawled, sounding bored.

Djetth winced.

"What now? Now that she has . . . ah . . . chosen to reject him, will he face death?"

Djetth silently called on The Great Originator to bless the Saurian Dragon, for forcing the issue in public.

"What business is that of the Saurians?" Django snarled. The effete old Prince had more testosterone than wit.

"I believe we Saurians have a treaty with Djetthro-Jason Djinnmagister's branch of the family," replied the disguised Saurian Dragon, whose true name was Ala'Aster-Djalet Djinnmagister.

"So the Saurians were aware of Djetthro-Jason's existence?" Tarrant-Arragon riposted.

If Tarrant-Arragon and the Dragon hadn't been discussing his fate, Djetth would have enjoyed hearing them try to interrogate each other. They were well matched, those two.

Djetth's musings were interrupted. Out of the corner of his eye he saw Grievous moving in his direction. Grievous's most recent job description was "Djetth's minder," which was a polite English euphemism for "Djetth's jailer."

Nevertheless, Grievous's arrival was a relief of sorts. It implied that he, Djetth, would be going back to jail.

"I warned you, Sir. It was a bad idea to shave off all your long blond hair," the Englishman said, bending forward and bracing his hands on his flexed knees like a kindly drill sergeant. "The ladies don't like a chap to be bald before his time."

Djetth ran his palm over his clean-shaven pate. "You don't like it?" he inquired, ironically.

"What I like isn't the issue, is it, Sir?" Grievous snorted. "Your life was supposed to depend on pleasing Princess Martia-Djulia. Shall I help you up?" He extended a hand. "If you don't mind my saying so, what with that and your new goatee, you look like Emperor Ming the Merciless from the remake of *Flash Gordon*. You're better built, though. Or were, before you lost weight."

"I'm still better hung," Djetth retorted.

"Since you're a seven-foot-tall Great Djinn, and Ming was played by an average-sized English actor, I dare say you are better hung, Sir," Grievous said politely, his helping hand still on offer.

"Between you and me, Grievous, I thought the Ming look was a brainwave. I had to do something with the wild tangle that grew under that bloody half-mask."

Djetth had spent four weeks with the lower half of his face in a rigid mask, under which a beard had grown, itching like crazy. The mask concealed his extraordinary resemblance to Tarrant-Arragon, which no one had noticed. When it came off, he hadn't needed a new disguise, thanks to the wild beard, until he was required to clean himself up for his Mating.

"I shaved my head on purpose. A calculated risk," Djetth confided. "Given that my task is to convince the Princess Martia-Djulia to love me even though I am *not* the late traitor Commander Jason, my blond locks had to go."

The Earthling nodded sympathetically.

"Gotcha, Sir. You vowed to change your identity, and you kept your word. Ready to move out? It's back to the *Ark Imperial*'s brig for you, Sir."

"Oh, good," Djetth remarked in a very English drawl.

He took Grievous's hand and allowed himself to be helped to his feet.

"I say, old chap." Djetth played up the British, officer-and-aristocrat accent. "You wouldn't happen to have any more Disprin on you, would you?"

Djetth had tapped Grievous for the low-tech British aspirin for weeks since his surgery, using the macho excuse that he really was in pain but he'd be damned if he'd let the bloody aliens know it.

Also, Disprin came in neat little blister packets. A third person couldn't easily spike them, or switch them for something more dangerous. With a brand-name blister packet, you knew what you were getting.

"Not 'on me,' Sir, but I think we could take a look in Storage Bay One. We've still got Princess Djinni-vera's household contents down there. I dare say there'll be some Disprin in one of her medicine cabinets, if you don't mind taking a chance on the expiry dates."

Djetth hid his intense interest. A lot of his stuff had been left with Djinni-vera for safekeeping, thirteen Earth years ago, when he left the sanctuary of Earth to infiltrate Tarrant-Arragon's star forces as "Commander Jason."

If Djinni-vera's entire household contents were aboard the *Ark Imperial*, and if he could get at a certain antique tailor's table unobserved, there was a secret compartment where he'd stashed the long-lost Rings that had belonged to an Emperor or Crown Prince in his ancestry.

An Imperial Heir's three Rings were the Tigron Empire's equivalent of the means and the license to kill. If only he could get his hands on them.

Chapter Five

ARK IMPERIAL, Storage Bay One

There it was! Djetth's gaze locked on the lightweight mahogany table that had once been his own. The hiding place was within reach. Were his Fire Stone, Ring of Gravity, and Death Ring still hidden inside it?

When he'd left the sanctuary of Earth, it had been to infiltrate the enemy Tigron Imperial Star Forces. There was no better training ground for a future Throne Contender and potential usurper.

However, he'd enlisted as a mercenary. By unwritten definition, mercenaries fight for money. Since their motives are murky, mercenaries also get cavity searched, shorn, disinfected, and scanned. Therefore, Djetth's valuables had to be left behind, also all possessions that would attract attention or betray his genetic identity.

He'd gambled that a mercenary's collection of primitive firearms wouldn't raise eyebrows, but it would have been arrogant folly to use guns to smuggle more dangerous items.

"Here you go, Sir. It's pretty much all here." Grievous

gestured expansively with his right arm, like a stocky, crew-cut 007 tossing his bowler hat onto the rack on the other side of the secretary's office.

The *Ark Imperial's* Storage Bay One was as vast as a small English beach with the tide out. All Djinni-vera's possessions were laid out—room by room—as if ready for a forensic inquiry into some sort of disaster.

In a way, it was a disaster that Tarrant-Arragon had captured all this potential evidence about Djinni-vera's side of the family.

"You'll be looking for medicine cabinets," Grievous said patronizingly, but then, Grievous probably had no idea that Djinni-vera's home had once been Djetthro-Jason's, too, and that many of "her" possessions were his own.

"Try among her bathroom things first, Sir." Grievous pointed. "That lot, there, would be from the bathroom nearest her room."

Djetth scanned the bay. Grievous hadn't commented, but, like most homes in Rock Road, the Djinnmagisters' house had had two baths, one half-bath, and five bedrooms.

Recognizing beds, Djetth ran a mental checklist. His, the twins' bunks, 'Rhett's, the master bed for the Saurian Dragon when he was between wars, and Grandmama Helispeta's for when he was not. Djinni-vera had shared Grandmama's room until she was five and Djetth vacated the attic room with the dormer windows.

"Why did Tarrant-Arragon store all this?" Djetth asked, trying to sound idly curious.

"There's no saying why, or what he thought he might look into one day, Sir. Of course, it'd have been a shame to burn her treasures. The house had to be razed to the ground to wipe out all proof that she'd ever existed."

"Of course," Djetth agreed, mirroring Grievous's conversational style. "It would've been a crying shame to burn those." He nodded at two turned-oak umbrella stands, which were showy but not particularly valuable.

It was a test. He knew that Grievous was impetuous, speaking his mind first and thinking belatedly. Grievous would correct him if Grievous knew antiques.

Apparently, Grievous did not know antiques.

"Or this. This is a nice piece." Djetth casually patted the tailor's table, watching Grievous closely for any sign of uneasiness or suspicion.

"Is it, Sir?"

If Grievous had an inkling what might still be in the table, or if he'd already removed the lethal treasure with or without Tarrant-Arragon's knowledge, he'd be nervous.

"Do you know what it is, Grievous?"

"A games table, we think, which Princess Djinni-vera had by her bedside," Grievous said without a whiff of artifice.

Djetth nodded. Most people mistook a genuine, antique tailor's table for a foldaway games table.

"Look at this!" Grievous darted to the table, reverently lifted and flipped back the four envelope-fold panels, doubling the working surface and revealing a smooth, green baize square surrounded by four shallow, tea-bowl-shaped recesses.

War drums pounded in Djetth's head. If Grievous found the Rings, he'd have no choice except to kill the Earthling.

"Princess Djinni-vera kept rune tablets in here, like game pieces, hidden in plain sight," Grievous said.

"Really?"

There was a special space hollowed out underneath one of the four screwed-in bowls. Djetth ran a casual, exploratory forefinger around the rim of the one nearest him. He could tell that it hadn't been touched in a very long time.

Like Martia-Djulia.

"Tarrant-Arragon gave the runes to his Codes and Ciphers chaps when he realized she used runes for sending secret messages," Grievous added confidentially.

"If I were still Commander Jason, I'd be most concerned to hear that Tarrant-Arragon had cracked a secret Saurian code," Djetth retorted. "As Prince Djetthro-Jason . . ." He shrugged. "I don't think I'd get very far by writing love letters in secret code to Martia-Djulia, do you?"

"Love letters in code, Sir?" Grievous looked sharply at him, then thrust out his lower lip in a begrudging, upside-down grin.

"Ah. Right. They do say Princess Martia-Djulia is not the sharpest knife in the drawer. Dare say, if she were, she'd have married you like a shot."

Apparently, Grievous attributed the remark about Martia-Djulia to pique. Possibly he also put Djetth's finger-circling of the bowl rims down to masculine embarrassment.

Or to carnal nostalgia.

"What did Tarrant-Arragon make of Djinni-vera's things?" Djetth inquired, as if out of idle curiosity. He turned back to the nearby umbrella stand, which held 'Rhett's old fencing foils, a brace of grouse-shooting guns, a rune-inscribed, ceremonial Saurian Knight's sword, also a five-iron golf club, sometimes known as a mashie, and a few poster rolls.

"Fascinated, he was."

Grievous's voice changed subtly.

Djetth wondered whether Grievous was going to open up. The topic should have been irresistible to a gossiping man.

"She's got some very surprising stuff for a virginal little miss. The Saurian sword you'd expect. Maybe the shotguns. She was supposed to be a fighting Saurian

White Knight, after all." Grievous pursed his lips as if considering an indiscretion.

"Although we looked at Princess Djinni-vera's posters of Tudor armor, and of strange-looking animal penises—in those rolls, there—I didn't make a point of showing His Highness her collection of seventies' girly magazines. Saw no earthly use in Tarrant-Arragon knowing she'd a taste for porn."

Djetth raised a quizzical eyebrow, and toyed with the notion of "borrowing" some of them . . . to warm up Martia-Djulia, of course.

"I dare say, Princess Djinni-vera had them for inspiration for her sexy oil paintings."

"Very likely." Djetth smiled. The porn was his. So were the guns. "May I?" Without waiting for Grievous's permission, he shouldered one of the shotguns and squinted down the once-familiar long, twin barrels.

About now, it would be late August on Earth. How he yearned to be back there, and free to spend windswept hours on a well-managed grouse moor, shin-deep in purple heather.

With his inbred Djinn powers and shark-like senses, Djetth had an advantage over humans. He'd hear the whirr of wings before the grouse rocketed explosively into sight. His vision could slow the birds scudding low over the heather at speeds approaching ninety miles an hour.

He'd been a "demon" shot. Djetth acknowledged a twinge of regret. If *he* had been the assassin who'd aimed a gun at Tarrant-Arragon's head, he wouldn't have missed, with or without Djinni-vera trying to put her hand in the way of the bullet.

If he had shot Tarrant-Arragon, he would now be Emperor Djetthro-Djason IV, with the extra silent Royal D prefix. It wouldn't be an issue whether he loved Martia-Djulia or Djinni-vera. He'd have had them both.

He would not now be suffering punishment for a High Treason he had neither intended nor attempted.

Djetth's acute Djinn nostrils picked up the sharp change in Grievous's body odor, as the human's adrenaline production kicked into high gear. It took a moment before he figured out what had made the man nervous.

"Have you ever had a go with one of these, Grievous?"

"Clay pigeon?" Grievous asked laconically.

"Red grouse!" Djetth replied.

He put the gun back, and heard a slight nasal whistle as Grievous exhaled in relief.

"You a shooting man, Sir?"

"Not as often as I'd like, Grievous."

With luck, the Englishman, who was no fool, had inferred two things from the byplay.

Firstly, Djetth was a very good shot. Secondly, since Djetth hadn't taken advantage of the loaded gun, Grievous could safely turn his back on him.

"I'm from Dorset, Sir. Not the best moor country," Grievous said. "I was in the Special Air Services, not as a crack shot, though. I specialized in demolitions."

Djetth smiled. "So, you know Wiltshire and Dorset. The Dorset schools are better, don't you think? Where did you go to school? Bryanston?"

"Clayesmore." Grievous named a rival public school.

"Small world!" Djetth said, giving the totally false impression that he and Grievous had an old school in common. He'd been to Harrow, Eton, and—for three years—to St John's College, Cambridge. "Come to think of it, there's no reason why you should remember me. You're a bit older. I dare say you'd have been in the Sixth Form when I was an Upper Third. But you weren't called Grievous."

"I was Greg Harmon. What did they call you, Sir?"

Djetth wasn't about to answer that.

"You wouldn't have noticed me. Swimming team, but not until the Lower Fourth. Do you remember we had a lifesaving team? I was on it. The things little boys do! Competitive lifesaving. About then, I developed broad shoulders. My shoulders made me a good arm, so I ended up on the track-and-field teams, too. Javelin. Triathlon. Decathlon. Later, cricket, of course."

Having proven himself to be a gentleman and a school sports hero, he looked for an excuse to get Grievous out of the way.

"Well, Grievous, we came to look for old-fashioned painkillers. Didn't you mention that there were more than one set of bathroom cabinets?" he asked.

"There were built-ins. I thought the contents were all herbals. They went in a box," Grievous said, setting off. "No harm in our having a look, Sir, but we can't tell her all her old stuff is down here."

"Oh?" Djetth pretended an interest in an architectural calendar from one of the poster rolls, spread it over the tailor's table, and underneath it, pressed down and pushed on the lip of each bowl until he found the one he was after. The one that would push down and unscrew like a child-safe prescription-pill bottle.

"Nah, Sir. His Mightiness might not have got around to telling her he helped himself to all her worldly possessions. Let's see what we have in here."

Grievous squatted over a box.

The bowl loosened. Djetth lifted it, reached underneath. His fingertips felt the Rings. One rolled away inside the hollow tabletop.

"No luck here," Grievous reported. "How're you getting along?"

Djetth needed just a little more time.

"You've got everything but the kitchen sink," he quipped.

"Got that, too, Sir."

"Really? I seem to recall hearing Djinni-vera say that she had quite a nice acoustic guitar. Do you happen to have seen that?"

While Grievous glowered thoughtfully, Djetth hooked his third finger through the third Ring. He had all three. In one fluid movement, his hand was out from under the poster and his Rings were deep in his pocket.

A small push, a twist, and the receptacle was back in place. After thirteen Earth years of being at a disadvantage, the Great Djinn Prince Djetthro-Jason had his ancestor's Rings again.

If he were to meet Tarrant-Arragon face to face, hand to hand with no innocent bystanders around, he'd no longer be the underdog.

PART THREE

SURVIVAL OF THE FITTEST

EARTH DATE EQUIVALENT: NOVEMBER 1994

Chapter Six

The Bright Side, Pleasure Moon of Eurydyce
Two months later

The Empress Helispeta liked to eavesdrop on strangers' conversations. It was an inbred Great Djinn family trait, made all the easier and more interesting because the Djinn had six—or seven—senses, most of which were as sharp as an efficient predator's.

So, instead of spending her time watching early practice for the jet-racing events from the pit wall, or in her twin grandsons' hospitality suite, Helispeta quietly gatecrashed the Pleasure Moon's equivalent of the Press Enclosure.

Newly arrived from Earth, she sat nodding among the aliens, soaking up sun and the scandals. If they were to notice her at all, any gentleperson of the Communicating Worlds' press would assume that she was just someone's grandmother.

In fact, she was A Somebody's grandmother. She was the recently royaled Princess Consort's Grandmama. Also, she was the Saurian Dragon's mother. It was possible that she was also the grandmother of the rightful Tiger Emperor of Tigron. And there was a huge price on her head.

Ninety-three Imperial gestates, or the equivalent of seventy Earth years ago, she had committed High Treason by running away from the Emperor Djohn-Kronos with the Emperor's identical twin brother.

Only the abduction of Djinni-vera, and the almost simultaneous disappearance of her grandsons Djarrhett and Djetthro-Jason, would have intrigued Helispeta out of her delightful exile and safe sanctuary on Earth.

That, and . . . a niggling suspicion that she might be in possession of an extremely dangerous secret, which should not be permitted to go with her to the grave. Djetthro-Jason had a right to know.

From time to time, liveried jets whizzed by. Truly, jet racing was unremarkably similar to Earthling motor racing, except that it was much faster, quieter, off ground, and infinitely more dangerous because of the Pleasure Moon's shifting magnetic fields.

As if to contradict her thought about the relative quietness of jet racing, a distant scream tore into her consciousness. It must be a new engine, but it sounded distressingly "human."

The Empress Helispeta wore wraparound sunglasses of the same gamblers' green as the visors worn by some of her fellow professional card sharks back home on Earth. Green was the perfect disguise for her mood-shifting eyes, which turned from deep violet to silvery gray when she was excited. Such a giveaway would never do at bridge or blackjack tables.

Helispeta felt that her time in the Press Box was well spent. In short order she had overheard the news that her grandson Devoron had neglected to report during their boring, slow, seven-week-long journey from Earth.

Tarrant-Arragon had married Djinni-vera, and got her pregnant immediately if not sooner. Tarrant-Arragon had been seen on the Pleasure Moon less than two gestates before his Mating, incinerating Scythian pirates on the Dark Side. Some said in his defense that the sexually sadistic pirates had tried to attack the future Princess Consort.

Naturally, there was talk that the Royal Mating had been a terrible setback for the Saurian Dragon and his Knights. There had been at least three disowned Saurian Knights who had tried separately and jointly to assassinate Tarrant-Arragon. The Saurian Assembly was in disarray. There were whispers of impeachment of the Dragon—no one knew why.

Hearing that, Helispeta repressed a snort. No doubt that explained why Ala'Aster-Djalet had been avoiding contact. He did not want to hear a motherly "I told you so!"

Of local interest, nearby An'Koor had lost its war-power status, its King had been banished, and the planet was under blockade. Helispeta listened intently because Djetthro-Jason had infiltrated the An'Koori Star Forces.

Apparently, all An'Koor was being punished because of corruption, draft dodging, and the fact that one of its war-stars had harbored a traitor. Now its alien mercenaries had been sent home, and the old war-stars were to be used for prison hulks or terraforming.

Further afield, back in the Tigron Empire, a "Prince" with the improbable old name of Djetthro-Jason had been produced from nowhere, because, it was whispered, Princess Martia-Djulia urgently needed a Mate.

Much to Helispeta's frustration, the entertainment media had no interest in where Tarrant-Arragon had found this so-called "Prince" Djetthro-Jason, whom they dismissed as a bald, thin, limping pretender. Martia-Djulia made far better copy, especially since her disappearance.

All the Communicating Worlds wanted to know why Martia-Djulia had rejected a willing Mate; from whom she'd inherited the power to blast her unwelcome suitor onto his scrawny butt without a Ring; whether or not there had been a gross miscarriage of justice many gestates ago when her first Mate had been summarily sent on a suicide mission.

Who, the chattering Worlds wanted to know, was the father of Martia-Djulia's sons? Resemblances were seen or imagined concerning Prince Henquist and an unmentionable senior member of the royal household. Charitable voices reasoned that it wasn't necessarily scandalous for a son to look like his mother and her relatives.

The distinctive, screaming engine had been silenced.

". . . there's . . . contract out to kill her."

Seen out of her Imperial context, the Empress Helispeta might easily be mistaken for an An'Koori or a Tigron. The clawed, hairy Scythian had no reason to think his hoarse whisper could be overheard and understood by the little old lady dozing in the sunshine.

Helispeta flicked a green-shielded glance around the Press Enclosure until she located the speaker. She was not surprised to hear a Scythian pirate discussing murder. That he was discussing it with a Volnoth was odd.

"Killing the newfound Prince would make more sense," the Volnoth argued.

Helispeta was all ears.

"He's . . . bastard with . . . courtesy title for appearances. No one believes he's anyone. It's . . . cover-up."

Gossip, Helispeta reflected, was often inaccurate, if not downright wrong.

"Why kill Princess Martia-Djulia?" the Volnoth asked.

"Maybe she's pregnant?" Said with the verbal equivalent of a shrug, it was a theory, not an explanation.

Again that rumor. Again the linking of Djetthro-Jason's name with that of Martia-Djulia. Was there some truth in it?

The whisperers moved away, leaving the Empress Helispeta mystified until other low-voiced conversations informed her, piece by piece, that a rim-world mercenary named Commander Jason had gone mad and had been blasted into space dust for various crimes including—it was said—impregnating Princess Martia-Djulia.

Unreliable gossip maintained that "Jason" had ripped out the entire front of the Princess's ballgown from bodice to hem, exposing her—and the fact that the scandalous Princess did not wear underclothing—on a public balcony at a Virgins' Ball, of all venues. He'd torn open his An'Koori uniform, taken out his very small An'Koori penis, and deployed it—apparently effectively, despite the difficulties One might expect—until a Saurian Ambassador intervened.

As part of the cover-up, the gallant Ambassador had been beaten and arrested, never to be seen again. . . .

Helispeta assumed that the Ambassador was Djarrhett, who was better known as 'Rhett. This accounted for Djarrhett's disappearance. Otherwise, she did not believe a word of the account of "Jason's" doings. As a grandmother who had occasionally changed her grandsons' diapers, she knew that no one in a position to see Djetthro-Jason's positor would ever describe it as small.

"It's Petri-Shah!" someone was shouting, as chaos erupted in the Press Enclosure and everyone either rushed to look over the parapet, or made for the exit to the track.

The name rang a distant bell. Helispeta could not place it. She lifted a hand, removed her sunshades, and stopped a rushing reporter mid-stride.

"What is it?" Helispeta murmured, fixing her compelling gaze on him.

"A local girl has been horribly murdered," he answered. "They're saying she's been tortured."

"Is that unusual?"

"Yes. Petri-Shah was one of Madam Tarra's girls. Why would anyone want to interrogate a courtesan?"

The Empress Helispeta released her informant, and he ran after the "story."

A girl was dead. A girl whose name the Empress had heard before. A girl connected to Madam Tarra, who was not generally known to be Princess Martia-Djulia's mother, and also Djetthro-Jason's spymaster.

It seemed, One had arrived not a moment too soon.

Chapter Seven

Overflying Freighter Island, the planet An'Koor

"This won't work."

"What won't?" Djetth asked, keeping his patience. The J-shaped hand control of the borrowed two-seater Thorcraft was sensitive, so any white-knuckled reaction to Martia-Djulia's petulance might result in dead fish in the shallow sea below them. Or worse. It depended whether or not Tarrant-Arragon had let him take Martia-Djulia sightseeing in an armed starfighter.

"This . . . this . . ." Martia-Djulia gestured off to the west, where Tarrant-Arragon's single-seat Thorcraft had veered out of formation. "What is he doing?"

"Circling a small island?" Djetth suggested facetiously.

"He is soooo unsubtle. I suppose he thinks it's funny that that island is shaped like a phallus."

It was a good analogy, but Djetth wasn't in the mood to compliment her. Compliments should have some chance of being reciprocated, or at least accepted graciously.

"It looks like a cuttlefish to me," he said, knowing that the untraveled Tigron Princess had no idea what cuttlefish looked like, and also that she wouldn't admit her ignorance. "I don't think Tarrant-Arragon expects that the sight of it will inspire you with romantic ideas, if that's what you meant by 'This won't work.' "

"I was talking about how he finds excuses to leave us alone together. Also, this stupid pretense that we are making a royal progress around the Empire to show you our Worlds."

"Thrusting us together should work, eventually."

Out of the corner of his eye, he saw her wince. Martia-Djulia didn't seem to like "thrusting" as an expression. He did. Every time he used it, he imagined himself thrusting into her. Long and hard, and deep. Fast in, sloooow out. Sometimes giving her a frenzied stabbing. Sometimes a long-lasting, leisurely screwing.

"You flatter yourself."

"Do I? 'Pheromones! Nothing more than pher'-mones,' " he sang to the tune of a vaguely remembered Las Vegas crooner's lament about his feelings. " 'Oh woe, woe, pher'mones—' "

She threw him a look of scornful incomprehension. Oh, she knew what pheromones were, but on her world—on Tigron—music was reserved for State occasions. No one sang songs about unrequited love and orgasms.

Djetth censored the next line of the lounge singer's song. "Wish I'd never met you, dear" might or might not be an accurate reflection of his sentiments after two months of unsuccessful courting.

As for "You'll never come again," he could only hope that the female to whom he was bound would stop pretending to be frigid pretty damned soon. He knew she wasn't.

"You forget that we are full-Djinn, my dear."

"I never forget my status!" she retorted haughtily.

Not quite true. But she did not know that he knew what she was like in bed.

Djetth turned his head and smiled across the cockpit

at her. Whenever Martia-Djulia made a particular effort to be royally obnoxious, he'd taken to imagining her reaction to the outrageous and colorful rock stars he remembered from his youth during Earth's seventies.

One day, he'd take her to Earth and introduce her to Hair Bands, if there were any left. Lots of long, wild hair, tight spandex, and thin, bare chests.

When he tried really hard, he could imagine Martia-Djulia head-banging her platinum blonde hair out of its tight, formal "do" and shimmying her bountiful curves until her beautiful soft bosom bounced out of her restrictive scarlet-and-black corset. She'd be wild for rock concerts.

He'd never done it from behind to a girl while she was standing up and thrashing to a live stage performance. Martia-Djulia was a big girl, though. She could take it.

Djetth glanced at her stony profile, and grinned. If she only knew what he was thinking!

"I never forget who I am!" Martia-Djulia reiterated, apparently determined that he should not enjoy his thoughts.

He hoped she was enjoying her latest low-key hissy fit. Someone should.

"The crude and brutal truth, sweetheart," he said with a deliberate Bogart lisp on the endearment, "is that sooner or later you will become deliciously rut-rageous. I'll detect your wildly arousing scent and be overcome by raging passion. Being rut-raged, I'll sweep you off to bed, rip off all your clothes, pin you down with my hard body, and make violent love to you. You'll love my masterful behavior, and submit eagerly to whatever I choose to do to you, and we'll all live peacefully, if not happily, ever after." *Including your bloody big brother with my Djinni-vera.*

Martia-Djulia muttered something unintelligible.

"True," he agreed, though he had no idea what she'd said. "It should have worked by now—after two cycles of being thrust together—if it was going to work. Either you don't exude a fragrance when you are fertile, or my saturniid gland isn't functional."

Djetth felt a twinge as his jaw tensed. One of them was sub-fertile. Was it he? Was there some foundation for Martia-Djulia's taunts? Had Djinni-vera betrayed his trust in Tarrant-Arragon's operating theater? Could it be that he was no longer a "full" Great Djinn?

No!

He glanced speculatively across at Martia-Djulia again, and then back at the watery horizon. The way she dressed, there was no way a male could check out her satiny belly to confirm or refute another possibility that Djinni-vera had mentioned in the operating room.

"You wouldn't happen to be pregnant, would you?" he asked, trying not to sound hopeful.

It was an awkward thing to ask, because as far as he knew, Tarrant-Arragon had done a superb job of suppressing any whisper of a rumor that Martia-Djulia had docked with "the traitor Commander Jason" or with anyone at all in the sixteen years since she'd been widowed.

Although Martia-Djulia had called him "an impostor" on their aborted wedding day, since that moment, she'd never said anything to imply that there had been a lost lover.

"Naturally, I'm not pregnant," Martia-Djulia snapped.

"Pity!" he retorted. "Menopausal?"

The Royal genealogy* was a matter of public record. In Earth years, Martia-Djulia would be at the young end of thirty-six. His own age.

He heard an outraged intake of breath. A clatter of bracelets and a flurry of pastel sleeve-flounces warned him that she'd lashed out in a cross-body attempt to slap him.

He was lucky that she was left-handed, elaborately and restrictively dressed, and that her seven-point seat harness kept her shoulders securely against her seat back. If she'd used her right in an uppercut, she could have done damage to his still-fragile jaw.

"Hey, don't hit the pilot! If we ditch—"

"Ditch?" she questioned, but from the way her fingers gripped her armrests, he inferred that she had a fair idea what "ditch" meant.

"Crash into the sea." Point made. "Look down there." He nodded his head at the bruise-dark shadows on the sandy sea floor and the streaming, iridescent swirls in the water.

She peered down.

"What is it?"

To his surprise, she did not seem enraptured by the bright arabesques of peacock colors.

"In fact, it's phosphorescent ejaculate from those large mollusks." Djetth turned their starfighter and circled lower than he should. "At this time of year, the males spray billions of sperm in great concentrations, with immense force. As the semen shoots over the females, they're stimulated to open up and release their eggs. Isn't it a spectacular sight?"

She'd be a spectacular sight if he got to do something similar to her.

"How slurrid!" she said. "Is that what you brought me all this way to see? Well, I do not wish to see it. What's that light for?"

Warning lights had come on.

Warning, the flight computer's modulated male voice intoned dispassionately. *You are flying too low, my Lord.*

"I've seen enough!" Martia-Djulia gasped, losing some of her ice princess hauteur, and also her affected, formal speech. "Take us back to a safe height."

"Scared?" he teased, enjoying the upper hand for once. After two months of being henpecked in public, he wasn't about to take orders in the privacy of a starfighter. "Watch this. I'm going to excite them. Look at that!"

He skimmed lower over the water so that the vortexes of air thrown off his wing tips would create turbulence on the water and make the minuscule aquatic organisms flash.

Warning, my Lord.

"I will not look. I don't like water," she gritted, bracing her hands on the arms of her seat. She pushed her too-perfectly coifed head back against the headrest, and turned her lovely face to one side—away from him, naturally.

The craft bumped on a little turbulence. Beside him, Martia-Djulia gasped.

Warning, my Lord.

"Yeah, yeah. I know. I'm too low."

You are under attack, my Lord.

"What . . . ?"

His heads-up display was alight with options. Too much information to process. His rear scans showed that Tarrant-Arragon's Thorcraft was roaring up behind them. The computers clamored silently that some unspecified type of weaponry was locked on to them.

"What the fuck . . . ?" Djetth let fly an Earthling curse from his youth.

"What the what?" Martia-Djulia snapped, gripping the armrests so tightly that he heard one of her perfectly impractical nails fracture. "Why would anyone attack us?"

He ignored her.

No time for pleasantries. Something winked in the missile cradles of Tarrant-Arragon's Thorcraft, which was in the classic six-o'clock position of a surprise attacker. Was the flash a trick of the light?

Warning, my Lord. You are under attack.

"Oh, who is attacking us? Who could possibly want to . . . ?" Martia-Djulia squirmed in her seat restraints, looking everywhere but behind her for an attacker.

There! The rearview scanner magnified a stream of particles arcing toward them.

"Quiet!"

The blood raced in Djetth's veins, drummed in his ears like Hollywood Western war drums. *Pump pump-pump-pump. Pump pump-pump-pump.* He could feel himself thinking faster. The data on his display seemed to dance slower, though of course they did not.

He was in the zone . . . as they said on Earth. His heightened senses did not need magnified distractions. By now, there was an overload of information on the heads-up display. It was like trying to keep track of autumn leaves in a high wind.

Select evasive maneuvers, my Lord? the warning system suggested.

"Damn it, I'm too low for evasive maneuvers," Djetth snarled. With a jab of his thumb, he muted the computer. At the same time, he moved his control hand to bring his Thorcraft's nose up, and turn away from the island.

He heard an odd mechanical clunk, like a magnet clamping onto another.

Milliseconds later, it seemed that there was an indefinable sluggishness in the controls. Peripherally, he thought he saw his auxiliary wings slide and lock. Why . . . ? Did the craft automatically trigger Landing Mode below a certain altitude?

Fewmet! Surely not in the middle of a dogfight! No way to retract the auxiliaries . . . maybe if he took off skyward . . .

"Pull up, slack-damn it," Djetth swore at his unresponsive Thorcraft.

A dark, shark-nosed shadow nudged out his daylight. Looking up, Djetth saw Tarrant-Arragon's long nose cone about thirty inches above his canopy, and creeping forward.

Martia-Djulia wailed.

All the while, he was being forced down, down. With his Nemesis riding his back, it was all he could do to keep his starfighter level.

The alternative was to let one wing drop, and if it went in the water it would sheer off, and they would flip, cartwheel, and drown. Chances were, they'd clip Tarrant-Arragon and take him down, too.

"If he's trying to kill us, he'll do it," Djetth muttered grimly.

"But why? Why here? Why now?" Martia-Djulia moaned.

"Good question."

With a double click of his thumb, he opened communications.

"Djetth to Tarrant-Arragon."

No answer. Absolute silence, unlike the static one heard when there was a gremlin in the spacewaves. So silent was it, Djetth knew that Tarrant-Arragon could hear him perfectly, but chose not to answer.

"You bastard! What the Carnality are you playing at?"

His Royal Highness had gone mad. The *Ark Imperial* should be warned. A sudden sinister thought flashed into his mind. The *Ark Imperial* had been cloaked for their supposed Royal Progress? No one knew where they were.

He flipped a connection with his thumb.

"*Ark Imperial*, what have you . . . ?" he began.

He heard hissing, sizzling silence, as if someone had walked out on him and left the phone off the hook.

Beside him, Martia-Djulia was looking up and screaming silently at the cloudless, blue-violet sky.

Tarrant-Arragon must have dropped back.

Djetth turned his head to look for his enemy, just as the crazed bastard shot alongside them. His cockpit drew level. Tarrant-Arragon turned, smiled, and raised his free hand in an ironic wave. Then he sped ahead.

Easy for him. His Thorcraft's wings were swept back and zooming. He wasn't locked down in Automatic Landing Mode.

"Hold tight," Djetth said to Martia-Djulia. "I think he just waved goodbye."

Ahead, Tarrant-Arragon's Thorcraft dipped lower, sucking up rooster tails from the sea not so very far below their racing craft.

The first wave of spray spattered their canopy. Then it hit them like a fire hose.

"He's pissing in my wind on purpose!" Djetth said. "Can you believe it? Tarrant-Arragon's slashing all over us."

Phosphorescent water as colorful and dangerous as spilt gasoline was spraying over them.

Belatedly Djetth understood. First Tarrant-Arragon had stolen his "lift;" now he was buggering up his coefficient of drag. Water and turbulence buffeted their diplomatic-model Thorcraft. It was hard to see, harder still to fly. But, from the *Ark Imperial*, high above the atmosphere, the whole thing must look like a couple of macho Princes trying to out–top gun each other.

Whatever dirty trick Tarrant-Arragon was pulling with his superior, undiplomatic Thorcraft, Djetth was determined to fight back. Except he couldn't fight back. He felt his tail drop. He was going down fast.

He glanced at his power levels and made calculations. Where had the power supply gone? There wasn't enough juice left for a getaway. Not enough to explode, either. A crash might be survivable, after all.

His situation reminded him of a pirated reality TV show he'd seen with Grievous recently. From a pursuing helicopter, Earthling police had the technology to cut the power to the engine of a stolen car on the ground.

Obviously, Tarrant-Arragon had pirated more than the show. He'd appropriated the idea. What the hell to do?

"Brace yourself," Djetth warned, though he doubted that Martia-Djulia was listening.

If he'd been alone and over land, he might have ejected

long ago, low though they were. Ejecting was out of the question with Martia-Djulia, and even if she hadn't been too inexperienced and borderline catatonic with terror, it was impossible now they were being hosed.

As suddenly as it had started, the deluge stopped. Droplets of water streaked off to the outer edges of the canopy, like shooting stars. A darker streak might have been Tarrant-Arragon, peeling off.

Djetth could see again. He had the controls, but it was too late. He had to land. Ha! Land? There was no land. It'd have to be a water landing—a hard landing—as close to the island as possible.

"Might be a hard landing. Keep your belts on." His voice was calmer than he felt. "This is it."

CHAPTER EIGHT

Freighter Island, An'Koor

No. Oh-oh-no. . . . He couldn't slow down!

Snatches of half-remembered rock lyrics roared in Djetth's head as he fought to control the inevitable crash. The landing gear wasn't down, he was keeping the wings level. If the auxiliaries had retracted—as they should have—on contact with the first spray of seawater, there was nothing to snag on the waves and flip the Thorcraft.

All he could do was head into the wind, what little there was of it, watch his altitude, use the throttle, and pray that they wouldn't stall, that the wind would not shift at the last minute.

"Fifteen feet, thirteen, eleven . . ." he counted down. Too late to respond if the wind shifted.

"Ten. . . . Come up, damn it!" Djetth's biceps and wrists burned with the strain of pulling the J-shaped yoke back towards him to keep the Thorcraft's nose about ten feet above the water, five degrees above the blue horizon.

"Nine, eigh—ahhh!" *Tail's down.* Djetth's head

whiplashed forward and banged back against his head-rest. His belts dug sharply into his armpits and thighs.

That's the nose! Djetth registered the second of two almighty jolts in rapid succession. First the back end of the long Thorcraft hit the water, and then the nose bounced. His senses flooded with impressions of tortured metal noises, hot water-and-wiring smells, jarring pain.

"We're down." He stated the obvious, partly out of relief, partly to reassure Martia-Djulia. "We're down." He struggled to remain conscious. His eyeballs hurt. His vision spun. His head hurt. His jaw—had the impact broken it again? He hurt all over. He didn't want to move. He rolled his head back and closed his eyes.

Pounding at the back of his mind was a rock song about being unfairly grabbed by the balls.

"Oh, shit! We're sitting ducks."

Djetth forced himself into action. No time to sit, stunned, on the choppy, sloshing water. No time. For all he knew, that unpredictable bastard Tarrant-Arragon could be circling back for a sure kill-shot.

We've got to get out.

He shook his head to clear the dazedness. Not a smart move. Above him, the sky seemed clear. Below him, the hull was intact for now. How deep was the water? Only one way to find out. The Thorcraft wouldn't float for long.

"Got to get you ashore, Princess," he gritted. "Are you all right? Martia-Djulia?"

She didn't answer.

Djetth took a deep breath and deployed all his sea-predator senses. There was no smell of blood. She was breathing. She appeared to be catatonic with shock, but she was conscious. He could tell from her trembling, white-knuckled grip on the seat armrests.

He unfastened his seven-point seat harness. Still seated, he unlocked and slid back the heavy, domed canopy, felt the heat of the sun, and filled his lungs with fresh, sweet air. He hadn't realized how stifling the air inside their cockpit had become until that moment.

He could hear the soft slap of ripples against the metal bodywork of the Thorcraft. The sound was incongruously peaceful. He patted his crotch to check that his Rings of Imperial Authority were safely stashed in their hiding place before he moved his legs.

"Martia-Djulia?" he tried again. Glancing at her, he noted the gentle rise and fall of her magnificent chest. As he watched, she swallowed convulsively. She just needed a little more time to get a grip.

"Okay," he said to himself. "Now what?"

Map, compass, whistle, signal mirror, flashlight. . . . A must-have checklist from his adventure years on Earth flitted into his mind.

Not! He thought. To whom would he signal? His enemies? The bastard who had just forced him down? Rescue was probably not an option.

Water purification tablets, water bottle, plastic bag . . .

Containers of all kinds would be useful, but could be salvaged later. Ditto copper wire. Some diving might be involved if the Thorcraft sank, but the seas of An'Koor were shallow and warm, like the Tethys Sea on prehistoric Earth.

Matches, foil survival sheets, extra clothing . . .

Hah! Martia-Djulia was wearing enough for two. However, it was the wrong sort of dressing for two. A serious thought crowded out the whimsy.

They might be marooned for months, years. What if she were already pregnant, despite her denials? What if he got her pregnant and no help came? Could he deliver a baby safely? He fought down the stirrings of male panic, took refuge in his checklist.

First aid kit, sewing kit, pocket knife . . .

Check that. Check. There ought to be a knife in each of the seats' side pockets. One was always there in case the seat belts locked. There was also an emergency kit zippered into each seat. Communications equipment was there too, in waterproof packaging. Djetth took it.

He frowned at Martia-Djulia's seat belts, which she'd made no attempt to remove. Not a lot of play there.

Four neat knife slashes ought to free her and restore circulation in her arms and breasts. He cut the belts and resumed quartermastering.

Parachute or nylon line, non-lubricated condoms . . .

As if!

Actually, condoms would be a good item to have for their intended, prophylactic purpose, aside from their survivalist uses for collecting water.

"I don't want to rush you, darling, but it's time to go," he warned Martia-Djulia. He hauled himself up and over and out onto the wing. Sitting with his legs dangling in the tepid water, he first filled his multiple pockets, then unzipped the front of his flight suit, stuffed whatever would fit into the improvised carryall, and zipped it up again.

Experimentally, holding on to the side of the Thorcraft with one hand, he took a deep breath and jumped. He went under. His feet touched bottom, he straightened his legs and found that if he stood on tiptoe his chin was above water.

"I'm standing," he announced, not complicating matters by pointing out that he was a critical foot taller than she was. "It's less than a tiger's length here."

His pants clung to his legs and his erection, with pockets of heaviness dragging him down. His boots were full of water, turning baggy. Beneath his soft-booted feet, he felt ribbed sand. He hoped to human Hell and back that no spiny-backed Venomfish lay between him and the shore.

"Come on, sweetheart," he coaxed. "Take my hand. You can trust me."

"I can't," she whispered.

"You can't stay here."

"Maybe help is coming." She peered worriedly around, like a fluffed-up bird in a suddenly exposed nest.

"I'm the help."

He heard it then, too: the distant roar of an approaching craft. He felt shock waves in the sea, and the floating Thorcraft in the water beside him rocked. Waves lapped over the wings.

Tarrant-Arragon shot by. Djetth could have sworn he saw His Highness make an ambiguous Star Forces gesture with one hand, just before a wave of seawater slapped him in the mouth and sloshed its frothy cap into the cockpit.

Djetth spat.

"Come on. Take my hand and jump into my arms. If he does that a few more times, this Thorcraft will sink."

Martia-Djulia remained frozen. Something was wrong.

Djetth flared his nostrils. There was a strong taint of fear. She'd been smelling that way since before the attack began. Adrenaline, urea, sweat, too damn much of the signature perfume she splashed all over herself.

Also, there was a faintly acrid, brothy tang.

"What's the matter? You can tell me."

She shook her head so slightly that the movement could have been a violent shudder. There was no point telling her that he'd figured out what was the matter. From what he knew of the shy and private Princess, she'd take no comfort if he were to assure her that fear in combat takes many outlets, and that wetting herself wasn't the worst.

Her brother might—or might not—have just tried to kill her. Did she really think that the worst thing in the world was that she had wet her ridiculous, beautiful dress?

Martia-Djulia refused to tremble. By sheer force of will she sat rigidly in her seat and waited to die.

If she sat very still, surely death would come suddenly, and no one would know of her final disgrace. If she squeezed her eyes tightly shut, she wouldn't see death coming.

Why can't Djetth give up? Go away? Save himself and leave me alone?

Keeping her eyes closed with difficulty because she was faintly curious, she was aware that Djetth was doing things to rock their flimsy craft.

But it wouldn't be dignified to complain.

He seemed to be tugging at this and that on the back of her seat, and whatever he was doing tickled in a vaguely sexy way. He was groping around her seat like a looter, dripping seawater on her, fumbling. Every so often the back of his hand brushed her arm or the side of her thigh. What was he doing?

Strange, disquieting feelings roiled through her belly, all of them unwelcome, especially the notion that there was something oddly sexy about being strapped down and helpless while an unseen, too-gorgeous male was telling her what to do and dripping on her.

Clumsy, inconsiderate, careless . . . couldn't he accept that their situation was hopeless?

"You're not afraid of getting wet, are you?"

He was at it again. Trying to dominate her.

Martia-Djulia felt a sudden heavy slap of wetness on her belly and then on her legs. The shock of such an assault made her gasp, and she opened her eyes. He'd splashed her! With seawater.

"See? Wetness is heavy, but it doesn't hurt." He scooped up another handful and dumped more water in her lap and between her legs. And more.

She knew what he was doing. He was trying to force his perception of the world on her.

"How dare you!" Martia-Djulia gasped in shivering outrage, as the wet weight of the pool of seawater in her lap pressed against her sensitive groin and the wetness between her legs reminded her of sex.

Nothing so undignified and humiliating had happened to her since she'd given birth to her firstborn, and her Mate had insisted on watching his son's head come out of her body.

"Water won't hurt you," the insensitive, unrepentant brute said, splashing her legs again with his dirty, filthy water. Did he assume that she was hysterical? "You're wet now. Get used to it. The first wetting is the worst."

His bullying words brought to mind a distant memory of another male voice, not as deep, not as mellifluous, but just as urgent. The dimly remembered voice was telling her that his semen depositor wouldn't hurt her.

"Soon you'll be so wet that you'll be beyond worrying about it. Now come."

Martia-Djulia stared down at the pool of water that had forced a deep depression in the thick fabric between her knees and was slowly soaking through her skirts.

"Oh, slurrid! There are bits of brown stuff in it. Dead, rotten, slimy, leafy things."

She half expected to see some alien aquatic life form thrashing around in the nasty puddle between her thighs.

The unpleasant wetness seeped through her skirts and other garments, trickled down her legs into her seat, and pooled coldly under her bottom. If she moved, she would squelch.

"Come on, sweetheart. Come to me. Come over the top. I'll catch you. I've got you," the ridiculous male urged.

Over the top, indeed! He had not "got" her. He didn't have a hope of "getting" her.

He didn't know that she had a knife in the flat, front part of her corset, like an extension of her sternum. He could not know that two of the six long "bones" of her corset were lethal bodkins.

Did she really care if he heard her squelch? No! At least he would never know she had wet herself.

Scorning his outstretched hand, she grasped the open side of the canopy with one hand, pushed on an armrest with the other, and got unsteadily to her feet. It wasn't such an effort as she had expected, despite the drag of her semi-saturated clothing.

Water cascaded off her.

Her hands were shaking. Her knees were shaking. Her stomach had knots in it, her head was spinning, and she had a headache and a pain where the hollow under her cheekbones should be.

As she stood braced against the rocking of the Thorcraft on the moving surface of the sea, she couldn't resist a quick backward glance down at where she had been sitting.

With an arrogant caterwaul of power, Tarrant-Arragon's Thorcraft hurtled past again.

How dare he! He didn't have to make so much noise. The noise was a battle option, designed to terrify enemies on the ground. Wasn't what he'd done enough? Did he have to deafen her?

She heard a metallic click and an explosive whoosh. Twin missiles whistled through the air and exploded far out to sea with an eruption of reddish spray and a surprising concussion.

"Oh, Carnality! He really is trying to murder us!"

When the heaving water beneath her subsided, Martia-Djulia slowly raised one hand. Her body moved considerably faster than she was used to. She felt feverish and uncoordinated. She needed the other hand to cling to the canopy rim.

Oh, she was angry enough to aim a two-handed Fend-Off and an enraged scream at Tarrant-Arragon, and see whether she had the power to knock his Thorcraft out of the sky the way she'd blasted Djetth off his feet on their aborted Mating day.

She used her raised arm to shield her eyes from the sun. Should she try? Could she? Could she bear the humiliation—and worse—if Djetth saw her try and fail?

What might he think of her if she succeeded? What good would revenge do her? She'd still be trapped on a terrifying, watery world with a very large, single-minded, sexually menacing male.

She was, to quote an expression she'd heard Tarrant-Arragon's annoying Earthman, Grievous, use, "between the Devil and the Deep Blue Sea." Which was "the Devil"? Her wicked, sororicidal brother, who was playing with them like a tiger with a wounded peccarian? Or Djetth, who looked the part with his gaunt, depraved-looking face and beard that emphasized his evil, oversexed sneer?

Either way, she was more afraid of the sea, though she couldn't recall why. Whole segments of her life were a blur. Something horrible had happened to her in a sea. She feared large bodies of water as much as she feared having Djinncraft used against her by a rut-raged Great Djinn. Yet, for now, it was the sea's embrace that couldn't be avoided.

"Come on," Djetth urged.

Martia-Djulia took a deep, resolute breath, stepped onto her seat, then swung one leg over the canopy rim. It took less effort than she'd expected. Her wet skirts were heavy and cumbersome to lift out of the cockpit without snagging them, and without showing Djetth too much of her legs, but she managed.

"Take your shoes off, or your heels will go through the bodywork," Djetth ordered. Why he cared about the bodywork of a sinking, stinking starfighter was beyond her!

Seething, Martia-Djulia shifted her weight back onto the foot still on the seat, and kicked her left shoe off in his general direction. It soared past his leering face, flying higher and further than it should have, and splashed into the sea.

Another weight shift, more inelegant scrambling, but she avoided having to sit down hard on the thin cockpit rim. It seemed a little easier to be athletic on An'Koor. The right shoe she shook off and left on the sodden seat.

Crouching, she eased out onto the wing, and as she did, she felt the Thorcraft tilt. Instinctively she straightened, but, thanks to her corset, her center of gravity was pushed up too high and too far forward.

"Oh-Oh-Woah-Woaaah!" She gave a wailing battle cry as, her arms wheeling futilely, she began to fall.

She fell slowly enough to notice heroic Djetth move out of the way, making no attempt to catch her. *So much for his promise to catch me. So much for trusting him!* She saw shadowy little fish circling in the sea. She closed her eyes.

Djetth had slipped into the water without a splash, like a diving bird in the dangerous waters around Tigron's Island School for Princesses, where she remembered being, briefly, before her first, inglorious nuptials. The water slammed her. She registered the acid pain of being winded, the stinging blow to her face and midriff, the blue-green blur of water pressing her eyeballs, and the desperation to breathe, all at once.

Thick, stinging water was in her nostrils. Her mouth filled. She was gagging, struggling, sinking, dragged down by her heavy clothes, and she didn't know . . .

Suddenly her hair was wrenched from above and behind, and her face broke the surface. The light! Air! She gasped, then choked and spluttered, and flailed her arms for something to hold on to. One hand scratched something. Her foot kicked something solid.

She had to grab hold and push herself up and out of this horror. As the thought formed, she went under. She fought. Her foot brushed something soft and yielding beneath her.

Something firm snaked around her waist. Again she was lifted to the light, again she sucked in air. This time, her clutching hands made contact. She tried again to climb him.

"Stop it!" She heard a voice of authority. "Stop fighting me, or you'll drown us both."

Every rational instinct told her to obey. Panic overrode reason. She continued to scrabble and flail and fight to climb on top of him . . . to get away from the water.

Pain exploded in her head. Bright stars sparkled and shot across her eyelids. Waves of blackness broke over her. She wanted to live. She wanted to fight for her life.

She wanted to cease the struggle, too. He hadn't left her a choice. As she sank into unconsciousness, and the warm sun caressed her face and bosom, a thought floated through her mind like the last bubble from a drowned child's lungs.

He hit me.

The neutral Pleasure Moon of Eurydyce

"Trouble comes in threes!"

The fortune teller sighed. Unfortunately, she was reading the cards for herself.

"*An unwelcome visitor.*" Madam Tarra placed an Inquiry card face up across the card to the East, where situations arise. "Hah! Not only 'unwelcome' but in possession of *a dangerous secret.*

"*A male who is not what he seems.*" She didn't bother to inquire further of that particular card. In the convoluted Who's Who of the Djinn family tree*, none of the Great Djinn was what he seemed.

Worst on the officially legitimate "Imperial Tiger" side was her Emperor's half-uncle, Django-Ra, who had fooled everyone about his sexual "bent," then raped the Empress Tarragonia-Marietta when she came unexpectedly into season soon after Crown Prince Tarrant-Arragon was weaned.

On the exiled "Dragon" branch, there was her "protector" Ala'Aster-Djalet—who did not officially exist. The Free Communicating Worlds would not have elected Ala'Aster-Djalet to lead them in the wars against the Imperial Tiger Djinn if they'd known that their Saurian Dragon Elect was not only a rogue Great Djinn, but also the enemy Emperor's cousin.

The thinly disguised, fugitive Empress Tarragonia-Marietta shook off her memories and tapped the third ominous card with a beautifully manicured forefinger. It showed an androgynous figure face down in the dirt, impaled by swords.

"*Someone close to me . . . in mortal danger.*"

Who was close? Did closeness refer to biology? Physical proximity? Or emotional affinity? As a clairvoyant, it was not easy to See Oneself, or One's loved ones . . . whatever "loved ones" meant!

Her sentiments were warmer for Ala'Aster-Djalet's boys than for her own three children, especially for her favorite, Djetthro-Jason, although there had been occasions when she'd felt in fear of her life in his exciting presence.

Could her terrifying son, Tarrant-Arragon, be defined as "a loved one"? Did she have any natural feelings for her eldest child, Electra-Djerroldina of Volnoth?

Tarra closed her heavy-lidded eyes.

Then there was her bastard youngest, Martia-Djulia, of whom she could not think without a shudder of horror and shame. Martia-Djulia would forever be seared on her mind as pinched-looking, with a galaxy-white shock of hair, the spitting image of Django-Ra.

The premature baby Princess had entered the world emitting blue sparks of static. Everyone whispered that she'd die, just as an infant Prince of an earlier generation had died.

Martia-Djulia hadn't died after her mother abandoned her. She'd grown up, an undiscovered cuckoo in the Imperial nest. Then, half a gestate ago, handsome, intimidating, appalling Tarrant-Arragon had paid his mother a visit, and she had blurted out the secret.

Perhaps One should not have. . . . Sometimes One wondered . . .

Tarra sat back in her wheelchair, distancing herself from myriad nameless regrets. One felt so helpless. Moreover, her most reliable couriers had not returned from their errand to Freighter Island on An'Koor.

Chapter Nine

Freighter Island, An'Koor
Later

Djetth sat on an improvised throne made of half a giant clam shell. It wasn't exactly comfortable, but it was dry and warm from the sun. Its stored heat felt pretty good on his overworked and underappreciated butt.

He was tired, and almost beyond caring.

He glanced across the shimmering beach at Martia-Djulia, who was behaving like an offended, fluffy cat, glaring at him when she thought he wasn't looking at her, then folding her arms and turning her tousled head away when he tried to meet her hazy, autumn-sky blue eyes.

He'd damned well saved her life!

"Textbook lifesaving!" he shouted at her, wondering why he was letting her make him feel he owed her an explanation. "Reach; Throw; Wade; Row; Swim; Tow," he quoted from some vividly remembered, black-crested, pale blue paperback, the *Royal Lifesaving Association Manual*. "Knock the damned fools out if they don't have the sense to lie back quietly and let themselves be saved."

That last wasn't an accurate quote, but the gist was spot on.

He could have waded, if Martia-Djulia hadn't panicked, forcing him to render her unconscious and cooperative. He'd towed her to shore and then, leaving her in the textbook coma position, he'd ventured back out four times.

He'd collected both of the seats, though they'd need a good day or two in the sun before they were dry enough to sit on, and the military hammock, complete with its clear, plastic-type protective covering.

Narrowing his eyes, Djetth wondered if it was worth the trouble to calculate the stresses they would impose on the hammock, if he were to be actively on top of—and in and out of—Martia-Djulia for a sustained amount of time.

He wasn't confident that the hammock was strong enough to hold Martia-Djulia and himself, even side by side, even if they were careful and very still. However, if her present mood didn't improve dramatically before dark, Martia-Djulia was unlikely to lie still for him in any case.

Mentally shrugging off the notion of celebrating their survival by having irresponsible sex, Djetth refocused on more practical matters.

He'd gathered up the cargo netting; some wire, enough anyway to make squirrel-type traps; the tool kit, and the canopy—which would make a good-sized water tank.

Hell's Teeth, he was tired, and he still had a lot to do before dark. The only silver lining so far was that An'Koor's gravity was a bit less than Tigron's—and the *Ark Imperial*'s. It made heavy work a little less heavy.

Clothes, shelter, fire, water. . . . He ran another checklist in his mind. Not necessarily in that order. The textbook order had been written with Earthlings in mind; modern Earthlings who'd got themselves lost while hunting or hiking in the woods, and who had a reasonable chance of being rescued within days.

Water. They needed water. Not immediately, but soon. If they'd been marooned on a naturally formed land mass, he'd look for fresh water bubbling up in the lushest, greenest part of the island. But, knowing Freighter Island's history, he didn't expect to find a freshwater spring. Therefore he had to start collecting and purifying water hours before they were desperate to drink it.

As for bathing—Djetth glanced at his fastidious, and very clean, Princess and smiled at his memories of being intimate with her.

Although wild and wonderful in many other respects, she didn't like any part of her body to smell of anything natural at any time. He foresaw problems. They were going to need a lot of fresh water.

Djetth surveyed the beach, trying to calculate how long they had been there, where the high tide mark was, and when the tide would be at its lowest. Low tide would be the time to dig a beach well for water.

Low tide would have been a better time for salvaging, too, but with his luck recently, the Thorcraft could have been in the path of a rogue riptide, and his stuff could have been washed a few hundred yards into deeper waters.

Deeper waters were exponentially more dangerous. There were carnivores in the sea. Big ones! Plenty of them had been attracted by the one that Tarrant-Arragon had so thoughtfully killed.

At first, Djetth hadn't realized what Tarrant-Arragon had been firing on. He'd been puzzled, until his fourth—and final—foray back to the Thorcraft, when he'd smelled blood and seen signs of an offshore feeding frenzy. Then he'd understood what Tarrant-Arragon had done, and perhaps why.

The sea monster's massive carcass would keep the other monsters busy for only so long. He and Martia-Djulia were imprisoned at Tarrant-Arragon's pleasure on this island with no way to escape.

They were like a male and a female of a rare species in a zoological society's breeding experiment, trapped in a small enclosure to force them to breed.

Just to make sure, Tarrant-Arragon had dropped them at a time and place where there were aphrodisiacs in the water. Damn him!

Who is he? What is in his mind when he looks at me so fiercely?

Martia-Djulia stole another glance at Djetth, *The Mysterious; Djetth, The Surprisingly Masterful—when no one else was looking. Djetth, The Savage.*

He terrifies me because he is a Great Djinn. He mystifies me because he doesn't talk like any Great Djinn I've ever met. He reminds me too much of my lost love.

I hate Djetth, if only for no better reason than that he isn't Jason. If only he'd give me a good reason to hate and despise him!

The trouble was, her brother had just tried to murder both of them. That was something she and Djetth had in common. It should make them allies.

Who are you, Djetth? she wondered. *Who—or what—are you that my brother would want to kill you so badly that he'd have no qualms about killing me with you?*

She wasn't going to ask. She wasn't going to show the slightest interest in him. He'd hit her! He kept secrets. He used words she didn't understand. For all she knew, such incomprehensible alien expressions as "fuck" could be words of enchantment, like a lesser form of Djinncraft.

Djetth could not be trusted. Never, never would she trust a male who was willing to take her to mate, sight unseen. She would have to be a complete and utter fool to make that mistake a second time.

She shivered at the memory of her unlamented and barely remembered first Mate, War-star Leader Titanus.

The Princess Martia-Djulia was not the vain, frivolous fool that the Princes of Tigron were pleased to assume she was. It was her private rebellion to validate their condescending, alpha-male assumptions. As long as Django-Ra thought her mind was too dull to read, she had been safe . . . until she'd had "inappropriate" sex with Jason, and made the fatal mistake of drawing Tarrant-Arragon's attention to her love life.

Why would a Great Djinn take a mercenary traitor's abandoned mistress to mate? Why would a male like Prince Djetthro-Jason want her? What bribe, or threat, or secret agenda would make a Great Djinn Prince—if Djetth truly were a Prince—overlook the fact that his bride was well past virginity and not known to be rut-rageous?

Djetth was staring at the sea. She did not know why he was doing so, but his focus on the water gave her an opportunity to watch him.

He'd stripped off his dark jewel-blue and yellow flight suit. One could tell a lot about a male from the way he treated his clothing when he undressed. Commander Jason had been tidy. Djetth was, too. He'd removed his outer garment with firm, efficient movements, and had hung it up to dry on a contraption he'd invented from some thin rope tied between two sturdy, long-stemmed, overgrown shrubs.

If she had wanted to draw conclusions about Djetth's disciplined upbringing and background, she could have. Naturally, she did not want to do so. She did not need yet another take-charge, military male in her life.

Djetth had glanced meaningfully at her as he split two thumb-sized sticks vertically with a knife, making them look like fat little females with his knife between their legs.

He'd looked at her again as he forced his female-shaped sticks to "sit astride" his rope and his wet clothes.

Everything he did could be interpreted as a low-key sexual threat.

She could tell that Djetth had been mentally undressing her. It was only a matter of time before he'd do more than throw meaningful glances at her. Sooner or later, he'd have the impudence to suggest that she should take her own clothes off. Males always did that if they thought the female might be available, and they were sure her protectors were too far away or too busy to kill them.

Naturally, she would defy him, just as she always found unnoticed ways to defy everyone else. She had courted the lightning for gestates, fully expecting that one day her quiet subversiveness would be noticed and punished.

Finally, out of An'Koor's blue sky, it had happened without warning or obvious provocation on her part. The brother who should have been her protector had tried to kill her.

Martia-Djulia plucked at her heavy, wet skirts, trying to spread them more advantageously so they would dry on her body, the way Djetth's remaining clothing was visibly drying on his body.

His upper body undergarment—which when wet had been indecently transparent and had stuck tightly to all his impressive bulges—now looked loose, white, and shapeless, although its cut seemed to suggest that it might have been intended to cling to broader shoulders, and drape teasingly over even more well-developed chest muscles.

Near-sighted she might be, but she could tell good tailoring from any distance, and his sloppy garment was not fit for a Prince.

It had short sleeves and a round-cut neckline. Most of the time, apart from the occasions when Djetth brazenly scratched himself, the hem fell decently below the top of his legs, but she had glimpsed a strange, short-legged, obscenely fitted, outrageously white garment with some kind of lumpy decoration in the most shocking place imaginable.

No, he was nowhere near as scrawny and diseased-looking as she had supposed on the disastrous day of their Mating ceremony. His arms and thighs were very attractive, really. It would be interesting to see what his face would look like clean-shaven.

He's looking my way! Getting to his feet . . .

Quickly Martia-Djulia covered her eyes with an elegantly languid hand, exaggerating her headache as she peeped through her fingers, but angling her hand so that he could see the discoloration and swelling on her jaw where he'd hit her. The bruise felt like a rotten soft fruit. In fact, although that side of her face tingled from her jaw to her eyelids, it didn't hurt very much, but she hoped that it looked dreadful.

She was glad that his mistreatment of her had left a mark. In fact, the next time he went out of sight, she might rub some berry juice on it, to make it look even worse. She wouldn't risk it yet, not while he was squatting on his haunches and digging a big hole in the sand using a hideous shell that looked like a mummified god's foot with long, white bones set in hardened, blackened flesh.

Was it logical to hope that a brute like Djetth would be patient if she claimed to have a headache? What Great Djinn ever was?

However, if Djetth were to rape her, he would give her the reason she needed to hate him. Perhaps then she'd find the heart to fight back.

Djetth took stock. Again. The short An'Koori day was still warm. He frowned at the horizon, estimating how long before the temperature dropped and night fell.

There was still a lot to do, and like the Little Red Hen of Djinni-vera's nursery-school stories, he'd have to do it all himself, though he had no doubt that he'd have company when the fruits of his labors were ready to be enjoyed.

Screw being the Little Red Hen! Djinni-vera's nursery-school stories were sexist. Why were there no immoral stories about Big Red Cocks?

His "beach well" was dug and lined with stones and shells to stop the sandy sides from collapsing inward as it filled. Water was seeping into the hollow, although it would take time before enough water had collected and the fresher water rose to the top.

At that point, the water would have to be scooped up and poured through a triple filter, and finally boiled. He would risk no shortcuts. Whether or not boiling would be enough to neutralize the aphrodisiacs in the water remained to be seen.

After months of enforced abstinence, he wanted sex badly. Just as badly, he wanted to thwart Tarrant-Arragon. After everything that had been done to force his hand, if he had sex with Martia-Djulia, it was going to be on his own terms, and with his eyes open. Unless or until she gave him the rut-rage.

Seeing Martia-Djulia's red corset again was going to severely test his willpower. Djetth glanced speculatively at his lovely companion.

One of the first priorities of survival in the wild is clothing. Dry clothing. Where the choice was between wet clothes or no clothes, one got naked. Two should not only get naked, but lie down together to share body heat! He would have to get Martia-Djulia out of her wet dress.

With hindsight, perhaps he should have undressed her while she was knocked out, but whatever else he might be, he wasn't that sort of male. He had ingrained, human scruples about what one could and could not do to an unconscious female.

Martia-Djulia worried him. The Martia-Djulia who'd let her hair down in bed with Commander Jason was a very different squirrel from the public Martia-Djulia of the last few months.

Jason had seen a secret side to her. Shy and inhibited she might be, but she hadn't hidden from Jason that she was an astute mischief-maker.

She wasn't as silly and superficial about her clothes and her appearance as she pretended to be. Nevertheless, if her pretense was for Djetth's benefit, she'd have to keep up her silliness.

His clothes were drying. Hers still had to be removed. They would be removed. However, he'd use force as a last resort. He'd really rather insert a little team-building between knocking Martia-Djulia senseless and stripping her clothes off.

"Would you like to help me make a fire?" Djetth called across the beach.

A fire ought to appeal to Martia-Djulia's frivolous persona. Fire was fascinating to watch and play with, and viscerally comforting. When it got dark, a fire was also romantic.

"Fire making is an art. I think you'd be good at it." He took a risk in saying that. He didn't honestly think the pampered Princess was good at anything except sex.

Fire wasn't as important, at least on temperate An'Koor, as dry clothing and shelter. However, not only would they need fire to cook with and to boil the water they collected, but before they could boil water, they'd need charcoal for water purification and filtration.

Later their fire would harden whittled stakes to make spears and javelins for when they went hunting, and its smoke would preserve fish if they caught more than they needed.

Djetth was thinking of the long term. Merely surviving wasn't his idea of revenge. He was going to live well. He was bloody well going to enjoy himself. Moreover, if he could, he'd find ways of enjoying Martia-Djulia without falling into Tarrant-Arragon's trap and making a lifelong commitment.

"Come over here. Help me select a good place for our fire," he tried again.

"You think I'm trying to lure you close to me so I can grab you for sex, don't you?" he guessed. "Forget it. Why would I waste time trying to trick you? You couldn't run far or fast in that big, wet dress. Right now, a good fire is a higher priority than sex."

Out of the corner of his eye Djetth thought he saw her toss her head. Hah! So she was listening.

"We want our fire site close to potential fuel, but not so close that a surprise gust of wind could blow sparks into those sparse woods and raze the island! We'd have charcoal out the *wazoo*, but we'd have to live on *sushi*."

Djetth deliberately peppered his conversation with Earth terms. Sooner or later, even Martia-Djulia would be curious enough to ask about one thing or another. Once he got her talking, she'd open up in other ways.

"Preferably sheltered from the wind, rain . . ." *Also from sea spray in case of a very high tide. Also from surveillance.*

Instinctively Djetth looked up. Presumably, somewhere miles above them loomed the massive, sinister bulk of the Tigron Imperial flagstar, *Ark Imperial.*

He raised an angry eyebrow, although his urge was to flip an obscene gesture into the ionosphere. Who was watching? Tarrant-Arragon? 'Rhett? Djinni-vera!

"Tarrant-Arragon fast-forwarded you, because you went at it so long." Djinni's comment had ricocheted for months in his memory. Was that criticism or praise? What had she meant? What had she felt? Was she sorry that his stamina had not been unleashed on her?

What he'd like Tarrant-Arragon to see—or not see—and feel was altogether different from what he wanted little Djinni to see and feel.

He wanted the damn lot of them to be sorry!

He glanced back towards Martia-Djulia, who was showing more interest in some sand-tolerant, flowering ground-vine than in him. On Earth the blue-flowering plant could have been a creeping, cascade petunia or morning glory.

Morning glory . . . he furrowed his brow, distantly remembering a psychedelic-era lyric. Was morning glory poisonous, or merely hallucinogenic like "magic mushrooms"?

"Don't eat—don't touch—anything you find," he warned. "Not everything that looks good is safe."

Martia-Djulia continued to stroke the delicate flower with her pampered forefinger. The pout on her expressive face looked a bit more pronounced. She'd heard him.

What a strange, contrary mixture she was! She wore a tight corset that set a male's imagination on fire, yet she rebelled whenever a dominant male told her what to do, or what not to do.

Had she known at the time that her marathon screw with Jason was being watched and filmed? There was an interesting thought for later!

"We'll want our fire near our shelter."

Even if she refused to join in the fire making, he was including her in the choice of its location, which would impact where they made their bed, whether she liked it or not.

"Shelters."

She had spoken! Djetth rejoiced disproportionately. Okay, she was arguing. She was stressing shelters, plural. She was drawing a little line in the sand.

"Shelters?" he fired back over his shoulder, studiously not looking at her. "Do you know how to build a shelter?"

"No."

"So, you think I'm going to build two tonight? After I've built a fire. And a fire reflector. All before dark?"

Sand scrunched. Wet finery scratched and sent shell fragments softly skittering. Djetth's senses told him that his Princess was moving towards him, but he did not turn to watch her approach.

Instead of smiling welcomingly up at her, he picked up a tightly closed, weed-encrusted, bivalve shell. Judging by its balanced weight, it probably had its dead owner inside. Djetth hurled the shell as far down the beach as he could, before resuming his tirade.

"As if I haven't enough to do after I've laid up fuel—all by myself—to keep the fire going all through the night. Caught dinner all by myself. Cooked the bloody dinner. And dug a *latrine*."

Her slanted shadow darkened the sand beside him.

Djetth was tempted to add, *I'm not going to share my bed with you if you're wet.* However, a threat like that would lose him hard-won ground, and would bolster her argument for a separate bed.

"What is a fire-reflector?" she asked. "Could we do without it for one night?"

"There are a lot of things we could do without for one night." *Dinner comes to mind. Sex.* Djetth grunted and rose to his feet.

The most natural thing in the world would have been to hook an arm around Martia-Djulia's tightly cinched waist, and point to the campsite he'd chosen. Instead, he put his left hand on his hip and pointed with his right hand.

"You see that little stand of trees—the ones with twisted trunks, which fork into three or four branches at about the height of my hip? Those two there will make good supports for the entrance to a shelter. I'll thrust a long, straight branch between their crotches as a ridgepole."

She looked doubtful, but Djetth was on good ground with his woodmanship.

"A '*crotch*' is where a tree *bifurcates*," he explained,

to make her think about crotches, and long, straight objects being thrust into them. "They're a good choice because their canopies lean inland, away from what becomes the obvious spot to clear for a fire pit. Do you agree?"

He took her silence for consent.

"Right. I'll start digging the fire pit. Could you find something we can burn? There are three types of fuel needed for a fire. Tinder is the most important." Chivalrously, he assigned the greatest importance to the easiest, most enjoyable, most feminine task.

"I can't start a fire without tinder," he added with strategic disregard for the fact that he was a Great Djinn in possession of three Rings of Imperial Authority, one of which was the laser-like Fire Stone.

"What is tinder?" she asked, sounding suspicious.

"Ahhhh," he drawled, overcome by a mischievous instinct. "Look here."

With his left hand he lifted his T-shirt, with his right forefinger and thumb he reached into his navel, confident that after eight weeks of hard exercise he had well-defined abs and a very deep and attractive "inny" of a tummy button.

He withdrew lint.

"Oh, slurrid!" his squeamish Princess exclaimed, predictably, but she stared at his lower abdomen and perhaps at the bulge in his trunk briefs with flattering interest.

"This fluff"—he placed it in the palm of his left hand as reverently as a scientist explaining an important specimen—"is created from the action of hard work. Friction attracts filaments of fabric from my cotton T-shirt, and works them into a flat, fluffy mat."

He moved his cupped hand closer to her.

"Good tinder needs to have irregular edges, plenty of air spaces." He teased his tummy-button fluff into a looser wad. "It must be dry. Would you like to touch it?"

He smiled, imagining what she was thinking behind her parted pink lips, and narrowed blue eyes.

"If you have any in your tummy button—which I doubt—yours would be too damp to be useful right now."

He could tell that she didn't know whether she'd been complimented or insulted. He grinned at her, lifted the hem of his T-shirt, and delicately put his well-fluffed lint back into his navel for safekeeping.

"Good tinder should look like that. You may find some birds' nests in the bushes." He pointed inland. "Or in the long grasses of that dune." He pointed seaward. "Birds line their nests with moss, lichen, and downy feathers. It's great tinder. Bring back an entire nest, if you find one."

"What if I can't find a nest?" She glanced at the tangle of woodland undergrowth beyond the first trees. "I don't think I want to go very far."

"I don't think you can go very far in bare feet, and in that ridiculous wet dress," he hinted heavily.

He could have offered to go with her. He'd have to go foraging for wood in any case. However, his top priority was to talk her out of her wet dress before it made her ill. "As I see it, you've got three choices. Your best option is to take off the dress and make yourself useful. Your worst is to keep the dress on and not help very much."

"You said I have three choices. What's the third?"

"I was hoping you'd ask." Djetth grinned. "Annoy me enough, and I'll rip that dress off you. Think about it."

Chapter Ten

Later

As if things couldn't get any worse. As if her body hadn't betrayed her enough for one day! Would this waking nightmare never end?

Martia-Djulia dropped the bird's nest that she had been carrying and pressed her hand low to her side until the sudden, dull pain subsided.

I cannot let Djetth see me like this!

She threw a quick glance back along the tree line to where she had last seen Djetth. He had been digging with noisy enjoyment; "singing," he called the barbarian roaring. Now he was nowhere to be seen. That did not mean that he couldn't see her.

Djetth asked too many intrusive questions. He took too much of an interest in her long-dormant reproductive system.

Another pang. She should lie down and hide amongst the coarse dune grasses. Though she'd missed taking her midday "remedy," her system should not react this soon. Her cramps might not be the curse she dreaded. They might be delayed symptoms of internal injuries from the crash. Or an intestinal reaction to this watery planet's lesser gravity. Or hunger. Or perhaps her bowels had taken a chill.

Normally, she would never lie down on the ground, but this was not a normal day, not a normal world, not a normal plight.

Thank the stars it was impossible Commander Jason could have left her pregnant! She had made sure she'd never been rut-rageous since her second son was conceived.

Her "remedy" prevented her from menstruating as well as ovulating. Now she was without her "remedy."

Slowly and carefully Martia-Djulia lowered herself to the ground and settled her damp, chilled stomach in the shifting sand. The stored heat lapped her sides. The gentle warmth was wonderfully soporific.

Martia-Djulia kicked the lower half of her legs free of the cold, damp heaviness of her dress, bent her knees, and idly swung her crossed ankles in the air.

The sun blazed softly on her bare shins, her damp back, and on some unknown plants which she could hear crackling in the heat. An intermittent breeze rustled the sharp, dry grasses.

Where are you, Djetth? What are you doing now? Martia-Djulia peered through the grasses, almost enjoying her low-lying, tiger's-eye view of this alien world.

Down by the water's edge, birds that she had at first taken for windblown leaves were playing daredevil games with the sea, chasing after the flat water as it retreated, then running for dry land as a new wave reared up and advanced.

If One were in a surreal mood, One might compare the birds to silly, infatuated young Princesses, and the sea to inexorable Djinn Princes.

So, her brother wanted her dead. Why? Because she'd refused to Mate with Djetth? A Princess Imperial wasn't an exclusive prostitute, by all the Lechers of Antiquity! One would not open One's legs to a stranger simply because One's brother wished this or that Mating upon One.

Defiance was easier, her troublemaking hormones whispered, when the candidate looked like he was newly released from a sick bed.

"Uh-huh!"

It was not the sort of grunt that Palace courtiers emitted. She'd never heard such a sardonic, ill-bred sound in her life, but Djetth's vulgar utterance seemed to say, "I was correct in my first impression of you, you useless, slack-witted female!"

By birth and breeding, I outrank you, Djetth. I don't respond to your grunts!

She picked up the nest and made a show of studying it. To scramble to her feet, to acknowledge his presence in any way, would signal that he had some power over her.

Martia-Djulia had never looked at a bird's nest before. At home, there were birds in the Palace, of course, but they nested and roosted high, where roaming household tigers could not reach them.

The nest wasn't as simple as it looked. Did birds collect plant matter at random? Did birds know what bits of plants would curl and shrivel as they dried, thus becoming interlocked?

A tiny, decayed leaf had a lacy lattice of reddish brown. Most of the sticks and grasses were drab shades, like the depressing brown once worn by Tigron's Badnewsbringers. The lining contained finer material such as long, twisted hairs which had been breeze-blown into complicated, single-stranded knots.

What's this? How did a vivid pink strand of something that looked like—but could not possibly be—a glossy thread of Volnoth's fine silk come to be on the island?

"What do you think you're doing?" Djetth drawled.

Martia-Djulia rested her head on her left hand, though

sandy grit dug into her elbow, and looked up at him. No appropriately clever retort came to mind, so she settled for silent insolence.

He'd adopted an aggressive stance, with his feet apart, powerful arms folded across his massive chest. His savage gaze seemed to be resting on her bottom.

Two could stare.

From where she was lying, Martia-Djulia had a very good view of his long, hard, muscled legs. Indeed, he was in very much better shape than the first impression she'd had two cycles ago.

She, on the other hand, had let herself go a little in the past two cycles. What, after all, was the point in looking her best for her beloved Commander Jason if Jason was never coming back? It would be foolish to make herself look as attractive as possible when she did not want the Mate who was sniffing around her.

What slack-mindedness to regret that she'd abandoned her weight-reducing diet! Of course she was not sorry, now. The more weight she carried, the more she could throw behind a blow, if she needed to hit him, or stab him.

"Do you want to have sex with me?" he asked abruptly.

"Great balls of fire, no! No!"

His bluntness had startled her into answering far more vehemently than she should have. A casual laugh and a "Stars, whatever gave you that idea?" would have been so much more effective.

"If that's true, why do you care if I see you half-dressed? If you aren't interested in arousing my sexual interest, what is it to you if I see you in your corset?"

Oh, stars, he *had* been mentally undressing her! Had he been stripping her mind, too? Why else had he chosen this moment to voice a coarse version of her own thoughts?

"I have no idea what you are talking about," Martia-

Djulia retorted with all the dignity she could muster. As she spoke, she sat up and drew her clammy skirts over her legs and feet.

Sand was stuck to her front, like an encrustation of thirsty beetles on a smooth-skinned, water-engorged cactus. She tried to brush the sand off.

"You don't much like that dress, do you?" he asked, sounding thoughtful as he watched her.

"I love this dress. Have you any idea how much work went into it? Have you noticed the cut? The detail? The muted colors are particularly flattering, I think."

"Then you should take better care of it," Djetth retorted. "That dress isn't going to dry properly with you wearing it. The colors will fade unevenly, more's the pity, if it doesn't rot and fall apart first. Sun, salt. Shit. It's inevitable."

He bent and reached out a hand to her. Martia-Djulia pressed the damaged nest into his hand, and hoped a snapped twig might dig into the fullness at the base of his thumb.

"I've got the fire going, our dinner is roasting, but it needs watching. Come along." He transferred the nest, and reached out again. Martia-Djulia ignored his hand and got to her feet without his assistance, staggering a little.

"Princess, the sooner you get your royal clothes off, the better," he remarked as his masterful hand caught her just above the elbow.

"Thank you," she said, intending her cool thanks as assurance that he could release his hold on her arm without further fear that she would fall at his feet.

He did not unhand her.

Djetth's reference to her "royal clothes" was more accurate than he could possibly know. Martia-Djulia used clothes the same way that she spoke in formal Court language around Djetth; to emphasize how sexually unavailable she was as far as he was concerned.

As he marched her across the beach, and she tried not to stumble, she eyed her tall, grim, formidable escort.

Her beautiful, formal, exquisite dress was an extension of her ego. If she gave up her royal trappings, she gave up part of her identity, and all of her inborn superiority over Djetth.

What superiority? a small voice jeered in her mind. *What precedence does an Emperor's daughter enjoy on an uninhabited island, on a blockaded planet?* What use was her blood-closeness to the throne if the Emperor's Heir Apparent could shoot her down with impunity and leave her to die?

Besides, if she removed her dress—given that she could remove it without the assistance of several servants—she would look like any other female. Would Djetth treat her respectfully if she looked no better than a commoner? Did he treat her respectfully anyway?

"Have you considered," Djetth began slowly after they had walked a little way, "what it will feel like to have diarrhea in that dress?"

Djetth was the most ill-bred person with whom she had ever been forced to converse. Not even the Imperial Court physicians spoke of such matters.

She would not dignify his question with a response.

"You should think about it. If you stay wet, you will become ill. You may become ill, anyway. Better half-naked for a day than wearing excrement, wouldn't you say?"

Martia-Djulia remained silent.

"Take it off, and we can dry it. Tomorrow, you can wear it again, if you want to."

She supposed that she should encourage the sudden polite turn that his remarks had taken.

"You may have a point about the logistics of physical necessity," Martia-Djulia conceded. She glanced at him, and hoped she didn't appear nervous. "Is there anything, anything at all, that I can wear for the sake of modesty?"

"Modesty?" he repeated. "Who is to see you? Apart

from ourselves, there are no arbiters of good taste and fashion here. No Court reporters."

He narrowed his eyes and looked at her with a slight lifting of his lip at one corner in an enigmatic shadow of a half smile.

"Haven't you got a simple petticoat or shift under all that? No, I don't suppose you have." He tilted his head to one side and seemed to consider. "My T-shirt is bone dry. I could lend it to you."

"I would not be seen dead in male underwear."

"If you die, I'll take it off you."

Martia-Djulia hadn't expected to laugh. Djetth's warped sense of humor took her completely by surprise. She found herself laughing aloud before she could reflect on the unwisdom of encouraging him.

"That would be acceptable," she said formally.

As they neared the fire, she straightened her back and lifted her chin. "Owing to the action of the seawater, I may require some assistance," she said with as much dignity and detachment as possible under the humiliating circumstances.

"Of course," Djetth said urbanely. "Your things have shrunk. I should have thought of that."

"Why should you?" she questioned, wondering whether he was mocking her. It was, after all, quite implausible that her clothes had really shrunk.

He threw her a disquieting look.

"Are we as close to the fire as we want to be for this exercise?" he asked. "Some of this stuff you are wearing could conceivably be flammable."

Martia-Djulia inclined her head in acknowledgment of his concern for her safety, then turned her back to him.

Nothing happened.

"My sleeves seem tight. I cannot reach between my shoulder blades. Please unfasten my dress at the back."

"Oh, yes, of course. Happy to." He sounded distracted.

Martia-Djulia felt his breath on the bare skin above

her scooped neckline. His warm, clumsy fingers brushed the curve of her hips and curled around the back of her waist. It was almost as if he held her from behind at arm's length while he bent to study the intricacies of her fastenings.

"Start at the top," Martia-Djulia suggested.

"Hmmm," he commented obscurely. Instead of obeying that simple instruction, he stroked his fingers up either side of her sensitive spine. "It seems to me that this fabric has not shrunk evenly. I think there would be less strain if I were to alternate."

Martia-Djulia didn't know what to say. She could hardly contradict herself and tell him that the fabric hadn't shrunk. Yet he seemed to be using shrinkage as a pretext to gently and firmly stroke her body around each successive—or alternating—fastening.

Up. And down. Up . . . It was most unnecessary.

His fingertips traced each of the rigid, vertical "ribs" of her corset behind her back. If she hadn't known better, she would have thought that he knew about the narrow knives.

His clever fingers returned to the small of her back, which had always been a secret, sensitive erogenous area, and lingered there. To her horror, a secret thrill began. Her inner thighs began to tremble.

Suddenly she felt the top part of her dress come loose. Just in time, she caught the front of her stiff outer bodice in both hands as it collapsed forward like the first thin slice of roasted meat under the master chef's carving blade.

She held the front of the dress against herself as her sleeves crumpled and avalanched against the insides of her elbows, leaving her shoulders bare and exposed.

"Whoa, that looks nasty!" Djetth commented.

She closed her eyes in humiliation. Assuming that he had seen a silvery stretch mark, or an out-of-place bulge of skin, she felt sick with misery and shame.

"Those seat belts did a number on you," he murmured. His rough-skinned fingertip reached over her shoulder to touch the exposed upper curve of her bosom.

Without understanding why she bothered, Martia-Djulia held her breath and inwardly tensed so that her arms and breasts would be as firm as possible.

"By the way—"

His fingers gently closed on the point of her chin, and he turned her averted face towards him. Although her eyes were shut, she felt his breath on her face as he inspected the bruise. For an incomprehensible, breathless moment, she thought he was going to kiss her.

She felt her lips part.

"For what it's worth, I'm sorry I got you into this," he whispered huskily.

An apology? Martia-Djulia's eyes flew open and she found herself staring into concerned, slightly frowning, stormy gray eyes.

Great Djinn never apologize. The Imperial Machismo did not permit a Prince of the blood Imperial to admit that he'd done wrong. No one who mattered had ever apologized to her. As far as she could recall, her father had never uttered even a word of regret for Mating her to War-star Leader Titanus.

What did this apology say about "Prince" Djetthro-Jason? Her suspicions had been correct. They'd tried to foist a bastard half-breed on her.

"Luckily, we have the emergency medical kits. I'll see what we've got for those abrasions. Don't go anywhere."

When she was sure he'd gone, Martia-Djulia eased her hands forward and stared at the exposed swell of her bosom. Where the seat belts had tightened, they had dug in cruelly, leaving ugly, red diagonal grazes on her breasts.

And he'd touched them!

* * *

Djetth was glad of the excuse to take a walk. Touching Martia-Djulia's soft skin brought back memories of the last time he'd undressed her, along with insane yearnings.

Presumably he was suffering some primitive reaction to the danger they'd come through; some vestigial evolutionary urge to celebrate the fact that he was still living by inseminating the nearest female.

Unfortunately for his primal instincts, Martia-Djulia was exactly the sort of female a caveman would go for. She looked gloriously fertile. Plenty of fat reserves in that big, firm, amazing arse. Those splendid, soft, white, mobile breasts were made for grabbing, playing with, and sucking.

Whether or not he liked her personality had nothing to do with it. His warrior hormones needed a release.

Do you want to have sex with me? he'd asked. She had said *No*. Therefore, he was obliged to behave himself.

Easier said than done!

It had been all he could do not to bite the base of her neck where a nervous pulse fluttered. Or grab her buttocks. Or hold her firmly by the hips and press himself against her lovely backside. Or slip his hands under her arms and cup her breasts while he swirled his tongue around the ridges of her ears, and sucked and nibbled her plump little earlobes.

How different from last time, when he'd ripped her clothes off with her frenzied assistance and the aid of a knife which she had produced from somewhere. Then he'd fucked her brains out. Also his own. If he hadn't, he might have been in the right place at the right time to stop Tarrant-Arragon from marrying Djinni-vera.

She must be wondering what I'm doing with the salve. Djetth snatched it up, turned towards the job at hand, and caught an eyeful of her back-laced, black-lace-trimmed, rebellion-red corset.

Think of something else, Djetth.

He glanced at his nearly dry flight suit hanging on the improvised clothesline, and decided that she might think it obnoxiously sexist if he were to be fully dressed while stripping her almost naked.

"You'd better do your front yourself, don't you think?" he said, joining her and passing the salve over her shoulder. "Er, you haven't been scratching yourself, have you? You don't want to do that."

He'd noticed a scattering of long, raised streaks criss-crossing her upper chest and cleavage. The seat belts hadn't given her those marks. Moreover, the tip of her nose and the high planes of her cheeks looked like she'd caught the sun, or wandered into a biting cloud of midges.

When the light slanted a certain way, a part of her face and chest took on a subtly pebbled texture, as if a workman on a ladder had slopped skin-colored stucco down onto her.

Since there were no workmen—on ladders or otherwise—the culprit was most likely pollen. Fewmet! She might have allergies. Just when he thought he was on top of things, life moved the goalposts.

Pacing in circles behind her back, watching her shadow's progress as she rubbed the stuff over her fantastic breasts, he had an idea. Assessing her garments for their value as survival equipment might be a good way to introduce emotional detachment into the tricky final stages of the process.

"Ready?" he asked. He took the tube of salve from her and tucked it inside his waistband for safekeeping.

"Oh, how slurrid," she said. "That is so unsanitary!"

Djetth wasn't going to discuss the contents of his trunk briefs.

"Hey, look at this," he announced, detaching some looped stuff from the lower part of her court dress and exposing an alien garment that reminded him of a bustle, or the reinforced insides of a full wig. "I've found a sieve! Or a colander. Now, if we could only find some wild rice to cook—"

"Fool!" she sneered.

"You're right. It's a good basis for our first water filter, though. This is nice," he continued, as he peeled off yards of netting. "We could probably catch fish in this, if we don't need it all for triple-filtering water, of course. You bring plenty to the party, don't you, babe?"

They were down to her corset and her lace trimmed, knee-length drawers.

"Do you want your, er, foundation garment that tight?"

"Yes, I do."

Djetth glanced at the position of the sun, and decided that he'd taken way too long coaxing her out of her dress. There wasn't enough daylight left to argue over the corset.

"Ah well, An'Koor has a temperate climate. The nights are short and cool, but not cold. I don't suppose your circulation will be massively affected if you keep it on. Raise your arms." So saying, he stripped off his T-shirt and dropped it over her head and arms.

"At least it is warm," she remarked. Her voice shook with a powerful emotion that might have been relief. Of course, she might have simply not known how chilled she had become. "White is not my color."

"It's not anyone's, is it?" Djetth retorted. He bent and tossed the bulk of her damp dress over his shoulder.

"It is not, now. My father's chosen livery is dark purple with silver. My brother's color is black."

"Of course," Djetth agreed sardonically, not expecting Martia-Djulia to understand. He doubted if she knew about the color coding for heroes and villains in old American Westerns.

Apparently, it hadn't occurred to her to pick up her

own discarded clothes. While she stood there with her arms crossed under her breasts, he used his elbow to roll up the yards of decorative netting, garden hose fashion.

"Upon his accession to the throne, my grandfather, the Emperor Djohn-Kronos, took white for his own exclusive color, which meant that all the virgins in the Empire had to wear pale green instead," she said chattily.

Tight-lipped, Djetth picked up the last item, the bustle, and strode towards his clothesline. He was not surprised that the status- and fashion-conscious Princess's focus switched from what color suited a person to what color was exclusive to her senior male relatives. She was very up on the history of Royal color choices. Very spoilt.

Did she honestly imagine that he was interested in what color virgins wore seventy years ago when her grandmother and his were girls? Hadn't she registered that Djohn-Kronos's color choice started a war?

Ever since the original Troodons founded the Saurian Orders, Saurian ambassadors had always worn the no-color, white. When the Emperor decreed that anyone except himself and his Mate would be put to death for wearing white, he violated intergalactic treaties that guaranteed peacemakers and diplomats neutrality as long as they wore white.

"So that is why We don't like white?" he snarled over his shoulder. His barbed use of the Royal Pronoun probably flew wide.

Martia-Djulia had never yet shown any interest in him whatsoever. She had not asked about his historic name, nor about his family, or indeed whether he had any living relatives. Not that he would have told her the whole truth, if she had asked.

Since she had only the vaguest idea who he was, there was no reason for Martia-Djulia to know how much, or why, his branch of the family hated hers.

However, as he had demonstrated before, and would demonstrate again before long, liking a person or her ancestors was not a prerequisite for great sex.

He grinned.

"Take heart, sweetheart. My T-shirt won't stay white on you for long."

Chapter Eleven

"Hey, sweetheart . . ."

Djetth broke off whatever ineffective spell he'd been chanting as he fastened her beautiful dress and all its trappings beside his flight suit. Martia-Djulia looked away, before he could turn and catch her staring at his finely chiseled buttocks.

". . . you need a nickname."

"I do?" Martia-Djulia knew that a nickname was a *name-shortform*. Djetthro-Jason was "Djetth" to his friends. The universally popular Djarrhett was better known as " 'Rhett." She'd heard that Djinni-vera called Tarrant-Arragon "Tigger" in private. A nonsense nickname meant that the nicknamer liked One.

"I can't go on calling you Martia-Djulia all the time," he said, casually wrenching a branch off a nearby tree.

"You do not do so, in any case." Martia-Djulia became painfully aware that at some point she'd clasped her hands over her pounding heart. *Why can't you go on calling me 'sweetheart'?*

"You realize that sometimes when I call you 'sweetheart' you are anything but . . . ?"

Sweetheart could be an insult? Oh!

She could tell nothing from his expression. Djetth seemed more interested in what he might do with his length of tree-wood than in whether or not her feelings might be hurt.

"So, sweetheart, do you think of yourself as a Jewel or as a Marsh?"

"Neither!"

One might as well have shouted defiantly at the sea. Djetth took a knife and began to chip the torn end of his branch into a pale point.

Martia-"Marsh." Djulia, "Jewel." How . . . obvious. Migger? Jigger? Digger? No, One had to admit, One was not a "digger"! Anyway, what was the point of a nonsense nickname if One made it up for Oneself?

"Those are my choices?" Even to her own ears, her demand sounded plaintive.

Martia-Djulia saw Djetth's lip curl in an expression of amused contempt. No doubt he was mentally placing bets that his frivolous, superficial, not-too-smart Princess would choose to be "Jewel."

If "sweetheart" was an insult, "Jewel" would be, too.

"Marsh, then! If you don't mean it when you call me a sweetheart, then you might as well call me after a treacherous bog."

If he'd been within reach, she'd have slapped the sudden grin from his wicked-bearded face.

"I like marshes," he said. "They're soft, lush, wild, wet places that a male could sink himself into and be lost forever!"

Disgusting male!

Why am I not disgusted? Martia-Djulia wondered. *Is it because I am almost sure he does it deliberately?*

Djetth missed no opportunity to insult, shock, offend, and patronize. It was as if he purposely displayed himself in the very worst light possible.

Why would he do that? Was it his idea of intellectual

honesty? Was he trying reverse psychology? Did he imagine that, if he behaved grossly enough, she would be moved to offer him advice on how she would prefer to be courted?

Or was Djetth cunningly mirroring a low distortion of her own tactics back at her? It was a depressing idea.

Fading with the An'Koori daylight was her last glimmer of hope. Hope of what, though?

That Tarrant-Arragon would have a change of heart, and rescue them? Tigers were more likely to sprout wings and develop a taste for cactus flowers!

That Djinni-vera would discover what Tarrant-Arragon had done, and would insist that the day's actions be reversed? That was unlikely, since Martia-Djulia hadn't had a chance to keep her promise to be pleasant to Djinni-vera. Although they'd been on the *Ark Imperial* for two cycles, she and Djetth had never once been invited up to the Imperial Suite.

That Commander Jason was not really dead? That, undetected, Jason had been following the *Ark Imperial* with a mighty rebel force, and once the *Ark Imperial* had gone, Jason would invade An'Koor and rescue her?

That was the least realistic hope of all!

Lifting her chin in forlorn pride, Martia-Djulia took in the site of her approaching—what?—Defeat? Humiliation? Downfall? Prince Djettho-Jason would assert his physical power over her. At the time and place of his choosing, there would be a swift and decisive return to male dominance and the subjugation of the female.

What was the worst he could do to her? Would it be so bad if only she could pretend it was Jason doing it?

Tonight would be the turning point. When darkness fell, Djetth would give her more than enough reasons to hate him.

"*I want to stain you all over. And over again . . .*"

As he continued his preparations for the night ahead,

Djetth crooned his own perversion of some dimly remembered seventies' lyrics.

Having whittled and fire-hardened the ends of four wrist-thick saplings, he began to pound stakes into the soft ground at an angle, while he imagined having Martia-Djulia on her back, and on her front, until his T-shirt was grass-stained all over. And not just grass stains.

He was in no hurry to be seen to consummate a Mating he wasn't sure he wanted. Princess Marsh had left him at the altar. Pulling out at the last minute, again and again, would be fitting revenge.

Good plan!

Keeping time with his song, he began to lift and stack logs against his newly erected stakes, forming an efficient firewood pile which did triple duty as a windbreak and fire-reflector, throwing heat back towards where the shelter would be. Shelter, singular. Bugger shelters!

He was only building one, and in the end the fastidious Princess would be glad to share his bed and his body heat.

Behind him, the fire crackled louder as fat dripped from the animal roasting on a spit. It looked even better than it smelled. And it was beginning to smell pretty good.

While he stripped offshoots from branches that would become sloping rafters for the shelter, he mentally debriefed himself.

"*Do you want to have sex with me?*" had been way too considerate, even if he had only been intent on frightening her out of her dress at the time. Commander Jason's "*I've got to have you!*" was the line that got the deed done. Unfortunately, he probably shouldn't recycle that exact phrase. She might remember it.

Djetth grinned as his memory fired up again.

"*Damn, Princess, I've got to have you!*" he'd announced, on a not-so-private balcony. As far as he'd remembered, he'd danced with her in the ballroom below, then he'd gone off to get drinks, promising to join her on the Imperial balcony to look down on the guests and criticize their fashion sense.

He'd probably tossed back a couple of strong slugs from his hip flask before returning to sip fizzy wine with her; he might have been slightly "in his cups" as his Grandmama would say with regal disapproval. If he hadn't been drunk, who knows what would have happened next?

Grandmama Helispeta was probably right. He drank a bit too much, posed a little too recklessly, and put too much swagger into living up to his chosen image as an action-stud. Deep down, perhaps he was not naturally the flashy top gun, but he always looked the part. He was an excellent shot, and had a cool head in a crisis. When sober.

When he wasn't sober, he was a lightning rod for trouble.

He stood, rested his fists on his hips, and leaned backwards to stretch his heavily worked abs, before getting down to the next job on his To-Do-Before-Bed list.

He'd selected the longest branch to be a ridge pole, wedged between the two trees he'd identified earlier, and against which he'd lean and lash the "rafters." However, given the lack of headroom, he'd frame the bed before he constructed the shelter.

Djetth rolled his sore shoulders in a doggy-paddle motion, showing off a little, knowing that Princess Marsh had been watching him for some time. He turned his head and smiled at her.

She dropped her gaze.

"What is that?" she asked, as if she'd been staring at the mystery roast, and not at his physique at all.

"It's the best I can do for dinner tonight. Do you want to know what sort of animal it was?"

Considering how squeamish she was, he'd gone to some trouble to render their dinner anonymous. The marine iguana-like creature that he had caught sunning itself on the beach had skinned well. Minus crested head, clawed feet, skin and tail, it could have been a very large rabbit.

Princess Marsh hadn't seen the capture, the kill, or the preparations because she had been sunbathing in her wet dress in the long dune grasses.

"No," she agreed.

"Didn't think so."

The big, ugly tail was cooking separately, caked in a ball of mud and buried in the ashes. Owing to the absence of loose folds of excess skin in the muscular tail, it had been too fiddly to skin. He'd sliced it off.

It would probably be the best bit, but it would also take longer to cook, and they were both hungry.

Djetth had eaten An'Koori iguana before. Roasted, it would be tough eating, but it wouldn't poison them.

Having positioned four long, straight branches on the ground to make a rectangular bed frame, he strode to the fire to turn the spit. His thoughts, naturally, considering where one puts a spit, turned back to sex.

How many times he'd gone over that balcony scene in his mind, wondering which of any number of possible elements had gotten him into bed with Tarrant-Arragon's sister.

Her Highness should have slapped him for his insolence. As far as the Communicating Worlds were concerned, he was a low-born mercenary, not fit to kiss her feet. When she'd lifted her chin and given him a haughty stare, he'd expected a stinging rebuff at the very least.

For some reason, she'd gaped at him as if he were a god. It was the faintest shimmer of encouragement. He'd taken it and pressed his hips as close to hers as he could get. In the same bold move, he'd thrust one thigh between hers, brushing her delightfully soft crotch, which was trembling with submissive passion. Or so he'd imagined at the time.

When she still didn't object, he'd seized a fistful of

hair at the back of her neck, and plunged his tongue between her lips. The rest was history.

By All the Lechers of Antiquity, it was time for history to repeat itself. Why not? What had Martia-Djulia fancied about Commander Jason that she did not go for in Djetth?

With Commander Jason, Martia-Djulia had seemed to fall for the sexually assertive approach. Of course, it might not have been Jason's conversational prowess that turned her on. She might have liked the decadent thrill of doing the deed with what she thought was a lesser being.

"How long will it be? Before dinner is cooked," Marsh added, as if she thought he might have misunderstood what she was talking about.

He had just stepped back inside the bed frame.

"If you want to know that, sweet . . . Marsh, grab hold of one of its legs and pull." Ignoring her look of disgust, he added, "It'll be ready when the legs loosen. Meanwhile, you'll find time passes more quickly if you work. Would you like to take charge of turning the spit?"

Djetth kicked at high spots on the ground, making sure that the groundsheet wouldn't rest on stones, or ants' nests. They'd be uncomfortable enough, this first night, without that sort of annoyance.

Casually, as if he didn't care whether or not she lent a hand, he waved a hand at the pile of discarded twigs. "Maybe you could peel off strips of flexible bark from those so we have ties for lashing poles together."

He had no imminent need for bark strips; he could rip strips from her dress if he ran out of rope-like materials rescued from the downed Thorcraft. However, he preferred not to ruin a good length of anything, and Princess Marsh needed an easy task.

"It's getting cooler," she remarked, as if that were her reason for moving closer to the fire.

"That's because it's getting late."

Djetth glanced at the An'Koori sun, which was well on its way to setting in the sea behind them, turning the sky from turquoise to swimming-pool blue.

As the short day came to an end, a cool breeze had blown up off the sea, which was why he'd changed his mind about skipping the fire reflector. Since consensual sex didn't seem to be a realistic expectation, he wasn't about to waste his time and energy on making her a comfortable bed.

Out of the corner of his eye he watched Marsh make herself mildly useful for the first time since he'd met her.

How ironic, he reflected. *Less than six months ago, I thought conjugal bliss meant a soft, curvy, auburn-haired Mate ready and waiting for me on my bed at the end of every day. She'd have hero-worship in her violet eyes; a willing mouth; and she'd wear flimsy, see-through stuff that I could do all sorts of sexy things with and through.*

And what do I get?

Christmas angel blonde, blue-eyed, scarlet-corseted, Princess Marsh blinked reproachfully at him. She had the temperament of a Tasmanian she-devil and the beginnings of a Take-It-Or-Leave-It pout on her full lower lip.

She'd probably snapped a fingernail.

"Why is the sky that color?" she asked nervously.

"It's normal. For a short time, the sky goes green at dusk. It's something to do with 'excited' molecules of ionized oxygen returning to their ground state."

He took the military hammock out of its waterproof bag, shook it out and draped it over the newly stacked, multi-purpose wood pile.

"That's here to get warm for later," he explained in case she thought it was for her to sit on. It wasn't.

She made no comment.

Djetth had designated the hammock as a blanket. There were two gold foil survival sheets, but they'd use neither in the way intended by the Tigron High Command. One of the heat-reflective sheets would act as a ground sheet. The other was going into the roof of their shelter, to mess with the *Ark Imperial*'s thermal-imaging surveillance.

Djetth hadn't decided which he wanted: for Tarrant-Arragon to think he'd got lucky, or to fret that perhaps he hadn't. His motives seemed to change every four minutes, every time he thought about sex.

Well, Fewmet! Being shot down did nothing to clarify which Princess he loved. It simply put the easier lay of the two completely at his mercy.

ARK IMPERIAL. Bridge

Not even the most accomplished Saurian diplomat would be fool enough to remonstrate with the First Warstar Leader of the Imperial Star Forces, Prince Tarrant-Arragon, on the fully staffed bridge of the *Ark Imperial*.

'Rhett bit his lip and approached his brother-in-law, who was on his feet, albeit leaning with his well-maintained hands taking his weight on a bar-like console.

His Imperial Highness's stance reminded 'Rhett of an implausibly handsome movie CEO leaning menacingly on a long boardroom table, stiff-armed and sneering, looking for any excuse to ream out a seated subordinate.

Except no one on the bridge was sitting around asking for trouble. The *Ark Imperial* was without a doubt the most efficient, disciplined—and happy—military vessel that 'Rhett had ever seen.

Between Tarrant-Arragon's hands was a flat monitor, like a high-tech version of the recessed screens that human news anchors were starting to use instead of paper scripts.

He was watching dark squadrons of starfighters streaming out of the *Ark Imperial* in triple chevron formations. 'Rhett had heard that their small-bore cannons were armed with specially prepared ice pellets.

"Is it true that you're going to 'seed' the clouds to make it rain on the happy couple?" 'Rhett injected amusement he didn't feel into his raspy voice.

"Something like that," Tarrant-Arragon replied silkily. An unpleasant smile curved his thin lips as if he silently dared 'Rhett to call him sadistic.

"I suppose it is absolutely necessary to soak them on their first night?" 'Rhett imitated the aristocratic drawl of a grinning senior who deprecated, yet thoroughly enjoyed, the ritual torment of first-year initiates into an elite society.

"They need fresh water." Tarrant-Arragon's answer did not come across as defensive.

"The rain will be fresh water, then?"

'Rhett could not conceal his skepticism. Tarrant-Arragon was high-handed, arrogant, and unscrupulous. If he wanted "the happy couple" to mate, the ice "pellets" might well be a frozen testosterone cocktail.

Tarrant-Arragon lifted a supercilious eyebrow, neither confirming nor denying anything. His middle finger touched a control, and a patchwork of spy images appeared on the screen between his hands.

"Djetth has accomplished a great deal more than I would have thought possible," he said, passing over water quality as a topic. "He even had the foresight to set out receptacles in case it rained naturally. Observe."

'Rhett leaned forward to look, but his gaze slipped to the Rings of Imperial Authority on his sinister brother-in-law's right hand. One was still missing.

On the signet finger, Great Djinn Crown Princes and Emperors of Tigron wore the saber-toothed tiger skull of the Death Ring. This Ring was a symbol of the wearer's Right to take or spare lives at his pleasure. This Ring was missing from Tarrant-Arragon's hand.

The unformed chunk that represented dark matter was the Ring of Gravity, and was worn on the third finger.

Most dangerous of all the Rings was the cunningly

faceted blue-crystal of the Fire Stone. Much more than a symbol, this Ring was a laser weapon which—with the proper concentration, strength of mind, and skill—could be fired from the forefinger.

Tarrant-Arragon tapped an image on the screen.

"Do you see what that is?" A decidedly wicked smile transformed Tarrant-Arragon's grim features as he spoke.

"Is it Martia-Djulia's dress?"

"Indeed it is. The chances are better than eighty percent in my favor that Djetth will neglect to shelter that preposterous dress before he goes to bed. It's damp. Where will he put it?"

Instead of hazarding a facetious guess, 'Rhett whispered an equally rhetorical, "Where indeed?"

"I thought it would help matters along if we kept her clothing wet for another day."

Two people's lives are on the line. This isn't a joke!

Sometimes 'Rhett wondered whether he was too responsible for his own good. His half-brothers and cousins called him "anal," "officious," "a born sneak."

"Born" might be an exaggeration. More likely, 'Rhett owed his wary ways, not to mention his hoarse voice, to the human childhood illness that had killed his mother and destroyed an important assortment of glands and organs in his face and neck when he was nine Earth years old.

"What if she gets ill?" Whatever the risk, he had to ask. Martia-Djulia was not exactly Princess Congeniality, but she was his sister-in-law.

"There were two portable communicators in perfect working order in their Thorcraft. They are still working. In the unlikely event that both were to fail, Djetth has only to trace 'HELP' in the sand."

"Did you tell him that before you shot him down?" 'Rhett asked more sharply than he intended.

Unexpectedly, Tarrant-Arragon's mouth curved into a

smile of genuine amusement, softening his harsh features.

"I told him nothing. You virtuous Saurian ambassador types have heard of the concept of plausible deniability, haven't you? If Martia-Djulia were to confront him, Djetth would be able to reply with absolute innocence."

An incongruous concept, that . . . porn-loving, penis-tattoo-sporting Djetth as an absolute innocent. 'Rhett did not share his disloyal thoughts.

"The Thorcraft I lent them was unusually well equipped," Tarrant-Arragon continued urbanely. "The island has been stocked in advance. And we are . . . watching over them."

I underestimated Tarrant-Arragon, again! I should never forget that he is a consummate actor when he chooses to play the villain.

"Why have you precipitated matters?" 'Rhett asked.

"Ahhhh. Political expediency. Djetth was getting tired of Martia-Djulia's rudeness. She can be . . . ah . . . 'tiring.' If she should happen to be hiding a pregnancy from us all, then Djetth must be the father officially. A Princess Imperial cannot remain unMated until she is so far along that her pregnancy is a scandal."

"Is she pregnant?"

If Martia-Djulia might be pregnant, the rut-rage didn't work the way Great Djinn legend said it did.

'Rhett couldn't exclaim over this discrepancy without revealing that he'd had a much greater part than anyone knew in a recent plot to disgrace and destroy Tarrant-Arragon.

"We don't know," Tarrant-Arragon murmured. A flicker of his eyes indicated that some topics were not for discussion on the bridge. "However, there is an anomaly in my sister's urine."

CHAPTER TWELVE

Freighter Island

"If I have sex with you, it won't mean a thing to me," Martia-Djulia announced, taking the proverbial Tigron Hunnox by the horns.

Since there was nothing remotely sexy about eating an unknown animal's recognizable body parts without utensils, Martia-Djulia thought she had chosen a safe time for a difficult conversation.

"Meaningless sex can be fantastically liberating," Djetth answered evenly. He spat something—she could not discern what—into the fire and continued to gnaw the back end of his half of the roast.

"I do not want to be fantastically liberated."

"Really? I'll take that as a No, then. I'm *shagged out*, anyway."

Martia-Djulia had no idea what "shagged out" meant, but she was beginning to know Djetth. If she were to ask, he would tell her. The mystery words would turn out to be something to do with bodily functions or sex.

"Do you often have meaningless sex?" she asked him.

It was a foolish thing to say. She knew it. It was also unpardonably rude.

"Not recently," he replied, sounding both rueful and amused, but not in the least offended. "Why don't you want to be fantastically liberated?"

Martia-Djulia did not know what to say. She fought back an insane urge to tell Djetth that she had tried being fantastically liberated once—with Commander Jason—and the Imperial repercussions had broken her heart.

Instead, she pointed at the remaining foreleg and chunks of rib meat on her leaf plate.

"It's a little tough."

"There are techniques to soften up your prey. All in all, I'd rather kill my dinner humanely, and chew it well," he replied evenly.

There was no answer to that. One did not wish to know what kind of cruelty he had in mind. Having lived in a Palace with pet tigers, she knew how tigers sometimes played with their live food. She picked up another morsel and nibbled at it.

All that Princess Marsh had said was that her meat was tough, Djetth told himself, trying to understand his sudden impatience with her. It was the truth. Had he expected a compliment? Or was he frustrated that she'd shied away from a very promising subject?

Djetth's gaze dropped to her gracefully restless hands as she delicately prodded and rearranged the meat on her plate. If he were to compliment her, she wouldn't believe that he was sincere, now that her fingernails were broken.

She saw beauty in a perfect manicure. He saw beauty in the animated way she pointed all the time at things that interested her, without realizing she was doing so; and in the way she reached up with her left hand as if in an insolent salute and swept a stray lock of hair from her eyes to hook it behind her ear.

Her hands were like butterflies. He longed for them to alight on his erection.

What are my chances tonight, babe?

Wordlessly he offered to pass her his hip flask, which he'd pretty much left untouched all day. She shook her head.

"Look, take it. It's all I can offer you to drink tonight. It won't kill you. If it goes to your head, I give you my word of honor—"

What the blue star-blazes am I saying?

"—my word of honor, I won't take advantage of you. Yeah, dinner's tough. It's dry and salty. You're not used to this. You could do with something to wash it down."

Shit!

"Your word of honor?" she repeated. She held out her hand and took the flask. "I will chance it. I confess, I am extremely thirsty."

Well, that tore it. Even if the alcohol inspired her to spread her surprisingly slender legs, which always seemed to be pressed demurely together at the knees and ankles, now he'd have to tough it out. He'd given his word.

Marsh was free to let him impair her better judgment with a few potent swigs of fermented cactus liquor, but he was not free to enjoy a sexual quid pro quo.

"I have had enough. That was a good dinner under the circum—. Thank you," she said with more courtesy than conviction in her voice. She handed back the hip flask.

He could tell from the feel of it that it was all but empty. She'd be asleep within the hour, awake and parched with thirst at midnight, and she'd have a killer headache in the morning.

"Are you sure? I've got a juicier piece of tail in the fire. Should be just about ready."

"Ummmm," she prefaced whatever she was about to say next. She gasped and flinched, as if she'd just fought down a boozy hiccough.

Djetth put on what he hoped was a reassuring smile.

"About that hole you were digging on the beach, in full view—"

Marsh's luscious lips pursed as if blowing a kiss through the perfectly enunciated last consonant of 'view,' then snapped back into a wide, ambivalent grin. She did that a lot, especially when she was embarrassed.

"—I hope you weren't digging there for the same reason that a big cat would dig a hole?"

Do big cats bother to bury their dirt? Djetth mused. *Tigers aren't the apex predator on Tigron, so maybe they do.*

"Fewmet, no! That's our drinking-water well. You didn't?" he asked, torn between exasperation and amusement.

She shook her head vigorously, and a stray lock of platinum blonde hair flopped over her eyes.

"No, but I want to. Not there, of course. . . ." Her voice trailed off. She took a breath. "You seem to have thought of everything else. Did you think of that?"

Obviously she hadn't understood the English "*latrine*."

"Have you any reason to think I would not think of that?" he teased, enjoying her discomfort.

"Male anatomy."

She said it in such a lugubrious voice and pulled such a face that Djetth burst into surprised laughter.

"Permit me to escort you to the pit stop." He stood, a little awkwardly, as his muscles were beginning to stiffen and ache from a long afternoon of hard physical labor.

"In that stand of small saplings"—he nodded to it and, with incongruous gallantry, offered her the support of his bent arm for the short trek—"I've dug a trench for the purpose you couldn't quite bring yourself to mention."

He saw her horrified expression, and got in first with the critique. "It's not fancy. Tomorrow I'll bend a sapling or two and make a throne over it for you. All right, Marsh? If you feel like brushing your teeth, simply chew on a stick."

While she was about her business, he returned to the fire and ate the iguana's fat tail. It was fair. He'd done all the work, and he'd given her his liquor. The tail was fair dues. He didn't feel guilty at all.

"Oh, slurrid!" she squealed in the semidarkness.

"You all right, Marsh?" he responded.

"What is this green stuff?"

"Nature's *wet wipes*," he replied, smothering a laugh. "Pull up some grass and use that if you'd rather. Seaweed is softer, though. Does a better job. Just remember one thing. What you use, you replace tomorrow."

There was silence. Not that he was listening. He was remembering an early situation-comedy TV show that had never struck him as particularly funny.

Here he was, living out the worst-case scenario of *Green Acres*. Or, at least, if he were to settle for Marsh, he would be. He wouldn't mind life as a farmer, providing he could figure out how to make a distillery.

He'd have moonshine, hunting, and a guitar.

Too damned right, he'd have a guitar! Once he'd got the camp built and the food and water sorted out, he'd make a guitar, and wow her with rock star impersonations.

But how could Princess Marsh—the terminally vain designer doll—bear life as a farmer's helpmate, especially if there were no private jets to whisk her back to her Imperial city home?

"What is the big shell for?" she wailed.

"All the better to bury what you have done, my dear," he called back in his best Big Bad Wolf voice. "And when you are quite ready, come to bed."

ARK IMPERIAL (officers' gymnasium)

"If you neglected to warn Djetth beforehand that you were going to shoot him down, Your Highness, he may consider you in breach of contract."

"Is this a warning, 'Rhett?"

'Rhett glanced at Tarrant-Arragon, who had performed several hundred crunches with silent efficiency, and was showing no sign of resuming the conversation that they'd adjourned on the bridge.

"It's an unsolicited legal opinion from one lawyer to another." 'Rhett knew his answer was pompous, but lawyers and court jesters could criticize—or warn—Royalty with relative impunity. "Djetth's choice was to marry Martia-Djulia under a new identity, or be put to death. If Djetth believes that you tried to kill him today, he might feel free to tell Martia-Djulia that he was Jason."

"Do you really think so?"

'Rhett wanted to ask what was in Martia-Djulia's urine. The topic was like a hippopotamus with a hard-on at a garden party. One did not know quite how it got there, everyone was studiously avoiding it, and unless the host explained it, one did not want to be the first to comment.

On the bridge, Tarrant-Arragon hadn't let slip the mention of the anomaly by accident. Tarrant-Arragon was an experienced interrogator, and an Intergalactic Chess Grand Master. Martia-Djulia's urine—as a topic—was almost certainly a trap of some kind.

The question was, what did Tarrant-Arragon think 'Rhett might be tricked into revealing?

"Three thousand!" Tarrant-Arragon announced the end of his set, as he sat up and rested his forearms on his knees.

Ignoring the contemptuous curl of his muscular brother-in-law's lip, 'Rhett concentrated on specialized exercises of his ankles, knees, and wrists. A swordsman did not need eight-pack abs.

"I hope he won't tell her as long as Django-Ra lives," Tarrant-Arragon said coolly. "Besides—"

"Is Django-Ra dangerous, then?" 'Rhett was surprised into lowering his épée and asking a question outright. He'd heard the usual rumors, of course, but assumed that the old Prince was a shade nastier than the average Tiger Prince but more snarl than bite.

"Aren't We all?" Tarrant-Arragon smiled mockingly, as if he'd set a trap and 'Rhett had fallen in.

'Rhett bowed his head, one duelist to another, silently thanking Tarrant-Arragon for the reminder. They might be related both by marriage and by birth, but the Saurian Dragon had not signed any peace treaty.

Officially, they were still enemies, and if 'Rhett were to remove his white Saurian ambassador's uniform, his status could change in the snap of Tarrant-Arragon's fingers, from guest to captured spy.

"As I was saying," Tarrant-Arragon added smoothly, "if Djetth tries to tell Martia-Djulia the whole truth, now, after two Imperatrix cycles, would she believe him? Is there any proof he can offer?"

Rhetorical question. A truthful answer wasn't expected.

'Rhett imagined Tarrant-Arragon's reaction if he were to suggest that Djetth's bioluminescent, interactive penis tattoo would prove quite a lot to Martia-Djulia, providing she'd seen it.

"Presumably," 'Rhett said instead, "if Djetth put his mind to it, he might be able to describe some intimacy that only Commander Jason and she could know about."

"Not when Martia-Djulia recorded their intimacies. When she changed her mind about using the tape to blackmail Jason into a lifelong commitment, she asked me to erase the footage. She knows that I saw everything, and that I could have briefed Djetth on any memorable details."

"Would she think of that?"

'Rhett saw Tarrant-Arragon's calculating expression and knew that he'd made another misstep.

"My little sister is shallow, not stupid," His Imperial Highness said. "She has been betrayed so many times that I would imagine she's learned not to trust anything anyone says to her."

"I stand corrected," 'Rhett apologized, hiding his surprise. He didn't know of anyone who had ever heard Tarrant-Arragon defend his younger sister.

Above their heads and reflected in the mirror wall of the gymnasium, the lighting changed to the ceiling color code for the next watch. It was late. Bedtime.

Hundreds of miles below them, it would be raining down on Djetth's and Martia-Djulia's flimsy shelter.

"I feel sorry for her," 'Rhett said in a last-ditch attempt to turn the conversation to whether it was possible for a Princess who wasn't rut-rageous to be impregnated by a Great Djinn who was, apparently, rut-raged. "Do you think it is quite ethical to subject a pregnant female to the rigors of desert island living?"

Tarrant-Arragon smiled.

"I said there was an anomaly. I didn't say she is pregnant. She's been asked, and she denies it. She's been offered my gynecologist's services, and has refused. If she doesn't know and doesn't want to find out for sure . . ." Tarrant-Arragon shrugged, got to his feet, and swirled his robes about him. The interview was over.

At the portal, His Highness looked back. "Besides," he drawled with the callousness of a mortgage banker, "it would be a very inconvenient pregnancy."

'Rhett felt his jaw drop. Why was he surprised that Tarrant-Arragon had given him a glimpse of his Machiavellian side? "The Terror of the Dodecahedron's" dark reputation was not all smoke and mirrors.

"Tarrant-Arragon! Wait!"

Tarrant-Arragon lifted an eyebrow, but did wait.

"How does Djinni feel about this . . . ?" 'Rhett left it up to Tarrant-Arragon to complete the question.

"Djinni doesn't know."

'Rhett's heart soared with relief. He'd staked his life and his career on his little sister's integrity. He should never have doubted for an instant that she would condone the endangerment of even a rival's pregnancy.

"She thinks the Mating Ceremony took place as planned. She wants to invite them up for dinner."

Tarrant-Arragon smiled ruefully, and 'Rhett understood why Tarrant-Arragon had lingered late, first on the bridge, and then in the gym.

"She does?" No diplomatic language came close to expressing the malicious delight bubbling up in 'Rhett. Only an Americanism did justice to what he felt. "Your Imperial Highness, you are in deep shit!"

CHAPTER THIRTEEN

Freighter Island
Midnight

There were three devastatingly handsome males in her bedroom. The symbolism of three escaped her. There wasn't room for all of them.

Martia-Djulia recognized the dream. She'd had this dream before, although this time, her bed seemed unusually hard, and she couldn't understand why an unseen chaos of small-footed creatures were stampeding above the mirrored ceiling and outside the golden walls, making a scurrying, pattering noise.

One male was Djinn-tall, dark-haired, star-tanned, very muscular, and very naked. He was sitting, like a maternity-bed visitor, halfway down the bed, in the hollow where her knees bent away from him. She was on her side with her back to him. His left hand rested possessively on the curve of her hip.

The pounding in her head was not in her head. The regular thumping sound was coming from her warm, hard, lumpy pillow. What . . . ?

Her eyes flew open.

Oh, Great Originator! There was a loosely clenched fist in front of her eyes. The fist was attached to the powerful arm on which her head was pillowed. She was lying with a male. There really was a male in her bed.

She lay still and willed her throbbing mind to clear.

His living warmth pressed against her all along her spine. His legs nudged up against the backs of hers. His exhaled breath stirred the hair on the top of her head. She was on her side on the hard ground, and he was cuddled up to her. The long fingers of his left hand splayed over her hip bone.

Djetth!

How had she got there? What had happened?

She tightened her buttocks, pulled in her stomach, and clamped her inner muscles, expecting to expel a gush of wetness, or feel soreness, or find some evidence that he had used her while she was unconscious.

She was dry. Nothing ached . . . nothing that mattered. Her feet hurt, but gods didn't have sex with feet. She parted her knees. There was no wetness between her legs, not even dried stickiness.

How could that be? How could he not have had her?

Her unbelieving mind signaled her hand to reach down and touch herself, but her hand met soft, webbed resistance. She registered the odd tightness around her body and thighs. Had he bound her so she couldn't fight back? Had he . . . ?

Ah. She remembered.

She had rolled herself in the hammock. It had been a stupid thing to do. She'd thought so at the time. She should have put on her wet dress, if she could have managed it by herself.

What else? Her memory was a little hazy.

She could recall stumbling back from the primitive trench that he called a "latrine," and realizing that she was so inebriated that she couldn't even walk a straight line back along the beach. Whatever evil concoction he'd given her to drink had kicked in.

She had known it would. She'd delayed returning to the camp until it did kick in. She could remember everything she'd thought and feared up until the alien alcohol took effect.

She'd known how it would be when she had accepted his offer of the flask, never trusting for a moment in his "word of honor." What Tiger Prince of Tigron ever kept his "word of honor"?

That was partly why she had accepted his drink—to take the edge off the inevitable betrayal. She'd chosen to play along with the "civilized" approach of getting her drunk, rather than risk being bedjinned if she misjudged how much pleading and struggling would please and arouse him.

Now, she was paying the price. Her head throbbed. She was desperately thirsty.

Why, oh, why had she drunk so much of his alien liquor? From the first gulp, she had known it was as potent as any Great Djinn.

Martia-Djulia could remember exactly why she'd decided to drink it all, regardless. She'd been prompted by a certain measure of malice, also a degree of self-preservation.

What she drank, he couldn't have. She preferred that Djetth should be sober while he took sexual advantage of her helplessness. He'd be more quickly satisfied.

Well, that made sense.

Why had she rolled herself in the hammock? Her thinking had not been so clear at that point. She vaguely remembered stumbling against the log pile, and touching the hammock. It had felt warm and soothing. She was cold and friendless, and scantily dressed in the short "T-shirt" that showed too much of her legs.

Perhaps rolling herself up in the hammock had seemed like a passive form of defiance, so he'd have to unwrap her to get at her. Passive defiance had been her lifelong specialty.

Spreading her fingers, she could now see that the hammock was a purely symbolic barrier. He'd have had trouble getting her legs apart, but otherwise its wide, flexible webbing was no protection. Djetth could easily have rolled her onto her back, pushed her knees to her chest, and thrust through it and into her, if he'd felt like it.

But had he felt like it? Whatever his intentions might have been, how could she hate him for falling asleep as soon as he lay down beside her after a thankless day of saving her life?

"Go back to sleep."

"Did I wake you?" Martia-Djulia asked breathlessly. Perhaps her movements had disturbed him.

"Mmmmm," he agreed, drawing her closer to his body.

"Djetth?" she said. "Djetth, what's that noise? Why is the fire spitting? Are we in danger?"

"It's raining."

"Rain sounds like that?" Rain fell on the Common Side of Tigron, but not on the arid Royal Side. If it had rained during her short time at the Island School for Princesses, she'd never have heard it because of the overarching biodome. "What shall we do?"

"Go back to sleep."

"I can't. Help me out of this hammock, I have to go out."

"You're going out in the rain?" he protested.

"I have to."

"Do you? Ah." He sounded more awake. She felt a tension on one end of the hammock. "You unroll until you're free. I'll take up the slack. I wanted some cover, anyway."

At first, she didn't understand, until she was free and saw that he was wrapped up in the hammock.

"Do you think I can drink some rainwater? I am terribly thirsty," she asked, as if that were her only reason for going out.

He grunted. "Rainwater is about as fresh as water here is going to get. Your best bet might be a puddle in the gold-foil roof, there. Dip my flask into that bulge above us."

Only after she'd returned from the latrine, slaked her thirst, filled the flask, and lain nervously back down beside him, did she realize that he couldn't have been half asleep as he'd seemed.

A little later, her suspicions were confirmed as she drowsed, curled up and cold. She felt him tuck the warm hammock over her and draw her into his arms.

He'd passed up at least three opportunities to make her hate him!

Tarra's Pleasure Palace, The Pleasure Moon of Eurydyce

"I am here on a quest," the Empress Helispeta said, as soon as she could decently broach such a serious issue.

It would have been bad form to blurt out an unknown person's murderous plans for One's hostess's long-abandoned daughter before all the courtesies had been observed.

Since Helispeta's—somewhat upstaged—arrival at the Empress Tarragonia-Marietta's palatial brothel, she had complimented her on the "palace" fortifications—worthy of an American presidential nuclear bunker; on the extraordinary displays of dildos; on the one-way mirrors to protect the expensive courtesans; and on how healthy and happy the girls professed to be! With less success, she had congratulated Tarragonia-Marietta on how "well" she looked, and on the attractive cushions on her wheelchair.

Privately, she could not help wondering why

Tarragonia-Marietta did not embrace a less primitive solution to her injury-related disability. Surely, bionic legs would be possible.

Now, rested and refreshed, Helispeta and her still-tearful hostess sat in the exotic, scented dimness of "Madam Tarra's" fortune telling parlor.

Under the sad circumstances, it would not be tactful to say, "I intend to prevent a murder from taking place." The murdered girl from the racetrack had been one of Tarragonia-Marietta's most loyal courier-courtesans. Helispeta rephrased.

"I intend to stop a murderer."

"It might be a dangerous quest," Tarragonia-Marietta said, frowning at a Tarot card. She turned another card over the first. "Especially since it seems that I am destined to assist you."

"And, you add danger to my quest because . . . ?"

"My enemies are younger than yours. My Emperor is still living."

"If we are in danger, perhaps you should start calling me Hell, dear. Although grossly improper, it would be safer, and more succinct. As you may have noticed, I have already stopped using The Royal Pronoun in conversation."

"My clients call me Madam Tarra. You—"

"Tarragonia-Marietta, I will not call you Madam! If I may, I will call you Tarra?"

Tarra smiled. "Very well, Aunt Hell. Do you have a victim in mind? Whose murder are we going to prevent?"

"Just before poor Petri-Shah was found, I heard talk of a plot to kill a junior member of the Royal Family."

CHAPTER FOURTEEN

Freighter Island
The next morning

"I propose a sexual experiment," Djetth announced without warning, shortly after she joined him by the fire and sat down to watch him prepare their breakfast.

"You slept well, I take it?" Martia-Djulia retorted. He'd been busy, and he'd more than kept his word. The latrine now had a seat with a hole so neatly cut that she couldn't imagine how he'd done it without a laser. There had also been a shallow giant half-shell full of seawater for a washbasin.

Water was bubbling on the fire in two large, white, many-spiked shells. Two similar shells had been set off to the side to cool.

Martia-Djulia reached forward, took the nearest one by one of its spikes, and sipped hot, tangy water from the shell's pink, contoured lip. She was thirsty.

Judging by the wet, sharpened sticks and the bright-eyed, iridescent corpses on a broad, deep green leaf,

Djetth had been up early, spearing fish in the rising tide while she overslept.

Martia-Djulia shifted her position and one-handedly combed back her hair with her fingers. Djetth looked different—rougher, dirtier, and sexier. A dark shadow on his jaw softened the harshness of his odd-shaped beard. He'd knotted a folded square of parachute fabric around his head, possibly to protect his bald scalp from sunstroke.

Although he must have been aware of her puzzled scrutiny, he didn't look up from what he was doing. He had a fish draped across the palm of one hand and was carefully inserting a very sharp knife into a small hole in its lower abdomen.

Martia-Djulia did not suppose for a heartbeat that his proposed experiment had anything to do with fish.

"This experiment would involve *having* sex, I assume?" she replied sarcastically.

If another conversation about sex was inevitable, she was grateful that he'd chosen to broach the topic in broad daylight and on the far side of the fire.

"Don't you want to know whether you are ever again going to be capable of enjoying one of life's greatest physical pleasures?"

"Speak for yourself," she sneered, watching as his knife hand moved rhythmically, slicing open the fish. "Life's greatest pleasure, indeed!"

"Shall I rephrase? Are We maintaining a polite fiction that you have never enjoyed sex, sweetheart?"

There was a disquietingly odd note in his voice that suggested he knew otherwise. Not for the first time, Martia-Djulia wondered whether her untrustworthy brother had told Djetth about her interlude with Commander Jason. Or worse. What if Tarrant-Arragon had kept a copy of the recording?

She spread her arms in a Look-Around-You gesture that ended in a shrug.

"What?" Djetth said, tossing down the now-gutted fish into a water-filled half shell.

"Sand. Insects. We're salty. We can't wash. We wipe ourselves with grass and seaweed. We clean our teeth with sticks. You have a beard. Sex is impossible."

"Details." He brought his flask to his lips, and threw back his head. His throat moved as he drank. For a dismayed moment, she thought he might be drinking irresponsibly. Then she remembered that she'd filled that flask with rainwater during the night.

"Details are important to me," she said with regal finality. The distasteful conversation was over.

"Here are some details, then," he retorted, undeterred. "I'll take you firmly by the hand, and lead you over the soft, shifting, midday-hot sand to where I have positioned one of our rescued plane seats in the shade."

Why wait for midday? she would have liked to jeer, but didn't dare.

"Maybe we'll run, laughing like eager, horny teenagers in our excitement. Maybe you'll be hesitant and I'll take both your hands in mine and pull you, stumbling and shying back, like an untamed mare. When I've got you under the gold-tented, sparkling shade—"

"Why would we be under gold-tented shade?" she asked, her curiosity getting the better of her.

"To protect us from birds," he said cryptically as he reached for his next victim.

"Birds?"

"Incontinent birds flying overhead."

"Oh!"

He was silent, concentrating on the task at hand, as the tip of his knife penetrated a fishy body opening. Martia-Djulia couldn't help wondering if Djetth watched what he was doing with such intensity whenever he eased his positor into a new lover for the first time.

Just then, he looked up and grinned at her.

"Where was I? In my love shack, with you cornered

between me and the tightly upholstered seat back? I'll turn you around, so I am behind you with my legs astride yours. Placing one hand under your belly, and the other squarely between your shoulder blades, I'll bend you over the back of that seat. Your hips and belly will be snugly cradled by the contoured headrest. Your bare bottom will tremble against my hard groin."

"Will you be dressed?"

He ignored her.

"I'll hold you down with one hand, and pin you firmly in place with my hips, as I reach over with my other hand and fondle your breasts until they are swollen and heavy, and you beg me to grab them with both hands and fuck you hard."

Martia-Djulia hoped that Djetth couldn't see the heat she felt in her cheeks. She raised the conch to her lips, cradling it in both hands with the fierce spikes sticking out between her trembling fingers.

"All this time, and I'll take so much time that your senses will spin, you'll brace your splayed hands in front of you on the resilient cushion, all the better to bounce on, and—incidentally—to push back when you want to urge me to thrust deeper, or faster into you."

"You think so?" she muttered defiantly, determined that if this "experiment" were ever acted out, she would pass out before she did as he expected.

"Or, maybe I'll stroke you slowly from the curve of your waist down the back of your smooth thighs to the delicate dimples behind your knees. I'll massage your luscious bare bottom for hours if I feel like it, until you relax and part your trembling legs.

"Then, I'll thrust my thigh between yours. I'll reach down with my long fingers, and play with your pussy for as long as I like, and when you're wet and moaning from that, I'll slide three fingers in—"

She had to interrupt. He was going too far.

"What exactly is this supposed to prove?"

"That I'm a considerate lover?" he suggested with a question in his tone. "That I can do you very nicely without breathing on you, or roughing you up with my stubble, or ramming sand into you. What else were you worried about?"

"Are you suggesting that we have sex simply to see if you enjoy it?" she asked, frowning at the tremor she heard in her voice. She'd have to keep her remarks short, or he would notice that she was not unaffected by his lewd conversation. "Everyone knows that males don't need to be in love."

"Do females?" he retorted, and again she wondered what he knew. By now, he had removed the next fish's internal organs.

Martia-Djulia swallowed, knowing that she had made a terrible mistake in mentioning love. No one was talking about love.

Smiling at her, Djetth held up the fish and explicitly pushed his three middle fingers into the cavity.

"A fish's insides flutter like a female having a small, long-lasting orgasm. Would you like to come over here and put your fingers in it, to know what you'll feel like to me?"

Martia-Djulia shook her head and stayed where she was.

"Maybe, sweetheart, we should have sex to prove to you that you can and will enjoy it."

"I enjoyed it once. I am very happy with my memories. I don't need you or your experiment to prove anything," she said stiffly.

"Once?" He raised an eyebrow. His lips twitched. Too late Martia-Djulia realized that she had just contradicted one of her earlier statements.

"The Aim of the Experiment is to discover whether or not we are sexually compatible," Djetth said loftily. She suspected that he was amusing himself by parodying a formal checklist. "Method: to have mind-blowing recreational sex using positions and techniques that mitigate or avoid unfortunate consequences. Expected Result—"

"What unfortunate consequences?"

"Insects in your hair?" he teased. "Sand in your baby box. A baby. Infection. Injury. Legal consummation of a Mating we might not want."

His gaze flickered. Martia-Djulia had the impression that his list was deliberately ordered.

"Injury to whom?" she asked, ignoring the glossed-over "baby."

"I've wondered why you haven't blasted me backwards onto my butt since our Mating Day. I've certainly deserved it."

"Yes, you have!" she agreed heatedly.

She trusted Djetth far enough to have a conversation such as they were having, but not far enough to admit that she'd no idea how she had blasted him that time. Or that she didn't feel strongly enough about him to try again.

"Yeeees," he drawled, sounding unsettlingly like Tarrant-Arragon. "I know I have."

She can't do it! It came to her in a flash what he was thinking. *Either she can't do it, or she really likes me!*

"I wonder whether I could make a condom out of fish skin?" he mused aloud, with a laugh in his voice. "Inside out, of course. It wouldn't be gentlemanly to give her the scales. Then, the tail would have to be on the inside. Maybe not. Animal guts, now—"

A few days ago, she might have squealed in exaggerated disgust. Now? Djetth was too interesting. Besides, he wasn't going to ignore her and leave her alone even if he were convinced that she was as frivolous as a nectar-sipping, gaudy-winged insect.

Apart from the fluttering body cavities of gutted fish—not a serious rival for his affections—she was the only action available to him.

"Conclusion?" he murmured.

Her mouth went dry at the notion that he might have been reading her mind, although that ought to be impossible.

"Conclusion: to be determined. If we're good in bed, it might be enough. Or it might not be," he continued. "We can't face the truth until we know what the truth is."

Fish-skin condoms? I know better than that! Scales out, or in . . . ? Fewmet! What was I thinking?

Having washed and wrapped the fish, and buried them in hot ashes to cook, Djetth stalked down to the sea with the bloody guts. He was stone-cold sober. More sober than he'd been in Earth years. So, why had he said it?

If only he could ask his smart-ass little half-brother, 'Rhett would put his finger right on his motivation. In 'Rhett's case, it wouldn't be so much the finger, as the safety button on the sharp end of his épée.

Okay. Imaginary conversation. Psychoanalyze this, 'Rhett. What WAS I thinking?

"Hmmm. Sabotage, maybe?" Djetth imagined 'Rhett saying.

No shit. And why, 'Rhett, you obnoxious know-all, would I sabotage myself? I almost had her eating out of my lap back there.

"You don't want to?"

What do you mean, I don't want to? Of course I want to . . . Don't I?

Knee deep in the waves and yards from cruising shoals of fair-sized fish, Djetth stopped blustering and gave the matter more thought.

That's the thing, isn't it? I like the idea that Marsh is loyal to Jason. Whatever else is wrong with her, there's a lot to be said for a loyal woman. If she's loyal to Jason, one day, she'll be just as loyal to me.

Around his shins he felt the tug of an undertow, which indicated that he was close to a part of the shore where the sea, for no apparent reason, scoured out deep pools in the sand in which fish, prawns, and crabs could be stranded from one high tide to the next.

Until he had time to weave crab pots and do the job properly, he planned to anchor offal here as bait.

So, in my heart of hearts I want to test her, but I want her to hold out. The longer she holds out, the more I'm likely to like her.

The bait was weighted down with stones. He washed his hands, and waded diagonally back the way he'd come.

Tricky thing, courtship, he reflected.

I can't tell her I was Jason. Maybe she'll figure it out if she recognizes my tattoo. That begs another question. Do I want her to figure it out? I wonder. Who would I be sabotaging if I were to "accidentally" let Marsh see my "lightning rod" in all its glory?

Near the top of the beach, as Djetth squatted to check on the water quality in his beach well, he noticed that his barefoot Princess was picking her way across the sand to join him. Though Marsh wasn't limping, she moved as if her tender feet were sore.

Her high-heeled court shoes wouldn't be practical beach wear, even if she hadn't kicked them into deep water in a fit of petulance. Retrieving them wasn't worth risking his life.

He narrowed his eyes and watched her run her fingers through her hair. She looked as if she had something on her mind, but was still rehearsing how she wanted to put it to him.

She'd knotted some of her soft, diaphanous, tulle fabric around her waist, sarong style.

Very nice!

When she was close, he got to his feet. "Ready to go exploring? We need some firewood."

Marsh nodded.

"That could be a useful chunk of driftwood." Djetth pointed to a dark shape where the highest water mark met the most salt-tolerant of the coarse grasses. "Let's head in that direction."

The small sun had almost risen high enough to glitter between the topmost branches of the tallest trees on the other side of the island. High on their beach, shadows were long and an indeterminate color between green and purple. Even lower down the beach, the rain-pocked sand was cool under their toes. It was a lovely morning.

"About the truth," Marsh began hesitantly.

Djetth stooped without breaking his stride to pick up the first twig of his collection. Whatever she was trying to say, he wasn't going to give her any help.

"You said, 'We can't face the truth until we know what the truth is.' "

"Did I say that?" He hated to sound like Tarrant-Arragon, but he could hardly explain. He shouldn't have said something so cryptic in the first place.

"What 'truth' were you talking about? You meant more than just whether or not we could be sexually compatible, didn't you?"

Djetth glanced at her in surprise, but was saved the necessity of lying. They'd come to the driftwood. Sea and sun had bleached it bone-white, and sea creatures had bored perfectly circular, peppercorn-sized holes in it.

"Stand back. Be ready to run for the water," Djetth warned, and gave it an experimental kick. Dust erupted out of it, but no tiny, angry An'Koori bees.

"Riddled. It'll burn too quickly. We'll need more," he said. "Let's walk on. We'll pick it up on the way back."

Bees. Honey! Djetth checked out Marsh's rear elevation as she forgot what she was wearing and bent from the waist, like a ballerina, to pick up a stick.

I'll have to keep an eye out for bees. I know of a very good use for honey.

Marsh's stick was a long, whippy reed, and she swished it, knocking the tops off coiled worm casts in the sand.

Djetth said nothing.

"You did not answer my question."

"No," he agreed. "I hoped you'd forgotten about your question."

He cleared his throat and decided to tell a watered-down version of the truth. Their relationship wasn't far enough along for them to discuss the rut-rage, although the question of whether or not he'd had it, and—if so, which Princess had set him off—was on his mind most of the time.

"It's a question of fertility, isn't it?" he said awkwardly. "Whether or not we could breed."

"Whether we *should* breed!" she amended. *Swish* went her stick, and a sharp-tipped shell skittered out of her path.

Djetth did a double take. Marsh's emphasis on "should" implied philosophical thinking, if not the ultimate in civil disobedience, given that the Great Djinn were close to going extinct.

"I see," he said when she didn't elaborate. "You have a moral, ethical or political objection to sexual activity that might result in a pregnancy. Is that it? Is *that* why you ran away on our Mating Day?"

Marsh met his searching gaze defiantly.

"Bad genes!" she muttered under her breath, which could have been an insult to his parentage, or to his persistence, or something else entirely.

Before he could demand what she meant by "bad genes," Marsh picked up a more useful bit of firewood than her whippy stick, and hurled it down the beach, toward the sea. Beneath the wet sand, startled worms spat miniature liquid eruptions out of their breathing holes. She had a good arm.

"Now, if you'd brought down a bird, or incapacitated one of those iguana-type creatures we ate for dinner last night, I'd call that a jolly fine shot," Djetth drawled. "Since our task for right now is to collect fuel . . ."

He shook his head.

"Oh." She pouted for an instant, then her fascinating, wide mouth moved again, and Marsh laughed.

Déjà vu! Djetth had a vivid memory of a moment at the Virgins' Ball, the night before Tarrant-Arragon's wedding. He'd happened to be watching Princess Martia-Djulia's mouth as she smiled, mimed a laugh, pulled a face, mouthed silent greetings and compliments on pretty dresses or handsome escorts . . . paying myriad flattering attentions to innumerable guests, all at once, all without saying a word.

What a hostess!

What a mouth! He'd imagined the pleasure such a wide, versatile mouth might give a demanding lover.

Then had come a private moment. Pausing in the shelter of a Great Djinn ancestor's statue with a hideously broken nose, the Princess had perhaps imagined that no one could see her. As soon as she was not "on camera," her animated smile had snapped off. She'd looked lost, lonely and miserable. An instant later, she'd passed out of the statue's shelter, and the broad, tooth-flashing smile was back.

That fleeting lost look had been an irrestible challenge to a male who wanted nothing more—nothing much more, at any rate—than to put a dazed, sated smirk and a sex flush on her thoroughly kissed lips.

"Why shouldn't we, if we want to?" Djetth asked, while wrenching up fistfuls of straw-like reed stems that were tangled up with dried, brown, leathery straps of seaweed. It'd be decent kindling.

He left it up to Marsh to decide whether he meant *Why shouldn't we breed?* or *Why shouldn't we make out?*

"Who says I want to?" She picked up a good-sized branch and waggled it fiercely.

"What are you going to do with that?" Djetth asked. "Here, I'll carry it for you. Give it to me." He held out his hand and added her branch to the growing bundle across his left arm. "Thank you. Correct me if I have got this wrong. So the problem—your not wanting to have sex with me—is nothing to do with me?"

He saw the way Marsh looked askance at him and bit her lip. Fancying him—or not fancying him—was part of the problem. But only part.

"Shhhhh. Talking of breeding . . ."

Martia-Djulia felt her heart thud hard. Her mouth went dry as Djetth suddenly gripped her upper arm, halting her.

"That's really odd. Look!"

She didn't know where to look. She did not want to ask where to look. She blinked at him, confused by his urgent tone, not understanding whether he had espied danger lurking in the sand dune ahead, or whether he was overcome by lust and wanted her to admire developments in his bulge-hugging trunk briefs.

Still holding her tightly with one hand, he bent in a stealthy manner, and laid his collection of firewood on the sand, then stood again.

"Look there!" he hissed, pointing with his free hand.

Following the direction of his finger, she discerned a fuzzy, sandy-colored, irregular shape ahead of them. "What is it?" she whispered back.

"Eurydycean desert bunnies. Two of them. Don't tell me you can't see what they're doing."

"There are two of them?" she questioned.

"You really don't see very well, do you?" Djetth gave her a quick grin. "The female is cowering low to the ground. The male is covering her. He's biting her neck. That's to hold her still, see? She's probably in some kind of a sexually receptive trance. His front legs are astride her, and his especially clawed forepaws are probably pinning her forelegs down. His hind quarters are pounding away for all he is worth. Can't you see his scut flashing?"

"I can see something pulsating."

"That's the male's back end, thrusting as deeply and as hard as he can. Copulating in the open is dangerous. He needs to pump all he's got into her as quickly as possible. Stay here."

With that, Djetth sprinted across the sand towards the humps. She had never seen anyone run so fast. As he got close, he launched himself, arms outstretched, and flew.

Sand sprayed around them, and the blurry, brown shapes seemed to heave, as if the creatures saw Djetth but were too surprised to part and scatter.

Djetth reared up onto his knees in the sand and dust, his broad back to her. The struggle went on for a long time. Martia-Djulia was glad that she was nearsighted. She sank to the sand and covered her ears.

"It's the damnedest thing," Djetth's deep voice greeted her cheerfully. "Creatures of lowly intelligence require a lot more killing than one might expect."

Looking up, Martia-Djulia saw him striding towards her. Blood had spattered his barbaric headdress. In each hand, he held a dangling "bunny" by its long back legs. Djetth slaughtered and butchered with the insouciance of a warrior. Or a livestock farmer.

Who was Prince Djetthro-Jason? Where had he spent his life? Doing what?

"Come on. Get up. Would you rather carry these . . . ?" He swung the bloody bodies invitingly. "Or will you carry the bundle of firewood?"

Martia-Djulia picked up the wood, and began to retrace her steps to the campsite.

"I thought we were having fish," she said over her shoulder.

"For breakfast, we are. We can't make socks—or condoms—out of fish skins. Besides, these won't be ready for hours."

Martia-Djulia did not have the faintest idea what "socks" were, but, given his obsession with whatever he could sink his sperm depositor into, she could guess.

"Did you have to kill both of them?"

"It was a bit unsporting of me, wasn't it?" Keeping pace behind her, he laughed. "Next time, I'll keep the newly impregnated female for a pet, if she survives being separated from her lover. Did you know that the male Eurydycean desert bunny literally gets his sperm depositor stuck in, once he gets a rhythm going? That's why these two were so easy to catch."

Gritting her teeth, Martia-Djulia walked faster. She'd rather step on broken shells than hear more.

"Her vaginal contractions stimulate the head of his sperm depositor to swell up like a mushroom-shaped plunger. Once that point is reached, he can't pull out until he's spent. I'm not sure what happens if only one of a pair is killed before the male is spent."

"I don't want to think about it!"

"Why not? Penises and positors are pretty fascinating."

"They are NOT pretty!"

"So, you have noticed? There's an incredible variety across the galaxies. Some are shaped like a corkscrew. Some have a whirling appendix like a weedwhacker on the end. Some are useful, and some are purely status symbols, like the false ones on dominant female hyenas. You should take an interest."

In yours, I suppose?

Martia-Djulia bit her lip. Only the day before, she had resolved not to ask him about himself, but some resolutions were made to be broken in an emergency.

"How do you know so much about desert bunnies?"

"I have an ahhh—acquaintanceship with the Pleasure Moon of Eurydyce," he began.

She noticed his stumble and hesitation, and wondered if "Ah" was the beginning of an indiscreet alien word, perhaps for a lover. He must have had many, many lovers. How else would he be so knowledgeable, and so . . . comfortable . . . talking about extraordinary genitalia.

All the more reason not to let Djetth dock with her.

He'd comment, unlike Jason, who would not have dared to make humiliating comparisons. For Jason, the honor of pleasuring an Imperial Princess was too sublime for words. He'd been tongue-tied with awe and excitement.

"The Pleasure Moon of Eurydyce is a neutral watering hole," Djetth was saying. "All the Worlds end up there at some stage in their travels. On the Dark Side, one gambles, feasts, and fornicates."

I was right! she thought.

"On the Bright Side, there's desert, target sports, jet racing, and sand boarding."

"And desert bunnies?"

"Deserts teem with life. It's only the top few inches of soil—or sand—that are scorching hot. Animals that live in holes or burrows do very well, even when there's no nightfall."

She had to ask. "If these desert bunnies are so, er, vulnerable when they, er . . . ?"

"Why don't they do it underground?" Djetth finished the question for her. "On the Moon of Eurydyce, they do."

"Why there and not here?"

"That's a good question. Maybe, here, it's too cold underground. Or maybe they haven't been here long enough to dig a decent burrow. Or maybe they're careless because they've never encountered a predator on this little island."

Martia-Djulia tossed her head to the misty shadow on the horizon, which she knew was the An'Koori mainland. "What about over there?"

"I can't imagine why the High Command would import fast-breeding desert bunnies to a 'bread basket' planet. They'd overrun the place, eat the seedlings in the nurseries, and undermine the vineyard terraces with their tunnels. Now I come to think of it, they'd drown in their breeding burrows if they dug deep. The water table's too high."

He knows a lot about An'Koor, too! Martia-Djulia's chest ached at another reminder of her Jason, who had been a Commander in the An'Koori Star Forces. *I wonder if Djetth and Jason ever met.*

"Did you know that this planet used to be a water world until our Djinn ancestors reclaimed part of it? This island we're on was created when a space freighter carrying topsoil overshot its drop zone and ploughed into the shallow seabed. That's why our island is such an odd shape."

"How do you think the bunnies got here?" she was able to ask, owing to the ingrained Royal habit of sustaining inconsequential chatter while thinking of heartbreak and ruin.

"That's a mystery, isn't it? I can't imagine desert bunnies venturing out into an unknown ocean to discover and claim new little worlds for themselves. They're not equipped for swimming. And although this is a relatively young planet, its ocean contains large life forms."

Martia-Djulia shuddered at the reminder of the shadowy, semen-spewing, giant mollusks that they'd been inspecting from the air before Tarrant-Arragon tried to kill them.

"Here we are," Djetth declared, shouldering his way past her to kick their smoldering campfire back to life.

She looked around for somewhere to put her bundle of wood, then quietly took refuge at the latrine.

While her back was turned, Djetth got out a knife and began to make sawing, squishy noises.

"Do you have to—" she began, until she saw what he was doing and swallowed. "Oh, Fewmet, what are you doing?"

"We can drink blood, so I'm trying to catch as much of it as I can in this shell," he said, elevating one leg of one of the bunnies and using some strips that looked suspiciously like they'd been torn from the looped panniers of her beautiful dress to tie it to a low branch of the short trees he insisted on calling "flowering cherry" although they had no flowers.

"She's still warm. Do you want a drink? It's good for you. No?"

Martia-Djulia pressed her fingers to her lips, not that she thought he would force her to swallow animal blood if she didn't block his access to her mouth.

He shrugged. "You're not feeling sick, are you?"

Djetth must be a brutalizing influence. She was not, in fact, nauseated.

"Now, since you're here, look here, and learn how to skin and gut large animals." He brandished a wicked-looking knife over the second bunny, which had not yet been strung up by a leg. "With smallish ones like this, it's easier to skin when it's cooled, so we'll wait."

He used his knife as a pointer.

"The first thing to do is cut its throat, which I've done already."

"I thought you said you'd wait."

He chuckled. "I'm going to tell you about it now. Then I'll talk you through it later."

"Why?" She did not defy him outright.

"Because I think it's time you learned how to take care of yourself. Unless, of course, you're pregnant."

Martia-Djulia refused to dignify his almost-question with an answer.

"All right, then. Next, place your animal belly up. That way, you can see what you've got."

"I don't want to see." Defiantly, she folded her arms and turned her back.

"I dare say you don't," he retorted. "I dare say, if I weren't here to take care of you, you'd simply curl up and let yourself die without even trying to fight back. You showed more 'spunk' on our wedding day."

His scornful words cut.

He looked up and grinned. "Not that I want you to

knock me down and run away. You should stick around. I'll lick you into shape eventually."

Martia-Djulia assumed that he meant something salacious. Yet, although it was grossly improper, the idea that he wanted to lick her was strangely reassuring.

He sighed, and abandoned any idea of teaching her gross butchery.

"Talking of which, after breakfast I need to rebuild the shelter and make a proper bed."

Leaving his untidy prey half hoisted by one leg, Djetth got to his feet, and started to stride back towards the beach, presumably to wash the blood off his hands.

"Are you just going to go off and leave them like that?" she called after him.

"It's best to give the parasites a chance to abandon ship. They will, when their host gets cool."

"Parasites? Oh, how slurrid!" She took a step back. "Those parasites won't attack us, will they?"

He stopped and lifted an eyebrow at her. "They might, mightn't they?" he said thoughtfully. "We'll have to get naked and run our fingers over every inch of each other's bodies. Checking each other over for parasites could be fun."

He laughed wickedly.

"We're in this together, sweetheart. We have to take care of each other. In every way."

CHAPTER FIFTEEN

ARK IMPERIAL
Morning (Imperatrix time)

"Does Djinni know yet?" 'Rhett risked asking when he encountered Tarrant-Arragon emerging from the officers' gym immersion showers.

From the darkness around His Highness's eyes, 'Rhett suspected that Tarrant-Arragon had gone to bed late and got up early to avoid an awkward conversation with Djinni. The tyrant in love slunk around acting like a guilty adolescent.

"You should tell her what you've done," he advised.

"Ka'Nych says she can't be upset." Tarrant-Arragon shrugged as he wrapped a short kilt around his hips.

"She'll be a lot more upset if she thinks you're lying to her," 'Rhett retorted. "What's the worst that can happen if you tell her? She'll throw you out of your Imperial bed?"

"We're already sleeping apart." Tarrant-Arragon snapped his glossy black communicator around his forearm without breaking eye contact.

The device resembled a high-tech version of the arm armor a Roman gladiator might have worn, but it functioned as a computer.

"You are?"

Tarrant-Arragon strolled along the long wall where the trophies of arms were displayed, as if he were considering which of the captured alien weapons to take down and use.

"My 'Imperial bed' is too high," His Highness said like a TV detective who has grown bored of toying with his suspect. "And there's too much equipment in it."

"Where is she sleeping?" 'Rhett asked, amused.

"In the Imperial bathroom."

'Rhett had seen Tarrant-Arragon's bathroom once. It was a most astounding piece of decadent extravagance, especially since the *Ark Imperial* was a spaceship. It had two of everything you'd expect in an on-planet bathroom, plus a small swimming pool of black herbal water which had similar buoyancy properties to Earth's Dead Sea.

The stated purpose of this "murk bath" was to give Djinni's half-Earthling system a respite from Tigron's slightly heavier gravity. Djinni had confided that this was only half the story. Tarrant-Arragon liked making love in the bath.

"You should tell her. She may imagine something worse. Pregnant females get depressed."

"So Ka'Nych tells me," Tarrant-Arragon drawled. "Damn!"

He glanced at a flashing display on his forearm communicator, frowned, and tapped out a response.

"In the later stages, pregnant females say things they don't mean." 'Rhett had no plans to stay around until Djinni was due to go into labor. "There'll come a time when she screams that she hates you, never wants another baby, would rather die than have sex with you ever again."

"Grievous was kind enough to warn me." Tarrant-Arragon sighed. "Since my own mother ran away soon after Martia-Djulia was born, I was already aware that my tolerance, and my elaborate security measures, might be tested."

"Would you like me to help you—?"

The recessed wall-top lighting flashed blue, which 'Rhett assumed was a general alert. Unlike purple-lighted Battle Stations, a blue alert seemed to open all doors.

"Slack-damn, she's out! Slayt!" Tarrant-Arragon spoke directly into his communicator. "Alert Ka'Nych. Report. Where is she?"

"*She* is right . . . here."

Djinni-vera's voice sounded faint, but furious. She staggered sideways in the open portal, toppling over to her right until her shoulder rested against the frame. Her hands were pressed against the cummerbund-like belt that curved under her pregnant belly, supporting the weight of Tarrant-Arragon's heir inside her.

On her left hand was a chunky ring. A fingerless, black leather glove sheathed the palm and back of her damaged right hand. Despite the Empire's best surgeons and the most modern medical technology, the injury to her right hand was slow to heal from the assassin's bullet that she had "caught" about four months ago, saving Tarrant-Arragon's life.

They all said—a little too often to be convincing—that her immune system was full-Djinn, although her mother had been human, and that her recovery would be rapid and full once the baby was born.

Tarrant-Arragon bounded towards her, hands out to catch her if her knees folded. 'Rhett held back. It would not be an overdramatization to say that an interstellar peace treaty hung in the balance. This was more than a domestic dispute, or could be. For the first time, Djinni had caught Tarrant-Arragon reverting to his old, high-handed, and ethically questionable ways behind her back.

'Rhett wanted to see firsthand how Tarrant-Arragon handled the situation.

Djinni's pallor was accentuated by the black, kimono-like robes she wore, and dark shadows emphasized her eyes, which flashed pale amethyst with weary anger. Her long, damp-tipped auburn hair hadn't been brushed.

"My love! How did you—?"

"Escape?" she snarled. "I've escaped from your suite before. I'll do it again. Don't touch me!"

Tarrant-Arragon looked as if he very much wanted to sweep her up in his arms and carry her back to bed. Instead, he propped his broad shoulders on the other side of the door opening, folded his arms, and frowned down at her.

"You shouldn't be balancing on stacks of books," he reproved her mildly.

'Rhett inferred that Tarrant-Arragon had a very good idea how Djinni managed to reach the Imperial Suite door control pad, which was above the lintel. A seven-foot-tall Great Djinn could reach it easily. Females and shorter mortals were effectively trapped. Or not, if they were as resourceful as Djinni.

"*You* shouldn't be endangering lives without consulting me. Promise-breaker!"

Djinni-vera balled her left hand and shook her fist under his nose. The point of her gesture, 'Rhett supposed, was that on the third finger of her left hand she wore Tarrant-Arragon's Death Ring.

Symbolically, Tarrant-Arragon had put his Right to take or spare lives into her hands. He'd slipped it on her finger after the duel with Djetth, and Djinni had repeated the irrevocable Imperial Mating vows, in full knowledge—that time—of what she was saying.

Given her Anglo-American upbringing, and the context, Djinni might well look on that Ring and all its significance as his wedding gift to her.

"Nor should you endanger lives, my love." Tarrant-

Arragon glanced meaningfully at her belly. "Shall we sit down?"

"I can't fight sitting down," Djinni snapped.

"I know," Tarrant-Arragon agreed. "Shall we sit?"

She glowered and stood her ground, trembling with rage.

"All right," the tyrant conceded. "Tell me what I've done to deserve your anger. Then we'll sit down, so you can give my defense a proper and fair hearing."

So far, Tarrant-Arragon was smooth. He admitted nothing.

"You have no defense. Your actions are indefensible." As if she felt the need to punctuate her accusations, but didn't quite dare poke His Highness's bare chest, Djinni jabbed the air between them with her forefinger.

"Perhaps." With the reflexes of a suddenly annoyed tiger, Tarrant-Arragon lashed out, caught her little hand in his, and kissed her imprisoned index fingertip.

"Nevertheless, I think I can mount a defense. You will permit me to try."

"Why are we still orbiting An'Koor?"

'Rhett felt his eyes widen. He hadn't expected such a cleverly loaded question from his little sister. Tarrant-Arragon could dig himself deeper into trouble if he lied.

"Lying," Tarrant-Arragon murmured, prevaricating, perhaps to give himself time to consider how much of the damning truth to volunteer. "We're lying over An'Koor. We're not strictly orbiting, because we are surveilling one particular island."

"Why?"

"For the protection and safety of my sister and your erstwhile fiancé, who are . . . ah . . . enjoying an enforced sojourn on that island."

"You marooned them!" The knives were out.

"I did."

"You shot them down." Djinni's accusation shook with indignation and fury.

"With surgical precision, my love. I'm an extremely good starfighter pilot. So is Djetth. . . ."

Smart move, 'Rhett thought. *Almost as manipulative as Mark Anthony's "I come to bury Caesar, not to praise him" speech, only it's the other way around.*

"Shooting Djetth down was more . . . interesting . . . than I had thought it would be. At no time, before, during, or since, did I consider that I might endanger their lives."

'Rhett would have been tempted to give His High and Mightiness the benefit of the doubt, if not for the fact that Tarrant-Arragon's remark about "a very inconvenient pregnancy" kept coming back to his mind.

"Indeed?" Djinni sneered.

A spasm crossed her face, as if she felt a sharp pain. Tarrant-Arragon must have relaxed his grip on her hand. Suddenly she snatched it free, and pressed both hands against her belly.

"You shot down a pregnant Princess. When I was four months along, you wouldn't let me leave the *Ark Imperial*, not even to go to your sister's and Djetth's wedding. Of all the callous hypocrisy! It's unconscionable to shoot down a pregnant female. She must have been terrified. The stress—"

"We must talk very seriously about stress, my love," Tarrant-Arragon crooned. "Won't you sit? It's dangerous for you to excite yourself."

"Excite myself? Excite . . . ? Oh! I'll give you excite—"

As tears ran down her flushed cheeks, Djinni's injured right hand tugged at the chunky Ring on her left.

'Rhett watched, holding his breath. Tarrant-Arragon, too, was very still.

The Ring did not come off. The moment of drama passed, allowing everyone to pretend that Djinni had not wanted to fling Tarrant-Arragon's Ring at him. 'Rhett exhaled silently. Either pregnancy had made Djinni's fingers swell, or her right hand wasn't strong enough.

"You must rescue them at once!" Embarrassment, perhaps, made her voice shrill, her tone imperious.

"I think not." Tarrant-Arragon's voice was as hard as space ice. "We will wait for Djetth to enjoy the rut-rage."

"Enjoy . . . ? Oh!" Djinni winced. 'Rhett wondered whether she might be having painful contractions.

"Tarrant-Arragon, how dare you assume"—her voice shook, but she seemed to be trying to contain her fury—"that to have the rut-rage on a desert island is not dangerous?"

Tarrant-Arragon couldn't win. He was in hot water with Djinni if Martia-Djulia was pregnant. He was no better off if Martia-Djulia was due to ovulate.

"Don't you bloody males realize that Djetth could seriously hurt Martia-Djulia?"

"My love, I must point out that if it hadn't been for your intervention, Djetth would not be capable of the rut-rage."

Tarrant-Arragon had a fair point.

"He won't get it if she's pregnant," Djinni snapped. "You know that."

Tarrant-Arragon tapped another message on his forearm device. Then he smiled tolerantly at his mate.

"I do know that. What We do not know is that Martia-Djulia is pregnant."

"She already gave him the rut-rage once. She must be pregnant." Djinni looked genuinely puzzled. Her voice was normal, but tired. "If she is not pregnant, why isn't she?"

"Birth control, perhaps?" 'Rhett murmured.

By entering the fray, albeit with a diplomatic "red herring," 'Rhett tested the dynamics of the Imperial couple's relationship. He'd already observed the loving latitude that Tarrant-Arragon gave Djinni.

Now, when confusing new information muddied the waters, Djinni looked inquiringly at Tarrant-Arragon for support.

"That raises a question—" Tarrant-Arragon began. "Ah, good, here's Ka'Nych."

The Imperial gynecologist and his medical entourage filled the corridor behind Djinni. With them was a contraption like a cross between a dentist's reclining chair, a gynecological examination table, and a hovercraft.

"Your Highness," Ka'Nÿch addressed Djinni, "too much exertion could bring on early labor. It would be prudent—"

"I know. If I'm very careful I can carry on until I explode." She sighed, and sat heavily. "I didn't really mean that. 'Rhett, will *you* come with me? Tarrant-Arragon, we're not finished," she added ominously.

Tarrant-Arragon's eyes lit up with amusement. "My love, I'm delighted to hear you say so."

Chapter Sixteen

Freighter Island, An'Koor

I'm a tiger when I want love,
I'm a snake when we disagree.

Djetth's testosterone roared through his veins as he emerged from the woods. Sex was in the air. Everywhere he looked, in the woods, on the shore, birds, beasts, and insects were mating. He'd found plenty of bedding material, and Marsh looked as if she'd been cleaning herself up for his imminent benefit.

They'd had a couple of great conversations about sex. She'd seemed cautiously interested. Why shouldn't she have changed her mind? Girls did that. If she still had doubts, maybe the soft, bouncy bed he was about to build for her would tip the balance.

If not, he'd melt her heart with a really useful and touching gift—homemade socks cut from the ejector seat upholstery to protect her big, beautiful feet!

He checked her out.

Marsh had the best-looking feet he'd ever seen, and

he'd seen a lot of girls' feet. He'd spent his youth rebelling against an Earth culture that idealized small feminine feet, and equated large shoe size with large penises in men. Where he'd most like Marsh's well-formed feet, right now, would be hooked tightly around his waist, or braced against his shoulders.

Instead of looking up with a smile of welcome, Marsh seemed intent on cleaning her fingernails with the sharp end of a flat, knitting-needle-like weapon.

Where she'd found it, he'd no idea. From the unimproved state of their campsite, she'd spent all morning grooming herself from head to toe.

"Remember this?" Coming closer, he dropped the worm-eaten chunk of driftwood they'd seen that morning. He'd made a detour to the beach to pick it up.

Marsh looked away as the log landed with a soft thud and a cloud of wood dust.

Djetth saw his chances receding. If she wasn't interested in sex, why the Fewmet else had she used up a day's supply of "wet wipes" at the latrine? Why did she need finger-combed curls and clean nails if she had no plans to scratch his back?

Cutting and hauling branches was thirsty work. He looked for a shell of boiled water. The shells lay empty. She couldn't even boil water for him!

Tight-lipped with annoyance, he moved to the tripod he'd set up that morning—while she slept—to filter rainwater, and which he'd refilled before leaving to gather material to make the bed and thatch the shelter.

What the Carnality! It was rain. I'll chance it. He drank an unboiled shellful, filled four conch shells, and put them one by one on the fire to boil. Then he ladled untreated water into the top of his filter system.

Had she noticed that he'd used her bustle-like bottom enhancer, and cut up some of her petticoats to make the three different layers of his filter system? Was that why she was mad at him?

He *had* warned her. Securely lashed triangles of petticoat fabric were great for the first, grass, layer of filtering. The second level bulged with sand and bustle was perfect to hold the charcoal he'd harvested first thing that morning from the fire embers. Okay. It wasn't a pretty sight. It looked like he'd turned her precious finery into big cat's litterbox.

He'd left some spare strips of fabric hung over an offshoot fork. Automatically he picked them up and wrapped them around his wrist for later.

A thought crossed his mind and he looked speculatively at Marsh.

When Tarrant-Arragon had ordered him to marry her or die a traitor's death, he'd been willing to take her on with all her faults—bitchiness, bad temper, and superficiality among them—because she'd once made him feel that he was the most potent lover in all the Communicating Worlds.

Moreover, with her lush beauty and submissive bedroom manners, Princess Martia-Djulia had been his idea of what a feminine mate should be, until she blasted him onto his butt. It was high time she refreshed his memory of why he'd agreed to take her for his mate.

"Are you hungry?" he asked abruptly. He kicked the log a little closer to where she was sitting, and sat down on it, being careful not to squash the berries he'd picked and put in one of the thigh pockets of his flight suit.

"After all the fish we had for breakfast? No." Marsh continued paring a shredded fingernail, as if this were her most critical task of the day.

"We can't survive on just protein," he lectured her. "On Earth, they warn Outward Bound adventurers about 'rabbit starvation.' We need fats, sugars, and starches. When you're starving and don't know it, one of the first things to go is your judgement."

"I have noticed," she sneered. "I might as well tell you that I have come to a decision. From now on, I refuse to eat—or touch—anything with testicles. I refuse to skin them—" She waved a languid hand at the dangling desert bunnies. "I won't eat them."

"A pity," Djetth retorted. "I was so hoping. . . . Female parts are all right to eat, I presume?"

"No!"

"They're especially fun to eat drizzled with honey." *Or so I hear.*

She didn't seem to know what he was talking about, which was quite possible. The Great Djinn weren't known to lower themselves. He'd never tried cunnilingus either, but he had heard about it.

"It's lucky I brought you this log, then, isn't it?" he fired back. "It's a living larder, full of sweet ants, grubs, and maggots. Let's take a look. . . ." Feeling perverse, Djetth made a big show of closely examining the wriggling rear end of a fat, cinnamon-colored grub. "Ha! Here's something that doesn't have any genitalia at all. How about eating this?"

He leaned towards her and held it out, as if he seriously expected that she might look at the grub, or better still, nibble it.

"I am not going to examine sex organs!" Marsh jumped to her feet and stamped a foot in defiance, just like a petulant female lead in Shakespeare's *Taming of the Shrew*, a play Djetth remembered only because of how violently he disliked the way the "hero" treated the "heroine" once he'd married her for her father's money.

Djetth grinned at her, but a balanced diet was no laughing matter. "You can't starve to death because you're picky. If you won't eat meat, what will you eat?"

She did not answer.

He slipped his right hand into his thigh pocket, and rolled the firm, grape-shaped, nightshade-black berries between his fingers like suede-covered marbles.

"Do you agree that we'd better find out what is edible while we are as fit and well fed as we are likely to be?"

"Maybe," she answered in a low, sulky voice.

"Are you sure you're not pregnant?"

He stared at Marsh through narrowed eyes, weighing her up. They had water. Not eating for forty-eight hours wouldn't hurt her. A bout of diarrhea and vomiting wouldn't hurt her, either.

He, on the other hand . . . if he were incapacitated, they'd both die, because Marsh didn't have a clue how to take care of herself.

"It's important that you tell me the truth. Are you absolutely sure?" he asked again.

"Of course I am sure." She glared at him. "Why?"

"Because I'm going to do things with you that I wouldn't do to any pregnant female." *Let alone to one who is carrying my child.*

Instead of running away, she sat on the log, although as far from beside him as was possible.

"If you tell me that you *are* pregnant, I'll take care of you," he said, meaning every word.

"And if I'm not?"

"Then, sweetheart, you are fair game. You cannot sit around all day playing the Princess—"

"That is not fair!" she interjected.

"And acting all finicky about what you will and will not eat," he continued inexorably. "Attitude won't get you fed and watered, Your High-Maintenance Highness."

"How dare you presume to threaten me, sexually!" Marsh hissed, leaning forward with the heels of her hands pressed together on the log. Her upper arms squeezed her glorious breasts together, creating a deep cleavage that his tongue ached to explore.

"Did I threaten you sexually? Did I say I'm prepared to wait on you hand and foot in exchange for sex?" He laughed. "As long as you don't give me the rut-rage, I'm perfectly capable of taking care of myself sexually."

She looked puzzled and taken aback.

"I thought you wanted a sexual 'experiment.' "

"I don't mind experimenting, but what I want is sexual certainty," he retorted.

I want . . . sexual certainty. Oh, the refined menace in his voice as he said that! The carnal gleam in his dark eyes, the brazen way his hand moved deep in his pocket, playing with himself, no doubt.

Martia-Djulia shivered with excitement and fear. She felt safe with Djetth, and she did not. She didn't know what he was going to do next. She couldn't wait to find out.

Where is he going? What is he going to do?

Her eagerly parted lips felt as rough as tree bark. She watched him stride across the beach to one of the seats he'd rescued from the plane. It was the seat he'd said he'd bend her over. . . .

He picked it up. He was bringing it to where she sat. Would he erect a gold tent, next? A fluttering began between her legs, just to think . . . She would fight him, of course. She would not let him strip her naked and seduce her over that seat back without a struggle.

"Sit on the chair," he commanded.

She shook her head.

"You might as well make yourself comfortable. No? Very well then." Djetth stood over her, looking as determined as a torturer.

She arched an eyebrow at him.

"We'll start now," he said, squatting down in front of her, his knees on either side of hers. He took hold of her left forearm and turned her wrist, so the back of her hand rested on his work-roughened palm.

"Start?" she questioned, trembling inside.

Irrationally, she felt glad that she'd washed all over, and done her nails, and chewed on knobbly little sticks until her breath smelled of their fragrant resin.

Was Djetth going to kiss the underside of her wrist? Might he kiss her fingertips? He could try. It didn't mean that she would let him kiss any further than the inside of her elbow.

A new pulse began to throb in anticipation.

She did not know whether it was An'Koor's slightly lighter gravity, the quantity of iron in the atmosphere, or the quality of light on An'Koor, but her senses seemed more acute on this fast-moving world.

Somewhere close by, a bird was chirring. Down the beach, the waves slurped and sighed as they sucked the shore. She could smell the smoke-and-flame of their fire; the sweet, crumbly wood of the log; and the salty tang of Djetth's crotch.

She breathed in through flared nostrils, savored her sensory impressions, then hurriedly reopened her eyes in case Djetth should jump to mistaken conclusions.

His face was very close to hers. She stared, noting the lean-cheeked, sexy look of a mature male. His eyes were a deep, purplish gray with long, dark lashes; he had four little crinkles—like tigers' whiskers—splaying out from the outer corner of his narrowed eyes, and a vertical crease between his eyebrows.

Whatever she might say about his wicked beard, and the smile it emphasized, Djetth was devastatingly attractive around the eyes. In color, his eyes were very like Tarrant-Arragon's, but Djetth's were the eyes of someone who could be trusted.

But trusted with what?

Martia-Djulia became aware of a cool, slimy sensation on her wrist.

"Oh, slurrid. What?" She tried to pull her hand away, but Djetth held her arm firmly. Looking down, she saw a watery black smear on her skin. "What are you doing?" She moved to rub away the disgusting juice with her right hand.

Quick as a predator, Djetth intercepted her. He held both her forearms with his left hand. "Don't interfere with the test, or I'll have to tie you up," he said huskily.

"What test? How dare you! Let go of me at once." Martia-Djulia trembled, but despite her choice of words, she was neither angry nor afraid.

Djetth had offered her the equivalent of a sexual ejector seat. If she truly wanted him to stop his perverted little game with her, all she had to do was tell him that she was pregnant.

"You had your chance, babe. Now, I am going to experiment on you. I shall do it slowly, very carefully, very methodically."

Martia-Djulia drew in a ragged breath.

Is he going to squash berry juice all over me and then lick it off? Slowly! Who knew Djetth could be so twisted? Her heart began to beat wildly.

"Don't hurt me," she begged, playing along. She found herself watching his mouth with new interest.

"You must tell me before it hurts," Djetth said, sounding serious. "If it tickles, or itches, I want to know."

"Itches?" *His beard might tickle, but itch?*

He raised an eyebrow.

"I'm starting with something that's probably safe."

"Probably?" she squealed. Her imagination ran riot. One couldn't live at the Imperial Court and not know of a few debaucheries and unsafe sex acts. Most involved large semen depositors and small orifices . . . not berries and beards.

"Berries like this are edible ninety-nine times out of a hundred. They seem to be pretty prolific, and I know wild creatures eat quantities of them with no ill effects. There wouldn't be any point subjecting you to what I am going to put you through for something scarce."

Martia-Djulia tugged a little. He did not relax his hold on her.

"What are you going to do to me?" she asked.

Djetth swung her arms gently.

"I'm going to leave that juice on your inner arm for a while. I don't want you rubbing it in or off, unless, of course, you are uncomfortable, in which case, we'll wash it off, and try something else. So far, you seem to be tolerating it quite well."

He dipped his head and looked narrowly at the smear. His exhaled breath rushed over her skin.

"It looks good. When I'm sure that nothing interesting will happen, I'll put a little berry juice on your lips and we'll see how you react. If all goes well—"

"Why are you doing this to me?" Martia-Djulia demanded breathlessly.

Is it possible that his explicit talk has stimulated me to ovulate already? Is he rut-raged? Will he declare he's desperately in love?

"I want to know what you can take. You see, there's no redness, no swelling. It doesn't itch, does it?"

"Did you think it would?"

"No. On the other hand, a poisonous berry might."

"What?" she shrieked.

Djetth chuckled. "If you're going to refuse the good and wholesome things I offer to put in your mouth, then we need to find out what you can eat. This is the safest way."

"NO!"

Experimenting with poisons? He wants to use me as a lowly food tester? Oh, the humiliation! The betrayal!

"Yes! It's like a virgin having her first full sexual intercourse. If we take it slowly, a little bit at a time, you might suffer some discomfort . . . some temporary incapacitation, but you'll survive it."

"No. I won't," Martia-Djulia protested, fighting him in earnest now. There was nothing sexy about being smeared with contact poisons.

Ignoring her protests, Djetth took another berry out of the pocket in his flight-suit pants, and brought his hand up towards her lips.

"Come on, sweetheart, be a good girl," Djetth

crooned as she turned her head this way and that to avoid his fingers and the berry between them.

"These come from some dwarf shrubs that have hairy white flowers and fruits in various stages of ripeness at the same time. If we can eat these, we'll have a constant and plentiful supply of fruit."

As she watched, Djetth pinched the fruit between his thumb and forefinger, and the skin split open, exposing dark, pink-tinted pulp and tiny teardrop-shaped seeds.

"I only want to put a drop of juice on the side of your mouth. For now."

"Not on me!" Martia-Djulia snarled. Lashing out, her shin caught him in the soft-and-hard place between his legs. Djetth fell backwards with a grunt, releasing her. She scrambled to her feet, turned, and ran.

"Damn! Fucking Carnality!" she heard him swear.

She had no plan, no place to go. Ahead of her was the sea. The fast scrunch of sand behind her told her he was coming after her. Without a doubt she knew that he would drive her into deep water if she stayed on her present course. The sea held no terrors for him.

He was closing as she turned to run parallel to the shore. His outstretched fingers raked her wrist. She shied away, and a pebble or shell grazed her instep. Her chest hurt. Her sides ached. She had only run a short way, and her knees felt weak . . . Martia-Djulia tripped in the uneven sand and stumbled forward.

"Got you!" Djetth grabbed hold of her arm, stopping her with a savage jerk and swinging her round to face him.

Although off-balance, she tried to throw a wild punch at his face, using her free hand. He caught her fist in his open palm. She felt the sting of impact.

Then in a move so swift she had no idea how he did it, her bosom and belly were crushed against his upper body, her arms were twisted and pinned behind her back, and his muscular arms locked around her.

Her chest heaved against his. She panted for breath.

"That was stupid," he rasped.

"I know it." It made no sense, but she was neither angry enough nor desperate enough to summon any of her powers. He was the same perfect height as Jason had been. How easy it would be to rest her head on his broad chest and submit to him.

Her heart pounded. Behind her back, Martia-Djulia felt him twist some kind of smooth fabric rope around her wrists and secure her. Apparently, Djetth did not take chances.

"We'll have to do this the hard way. Now, where were we?" Djetth growled, frowning into her eyes.

Another betrayal. Another letdown. The Worlds would be better off if she were dead. No one would be sorry. What difference would it make to struggle, scream, and curse?

"I thought you were a gentlemale," she said bitterly.

"No, you didn't. You think I'm a bastard."

Suddenly Djetth bent his head and pressed his open mouth over hers. She gasped in surprise. As fast as the mating of birds, his strong tongue darted between her lips and into her. Then, brief and violent as a black tiger mating, it was over.

Before she could take in the taste and feel of him, or register how it felt to be kissed by him, he was looming over her and glowering again.

"Last chance to tell the truth," Djetth said calmly, as if the kiss had never happened, or as if it had meant nothing to him . . . as if he had done it merely to prove that he could do anything he wanted to her. "*Are* you pregnant?"

"Why does everyone ask that?" She played for time.

"Does 'everyone' ask?" he asked softly, as if he found this fact revealing. "Could it be because 'everyone' knows all about you and Commander Jason?"

So, he knew.

He knew, and, even so, he wanted her. But, if she were

carrying Commander Jason's bastard baby, would he want her then? Did she want Djetth to want her?

Martia-Djulia gazed up at him. Her mind raced.

This was the third time he had asked whether she was pregnant. Each time he asked, the question took on greater importance. Whatever she replied, her answer had profound, far-reaching implications.

He'd made her choice clear. He would treat her differently if she were pregnant. He'd treat her better even though the child couldn't possibly be his. That was astonishing. No Great Djinn had ever made such a concession.

"Sweetheart"—his voice was gentle—"if you want to, you can buy yourself time with a lie."

Here was the ageless dilemma and test of character—whether or not to lie; whether to protect her physical comfort or her reputation and her freedom, such as it was. Martia-Djulia had no time to think about it.

For a Djinn Princess to be pregnant and unMated would be an intolerable situation. If such a rumor reached her father, she'd be Mated by proxy. Or quietly murdered.

Was that why she and Djetth were there? Was this all her fault?

"Oh my!" Martia-Djulia whispered.

Djetth brought the back of his right fist up to her face. For a moment she thought he might hit her. Instead, he stroked the previous day's bruised jaw with his knuckles.

Martia-Djulia blinked. Tenderness was unexpected.

"Tough choice, eh?" he teased. "What's it going to be, Marsh?"

Chapter Seventeen

ARK IMPERIAL (Imperial Suite)

"Tarrant-Arragon, in case we never meet again, I've decided to tell you something you may not know."

'Rhett stared into the golden depths of his wineglass, looking for a way to convey a warning without incriminating himself.

He'd stayed long enough. Now, he felt fairly confident that he was leaving his sister in safe, loving hands. While Djinni slept off her stress in the Imperial Suite's conversation pit with her head on Tarrant-Arragon's lap, he and Tarrant-Arragon had talked, mostly about Djinni, a little about benign non-enforcement of The Emperor's harshest laws, and about gradual reform.

" 'Rhett, are you leaving?" Djinni asked suddenly.

"Are you awake, my love?" Tarragon-Arragon murmured, unaware of how normal and foolish his query sounded. "What can I get for you?"

Djinni groaned faintly and tried to sit up. At once, Tarrant-Arragon rearranged the pillows around her.

"I didn't think morning sickness happened this far

into a pregnancy. I suppose there isn't any ginger-root tea, is there?" She sounded wistful.

"Grievous might know where to put his hands on some," Tarrant-Arragon said, rising. "I'll ask him."

Instead of using his forearm communicator, Tarrant-Arragon went to his master computer. 'Rhett took advantage of His Highness's temporary absence to perch on the parapet of the conversation pit for a private word with Djinni.

"I haven't forgotten that I'm mad at him," she confided. "But I have to stay calm if I don't want my baby to have his daddy's temper. He kicks."

She left it at that, but 'Rhett had a vivid impression of an opinionated baby with a taste for violence. If his Mamma and Daddy argued, whichever side the baby took in the dispute, it was Mamma who got kicked.

" 'Rhett, are you leaving the *Ark Imperial*?"

"Yes, I am." *Are you afraid of Tarrant-Arragon? Just say Yes if you want to be rescued from this marriage.*

"No. Are you going to see . . . The Dragon?"

"Eventually." *You haven't yet told Tarrant-Arragon that our father is the Saurian Dragon, have you?* "Do you have a message for him?" *Last chance, sis.*

"You might explain. . . ."

That you didn't mean to fall in love? That Tarrant-Arragon isn't the villain he pretends to be? I will.

Djinni nodded, as if satisfied. "While I slept—Stars, I slept!—did Tarrant-Arragon say you could go down to the island and make sure Djetth and Martia-Djulia are all right?"

"They're fighting," Tarrant-Arragon reported, as if he'd been part of the conversation all along.

"What?" Djinni gasped.

"Chasing each other, rolling around in the sand. He's tied her up, and she's sucking his fingers. It's normal, healthy courtship behavior."

"Healthy? Tarrant-Arragon, you have a very strange

notion of what is healthy!" Djinni threw a small pillow at him. "We never did any of that."

"We have time." Tarrant-Arragon caught the pillow and grinned at her. "So do they. Martia-Djulia is not pregnant. Do you remember what 'Rhett was saying, just before Ka'Nych came by and convinced you to rest? 'Rhett thought my sister might have been using birth control when she . . . ah . . . encountered 'Commander Jason'? He was quite right."

'Rhett shrugged. "It's an obvious precaution for a lady to take before jumping into bed with a complete stranger."

Djinni frowned at each of them in turn. "How do you know that? What changed while I was asleep?"

"Ours aren't the only toilets on the *Ark Imperial* that provide urinalysis. 'Rhett, Ka'Nych and I took a closer look at my sister's . . . ah . . . output. We ran a comparison over the last few cycles. If Martia-Djulia were pregnant, the anomaly in her system wouldn't be as consistent as it is."

"You shouldn't invade her privacy like that," Djinni chided. "People have a right to privacy."

"Not in my world, they don't," Tarrant—Arragon retorted. "Not on my war-star."

"Guests should," Djinni persisted.

"Djinni's right." 'Rhett sided with his sister.

"Very well, then," Tarrant-Arragon agreed. "As of tonight, guests' toilets will be deactivated. Now . . .'Rhett, you were about to tell me something I don't know?"

"No, wait. We're not finished with Martia-Djulia," Djinni insisted. "I don't understand. If Martia-Djulia's married to Djetth, why is she still using birth control? Is she afraid to give him the rut-rage?"

"They're not—" Tarrant-Arragon began.

"And, if she was using birth control when she made that film of herself having sex with Jason, how did she give him the rut-rage?"

Tarrant-Arragon's face had taken on an arrested look.

"It was a very *mild* rut-rage," he murmured, but his mocking words belied the narrowed eyes and the fingertips thoughtfully tapping his upper lip.

"It might not be safe to assume that Djetthro-Jason had the rut-rage over Martia-Djulia." 'Rhett took the plunge.

"But we saw them."

"Someone smelled rut-rageous in the Palace during my Mating Festivities," Tarrant-Arragon mused. "At the time, I thought it was Djinni. I was expecting her to come into season. I had no idea that I'd already got her pregnant."

'Rhett smiled. "It's a pity you erased Martia-Djulia's film. We might have been able to deduce something from it," he said unhelpfully.

"I do know that, thank you," Tarrant-Arragon drawled. "Martia-Djulia changed her mind about forcing Jason into a permanent Mating. She begged me to erase the footage, and never tell Jason—"

"Oh, Stars! Was it a secret? I told Djetth I'd seen the film. Do you think he remembers what I said?"

Tarrant-Arragon patted her shoulder. "He knows I spy on everyone. We don't care what he thinks of me. You didn't tell him that Martia-Djulia made the film." He turned back to 'Rhett. "My sister was ashamed of herself. So, I erased all surveillance—"

"No, you didn't," Djinni contradicted him. "I found you watching it shortly after Djetth's surgery."

"She keeps me honest, doesn't she?" Tarrant-Arragon threw a wry smile at 'Rhett. "That was a mere fragment, preserved by accident."

"I suppose this fragment didn't show whether or not the female assassin, Bronty, succeeded in planting a pheromone-soaked item on Martia-Djulia?" he asked.

"Is this what you were going to tell me?" Tarrant-Arragon asked in a cool voice. "Whose pheromones were they? Is there something else you have not told Us, 'Rhett?"

'Rhett felt as if a vise-cold, armored hand had clamped over his head and was slowly squeezing his skull. Djinncraft!

"'Rhett?" Djinni spoke quietly. "As we said on Earth, on a scale of one to ten, with ten being a certainty, how likely is it that Martia-Djulia smelled of me that day?"

The cold pressure stopped abruptly. Tarrant-Arragon stared at Djinni. The Imperial jaw dropped.

"Nine," 'Rhett answered, relieved that Djinni had leapfrogged the conversation—and the imminent torture—to what really mattered. *Thank you, sis!*

"Oh, no! 'Rhett, do you think Djetth knows that the scent might have been mine? Is that why he was so confused and angry? Oh, poor Djetth!"

"He can't 'know' for sure, sis. Bronty wouldn't have been told where the pheromones came from. She couldn't have told Djetth. We've all tried to make sense of why Djetth would try to rescue you from Tarrant-Arragon if he'd had the rut-rage with Martia-Djulia."

"That's right! Djetth should have 'fixated' on her if he'd had the rut-rage with her. Our family's fatal flaw wouldn't be a *fatal* flaw if the rut-rage was no more lasting than an aphrodisiac." Tarrant-Arragon began to pace.

"Yeeees," Djinni agreed. "I told myself that Djetth's strong sense of honor made him tear himself away from Martia-Djulia, in order to save me from you."

"'Djetth's strong sense of honor'?" Tarrant-Arragon snorted. "Correct me if my memory is at fault. Djetth's idea of 'saving' you included keeping you in his bed, claiming my child was his own, and killing me."

"Well, I've never told you this, dear, because I thought it would annoy you unnecessarily . . ." Djinni began mildly.

At this, 'Rhett hid an undiplomatic grin behind his hand.

". . . I read Djetth's mind back then. He meant to marry me because he thought he ought to, and Martia-Djulia because he wanted to. That's why I've been so sure he loves her."

"And you tried to excuse his behavior by saying that he didn't know what he was doing?" Tarrant-Arragon exploded. "That he'd had the rut-rage over my sister, and was confused? Hah!"

"Can a Great Djinn have the rut-rage with more than one full-Djinn female?" Djinni asked.

"That, sis, is something I hope the Empress-in-hiding, Tarragonia-Marietta, can answer." 'Rhett saw his exit-line and grabbed it. "That's why I'm going to see her."

"Do you know something about my mother that is not generally known, 'Rhett?" Tarrant-Arragon's singular turn of phrase warned 'Rhett to say no more in front of Djinni. "I would have thought that the exiled Empress Helispeta would have a great deal more to say—"

"I don't see why?" Djinni argued. "Grandmama Helispeta was, er, loved by twin brothers, one after the other. That's two Great Djinn with one female, and that's *not* what we're talking about."

"Hush, my love. We know. It was poor taste to mention your Grandmama."

'Rhett thought Tarrant-Arragon had done it deliberately.

"You may go, 'Rhett. Take one of my Thorcraft." Tarrant-Arragon dismissed him with a wave of a raised two-Ringed right hand. "Give my mother Our love."

'Rhett had been a spy too long not to take one final look back from the doorway, and to eavesdrop on what was said after his hosts thought he'd left.

"Tradition says the Great Djinn cannot love twice, my little love. The first scent-love is the one on whom One fixates. That's why my father, the Emperor Djerrold Vulcan, still secretly yearns for my mother after all these gestates. That's why—although he believes she must be dead—he offers an enormous reward to any bounty hunter who brings her back to him alive.

"That's why the late Emperor Djohn-Kronos never forgot Helispeta. There's a price on her head to this day. And this is why Djetth could be a problem for us for as long as he lives."

Tarra's Pleasure Palace, Pleasure Moon of Eurydyce

"Specifically, the 'contract' is to kill Martia-Djulia. I am sorry, Tarra, dear."

"There's a plot to kill Martia-Djulia? Why didn't you tell me so at once?" Tarra wailed. "We have wasted time!"

She could hardly reply that she had not been certain Tarra was at all interested in her daughter, and that she had since changed her mind.

"Space lag . . ." Helispeta murmured, following her maxim, *When in doubt, exploit One's age.* Blaming her age allowed Helispeta to ask the same question, or variations of it, more than once without arousing a suspect's suspicion that she might be an expert in painless interrogation methods. "And, of course, you were so upset about poor Petri-Shah. . . ."

Helispeta did not believe in coincidences.

"Think, Tarra, dear. Is there the remotest connection between Petri-Shah and Martia-Djulia?"

Tarra turned a card.

"Djetthro-Jason springs to mind," she said dreamily.

"Djetthro-Jason?" Helispeta repeated. It would not, after all, be good form for an Empress to appear unsurprised that her grandson consorted with prostitutes. However, it was not the reply she had anticipated.

"Or myself, I suppose," Tarra added.

Only an insider would know that Madam Tarra, employer of prostitutes, was the Empress Tarragonia-Marietta, mother of Princess Martia-Djulia.

"Djetthro-Jason—under his old alias as Commander Jason—had a reputation for enjoying courtesans prodigiously. Two at a time," Tarra continued when Helispeta did not speak. "It was a cover for his subversive activities. Petri-Shah and Feya visited his An'Koori war-star regularly, and were never suspected as Saurian messengers."

"As far as you know," Helispeta commented drily. "Where is Feya?"

"Feya is still missing. I sent Petri-Shah and Feya on an errand to An'Koor at Tarrant-Arragon's behest."

"Oh?" Helispeta questioned, drawing out the vowel to indicate slightly exaggerated interest.

"Tarrant-Arragon wanted someone discreet to plant mature fruits and vegetables, and release some flightless poultry and desert bunnies on Freighter Island."

"Why?"

"He mentioned an inconvenient pair of relatives, who would benefit from enforced isolation. I inferred, though he did not say so, that he planned to maroon Martia-Djulia's sadistic boys, Henquist and Thor-quentin."

"Really?"

"There's ugly talk about those young males. If half of it is true, I hope and pray that my girls got off Freighter Island before the Princes were dropped there."

Helispeta pursed her lips. Feeling suddenly restless, she rose from her chair to examine some of the extraordinary artifacts in Tarra's parlor by the flickering light of a number of large, mauve candles which gave off a scent like lavender sprinkled on warm elderberry wine.

"All in all, my dear," she mused aloud, "I think we can rule out your grandsons. In looking for a murderer, one must consider means, motive, and opportunity. Henquist and Thor-quentin may be vicious enough to contemplate matricide. One cannot underestimate the nastiness of our inlaws.

"However, underage Princes have neither the access to funds nor the opportunity to contact assassins. Someone older, wealthier, and more powerful wants Martia-Djulia dead. But who?"

Freighter Island
Darkest hour before dawn

Some things Djetth did slowly.

Too afraid to sleep, Martia-Djulia lay in his arms, with her hands tied in front of her, waiting to find out if Djetth had poisoned her.

Cramps like claws of fire raked her belly. Pangs similar to giving birth jarred her back passage. Her lower body ached dully as if from unaccustomed exercise, all through her thighs, and especially in her love handles.

She arched backwards, as if the change in position might expel the pain, yet clenched, afraid of what might happen if she bore down. Perhaps it was only premenstrual cramps and hunger pains.

Djetth had begun with the juice on her wrist. After an agonizing wait, during which he'd held her down, he'd touched her lip with a juice-stained fingertip. Later, his wet forefinger traced the corner of her mouth.

While they waited again, his wicked fingers stroked and teased her lips until under the erotic onslaught she forgot to grit her teeth and he slid two fingers into her mouth.

Dusk fell, and he would not leave her alone. Bound, helpless, and struggling, she could not stop him from slipping his fingers in and out of her mouth. Again and again he penetrated her, depositing his salty sweet juice on her tongue, and under it.

"I wonder," he'd murmured hoarsely, "why the textbooks don't recommend doing this to your pussy?"

Martia-Djulia did not know what tormentors' textbooks he meant, or in what way a pussy—whatever that was—would be useful. She hated that her treacherous body trembled under his gentle touch, and that he'd made her wet between the legs.

Finally, he'd cupped the point of her chin and forced a mashed, whole berry between her lips. Before she could try to spit it out, he bent his head and sucked her exposed, extended, vulnerable neck.

Up and down her sensitive throat, he nibbled, bit, and sucked, still holding her immobile for his twisted enjoyment. His free hand stroked her breast until her nipples were hard, and he trailed his mouth down her body, and suckled through the "T-shirt" until she gasped and cried out at the blinding pleasure.

She'd swallowed the berry without noticing.

"Just wait," he'd promised, with his mouth still over her damp nipple. "If you don't drop dead overnight, I'm going to give you seven more, at sunup, one after the other."

Without untying her hands, he'd carried her to his half-made bed and lain down with her, under gold foil sheets, under the stars. He must have known that she wouldn't be able to sleep for wondering what perverted ways he'd stimulate her to swallow for him seven times, one after another.

Djetth was determined. She had no doubt that when it suited him, he would do whatever he wanted to her, and she would open her mouth, or her throat, or her legs, for him again and again in spite of herself.

By firelight, Martia-Djulia glanced at strips of the expertly skinned desert bunnies which Djetth was drying over the smoky fire. What perversity, what self-destructive folly, had made her refuse to eat meat?

Had she been so truly disgusted that she was willing to die in protest? Had she been so desperate to pick a fight with Djetth that she would have seized any pretext?

Why? Was a painful, humiliating death preferable to meaningless sex with Djetth? If so, why? What did one more Mate matter?

This was turning into the longest night after the most miserable day of her life. Martia-Djulia sighed.

That wasn't true. Yesterday had only been the worst

day of her life since the day Tarrant-Arragon tried to trick her into Mating with Djetth, and she'd learned that her beloved Commander Jason was a dead traitor.

A tear slid down her cheek. The day before had been high on the scale of misery, too. Had it been only two days ago that her adored brother had tried to kill her? It seemed a lifetime ago.

For a while in the Thorcraft, she'd felt so humiliated and wretched that she'd wanted to oblige Tarrant-Arragon and die. Yet, when she lurched into the sea, her body had fought madly to escape certain death by drowning.

Later, when she'd found herself wet, miserable, and sore on the beach, she'd wanted to curl up and wait for exposure or starvation to end her loveless life. But her body betrayed her again when Djetth spoke of a hot meal.

And there must have been other bad days that were too terrible to remember—the day someone cut her, the first time she was impregnated. . . .

The self-pitying tears came thicker, faster. Djetth's arms were around her. Her aching bottom was pressed firmly against the heat of his ridged groin. His breathing was regular and soft. He was asleep. He didn't care how frightened, hurt, and unhappy she was.

She let her tears drip onto the leafy boughs beneath her. Now that her "remedy" must have worn off, her body was giving her more frequent warnings, but of what? Would she ovulate or bleed first? If she bled, how would she manage?

If she ovulated, would her reawakened reproductive system come back to life in an overpowering explosion of scent, like a smashed flask of perfume? Would her first season be mild after such a long hibernation? Or would her ovaries sputter and kick in at different times before a proper, regular cycle reestablished itself?

Either way, her body would humiliate and betray her again, one way or another, if Djetth's poisonous experiments did not kill her first.

Chapter Eighteen

Freighter Island
The next morning

She'd survived the night. It was a new day. Djetth was going to kiss and caress her body until she swallowed all of his berries.

Martia-Djulia opened her eyes and there beside her lay a pair of fluffy, furry, adorable slippers. He must have fashioned them for her from bunny skins and seat upholstery.

"Oh, Djetth! Djetth, you are so . . . capable!"

Not for a thousand worlds' tribute had she meant to exclaim aloud. Martia-Djulia would have clapped a chagrined hand to her mouth, but her wrists were bound.

Still lying on her side, she scanned the empty campsite, and exhaled in relief. Djetth was nowhere in sight.

"Spread your legs and I'll show you how *capable* I am!" his deep voice growled from above her.

Oh no! Martia-Djulia looked up. There he was up in a tree, looking as healthy as a god, grinning lustfully at her. For a moment, she was lost for words.

How commanding, masterful, and effective he was. There were times when a lonely fool could mistake Djetth for almost everything a Mate should be. But, she did not want sex with him if it would be meaningless.

And it would be meaningless. No self-repecting Princess could respond favorably to such a crass proposition. Martia-Djulia called on her Royal dignity.

"I outrank you!" she said with as much icy hauteur as possible, given that she was lying on her back in a glorified compost heap. "According to Imperial Protocol and the rules of precedence, it is not for you to suggest such impertinences."

Djetth's expression darkened. He jumped down from his tree with a thump, and advanced on her. She waited, shivering, for what he'd do to punish her.

Djetth could think of a dozen sarcastic retorts, any one of which would put the cock-teasing bitch firmly in her place.

I most certainly outrank you, my dear Marsh, *so how about it?*, for one.

Protocol wasn't a problem when Jason backed you against a structural pillar, parted your legs with his thigh, and swore he had to 'have' you, was it?, for another. *Oh, yeah? Perhaps I should thrust your gorgeous, high-class ass against a tree, and show you who's in charge here!*

She looked aghast, which inflamed him further.

Why the Carnality did you spread your legs so eagerly for Commander Jason, but won't for me? I'm the same bloody guy.

He couldn't say any of it. He could learn, though.

Giving her choices was obviously not the way to go. She chose not to take a risk at every turn. Except for that one time with Jason, which might have been because Jason hadn't given her a choice.

* * *

This is it, Martia-Djulia thought, as he stood over her, his lip curled, steaming with excess testosterone. *I've gone too far.*

"Fucking Jason was your idea, then, was it?" he sneered.

"How dare you!" she gasped at his savagery.

"Oh, I dare." Bending over her, Djetth grasped her by the shoulders as if to haul her bodily out of the bedding.

"Yes! Yes, it was my idea!" As she cried out, Martia-Djulia threw a wild, double-fisted punch at his face with her bound hands.

She missed. His reflexes were faster, his gallantry non-existent. He didn't just drop her and dodge, he thrust her hard back into the bed.

She landed sprawling in the branches. For a moment they stared at each other, both breathing hard, both furious, both wondering if he was going to throw himself on top of her and show her how little he cared about Imperial Protocol and the proper pecking order when it came to suggesting sex.

He turned away, came back; clenched and unclenched his big fists. From his tight, controlled movements, she could tell that he was very, very angry.

"Never," he snarled, "never hit me in the face."

Why the face? she wondered, staring defiantly at him. Traditionally, males were most annoyed by attempts to damage their tender testicles.

He strode to the fire, picked up a shell, and drank hot water. He picked up another and made a toasting gesture.

"You can have water. Do you want some?"

She nodded.

He went down on one knee beside the bed, pulled her into a sitting position, and held out the full, warm conch.

"What the blue star blazes did you see in Jason?" he asked, still forcefully but with his frustration and jealousy under better control.

Martia-Djulia drank before answering. She wanted to soften a serious answer with a note of rueful humor.

"For one thing, Djetth, *he* wasn't trying to kill me!"

"Kill you?" Djetth looked stunned.

His frown deepened, and his dark eyes stared intently into hers. He reached forward. The rough pad of his thumb stroked the delicate skin beneath her lower eyelid. "Is that what you think?"

As he spoke, he thrust his other hand into his pocket and held out a handful of berries.

She shrank involuntarily, thinking he'd force them into her mouth without the thrilling preliminaries. Instead, he ate them, one after the other.

"Sweetheart, I misled you a little. These berries are a staple of the An'Koori diet. I've eaten them often."

"Then, why . . . ?"

"You've a cute little rash that comes and goes. I've only noticed it since we've been on this island. I think you may have allergies, but I don't know what you're allergic to. I could eat a handful of fruit, kiss you without a thought, and you could die if you happened to be allergic to what I'd eaten. I don't think it's as bad as that, but your life's too precious to take chances."

"Oh!" *He thinks my life is precious?* Her reaction made no sense, but it was as if a whole new sun slid out from hiding. The An'Koori day seemed infinitely brighter.

Djetth watched as a broad, involuntary grin lit up her face, then morphed into a troubled pout as Marsh tried to sort out all the new data he'd dumped on her and come up with an appropriate reaction.

"Here, let me untie you," he offered, partly to give her an unobtrusive time-out, and partly because this was the first opportunity he'd had to release her safely without appearing to back down.

"Thank you," Marsh mumbled and twisted so he

could reach her wrists. "Djetth, I'm a female," she blurted out, while her face was averted.

"Uh-huh." Djetth refrained from any of the smart-ass comments that leapt to mind. She was shy. She had trouble using clinical terminology. One might well wonder how she communicated with her gynecologist.

"I'm having cramps. Oh, not because of the berry. I was having cramps before we started the test. That means. . . . I don't know how I'll manage when. . . . My body does slurrid things that a male never has to worry about. What am . . . I . . . going to dooooo?"

I'm going to be the father of her children. If I'm wrong about Tarrant-Arragon, I might have to deliver our baby on this island. I can talk about this.

"If we're discussing menstruation, we *could* postpone that problem," he began slowly. "If I got you pregnant."

"You cannot be serious!"

He shook his head and grinned. "Too drastic? You might be right. On Earth, some primitive cultures use moss."

"There could be things living in the moss!" she objected in a horrified whisper.

"And the 'things' wouldn't be pleased, would they?" he agreed. "A more practical idea is to cut strips out of the most absorbent fabric in your Court dress—or out of the ejector seat padding, if you prefer."

"What a waste," Marsh mourned, but she didn't refuse out of hand to be practical. She twisted the hem of his T-shirt around her finger, and peeped at him from under her long, dark lashes. "Oh, Djetth, I can talk to you about almost anything. You'd make someone a marvelous Mate."

"Yes, I would. Why not you?"

Did I just propose to her? Slack damn! I meant to sleep with her first.

"You don't love me—"

Do you really think Jason loved you? For some reason he didn't understand, he wanted to rebut her objections.

"—you can't possibly."

I would if we had the rut-rage, and it went the way it's supposed to, and then I'd know once and for all that it IS you I love and not Djinni-vera.

Fewmet! Marsh was looking shiny-eyed and expectant. She wanted him to say that he did love her, that it *was* possible. He wanted to tell her the truth. But truth and politics did not sleep well together.

A smooth bastard would come up with a nicely ambiguous "line" at this point.

"Sweetheart—" Djetth sighed. He was neither smooth nor a bastard. "I guess I know what you want me to say. Here's the problem: I'd probably be lying."

She looked shattered. He blundered on.

"You're right. It's not possible for me to love you. Yet." *Please notice I stressed Yet!* "We haven't officially had the rut-rage. I'm a Great Djinn. I'm supposed to go for a scent-love. So far"—*I'm leaving the door open*—"you don't smell right."

"In fact, I don't smell at all, do I?" Marsh hissed.

"I wouldn't go so far as to say that," he shot back, landing himself with the unenviable choice of discussing her body odor or his lost love. "Mmmm. If only we had some soap. If we went back up to the reef, I think I could find some real sponges—"

"Soap!"

It was a pity. Marsh seemed to be going out of her way to misunderstand him, while he was struggling to find the words to tell her that maybe the rut-rage didn't matter, that they could make love and be happy without being "in love."

He tried another tack.

"I once had a scent-love, or so I thought. Let's say I never got near her at the right time of her cycle. I hoped she might be you. . . . But you don't get fragrant, so it must have been someone else. Someone I can't have."

"So, you are saying that you agreed to Mate with me because you thought I might be your scent-love?"

"There was a little more to it than that. . . ."

Only I can't tell you that I'm the Jason you think you love. I've had proper, full-blown sex with three girls in my life, and you were my third, and the best by far. Even if I never love you back as you deserve, I could make you happy, and I could love our daughters.

From the look on Marsh's face, he wondered if he'd be sorry he'd untied her.

I'd better tell you something!

"Ahhh, let's add that I was very badly beaten up by a male who turned out to be slightly more alpha than I am. He got my scent-love. I got a jaw that keeps me from fighting."

Watching *Marsh*, he was pretty sure she'd figured out whom he was talking about.

"Is that why I mustn't hit your face?" she asked.

"Yeah. After he smashed my jaw, I couldn't eat, or speak for more than a month. It would be worse if it got broken again. Down here, I could die."

Freighter Island, reef end

"Am I dead?" Feya moved her head. "Oh, Fewmet, I smell like I am."

She cracked open her eyes, just a little. The world was bright. The outer corners of her eyelids were sore. She tried to stretch, and daggers of pain stuck her, all up her right side from her knee to her ribs. Her leg was still dislocated.

"How long has it been?"

Hunger gnawed her insides. Thirst burned her throat. It had rained on her, perhaps more than once while she'd been unconscious. Feya sucked on her wet clothes, ignoring the moldy flavor and the grit.

Her species did that—went into healing stasis when injured. It wasn't the most efficient evolutionary response in the modern Worlds. One could be raped, or buried, or eaten alive.

Feya scratched an itch where a bug had bitten her, then looked at her nails. They'd grown. She could tell by where the nail paint had grown out. It had been a while. If Petri-Shah was coming back with help, she would have been back by now, Feya realized.

Where was Petri-Shah? Feya gritted her teeth. If it had been the other way around, if Petri-Shah had been the one to dislocate a leg, they wouldn't have had to split up. Being bigger, Feya could have lifted her friend and mentor into the fast little shuttle on the beach.

Petri-Shah had tried. In the process, they'd dropped their communicators in the water. In the end, not knowing how soon the Royals would arrive for their adventure holiday, she and Petri-Shah had scraped a shelter out of a dune-side for Feya to hide in, and Petri-Shah had gone back to the Pleasure Moon to get help.

Would help come? If she kept her promise to Petri-Shah to stay where she was until help arrived, she'd die of starvation or exposure.

She would rather die slowly, naturally, than be found and shared by two voracious young Tiger Princes until their sexually sadistic attentions killed her. She'd wait as long as she could.

Chapter Nineteen

Freighter Island
Midnight

Fucking Jason was your idea, then, was it? He'd meant it rhetorically. Maybe he didn't do sarcasm as well as the lawyers in the family.

Yes! Yes, it was my idea!

Marsh's answer floored him. Had she really thought the idea was her own? Or had she wanted it to be her idea?

The very thought had been driving him crazy all day.

It had been a long, productive, hardworking day. Marsh had decided to help. Funnily enough, though she was useless at sewing or home construction, Her Ultra-Feminine Highness was quite a dab hand at whittling stakes and weapons. He should have been exhausted, but his mind was racing. His balls were full and aching.

Lying beside Marsh in the pine-scented darkness, he revisited that morning's heated exchange.

He'd been the aggressor in their first encounter at the Virgins' Ball. Hadn't he? Doing dishonorable business as Commander Jason, he'd swaggered up to her, growled,

"Princess, I've got to have you," and masterfully thrust his tongue into her mouth. His idea!

But wait. Rewind the memory further back. Martia-Djulia had been the one to approach him. She'd ordered him to dance with her. In fact, now he did think back further, he'd been showing an interest in an ambitious virgin, who was itching to be royaled, preferably by the biggest matrimonial game around.

Martia-Djulia had taken pleasure not only in whirling "Jason" away, but in doing so in such a way as to make the virgin heartily sorry that she'd put "Jason" down.

What had Martia-Djulia seen in Jason? What? Jason was an act that she'd fallen for. Dyed hair, attitude, scars, a shaven chest, everything but a spandex suit.

What was it about Jason: Was it a rock star-slash-groupie thing? He could definitely play the performer if she would make the moves.

He could dance around stark naked, with plenty of vigorous pelvic thrusting, sing "Can't touch this!" and his contrarian Princess would think touching him was her idea.

Masculine nerve endings sparkled and fizzed, neglected balls swelled and tightened with anticipation. Djetth let his imagination rampage.

Yeah! Given how unromantic their predicament was, and how squeamish Marsh was about dirt, sweat, blood, and nuts, "Raunch" was the way to go.

Djetth raised himself up on his elbow to watch Marsh in her sleep. Her cheek was pillowed on her right hand. Her left hand curled just below her nose. Though her features were too strong for her to be a conventional beauty, he thought she was a knockout!

He dipped his head and sniffed her tangled, lived-in hair. No joy. Not yet. She smelled sweet and sexy, but not of the faint, heady, white-flower scent-memory that he associated with his one, puzzlingly brief, rut-rage.

He could pretend, though. This forcible marooning

only made sense if his Vero-Nasal Organ and saturniid glands had left the *Ark Imperial*'s Operating Theater intact, and Tarrant-Arragon wanted Djetth and Martia-Djulia to have the rut-rage.

How easy it would be to overpower her, and blame the rut-rage if she didn't like being taken. But . . . he had his depraved grandfather's reputation to live down. All his life he'd heard stories condemning Djohn-Kronos, who'd gotten Grandmama Helispeta into bed by pretending to be someone he wasn't; who'd seized the throne before it was rightfully his; and a great deal worse.

Nostrils flared, he inhaled again half in dread, half in eagerness for a sign that Marsh was about to come into season.

If it had been Martia-Djulia's scent that had given him the rut-rage briefly, but long enough to keep him from disrupting Tarrant-Arragon's Mating, why hadn't it happened since, in the two cycles they'd been aboard the *Ark Imperial*? Was it possible that, if older females had such a thing as peri-menopause, Marsh was peri-fertile?

Inwardly he shrugged. He was unbearably horny, but he wasn't desperate to be reproductive. Careful not to wake Marsh, he eased himself over her, off the bed, and out into the night.

His eyes adapted well, even in the astonishing An'Koori nighttime dark, where there was no stray light from civilization, only the blue-white light reflected from one of An'Koor's two artificial moons.

It had rained earlier. The night was alive with the scurrying of insects and disoriented desert bunnies, the creak of branches, the rasp and chirp of backleg love signals, the snuffles and whuffles of insectivores hunting and humping.

Breathing in the night air, he registered that the flora of Freighter Island was similar to that of Earth's temperate, mixed woodlands. Who knows? Perhaps the freighter's cargo of topsoil had been stolen from Earth. It had to have come from a planet with a similar climate. Why not from the imported An'Koori people's original homeworld?

Other scents wafted to his nostrils. In his back-burner quest for guitar-making glue, he was boiling down various types of sap. One smelled like watered-down maple syrup. Another was pungently promising.

He checked it, and took it off the fire before moving into the cover of the woods. Though he was going to play air guitar with his flashy positor, he wasn't going to give the *Ark Imperial* a clear, unobstructed view of the performance.

Under the friendly trees, Djetth unzipped his flight suit all the way and let it drop from his hips. His splayed thighs stopped it from falling around his ankles.

Why do girls go for guitars? Is it the masturbating imagery of long-necked, phallic guitars that turns them on? Why? The body of a guitar is curvy like Marsh's luscious torso. And the hole part of the guitar with the vibrating strings across it . . .

Djetth closed his eyes to imagine Marsh, lying down, spread wide, with a tiny G-string thong pulled tight between her legs.

He imagined strumming on her string for hours. With his fingers. With his tongue. And after a very, very long time, when the thong was wet, and twisted, and chewed to a thread, pushing it aside and sliding past it with his Great Djinn positor.

Fewmet, who said guitars were phallic? Flutes, now . . . flutes were phallic.

He freed his positor, and rested its throbbing underside on the palm of one hand. Already the chromatophores in his bioluminescent tattoo flashed.

Flutes. He closed his eyes. Long, stiff, responsive to

the touch, especially underneath, just below the head. And, of course, flutes got blown. However, for a girl, a flute might not connote a satisfying thickness.

Thickness. He focused on his thickness, and how it had felt to push it into Martia-Djulia the first time, and then again and again, and what she'd felt like inside. Her softness, then her tightness when he was in deep enough to feel the pressure from her glorious corset.

Aaaah, that corset! Her corset was like the proverbial red flag to a bull. The laces . . . How many times had he felt an insane impulse to curve his fingers in the laces at the small of her back and jerk them as tight as they would go?

He wanted to find out what that would do to the feel of her from the inside. One day soon, he would.

He was in no hurry. If he wanted to, he could imagine Marsh in every corset he'd ever seen. Black leather. A dominatrix's corset. A submissive's corset. A corset with holes cut out and her beautiful swollen nipples pushed out where he could get at them, and suck them until she cried out.

A form-fitting, cloth chastity belt, with a hole for her shy little clitoris. She'd look fine in nothing but ribbons, too. He could probably fix her up in a lot of fun outfits, if he cut up her useless dress.

He visualized Martia-Djulia in all her Court formal finery, perfect makeup, and elaborately styled hair as she had appeared on their Mating Day.

Supposing that she hadn't run away in time, he imagined doing her, fully dressed, in front of everyone in all that get up.

How appalled she would have been that day if someone had looked into a crystal ball and told her that within a couple of months she'd be unwashed, barelegged and barefoot on a beach, wearing a man's white T-shirt that went see-through when she got it wet, and that clung every time her nipples got hard.

* * *

Martia-Djulia recognized her recurrent dream. Three gorgeous, mysterious males were misbehaving in her bedroom. She didn't know who any of them were, or why they were all there at the same time.

The tall, dark-haired "forbidden one" shouldn't be there at all. Since he was there, and since it was only a dream, she wanted him to watch her with the others.

One stood out of reach. Commander Jason's long, alien-yellow hair fell over his shoulders and across a face that should be scarred from the bridge of his nose, across one cheek, and down to his jawline.

His head was bent, watching his hands stroke his big, golden phallus. She couldn't tell if he wanted her to see it, or if he was wrestling with himself to hide it from her. Or perhaps he didn't "give a shit" what she thought . . . whatever that meant. How strange that one of Djetth's alienisms had infiltrated her romantic dreams.

His legs were spread aggressively, but she didn't feel threatened. She stared without embarrassment. His muscular chest glistened with a light sheen of perspiration.

She liked the rampant, musky smell of him. This was odd, because, at home, she didn't like sweaty males dripping on her and making a mess in her bed.

Her dreaming gaze drifted to the broad-chested third male, who competed, pose for pose, with the golden barbarian. He was more darkly star-bronzed, or else he stood in shadow. His muscles appeared less powerfully defined because short, dark hair curled on his chest, and ran in a V down his belly, then rioted thickly between his thighs.

His face was perfect, chiseled, with the classic, devastating-god-looks of a Great Djinn. His shadowed face sneered, his teeth were bared. He seemed angry, but she was not afraid of him. She should be. He was sexually on the very edge of his self-control.

Something glittered on his fingers or between his fingers, as he grasped his own massive sex organ. Even in her dreams, she could not see well. She couldn't discern what glittered.

His fierce glare dared her to approach him and take the consequences . . . lying down, between her legs.

Oh, he would satisfy her curiosity, and more. She would regret it for sure. Martia-Djulia imagined herself sprawled on her back. He was above her, his body on top of hers, one muscular arm braced, his splayed hand on the ground and on her loosened hair, pinning her down by the hair. She could feel the heat from his wrist in the curve of her neck.

His right arm was bent between their bellies. His fist was curled around his thick and heavy semen depositor, guiding himself for entry.

Martia-Djulia caught her breath. Though she knew it was a dream, her hips lifted, her stomach tightened, she arched to position herself for the inevitable, deep thrust.

She wanted this. Even if he didn't love her, she wanted this big, marvelous male to nudge her legs apart with his knee, to bring down the weight of his body on hers, and to thrust his big positor deep inside her, and throb and foin until the sun rose in morning glory.

Who was to know? If they docked for the pleasure of it, would they be irrevocably Mated? It would be her word against his.

Was this Djetth? But the god of her dreams had hair!

Martia-Djulia opened her eyes and turned her head. She smelled the fresh, tangy, bitter green smell of her woodsy bed, felt the rough-smooth bark of the boughs beneath her. She realized where her left hand was, and froze.

Oh, these dreams! Whatever would Djetth think . . . ?

As her eyes adjusted in the dark, she tried to focus. With every blink, she saw a little better, and she realized that Djetth wasn't there to embarrass her.

Martia-Djulia raised herself on both elbows and tried to see where Djetth might be.

Time passed and he did not return.

She pulled on the slippers he'd fashioned for her, and went to find out what he was doing.

"Mmmmm, come on, Princess, come and play with my tattoo . . ." Djetth crooned, picturing himself as a rock star.

He had the gear, the spotlight, the moves, and the attitude. Kneeling at his feet, he imagined bobbing heads of countless girls—all with Marsh's willing mouth and Marsh's deep, yielding, delightfully tight cleavage.

In his fantasy, he was singing sexually declarative statements about what he was going to do to her. She was sucking it up. He was enormously aroused for all the woodland world to see.

The way some performers extend an arm, bouncing in time with the beat, and point at happy members of the audience, he swiveled his hips and showed all points of the compass his tremendous pelvic thrusts.

"Picture this sliding into your clam, babe! It could . . . go . . . all . . . the . . . way!"

He could aggressively snarl the sort of sexist, sexually coercive stuff that would never be tolerated in modern Anglo-American society, if not put to music.

Once he got his act together, and glued and strung his guitar, he'd show Marsh a fine time. His tireless fingers would work fast on his instrument—like this—for hours. He'd do that until she was so worked up, she'd want him to put his fingers to work on her. In her.

The night air was cool, he had his boots on. He was in the zone. He was almost—

"Djetth? Djetth, are you there?"

"Al-most . . . you're just in ti—" *Oh, shit*!

"Are you all right? Djetth! What are you doing?"

It was too late. Marsh was right there, right behind him, looking at his bare arse and his straddled stance.

"I'm shaking hands with the unemployed, sweetheart."

He groaned, and turned around so she could see what he was bloody well doing. No way in Carnality was he stopping! He was too close. If he didn't, his balls would ache worse than ever.

"Oh!" she said, blinking rapidly and taking one hasty step back, then staring wide-eyed. She smelled like she was turned on and wet.

He liked her reaction. He bent backwards and performed a really showy air guitar riff.

"I propose to go on . . . pleasing myself. Unless you wanna please me," he said, breathing heavily again. He visualized Marsh falling to her knees, wanting him. "You can . . . watch. You can take over if you want to. Make . . . your . . . mind . . . up. Ahhh!"

He shouted at the sudden surge of pleasure. His climax claimed a tree trunk, a heavily fruited vine of some sort—pity about that—and a slow-moving, unimaginative and presumably deaf creature that had been minding its own business in a clump of grass.

"Too late. You missed your chance."

Recovering quickly, he bent from the waist and pulled up his extra-high-rise trunk briefs. "Now you see it, now you don't! Pretty much."

"What *was* that?" she whispered, putting a shocked hand to her flushed cheek.

"You're not that nearsighted, babe." Grinning, he pretended to misunderstand her.

Marsh curled her expressive upper lip at him, and then her gaze slid back to below his belt line.

"Have you ever seen a finer specimen?" he teased as if she had marveled at the size of his positor, and not the flashing chromatophores in his bioluminescent tattoo. "Did Jason have one like this?"

Am I crazy to ask her to remember what Jason's dork looked like? Do I want to spill the milk? Maybe I do!

It required some mental acrobatics to imagine what view she'd had of his genitals during their hours of intercourse some months ago. He'd been so caught up in the action that he hadn't worried at the time about where his bioluminescent tattoo had been when it lit up like greased lightning.

He hadn't thought about the mirrored ceiling, let alone the possibility that a high-tech surveillance camera might have been behind the mirrors. Could she have seen his unique tattoo, then or later? Could anyone else have seen it?

"I am not going to talk about Jason."

"Why not?" *Carnality, I've got to know. If I upset her now, what does it matter? It's five minutes past a great time to show her I'm the lover of her dreams.* "I want to know what you think he had that I don't have."

"He had hair."

"Hair?" *How could she be so shallow?*

Oh, slack damn it! My bandana's in the shelter. Who stops to put on a hat when sneaking out for a wank?

"What the Carnality has having hair got to do with anything?" he demanded, brazening it out and thanking his lucky stars it was dark, and she was staring as if bedjinned by the faint glow emanating from the bulge in his briefs. He was still turned on.

How much has it grown, anyway?

He passed an experimental open palm over his scalp, and felt three days' worth of hair growth. Since they'd crashed, he'd been too busy to think about how he looked.

Fewmet! Lucky she was near sighted. However, the *Ark Imperial* was not.

If a backward breed like Americans were well on their way to having long-range lenses able to see a basketball from two hundred miles above the Earth, it was a safe bet that the *Ark Imperial* could see faces from however far away they were.

His hair was growing. He should keep his head covered; a piratical headscarf today, sheikh-chic tomorrow, a turban next, and something fashionably creative the day after that.

"Do I have to explain?" Marsh folded her arms under her gorgeous boobs, which drew even more attention than her corset did. Her nipples were hard, judging by the jutting peaks and shadows on the T-shirt.

"Yes, you do!" he muttered.

"True Djinn don't go bald, which means either you have bad hormones, or you are diseased."

"Don't judge a Mate by appearances," Djetth quipped, light-headed with relief that he could solve her problem with him anytime he chose.

"Everyone does," she retorted defensively.

Djetth deliberately eyed her up and down. His insolent scrutiny spoke volumes, or would have if her night vision were up to following his gaze. He knew that Marsh was acutely conscious of her age, her weight, and her wonderfully exuberant figure.

"Do you think my brother would have been so determined to Mate us if there wasn't something wrong with you?" Her spectacular chest rose and fell with emotion. "You're Insufficient Mating Material."

"Insufficient Mating Material?" Djetth repeated.

"I overheard Tarrant-Arragon say it. He uses pompous language to be nasty behind someone's back. I expect it's to do with your being sub-fertile."

She'd misunderstood a conversation about an unwinnable game of chess. Djetth watched the agitated rise and fall of her bosom, and bided his time.

"Don't look so outraged, Djetth. They think I'm sub-fertile, too," she snarled, misreading his expression. "Tarrant-Arragon must think it's a wickedly cunning strategy to match us up. Unless one or the other of us dies young and the other Mates again, neither of us will ever produce a serious rival for his heirs."

"Is that what you think?" Djetth said gently. He heard the hurt in her voice, saw it in the tremble of her lower lip. She might have let slip hints in the past, but the penny hadn't dropped until now.

We both thought Tarrant-Arragon was trying to con us into Mating with a sexual slow poke. One day, we'll laugh about this.

"Well, of course, Djetth. Only, I wouldn't go along with the scheme, so he decided to kill us both."

"Marsh, sweetheart, you're wrong about what Tarrant-Arragon's intentions were the other day. I'm pretty sure that he wants the two of us to make babies and scandals. He should be careful what he wishes for." Djetth zipped his flight suit up to his midriff.

He was feeling mellow enough to touch lightly on his own heartbreak and resentment at the way things were.

"We Great Djinn have a time-honored tradition of cousins, half-brothers, and brothers running off with each others' Mates and trying to kill each other. You shouldn't take it personally. It's what we alpha males do."

"You can't. . . ." Marsh gasped a protest.

"I said we do it, I didn't say I like it, especially when it's done to me. When a Prince gets rut-raged, good intentions, dignity, and decency take a back seat."

Djetth checked out her breathing and the throbbing pulse in her neck, and decided she'd calmed down enough to be told what Insufficient Mating Material really meant.

"In war, or sex, or chess, it doesn't have to be win or lose, dominate or submit, fuck or be fucked. There's also the honorable draw, which sometimes results from having 'Insuffient Mating Material.' "

"*Having* Insufficient Mating Material?" she questioned.

"It's a chess reference. When a checkmate cannot occur by any possible series of legal moves, even with the most unskilled play, the game is declared a draw."

"It's a *chess* term?" Marsh sounded incredulous.

"A chess term," he agreed. "Tarrant-Arragon can't checkmate me. I can't checkmate him, no matter how many bad moves one or the other of us makes. It's nothing to do with your fertility or mine. Now we've got that out of the way, let's have a midnight feast."

"What will we eat?" Her voice bristled with suspicion.

"You're not afraid that I'll slip you some aphrodisiacal genitalia in the dark, are you?" He chuckled at how well she knew him. He did have something of the sort in mind. "Have you ever tried whitebait? It's tiny fish, fried. Let's grab a few yards of your old petticoats, a couple of flaming brands from the fire, and go fishing."

"In the dark?"

"Best time," he replied, taking her hand and swinging it lightly. "The fish will be attracted to the light, and we'll net them."

He might net her, tumble her in the waves, and reenact a notorious surf-and-sex scene from an old movie. He'd always wanted to thrust into a wet and shivering girl in time with the foaming surf as it pounded his backside. Marsh would be cold on the outside, warm inside. The contrast would be explosive.

"I'm afraid of water," she confided.

Scratch sex, then, he thought. *Doing it in the sea is probably overrated, anyhow.*

"You could manage to wade shin-deep, couldn't you?"

He assumed that she'd go along with him, since she continued to walk hand in hand with him, unfazed by what the hand now holding hers had been doing most recently.

"All you have to do is hold one end of our net in the shallow water. I'll do the rest. If we want lots of little fish quickly, the fastest way is for us to trawl."

Daringly he raised the back of her hand to his lips. As he expected, she smelled of his sex. He liked his smell on her.

In fact, he was beginning to lose count of all the things he liked about Marsh.

Freighter Island, reef end

It had rained twice, before and after the laughter.

The laughter changed everything. It was the good-natured laughter of a male in his deep-voiced prime, and the triumphant whoops of a happily surprised female.

Feya had no way to collect water, and nothing to eat except sand-hoppers and whatever coarse dune grasses she could reach. Last night, the aroma of fried fish had wafted up the coast.

Feya decided it was worth risking her life to eat again.

Freighter Island
The morning after

Djetth sniffed the ambient air. Some unknown and as yet undiscovered plant on the island must have blossomed. Its fragrance was pleasant and mildly intoxicating, like dogwood. He felt like a god. He was confident, talented, and damned fine-looking. He could do anything.

If only Marsh felt the same way.

He'd pretended to oversleep, to see what would happen if Marsh thought she had the beach to herself.

He visualized Marsh laughing in the dark the night before, fishing, and getting her legs tangled up in the net. He imagined the possibilities of the long, narrow strip of petticoat fabric that they'd used as a trawl net, and that was now looped over the log pile to dry.

If only he'd put it into her head to start something.

He looked down the beach. Marsh was squatting in the calm, outgoing sea with her T-shirt and drawers off, washing her clam. Djetth put extra water on to boil, and looked forward to imminent salty delights.

Chapter Twenty

Freighter Island

This was her idea.

Turning the tables on Djetth was going to be sweet revenge for the berries, and maybe for a few other indignities, too.

Trying not to giggle, Martia-Djulia crept up behind Djetth with the long petticoat-net looped low between her hands and trailing like the long sleeves of a ceremonial robe on either side of her.

Djetth had no idea. Oblivious to her naughty plans for him, he knelt by the fire. He'd surrounded himself with heaps of berries, bits of wood, charcoal, ash, different types of warm sap, and boiled-down fish-bone stock.

He was forever experimenting with something. Today he was engrossed in sticking-together experiments. He'd knotted strips of fabric to his wrists, so they'd be handy if he needed to wipe stinky, sticky stuff off his hands.

He called them his "quarterback towels." They made her think of tying him down, spread-eagled.

Perhaps she'd lash him to the fire reflector, sit astride his thighs, and shave him by force. Not that she minded his beard now that the growth along his jaw and cheeks had filled in, softening the hard, sinister lines. He simply looked slightly dirty and dangerously sexy.

Or she'd tie his wrists behind his back, and feed him the live grubs he'd wanted her to eat. She might even lick his flat, male nipples the way he'd kissed hers.

If he was docile, she'd blindfold him, pull off his underwear, and thoroughly satisfy her curiosity about his extraordinary-looking positor.

She could do some experiments of her own, and find out what made it flash, and if it flashed in different ways depending on how she stimulated it.

Closer. Closer. With a sudden squeal of laughter, she hurled the center of the net over his head and shoulders, and jumped on his broad, bare back.

In a flurry of hard-bodied action, he dropped his head, rolled beneath her, and the next moment, she found herself flat on her back, pinned down by the weight of his upper body across hers. Her own net was twisted and crossed around her, and between her breasts.

"Easy as roping a calf, my dear," he chuckled.

Martia-Djulia smiled inwardly. He'd left one of her hands free. The other was bent above her head and secured in such a way that if she moved it, she tightened a loop of the net around her bosom.

For the fun of it, she arched her back to see if she could dislodge Djetth, and quick as a snake, he passed the net under her and between her legs.

Masterfully disregarding her struggles, he set about tying knots, pulling the net tighter here, setting up a sinful friction there.

She felt warmth seeping through her hair. Their romp had spilled something. She hoped it wasn't the fishy gunk, but at the moment, she was having too much fun to complain.

Smiling arrogantly, Djetth reached across her body and stroked her in the exposed armpit, of all places.

"These perspiration stains are quite attractive, if you like white on white." With his thumb and forefinger, he tugged at the fabric in question. Cloth slid over the tip of her right nipple.

"You bastard!" She strained to put her arm down so he couldn't take further liberties with her armpit. Her bonds tightened, her right breast came under pressure, and she felt her nipple press against the white fabric of her T-shirt.

"That's interesting," he murmured, noticing. "Now your gorgeous nipples don't match. With your permission, Ma'am, I may have to do something about that. As I was saying before your nipple alignment distracted me, if you like wearing white, and if you focus on the double white border where the salt has dried—"

"I do not like white," she gritted. "I am sick of it!"

"Then I know just what to do. Have you ever heard of tie-dying?" He was using the deep, sexy voice he put on when he was aroused.

"What is tie-dying?" she asked. Her voice quivered with excitement. Her other nipple visibly peaked.

"I tie you up and stain you all over, Ma'am . . . as a fashion makeover."

An inexplicable thrill shuddered through her. She felt curiosity, mixed with something she couldn't define. He was saying all the right things. She wasn't afraid.

"What shall we stain me with?" she asked shakily.

"Whatever you like, darling. Berry juice, charcoal, tree sap." He licked his lips. "Anything else that comes to hand and seems a good idea at the time. Do you want to do it?"

Her mouth was too dry to answer. She was breathing hard; her chest rose and fell. She nodded.

"Where would you like me to start, Ma'am?" he asked, kneeling astride her, and staring at one of her taut nipples. "There?" He touched it lightly. "Would you like blue, or red?"

"Purple," she said, naming a third color at random to find out who was in charge.

"Yes, Ma'am," He dabbled his fingers at his side, and then put his forefinger back on her bound breast. "An excellent choice. I don't have a good purple made up. That means I'll have to make the color up at the site, once with the red berry juice, and once with the blue."

Martia-Djulia's insides leapt at the thought. She'd chosen purple without considering that a good purple would mean that he'd have to rub her breasts twice as much. More if the purple didn't turn out right. It wouldn't.

He traced a circle with a crushed red berry; the pressure of his touch wrinkled the material and his circle was imperfect.

"That won't do." He sat back and stared critically at her breasts. "I'm going to have to do a touch-up." He circled again, and nodded approvingly. "I like this," he said, taking a blue on two fingers, and circling her roughly and then lightly. "Almost a rainbow effect!"

"It should match." Martia-Djulia moaned, it felt so good. "You'll have to remove the wrong color."

"May I suck it off? That would be best." He dipped his head and his hot mouth suckled her through the T-shirt.

"We should converse," Martia-Djulia said. "We don't want to get confused about what we are doing. Oh, yes!"

"Mmmm," he mumbled with his mouth full, as he made the colors run and mingle. His other hand stroked up and down over her other breast.

"Who . . . are you?" Martia-Djulia gasped at how well he was doing . . . what he was doing. "Are you really a Prince?"

She could feel a pulse in her belly, but was not sure if the throbbing came from her, or from the male crotch resting firmly astride her.

"Absolutely, I am. What a time to ask!" He reared up to study the decorative effect he'd achieved so far. "What would you like between your breasts, Ma'am?" he asked.

"Russet. Try that reddish wood," she ordered. "Do you have an alpha name?"

"Like this?" Deftly he loosened a knot and moved netting aside, before he rubbed a thick, crumbly chunk of wood slowly up her belly and between her breasts. "I do, Ma'am. My Djinn-name you know. I have an alpha name, also a warrior, a god, and an Imperial name. I have an embarrassment of names. The usual. I don't care for most of them, and I don't tell them to anyone."

"Tell me," she urged.

"One day. Not right now."

He put a berry in his mouth, then shifted his weight, brought his mouth down, and licked the fabric over her navel, leaving a purplish swirl that was darkest at its center, where he thrust the tip of his tongue into her belly button.

As he decorated her with his mouth, his hands rubbed charcoal in the tight places that he got to by reaching under the net. She was getting well and truly streaked and she loved it. Martia-Djulia moved her head restlessly, and her legs fell open. She shifted her hips so that the net rubbed down there. It wasn't enough. She wanted more.

"What else can you use? We need moisture," she hinted. "The colors are too dry."

He turned his artistic attention to her most private area. He touched her, and she felt she'd explode.

"Oh, yes," she whispered. "Try there."

He caught her just below the knee, and pressed her bent leg to the ground, spreading her wide. She felt pressure, then release as he moved the net out of his way. He angled himself so one hand held her legs apart and one leg down, while his body pinned the other leg.

He slowly, sensually sucked three of his fingers while

she watched, fascinated. Her mouth went dry. What would he do? He held his fingers low and curved. She watched, shaking, as he brought them slowly to her.

"This is insane," she whispered. "It's broad daylight."

"We're only dying your T-shirt, sweetheart."

"Do you think there's something in the water?"

"Mmmm. It's occurred to me. I'm hornier after it rains. I think I have to have one more go at the purple, darling."

His open mouth came down on her erect, aching nipple, and he sucked hard. As she melted into the dazzling sensations, she felt his hand at the top of her drawers. She drew in her breath, and lifted her hips for him.

"Put your fingers inside me. I want you to swirl them around." She felt him nudge inside, dive inside her drawers, and explore her flesh.

She was embarrassed, nervous and excited. She swallowed hard. "Djetth? Who was your father?"

"Prince Djason-Merkur." He moved his fingers lightly between her legs; his tongue swirled heavily on her breast.

"I've never . . . heard . . . of a Djason-Merkur."

"*His* father—my grandfather"—Djetth gently used his teeth to tug—"didn't know he'd got my grandmother pregnant." His coarse beard scraped her through the dampened fabric. At the same time, she felt him pull her drawers down from where they were caught up over her hips.

"My father's father was . . . Djohn-Kronos." His fingers thrust deeply into her. "What do you think of that?"

Suddenly she was breathless; it felt as if he'd begun to slowly beckon deep inside her, and she couldn't think of anything but his fingers inside her. He'd impaled her so deeply and so hard that it seemed she could do nothing but flutter against him.

"How . . . oh my Stars, Djetth . . . how . . . can . . . that be?" She struggled to converse normally.

Djetth smiled. He pressed his free hand down on her belly, and looked down, watching his fingers slide in and out of her. The sensation blew her mind. She clamped around his fingers. Every time she felt his fingers pull out, she tried to tighten around them and make them stay.

"Didn't Helispeta run off . . . oh . . . with the Emperor's . . . twin brother?"

Breathing heavily, his fingers stilled in her, and he frowned. "You want to do this, don't you?" he rasped.

Martia-Djulia nodded.

"You're sure? Because talking about my grandparents does not turn me on. Let's try this." Leaving his invading hand where it was, he reached over to the side. His movement stretched her, and she gasped.

"How did you get that?"

His gaze flickered to the little scar on her mound.

"I don't remember."

From a pink-lipped shell, he trickled something sweet-smelling and dark brown onto her crotch and into the hand that was half inside her.

"I'm going to like this," he breathed. "Sap and you."

Before she realized what he meant to do, he thrust his face down between her legs, lapping at the sweet-smelling, sticky sap, probing and sucking her along with it.

She hadn't expected this and tried to protest, but her wriggles seemed to incite him to greater excesses. She felt a great, sparkling wave rising in her head. Her whole body strained.

"If . . . Helispeta had sex . . . with twin brothers . . . how . . . could . . . anyone possibly—oh yes— . . . know which brother was . . . the . . . father?"

Djetth stopped eating her, and rested his flushed face on her hip bone. He was breathing hard.

"You're kidding?" His eyes narrowed. "You're not?" He sighed. "Helispeta gave Great Djinn males the rut-rage when she ovulated. Therefore, when three or four months passed and Devoron-Vitan had not had the rut-rage, it was obvious that she must have been pregnant when she left Djohn-Kronos."

"But, all the same . . ." she interupted, then stopped. "So Helispeta gave birth to Djohn-Kronos's third son, and he was legitimate."

Djetth smiled lazily into her eyes. Watching her, he kissed the tiny scar on her mound. Without speaking, he seemed to say that he'd wait until she'd finished fretting over history. Then, he'd finish what he'd started.

"That means you are second in line to the throne after my brother. He knows, I suppose?"

"I rather think he does," Djetth agreed urbanely. "And now, Ma'am. . . ." He lifted with the fingers inside her, and her hips came up. He put his mouth on her.

"I wonder why he doesn't kill you."

Because I'm Mating with you, sweetheart.

The obvious answer wasn't tactful. If he pointed out that they were about to Mate, she might call a halt. They were well beyond the flimsy pretext of dying her T-shirt.

If he could remember the words of the Mating Vows, he'd grunt them over her, one solemn, irrevocable word for each deep, slow, claiming thrust of his positor.

He'd get to that very soon.

"I want a taste," Marsh whispered.

"Yes, Ma'am!" At once, he slipped his fingers out of her, moved up her body and kissed her, letting her taste herself and the sweet, warm sap from his lips.

He opened his mouth and she sucked his sticky lower lip. She became more adventurous. While her tentative tongue explored his, he took the opportunity to unobtrusively work his briefs down, freeing his positor.

"More," she ordered.

He went down to work her up for more.

"Djetth!" she wailed. "Give it to me!"

He gave her his open mouth again and this time she

drew his tongue into her mouth and sucked. It was all the permission he felt he needed. His heavy positor swung close to her warm, wet clam. He could feel her heat.

He could feel the flashing, jagged brilliance on the underside of his positor. His lightning was ready to strike.

"Let's do it," he murmured against her lips.

"Ohhhh, let's," she sobbed back.

"Jason? Is it really you?"

Time froze. For an instant, he couldn't think or move.

This could not be happening! Djetth turned his head. Fingers of dread squeezed his nuts and his throat. Beneath him, Marsh gasped in shock. Her legs snapped shut. Her hips slammed to the ground.

Lying behind him, on the beach, staring directly at the tattoo on the underside of his penis, was an old friend. She was gaunt, covered in sand, hollow-eyed, obviously in pain.

"Feya!"

Djetth leapt to his feet. A moment later he realized that Prince Djetthro-Jason should never have known Feya. It was too late. The words were out. Both Feya and Marsh had heard him.

"Jason?" Feya said again, sounding less sure.

Carnality! In all the galaxies, three females had been in a position to see his tattoo's fully aroused magnificence, and he was trapped on an island with two of them.

CHAPTER TWENTY-ONE

Freighter Island

"Feya, I'm going to have to put you in the sea."

How could he? Martia-Djulia's first instincts clashed. *He's going to drown her in the sea? That's so wrong! Yet, what a nasty, callous, brilliantly convenient idea.*

Her gaze flickered from Djetth to the stranger over whom he was squatting, still gloriously naked.

One's emotions were uncomfortable and unworthy. Martia-Djulia admitted to jealousy; frustration; suspicion; a desire to drive the trespasser back wherever she came from; a wish that One could turn back time, and take one of the many chances One had had to Mate with Djetth before a rival appeared on the scene.

Martia-Djulia sighed from the heart. Now that One had examined One's bad feelings, One rejected them . . . One supposed. She took stock. It was a little ridiculous to default to the Royal Pronoun and Court-formal language. There was dried fish glue in her hair. No doubt, twigs and leaves were permanently stuck to her head.

She had Djetth's tongue prints on her stomach and smeared rings around her nipples.

Her crotch was sticky. Syrupy sap was running down the insides of her thighs. All things considered, there was no point in getting sap in her drawers. Perhaps she wouldn't wear knickers ever again . . . just to keep Djetth interested.

She picked up Djetth's trunk briefs by the elastic, and sauntered over to the intruder.

"Damaged leg, may be dislocated; insect bites, stings—" Djetth was taking inventory of what was wrong. "Scrapes, cuts and abrasions. Some infected. Dehydration. Malnutrition. Is there anything else?"

"I don't think so," the stranger replied through cracked, swollen lips. "You're not Tarrant-Arragon, are you?"

"Whatever gave you that idea?" Djetth replied, with an edge to his voice that Martia-Djulia found puzzling.

"You look like him."

It was high time to establish who was whose.

"This is The Prince Djetthro-Jason. I am The Princess Martia-Djulia. We have been marooned here as a punishment for failing to Mate in public."

"Oh, Stars!" the newcomer whispered. "I am sorry to intrude, Your Imperial Highnesses." Feya's appropriate response turned the tide of Martia-Djulia's resentment.

"You may call me Martia-Djulia," she said, somewhere between kindness and condescension.

"Right, now we're all properly introduced, let's get on with it. I'm going to need a knife."

"Djetth, you can't!" Martia-Djulia said, grabbing his forearm. She meant it.

Djetth threw her an inscrutable look.

"I'd better cut off her clothes. Feya, it's up to you whether we take your catsuit off before we wash you in the sea, or afterwards. It's filthy, and we may not be able to save it, anyway. Seawater fights infection. It'll get you reasonably clean. We'll dab boiled water onto the areas that need to be scrupulously clean. Ready?"

"This is going to hurt, isn't it?" Feya hissed.

"Yes," Djetth told her.

"Wait!" Martia-Djulia held out Djetth's underwear. "Put your clothes on, Djetth. You are frightening us. And, if you're not frightened, Feya, I do not wish to know it. I will fetch a knife and some painkiller from the medical kit."

"Thank you." Feya's whisper followed her.

As Martia-Djulia poured a small amount of painkiller into a scalloped half shell, she was tempted to give Feya too much and put her out of her obvious misery, but, of course, she did not.

Pleasure Palace, The Pleasure Moon of Eurydyce

"Take Django-Ra . . ." Helispeta mused, sounding like a pleasantly mellow old lady who has enjoyed a little too much sloe gin. Of course, she was no such thing. Helispeta knew exactly what she was saying, and why.

"I would rather not, Aunt Hell," Tarra replied sharply.

Helispeta had waited for Tarra to shuffle her Tarot cards before beginning an oblique interrogation. It would be hard, even for Tarra, to hide trembling hands while mixing seventy-eight oversized cards.

"A little of Django-Ra goes a long way, doesn't it, dear?" Helispeta had no idea how intimately Tarra might have once known Django-Ra, but if she hinted that she knew everything, people tended to tell her a lot of things that she did not, in fact, know.

Tarra paled. Seven bright cards skittered to the floor. Apparently, Tarra had once known Django-Ra too well.

Empathy had never been Helispeta's long suit, but she knew when to back off. She poured herself some more liqueur, set the decanter close to Tarra, casually picked up the fallen cards without comment, and left it up to Tarra whether or not her glass needed refreshing.

"I am not proud to call Django-Ra my brother-in-law. Even 'half-brother-in-law' is too close for comfort." She spoke as if revealing something about herself, rather than probing into Tarra's past.

"All Djerrold Ramses's sons had cruel smiles that could twist a girl's insides, and strange, pale eyes which I always found hypnotic; even, I might say, sexually overpowering."

Although Tarra looked it, she was not old enough to know that Djohn-Kronos's and Devoron-Vitan's eyes were more often dark with passion. Not light at all. The lie was justified. Helispeta shook her head, as if at a regrettable memory, but she noticed Tarra's reaction to the mention of pale, hypnotic eyes. *Djinncraft!* Just as she suspected.

"Djerrold-Vulcan has pale eyes, too."

"So he does." Helispeta waved off Tarra's attempt to change the topic. "Looking back, I am quite sure that my Imperial Mates' generation did not scruple to use Djinncraft to get a girl where they wanted her. They were the Type."

"Do you mean Types as in Wands, Swords, Pentacles or Cups?" It was telling—and sad—the way Tarra grasped at Types as a diversion, and tried to demystify Types by sorting them according to the four suits of the Tarot's Minor Arcana.

Helispeta smiled.

"My secret policemen friends would refer to Typing as Profiling. On Earth, I play poker and bridge with some peculiar people. As a rule, if a new player reminds One of a known cheat, it is highly likely that this new player will turn out also to be a cheat."

Cheating at cards was not an alarming topic. Tarra's color returned. She relaxed too quickly.

Helispeta circled back. "There are Types who will always be a menace to females. Django-Ra is the worst of that Type. He believes he was born to the gods' Right to do wrong."

Tarra pressed one hand to her throat.

"Django-Ra is the Type to be very dangerous if he thinks he can get away with it. It would be helpful to our inquiries if we knew why he might have a deadly interest in Martia-Djulia."

"He is her father," Tarra said in a strangled voice. "Only Tarrant-Arragon, I—and now you—know it."

"What a pity!" Helispeta sighed.

Freighter Island
That night

Damn Feya! How am I supposed to explore my feelings for Marsh with Feya here?

Djetth threw a spear into the sea. He needed time to acknowledge his rage and frustration.

What timing! What bloody awful timing!

He'd made the connection that Marsh was responsible for the mildly intoxicating dogwood fragrance he'd picked up, and for his exuberant performance in broad daylight, which had been interrupted. It wasn't the "right" scent, but it would do. He could live with that level of excitement.

Damn and blast it, just as I was licking Marsh into fine shape, Feya turns up.

Doing Feya isn't an option. If I did, it would be because she's here and I'm horny, not because I have romantic feelings about Feya.

With her injury, she isn't up for it. Anyway, I've got no currency to pay her. It would be inhumane and immoral to make her ply her trade in exchange for food, drink, and all the extra work her arrival has heaped on my shoulders.

If I were to have a professional relationship with

Feya, Marsh would know about it. Her feelings would be hurt beyond belief. To think that I once seriously considered taking a small harem! What a nightmare.

Djetth hurled rocks and stones into the sea, and thought about all the things he could, and shouldn't, do.

Just when life was getting interesting, he had to dig deeper for more water, set more efficient fish traps, cobble together something for Feya to wear, and—since Feya would have to have the hammock—sacrifice his nocturnal privacy and pull the second foil sheet out of the shelter's roof.

Now that he'd had a taste of the rut-rage, twice, he could agree with those who said rut-rage was a fatal flaw. Here he was, saying and thinking all sorts of things he didn't mean, trying to work through what was going on.

Pleasure Palace, The Pleasure Moon of Eurydyce

In the brothel's entryway,'Rhett stopped to listen.

"Hell! Why did you say it's 'a pity' Django-Ra raped me?"

That's Tarrant-Arragon's mother's voice.

Instead of announcing his arrival at once, as he should have,'Rhett waited to hear more.

". . . deeply shocking . . . I spoke thoughtlessly, dear. . . ."

'Rhett wondered if Tarra was talking to herself. The second voice was almost identical, clearly that of a graduate of the exclusive Island School for Djinn Princesses, where Imperial elocution was instilled. In all the Empire and beyond, only four females spoke with such distinctive formality. And one—Grandmama—was on Earth.

". . . Out of disappointment I spoke thoughtlessly, dear. I said it was 'a pity' because I had quite decided that Django-Ra was my prime suspect."

This is *Grandmama's voice! What's she doing here?*

"Why does raping me clear Django-Ra of suspicion?"

"Anyone at home?" 'Rhett called, and shouldered through the magnetized, beaded hangings.

"The House is closed for business!" Tarra's voice quavered. "Oh, it's you, Djarrhett!"

"Hello, Aunt Tarra! Grandmama! By All the Stars, I'm glad to see you here," 'Rhett croaked, cheerfully advancing on the lumpy and overstuffed green chair in which Helispeta was ensconced. "I need to ask an indelicate question."

Helispeta arched an eyebrow at her diplomatic grandson, possibly not appreciating his tact in ignoring Tarra, who was as white as winter.

"So lovely to see you, too, Djarrhett. I am well, thank you. I trust you are in good health? And your father? Is Ala'Aster-Djalet sending you out to survey old ladies on indelicate matters these days?"

'Rhett laughed, and swept her an elaborate bow worthy of a Cavalier hero on the cover of one of the historical romances Grandmama Helispeta loved so much.

His white Saurian ambassadorial uniform with skin-tight pants, heraldic motif tabard, caped-and-hooded cloak, and rune-inscribed Saurian sword helped the effect.

White reflections swirled across the shiny surfaces of fish-eye surveillance mirrors and crystal balls with video monitors. Tarra's fortune-telling parlor was a scented, candlelit, deceptively low-tech-looking interrogation room within a room.

Visitors didn't know that the viewing gallery was there, because stepped-out and setback panels and layered, deep-folded curtains threw off a visitor's depth perception and gave a false impression of an intimacy that he did not, in fact, enjoy.

'Rhett answered Grandmama's questions in turn.

"I haven't seen my father recently. I didn't come from

the *Asgaard*. I've come straight from the *Ark Imperial*, a nonstop, hair-raising flight in one of Tarrant-Arragon's own Thorcraft, would you believe?

"I'm inquiring into my respected forefathers' sex lives for reasons of my own. I am sure Tarrant-Arragon would like to know what I find out, but I've no plans to tell him. I prefer to stay a step or two ahead of Tarrant-Arragon."

"A good rationale," Grandmama approved. "What do you wish to know?"

"Is it possible for a Great Djinn to have the rut-rage over more than one female?"

"Why do you ask, Djarrhett?" Grandmama Helispeta rubbed the one age spot on her hand, and glanced at Tarra.

"You heard that Djetthro-Jason's Mating with Martia-Djulia didn't go off as planned, I suppose? Not many people know this, but Djetth had the rut-rage over my sister's scent, which was accidentally planted on Martia-Djulia."

"How could this happen?"

"It's a long story. Unhappily, everyone who matters got the wrong idea about Djetth and Martia-Djulia. They were filmed *in flagrante delicto*, you see. When months passed and the expected romance didn't reignite, they were isolated on an island. Is it going to be possible for Djetth to have a secondary rut-rage—with Martia-Djulia—when whatever birth control she's using wears off?"

"Tradition has it that this is not the case. Great Djinn can enjoy having sexual relations with persons other than their first scent-love, but they only have the rut-rage with that one scent-love."

"Tradition* can't always be right, Grandmama. Otherwise, why was Djohn-Kronos able to have the rut-rage over you when you were not his first Mate?"

Grandmama stared. 'Rhett couldn't remember when he'd ever seen her lost for words.

"That," she said eventually, "is a good question. Hmmm. Tarra, did We consider the rut-rage as a motive?"

"A motive?" 'Rhett asked innocently.

Tarra had fumbled her pack of Tarot cards, and was staring as if she'd seen a very unlucky card. "Aunt Hell, if we are looking at the rut-rage and at males who do not behave traditionally, we ought also to consider 'a cover-up' as another potential motive."

"Motive for what, Grandmama?"

"For murder," she told him crisply. "Someone has offered to pay an immense sum to have Martia-Djulia murdered. That grin, Djarrhett, is hardly appropriate."

"You'd smile, if you knew where Martia-Djulia is."

"Do you know where she is?" Grandmama demanded.

"I do. Martia-Djulia and Djetth are on Freighter Island and guarded by the *Ark Imperial.*"

'Rhett's smile faded when he noticed Grandmama and Tarra exchange significant glances. "What is it?"

"Perhaps you have not heard this, Djarrhett. Petri-Shah was murdered recently. The last place she went was Freighter Island. We were unable to imagine any link between Petri-Shah and Martia-Djulia. It now seems that they have Freighter Island in common."

"And Djetth," 'Rhett murmured.

Freighter Island
Midnight

"We had a narrow escape!" Martia-Djulia felt awkward about commenting on the day's embarrassment; however, it was dark, and even if Feya were awake, she couldn't hear what was said at the dark water's edge.

There was so much she wanted to ask Djetth: *Who is Feya? How do you know her? Why did she call you Jason?*

For the first time, she felt that she had everything to

lose if she voiced the "wrong" question. The rut-rage seemed the safest thing to talk about.

"What got into us Djetth?" She slipped her hand into his.

"The rut-rage, I think."

Djetth leaned closer. She heard him sniff what was left of her glue-ruined hair. His hand swung hers. "It's a good thing you're not firing on all cylinders. If we had to devote a week to nonstop, round-the-clock lovemaking, we'd soon run out of water, food, firewood. . . ."

He called it "lovemaking"! Martia-Djulia pressed her free hand to her bosom, and felt her heart dance.

"And bedding!" she added shyly. "Our bed's not as comfortable as it was."

"Foliage withers."

"Of course it does. I can help with that. And I've been thinking, Djetth. Now we've got Feya to feed, I should stop being so pretentious about what I eat. From now on, I'll eat meat again."

She stood firm when the waves rushed over her toes and swirled around her ankles, and thought wistfully about making babies and scandals with Djetth.

"If the *Ark Imperial* is up there, watching us," she said, when Djetth showed no sign of suggesting they go back to bed, "Tarrant-Arragon must have seen Feya. Why hasn't he sent help?"

Djetth's hand tightened around hers.

"I imagine the cold-blooded bastard weighed up the pros and cons, and ruthlessly decided not to remove her. It's the sort of thing he'd do. Tarrant-Arragon is a lot better at dirty politics than I'd ever want to be."

"But, why? She's hurt," Martia-Djulia protested.

"I expect he wants to drive me crazy. Or, more likely, he thought her presence would drive you crazy, sweetheart." Djetth laughed harshly.

"Me, Djetth?"

"Tarrant-Arragon may think you're the type of girl

who only realizes she's interested in the good guy when there's a rival on the scene."

"Oh!" Martia-Djulia saw her opportunity, and took it. "He'd be right," she admitted.

Djetth kissed the back of her hand. "What are we going to do about it?"

Marsh flashed him an amazing smile.

"I don't know. It seems to me, there's nothing wicked or defiant or deliciously bad about having sex in front of an injured person. It would just be . . . rude."

Djetth laughed. He was tempted to tell Marsh that Feya was used to that sort of rudeness. One day, he'd have to find a way to tell Marsh who Feya worked for.

Tonight, he was more interested in skinny-dipping, if he could talk Marsh into the sea.

"There's a saying that it's better to be dirty than dead. Of course, the saying isn't about politics, or sex."

It was a feeble segue, but he didn't mind if they talked about body odors and what to do about them, or overthrowing tyrants, or whether or not they could find their place in a world dominated by Tarrant-Arragon.

"I ought to be grateful to be alive, and here I am, wondering how to smell like a king. A clean, fragrant king. Not a dead king."

"Why stop at a king? Why not wish to smell like an Emperor?" Marsh teased.

"Why not wish to *be* an Emperor?" Djetth retorted.

"Did you ever?" she asked.

"Ahhh." He exhaled through flared nostrils. "Did I wish to be an Emperor? The truth is, not really. However, I believed that I *ought* to want to. A lot of people thought—or seemed to think—I ought to be."

She nodded understandingly, but didn't interrupt.

"If one is not born in the right place and time, and one usurps the Throne—even with the best of intentions and to generally popular acclaim—there is a cost."

He smiled down at her. The more he got to know Marsh, the less good reason he saw to distrust her. The kicker was, although he reckoned it'd be safe to tell her that he'd been Jason, he didn't want to do it. "What about you?"

"Oh, I was doomed from the moment of my conception. What's the point in being a good person if one is Royal? The fate of a sister—or younger brother—is to sink lower and lower in rank and precedence as one's elder brother brings home a young Mate, and has children."

Her defiant expression told him, *So there!*

"You must resent Djinni-vera," he said neutrally. With hindsight, his old dream of having both Princesses was so bad it was laughable.

"Do *you* resent Tarrant-Arragon?" she fired back. "What if he and Djinni-vera had daughters? What would you do?"

"We'd have to have at least one son, or there'd be no point in doing anything." He kissed her fingers one after the other. "But I've got my heart set on having daughters."

"I've never had a daughter," Marsh breathed, sounding as if she'd always yearned for a daughter, but had never recognized her yearning for what it was.

"That," Djetth said, "is something to think about. Would you like to try for one?"

Chapter Twenty-two

ARK IMPERIAL, Imperial Suite
A half-cycle later

"My father's in danger!"

Djinni sat up in the murk bath. Her dream had been so vivid that for a vital moment between sleep and waking, she didn't know where she was or who was with her.

Tarrant-Arragon stirred, his arms still around her.

"Have you had one of your dreams, my love?" he asked, surging to full consciousness.

"I think I had three dreams. They were similar, and a bit confusing. I'd paint them—"

"That's hard to do in a bath. Just tell me," he said.

"This may sound mysterious," Djinni prevaricated.

"I'm used to it. My mother is a fortune-teller, remember. Fortune-tellers never reveal everything they see. If they were too accurate, they'd be found to be a menace to civilization."

Djinni smiled gratefully, and closed her eyes.

"I saw two distress calls, also an invitation. One was real. One was a decoy. Both involved a lie. One was from an enemy who said he did not want help, but needed it. The other was from a seeming friend."

She had sensed that Djetth was in danger as well, but withheld her impression. Tarrant-Arragon might react jealously if he thought she had a psychic connection with Djetth. Djetth had to be on his own.

"And the invitation . . . ?" Tarrant-Arragon prompted.

"That's a trap, too."

Freighter Island

"She's a brothel owner in a wheelchair? What else? Does she 'work'?" Marsh was questioning Feya about her employer.

Djetth was heartily glad that he was yards away, waist-deep in the sea, constructing a static trap out of sharpened stakes to catch shoal fish at high tide.

At some point, Marsh would begin to suspect that the psychic Madam Tarra was an alias for Tarragonia-Marietta, the mother Marsh had been told was dead.

A nice, broad streamer of green sea-sash floated by. Djetth snagged it, and wrapped it loosely around his neck to dry. They needed more toilet paper.

He didn't pay much attention as Feya explained how Madam Tarra's girls watched—through one-way mirrors or transparent eyes of portraits on false panels—while Madam Tarra "read" a would-be client's palm or Tarot.

Ostensibly the fortune-telling was to decide whether he was "safe" to be entertained by "her girls." In fact, while the psychic evaluation was going on, the girls would decide which—if any of them—was willing to entertain the paying guest.

"Feya, if you go out to a war-star for a date, and you don't want to go through with . . . whatever is expected, can you leave?"

"Of course!" Feya said.

"I wanted the same power," Marsh said.

Djetth wondered if this was the real reason, or the revisionist reason, why The Princess Martia-Djulia had run from the throne room on their Mating day.

Feya squealed, presumably with incredulity and delight to think that in one way a courtesan was better off than a Princess, and Djetth lost interest.

"Commander Jason had one, too!" When Feya giggled like that, she'd been set off by either condoms or what went into condoms.

Oh, shit! A cold chill ran down Djetth's spine. He'd had no idea that females compared notes. Things got tricky in a hurry, when your past ran into your future!

"You slept with him?"

Carnality! How could he have anticipated that Princess Marsh would be in a position to discuss his uniquely tattoed penis with one of the only two prostitutes he'd ever favored?

It was a disaster. Feya mustn't know that Jason was still around.

Brazen it out, Djetth told himself. *How?* He racked his brain for some plausible way to introduce his penis tattoo into polite conversation.

He might try coming right out and asking, "Ladies, I'm sure you must be curious . . . ?"

Fewmet!

An injury! For some mysterious reason, females seemed to find male injuries funny.

Was it absolutely necessary that Marsh see his "injury" take place? What were the logistics of staging a penis accident?

If a male came splashing out of the water, clutching himself, alleging that a fish had bitten him, Marsh and Feya might be maliciously amused. Surely, though, they would think it the most natural thing in the world for Djetth to examine himself.

Way to go.

"Something bit me! Slack-damn," Djetth swore volubly, clutching his crotch.

Feya giggled.

"Slack-damn it, it hurts like the blazes. I hope it wasn't the sort of fish that goes up inside. Sorry, Ladies. I'm going to have to inspect myself for damage."

Djetth threw himself onto his back on the sand, close to where the girls sat whittling stakes, thrust down his trunk briefs, hooking them just below his bent and spread knees. Nothing was worth the actual loss of his trunk briefs and the lethal contents in the secret pocket behind the appliqué frog.

"Whoa . . . that's horrible," he groaned, knowing that females like to see anything horrible. Moaning, he clutched himself with both hands, one behind the other, in a golf-club grip, the little finger of his left hand hooked into the forefinger of his right. Peripherally, Djetth saw the girls exchange glances. They were interested.

"Fewmetty thing. Why the blue blazes would a bloody fish want to bite me there?" he muttered eloquently.

The trouble with a bioluminescent tattoo is that the little organisms have a mind of their own. They only flash when life is gooooood.

"Would somebody help me, here?" he commanded.

Feya, being injured, was out of the running. That left the field wide open for Marsh. Djetth grimaced as she dropped to her knees at his side in a gritty spray of sand.

"What do you want me to do?" she asked.

"Could you look at it?" He closed his eyes and hoped. "Can you see teeth marks? Look closely."

Her soft breath caressed his skin.

He moved his hands. *She's staring. Imagine she's going to kiss it. That works. Think of asking her to suck imaginary venom out of an imaginary seasnake bite. Visualize her taking my cock in her warm mouth.*

He knew the instant she saw it. She drew in her breath. Her finger traced the dancing warmth of his tattoo.

"You've seen my tattoo?" he said hoarsely. "These bioluminescent blighters have no sense of occasion. They show up when I get hay fever, too. Histamines excite them."

Is she buying it?

"Really?" Marsh asked, still apparently looking for fishy teeth indentations.

"I got this on Earth. All pubescent males get one, you know," he lied through his teeth. "Have you ever seen one before?" he asked with careful innocence.

"I don't think so," she said, sounding puzzled.

She stroked his design. "What is yours supposed to be?"

"My lightning rod. It's a forking bolt of lightning. When it's doing the deed properly, you might call it Greased Lightning. It's a very popular design among human males. A cliché, almost. Of course, I didn't know *that* when I had it done."

Now he'd covered all the bases. He was home free. As long as she told Feya that there were a lot of tattoos like his about, and Feya believed her. But why not? When would Feya have ever got it on with an Earthling?

Oh, Fewmet! I forgot. Feya had "worked" on the Ark Imperial. *She'd been to see Grievous! Damn. Then again, what are the chances she'll ever see Grievous again?*

"Did it hurt? Having it done, I mean."

"Yes. Not as much as it hurts humans, though. They don't have a bone, so they have to keep themselves aroused." He covered up. The action wasn't going to go any further with Feya watching.

The Pleasure Moon of Eurydyce

"We keep coming back to Django-Ra," 'Rhett observed. "We just don't know why."

He'd settled in, run a few errands, and was in no

hurry to report the ugly news from the morgue. "I suppose Django-Ra never Mated?" he suggested. "Had a legitimate son, for instance?"

"Not that I ever heard," Helispeta snapped, without looking up from the bridge hand she was playing by herself.

'Rhett flicked a glance at Tarra, remembered the conversation he'd overheard, drew a conclusion, and moved on.

"No, I didn't think so," he agreed. "Aunt Tarra, I'm sorry to be the one to tell you this. It turns out that Petri-Shah was not only tortured, but raped simultaneously. And mutilated."

"Who would do such a thing?"

'Rhett saw no need to name names. They all knew who was on their short list of suspects.

"From the high sperm and chromosome counts, we know the perpetrator was Djinn. Since the authorities—such as they are—don't know that I'm Djinn, it would only have confused the issue to offer them my DNA."

Grandmama Helispeta narrowed her eyes. "It would have been a relief to be able to exclude Ala'Aster-Djalet." She sighed. "However, you were right to hold back."

"Are you rigging that deck, Grandmama?" 'Rhett moved a sturdy side table to her left, sat on it, and began sorting suits in the hand dealt to "East." "Do you need to win?"

"I have no intention of cheating anyone of their money, Djarrhett," Grandmama said primly. "However, I do hope to deal someone a hand that will overwhelm him with the desire to murder me."

"This'll do it!" 'Rhett grimaced. "Two points! Ummm, Grandmama, you don't seriously suspect my father, do you?"

"No, my dear, but when I consider who had the means, opportunity, and motivation to put out a contract on Martia-Djulia, two names keep surfacing. I can find no motive for either Ala'Aster-Djalet or Django-Ra."

"Why might you suspect my father?" 'Rhett persisted.

"Ala'Aster-Djalet always meant to overthrow the Emperor and install Djetthro-Jason on the throne."

"Surely you're not suggesting that he'd kill the bride to stop Djetth from taking a politically undesirable Consort?" 'Rhett loved playing devil's advocate.

"No," Grandmama mused. "Unless, of course, Ala'Aster-Djalet felt in some way responsible for Djetthro-Jason's plight. That seems unlikely. . . ."

'Rhett made a mental note never to underestimate Grandmama.

"There's a problem. Django may have raped Petri-Shah, and he may have put out a contract on Martia-Djulia. But he wouldn't have had to torture Petri-Shah to find out that Martia-Djulia was on Freighter Island. We're no closer to a motive that holds water."

"It is not impossible"—Grandmama's voice dropped so low that even 'Rhett's Djinn hearing strained to hear her above the sizzling of incense and the splash of a fountain—"that Django-Ra tortured her for his own pleasure."

'Rhett looked down as he fanned his cards. Until this moment, he hadn't registered that neither Empress had asked *how* Petri-Shah had been mutilated.

Grandmama laid the Dummy's hand on the table. Seeing the cards,'Rhett raised an eyebrow.

"I want to see if this hand is biddable as seven no trumps," she explained. "My enemy *must* be Dummy."

"Why, Grandmama?"

"To get his attention, dear. Then we will persuade him to tell us what his motivation was."

"How? You can't torture him."

"Oh . . . I think I can," Grandmama Helispeta replied.

ARK IMPERIAL, Imperial Suite

"No, I don't like the look of this."

Tarrant-Arragon stood in the bathroom doorway, facing the bedhead screenwall, which was in multiple-view mode. Too many lives depended on his judgment call.

He hadn't forgotten Djinni's exact words when she'd first announced her latest, prescient dream. "My father is in danger!" The rest was less clearly imprinted on his memory. Traps. Warnings. Distress signals. Lies.

Two screens were interactive. War-star Leader Slayt stood on the bridge, awaiting a decision. V'Kh sat ready at his console in Communications.

A vertical tower of screens showed a frozen image of The Saurian Dragon. Other screens displayed star-traffic maps showing concentrations of activity around The Pleasure Moon of Eurydyce, and also a long, ragged convoy off course for Eurydyce, but on course for An'Koor.

There was something odd-looking about the convoy.

"We need to reinforce our blockade of An'Koor. The *Ark Imperial* is not enough to protect the entire planet," Tarrant-Arragon decided.

"At once, Your Imperial Highness," Slayt agreed.

"V'Kh, now We will hear what the Saurian Dragon has to say," Tarrant-Arragon ordered.

He heard Djinni creep up behind him, and pulled her against his side. On the interactive screens, V'Kh and Slayt gave no sign that they saw their Supreme Commander put an arm around his Mate.

On the screen, The Saurian Dragon nodded. "A warning. If the *Ark Imperial* receives a distress signal, do NOT respond. There's treachery . . ." He staggered. "The *Asgaard* is under attack. Do not send hel—"

"Is that all we got?" Tarrant-Arragon asked. "V'Kh, was it enough to trace the signal and get a fix?"

"It was enough, Your Highness," V'Kh replied. "We were expecting it and were ready. He is not far away."

"Did he request our help?"

"No, Your Highness. As you heard, he specifically said that we were not to help him. He warned us not to respond to distress signals."

"I don't take orders from The Saurian Dragon, so I *will* help him. Slayt—" Tarrant-Arragon turned back to his War-star Leader, "Slayt, order the nearest war-stars to assist The Saurian Dragon."

"Tell them the *Asgaard* looks like a big meteor," Djinni urged. "It's coated with crushed asteroid and ice. The enemy is bombarding it."

Tarrant-Arragon smiled at Slayt, who was doing a fine job of looking impassive while Djinni revealed her surprising knowledge of how their greatest enemy's base was disguised. He'd hunted the *Asgaard* on and off for tens of gestates without success.

"You hear that, Slayt?"

He turned fondly to his little Mate. "I wonder whether it's a pity that we no longer have a Thirteenth Star Force patrolling the Eurydycean quadrant," he mused for her hearing alone. "Demilitarizing An'Koor and blockading it has had some unintended consequences. By the look of that star map, all the Communicating Worlds have decided to take a holiday here. The Pleasure Moon of Eurydyce must be a writhing mass of pleasure-takers. I had no idea that gambling and jet racing could be so . . . ah . . . lucrative."

"Doesn't that strike you as odd?" Djinni asked, furrowing her brow. "You and The Saurian Dragon have unofficially ceased hostilities, but you haven't made an announcement. How would the Worlds know that it's safe to take a holiday?"

"It is suspicious, isn't it?

"Your Highness," V'Kh's voice interrupted his musings. "We are receiving a distress signal."

"Ah, my love. Was The Dragon's message the treacherous gambit you foresaw, or is this the trap?"

"This one is the trap," she said.

"We will ignore this signal," Tarrant-Arragon purred. "Virtual Invisibility, if you please, Slayt. We are going to disappear and lie in wait for a while."

Part Four

Reversals, Fortunes and the Murderer's Hand

EARTH DATE EQUIVALENT: DECEMBER 1994

CHAPTER TWENTY-THREE

Freighter Island (reef end)

Two females and a male. The island on fire, Martia-Djulia thought, as she prepared to fight for her life against impossible odds. Their only weapons were what they carried—fire-sharpened stakes intended for fish traps; a few knives; the two gold foil sheets; the medical kits. Feya was on crutches.

Their only hope was the *Ark Imperial*, but Djetth wasn't waiting around for help to come. He was herding his females to the reef, which he said was defensible.

The *Ark Imperial* was overhead, a black eclipsing body against a corona of streaming lights haloing it. Djetth had heard what sounded like a storm in the upper atmosphere. He'd said that the distinctive pounding was the rhythm of a major war-star battle.

The *Ark Imperial* was not in danger. An'Koor was, he'd said.

The *Ark Imperial*'s gunners were deadly accurate. Every boom resulted in explosions and flaming, sparkling trails. It seemed like a thunderstorm in reverse, except that light traveled faster than sound, so the booms and thumps did not match up with the explosions of enemy craft.

"Won't the *Ark Imperial* pick them off?" Feya asked hopefully.

"There are too many. It's like shooting mosquitoes. Some will get through," Djetth said.

A stiff, unnatural breeze was blowing up from the east; thick droplets of rain spattered the ground.

"There they are!" Djetth pointed at what the *Ark Imperial* was firing on. "A skein of bomber-sized craft, at the right height and trajectory to be heading for the An'Koori mainland. It looks like an invasion."

"Then, won't they ignore us?" Feya protested.

"Do they look like they're ignoring us?" He pointed to more streamer-like formations passing overhead. A series of explosions lit them up, and Martia-Djulia saw them. One or two individual bombers appeared to be hit, spiraled lower, then took a new course, away from the mainland.

"What are those tiara-shaped things?" she asked him.

"Parachutes," Djetth said grimly. "Lightweight airbags for individual, air-to-ground transfer. Why would their planes double back, and drop warriors over the sea, away from the only place where an invasion would make sense?"

"What would happen if they landed here?" Feya asked.

"Assume that they will kill us if we don't kill them first," Djetth answered. "That's why I set the woods on fire. This island is too big for three of us to defend, so we have to force our enemies to land in the sea."

"How can we kill them? I've never killed anyone," Martia-Djulia wailed.

"You've wanted to, though." Djetth grinned at her,

and she grinned back, why she couldn't say. "Now's your chance, my love!"

A fashionista Princess, a professional submissive, and one Great Djinn. Three secret weapons, if I'm lucky. If Marsh comes through, Djetth reflected, as he carried first Marsh, then Feya, through the rising waters of the channel to the dry sandbar on the reef.

Spin everything!

He might feed the girls some heartening bullshit about the enemy not daring to jump into fire, but the fact was they needed help from the *Ark Imperial*. The burning island was a distress signal.

"We'll be on the sandbar, with a channel of sea as our firebreak, so we won't get burned," he pointed out. "Look what I've got!" He unzipped his flight suit, tore open the secret compartment behind the appliqué frog on his trunk briefs, and put on his Rings of Imperial Authority.

"Djetth! You had a Fire Stone all along?"

"For emergencies." Djetth flashed Marsh a quick grin. "It was a secret."

I could add, "but my secret's no good if I'm dead." It wouldn't boost the girls' morale to think of me dead.

Djetth eased the slings he'd used to carry the bulk of their supplies from his shoulders, and started to arrange the stakes in lines, like quivers of arrows.

"Marsh, let me tell you how you can be most effective. Remember when you blasted me from across the Palace throne room? You winded me and knocked me backwards. If I'd been wading through the sea, I think I'd have drowned. They won't have reckoned on you."

"Do you think I can?" she breathed.

"Oh yes!"

Oh my love! How proud I am of you, with your short, spiky, Punk Princess hairdo, your daubed camou-

flage T-shirt, long bare legs, and furry slippers on your feet, looking fierce, trying so very hard to be braver than Feya!

He scooped up a handful of dirt, and gave her bright hair an affectionate, darkening noogie. "More camouflage," he growled.

"I'm afraid," Feya whispered.

"We all are afraid. Only an idiot wouldn't be afraid, and we're not idiots. Those pannier things worked out well, didn't they?"

Although she needed crutches, Feya had figured out how to carry plenty, by wearing the skirts of Marsh's big dress, and using the panniers as multiple apron pockets.

"Here they come!" Feya pointed at the sky. More parachutes, swaying like obscene mushrooms in the heavy wind.

"Here's the plan," Djetth said. "First, we draw blood. Lots of it. We want to make our enemies bleed in the water. I'm betting that whoever told those bastards to jump over the sea didn't tell them about An'Koori sea monsters."

"There are monsters in the sea?" Marsh squeaked accusingly.

"In the deeper waters, yes. Tarrant-Arragon shot one the day he forced us down. You thought he was aiming for us and missed, did you? Your brother never misses!"

"Well!" she huffed.

"Feya." *Feya has to feel useful. And powerful.* "You've got great night vision. You're our spotter. See there."

He pointed to where the riptide was an eighty-foot-wide streak of fast-flowing death.

"See the break in the surf line, where the water looks streaked? The riptide's beginning to run. If you see a swimmer in there, don't worry about him. He's going to be swept out to sea, right into the jaws of our monsters. I'd like to put just one bleeder in that riptide."

Djetth scanned the sea and sky. The first parachutes were down and billowing like Portuguese men-of-war. Dark, hairy heads heaved in the choppy water as the invaders began to swim. Scythians!

"There!" Feya gasped a warning.

Heads. Within range.

Djetth picked up a spear, took careful aim for the whites of one set of eyes, and hurled it like a javelin with all the strength in his powerful swimmer's shoulders.

"Got one!" In the near darkness, he saw the Scythian mercenary lifted up and thrown back with the force of impact, the spear embedded in his forehead. "There'll be a lot of blood from a head wound like that.

"Take your time," Djetth encouraged Marsh. "They're short-legged bastards. They can't start to shoot at us until they can stand."

Out to sea, heads turned to see what had happened to their skewered comrade; eye whites flashed with movement. Djetth targeted another swimmer.

"Two! He's bleeding."

Slowly the pirates attempted to spread out.

Djetth took a third improvised javelin, held it at shoulder height, aimed with a straight left arm, and brought his right arm forward in a pitching action. The target might have seen it coming, but the Scythians were still too deep in the water to stand. The best any of them could do was lurch sideways. It was not enough.

"Three! In the jugular, I think," Djetth guessed grimly, as his target gurgled and hissed. "He'll bleed, too."

Everything was against the invaders except numbers. Djetth found his rhythm and made every spear count. Only one overshot. *Ten! There has to be enough blood in the water.*

Marsh seemed frozen.

"Sweetheart, who do you hate more than anyone?" Djetth suggested. "Think of blasting him. Or her. What's your worst nightmare?"

"Where I got this terrible gift," Marsh snarled.

"Several of them are moving towards the riptide!" Feya reported.

"Let's frighten more of them into it!" Djetth said.

"Hwoooyyyyy! Hah." Marsh was in action.

"WoooHooo!" Feya cheered as a Scythian was lifted head and chest out of the water and knocked backwards. His arms thrashed wildly. He sank and didn't reappear.

Djetth took his turn, with the Fire-Stone laser Ring on his forefinger. *Aim's off.* Nevertheless, a hairy arm ignited; its owner screamed, but quickly extinguished the arm. The stench of singed wet hair and skin was disgusting.

Standing on a spur well away from the girls, Djetth focused his Djinncraft to afflict the oncoming bastards with cramps, nausea, diarrhea, disorientation . . . anything to keep them in the water.

"More parachutes, but the wind's blown them off course," Feya shouted. "Riptide's picked up one of the bleeders. And look! Friendly fire."

An Imperial recon fighter screamed past, spraying shimmying death into the swimmers, and sending parachutes rocking, collapsing, and erupting in brilliant flames.

Djetth and Marsh fought on, he taking the right, she the left.

"I saw a monster," Feya sang out.

Sure enough, lurching swimmers would throw up their hairy arms, screech, and sink, never to resurface—sometimes with hardly a ripple, sometimes in a great, glossy swirl of wake and semi-submerged reptilian skin.

"Watch out!" Feya's cry held a new note of alarm.

One parachutist had a better class of device. It seemed to be motorized. He flew standing up, circled around, swaying as he dangled in a contraption that reminded Djetth of a gadget from an old James Bond movie. Something long and metallic projected at around his waist height.

At that instant, Feya screamed.

A low-tech kind of weapon chuntered like a slow, loud machine gun, throwing up chunks of reef matter even before the assassin was close.

"Let's get him!" Djetth trained both his gaze and his Fire-Stone Ring finger on the new threat. Though tired, he was in the zone. His perceptions were clear. The rest of the world was living, bleeding—and dying—in slow motion.

The swaying, hunched assassin might not have known which of the three of them was his target. Feya shouldn't have been there at all. With her informal garb and short shock of dirty hair, Marsh looked nothing like her old self. He had Rings which no one knew he possessed. Djetth sensed the assassin's pain, confusion, and fear as a distinctive smell in the air.

"Hwwoooyyyyy! Hah!"

Together, Djetth and Marsh turned their different Djinn powers on him.

In the second before Djetth ignited him, the assassin was thrown violently backwards. His flying contraption rocked; he screamed and thrashed, and his weapon—a cross between some fictional blaster and a Gatling gun—fell to the ground, jerking like a crazed snake spitting at the sea.

The flying device exploded into a brief burst of orange flame, and crashed into the wet sand. Instinctively, they recoiled from the heat and the stench of burning hair, hot metal, and melting rubber.

"That's mine!" Feya launched herself on the gun, and lay on her belly like a true military heroine, spraying hairy, buoy-like heads in the sea with large bullets.

"He was serious," Marsh said and darted hesitatingly—like a dog after a skunk—ever closer to the sizzling assassin.

Thank the Great Originator for Feya! Djetth thought, turning to watch Feya show what a markswoman she was.

"Don't go near him—" Djetth exclaimed, turning to see Marsh throw off the dark-streaked T-shirt. She drew in a deep, visible breath, and sprinted the rest of the way into the wreckage.

In only her corset, she knelt, reached her hands under her armpits, drew two whip-thin bodkins, and drove them deep into the dead or dying villain's staring eyes in a practiced, two-handed action.

"Bloody Fewmet!" Djetth swore. *She's right, though.* He bent, picked up a stake, and joined her. "Just to make sure—" He drove his spear through the assassin's rib cage where the heart should be.

The worst had come last. There were no more, and the short An'Koori night was over, too.

The world seemed strangely silent. No gunfire. No screams. It was a perfect High Five moment. Djetth glanced over at Feya, and looked again. She was lying in a growing stain of blood.

"Feya's hit," he said, ripping the piratical headscarf off his head. He unknotted the corners and wadded the cloth into a pad. "Take your corset off, Marsh. Now."

He knelt beside Feya. She was slumped, but conscious.

"Feya, we're going to put Marsh's corset on you and lace it as tight as we can to stop the bleeding."

He sensed Marsh beside him, holding out her satiny scarlet corset. It was a one-piece job, slightly fanned, but otherwise like a Japanese straw placemat.

"It hurts," Feya moaned as he slipped the broad, flat strip under her, and began to pull it tight.

"I know, love. You didn't notice it while you were fighting. You're a heroine. From the size of your wound, I'd guess you caught a ricocheted fragment, probably from an early shot while the assassin was firing wildly. Done!"

The corset was tied. It overlapped, so he'd had to tie the laces unconventionally, but it would hold her in.

He rose, stripped off his flight suit, folded it into a tight square, and knelt again to put it under her head.

"Feya, I'm going to bedjinn you to slow your breathing and so on. I'll be careful. I don't think we should wait for your own shutting-down reflexes. Soon, you won't feel a thing. You may not remember all your derring-do when you wake up, but you *will* wake up."

He pressed on the acupressure points in her neck, just as 'Rhett had done to him in the *Ark Imperial*'s operating theater. Then he wrapped her in gold foil.

"We could do with some help," he remarked, glancing from Marsh, who was wearing her T-shirt again, to the dark-mottled sky.

The tide was receding fast, carrying with it floating, red-haired corpses. Djetth picked up the assassin's gun and checked the magazine. There weren't many bullets left.

"Shoot the dead bodies if they move." Djetth handed Marsh the firearm, and knelt over the disarray of wickedly thin knives that she'd removed from her corset. "You were holding out on me," he said wryly.

Having chosen a flat, sharp blade, Djetth scraped the beard from his cheeks, upper lip and jaw until he was clean-shaven, and raw.

Marsh gaped at him. "You have hair! And, your face . . . ! How could I not have noticed?"

Peripherally, he spotted a black streak in the sky, coming straight for them. The streak became a two-seater Thorcraft. There were probably ten Thorcraft—maybe thirteen—in existence, including the one on the seabed a mile or so down the coast. All belonged exclusively to Tarrant-Arragon.

"H-e-e-e-re's trouble," Djetth announced in a low-voiced homage to a late-show M.C.

The pilot circled, and made a near-silent, elegant, vertical landing on the narrow sandbar, less narrow now the tide was going out. Shielding his face from the glare of the rising sun with his forearm, Djetth watched with slitted eyes, calculating. His right hand fisted on the ground, the Rings pressed into the loose sand.

Showdown time!

The canopy slid back, Tarrant-Arragon vaulted out, and dropped like a big cat onto the sand, landing on his feet, as he always did.

"We saw your flare . . ." Tarrant-Arragon's eyes widened as Djetth got to his feet, dropped his left arm, and stared his cousin in the face. "Ahhh," he murmured. "I see."

Martia-Djulia tasted the heady surge of testosterone in the still, smoky air as her brother and her not-quite-lover faced each other. She pressed her hands over her thudding heart. She was not the fool she'd played so convincingly for many, many gestates.

Suddenly, she realized, Tarrant-Arragon was seeing a resemblance he'd never thought to look for. He hadn't seen the self likeness when Djetth was bearded, bald, or gaunt. One sees what one expects to see.

Watching her brother, she saw the stunned, Oh-Fewmet look when Djetth oh-so-casually lifted his right hand and ran his fingers through his short, dark thatch. Djetth's Rings glinted in the sun. Djetth had a full set.

Martia-Djulia had no idea what Djetth felt beyond a certain triumphant sense of "thusness." She wondered whether she knew Djetth half as well as she'd thought she did.

"Soooo," drawled Tarrant-Arragon, lightly flexing his own Ring hand. "Who's going back to the *Ark Imperial*?"

Who goes? The implications cracked open and radiated like serrated world-shake lines. Djetth could kill Tarrant-Arragon, take his identity, go back to the *Ark*

Imperial, and live out the rest of his life as Tarrant-Arragon. With Djinni-vera.

Some would call that justice. Tarrant-Arragon had taken Djetth's scent-love. The only way for Djetth to get her back would be for him to take over Tarrant-Arragon's life.

Djetth had every reason to take Tarrant-Arragon's life. Everyone knew that Djinni-vera had been the last Djinn-line virgin anywhere. Djetth's lost scent-love could only be Tarrant-Arragon's newly taken Princess Consort.

Every word Djetth had ever spoken was scored on her memory. Also the alien words he'd sung because the angry, carnally inflammatory lyrics had meaning for him.

As for her, Djetth had seen her at her best and at her worst. He must regard her as a poor substitute for Djinni-vera. Nevertheless, she'd had her chances and blown them away.

Martia-Djulia's perceptions speeded up with her pulse; each muffled double-thump of her heart matched a gut-realization.

A two-seater Thorcraft. One true Prince. One once-thwarted usurper who looked just like Tarrant-Arragon. Two females on the ground who knew his secret. Two witnesses.

If he killed all three of them, Djetth could go back to the *Ark Imperial* alone and have his true heart's desire.

Martia-Djulia bowed her head and clasped her hands over the bumpy softness of her flimsily covered bosom.

"No-brainer," Djetth said.

Looking up, not daring to hope, Martia-Djulia saw a strange smile curving Djetth's thin but sometimes generous lips.

"Feya goes." He swept up Feya's inert, gold-wrapped body, strode across the sand and around to the far side of the Thorcraft, then lifted his burden into the passenger seat. "With you, Cousin."

Djetth reached over and began to strap her in, as if oblivious to Tarrant-Arragon's puzzled frown. "Shrapnel ricochet injury. Serious. She's bedjinned. Marsh's corset is keeping her guts in."

As the seriousness of Feya's injuries became clear, Tarrant-Arragon acted. He was back in the Thorcraft, buckled up, and with his hand on the control yoke before Djetth finished securing the patient.

"Have your best surgeon standing by." Djetth clapped Tarrant-Arragon on the shoulder, and stepped back.

Tarrant-Arragon nodded curtly.

"I'm Tarrant-Arragon. Power up," he voice-activated the Thorcraft. "*Ark Imperial*! Slayt, get Ka'Nych to the operating theater. Call the Imperial Escort Service on Eurydyce's Pleasure Moon. Ask Madam Tarra what Feya's blood type is, and have some ready. I'm coming in."

The canopy slid shut, and locked with a metallic double-thunk. The Thorcraft rose vertically, hovered for a heartbeat, then sped away.

Although her brother had ignored her, Martia-Djulia watched him go until he was out of sight. The brightening sky shimmered with broad swaths of storm-pink, blue-green, and purple, as if An'Koor couldn't decide which hue to wear for this stark, sparkling new day.

Who would have dreamed that a battle would have such an iridescent aftermath? There was dark matter, bright matter, smoke, fuel, and atomized particles of whatever starships were made of.

"Does it bother you that I'm the spitting image of your brother?" The harshness in Djetth's voice startled her.

Martia-Djulia turned, and saw that Djetth lay sprawled low on the steeply sloped beach, staring out to sea, with his upper body weight on his forearms and elbows and his heels in the surf.

Even the tide had been pulled down lower than usual.

"Why should it bother me?"

Oh, Malevolency! Don't answer me, Djetth. Don't think of all the Worlds' reasons we shouldn't be Mates.

He shrugged one muscle-bunched shoulder, his back still to her, his expression hidden. "I suppose it depends how you feel about him."

"I think you look nicer without the beard," she ventured shyly, avoiding a direct response.

"Nicer?" Djetth threw back his head and laughed, apparently not in the least offended by faint praise. "Come here!"

She grinned back. "Nicer" had been an outrageous understatement. Clean-shaven and dark-haired, Djetth was a heart-throbber—the god of her recurrent dreams. If she dared to, she might sit at his side forever. She'd dare anything for another chance to win his love.

She'd even brave the sea.

"Come!" His voice deepened, as if "Come" were a sexual invitation.

I'm imagining things. It's because this is the first time we've been truly alone together since Feya interrupted our short-lived, rut-raged excesses.

Her mouth felt dry. Her empty stomach fluttered. Martia-Djulia eyed the sand beside Djetth. The patch he was patting seemed to get wetter with every touch of his hand.

Though he seemed to want her to sit in wetness, she went to him. She stumbled as she stepped out of her slippers, and her suddenly trembling legs gave way when she would have lowered herself gracefully to sit at least a thigh's length apart from him.

"Stiff?" he commented with monosyllabic sympathy, like one warrior to another.

She swallowed hard and nodded. Suddenly, folding her legs elegantly under her so her T-shirt covered her thighs did not seem realistic.

With gentlemanly arrogance, Djetth reached behind

her back, hooked her slippers on his long fingers, and tossed them—without looking—up the beach.

"You don't need those," he growled, then surprised her by lying back and resuming his contemplation of the horizon.

Something's very wrong with my hormones! I could have sworn he moved my slippers out of his way because he meant to push me onto my back.

I wonder how it would feel to have him on top of me, holding me down, his forearms pressing down on mine, and my wrists pinned under his big hands, as he thrusts deeply into me. . . .

But he's not rut-raged. There's no reason to think of sex.

Since he showed no sign of wanting to force her to lie down, she reclined—gradually—alongside his longer, larger body. The warmth of his legs was like sunshine on her thigh.

To be companionable, she stretched first one foot, then the other, into the water beside his. It was ankle-dragging cold. She couldn't help gasping.

He glanced questioningly at her.

I can't say the water's cold.

"I was thinking. Earlier. Tarrant-Arragon was at your mercy. You could have . . ." Words failed her, but she could not simply ignore all the things he could have had—with his face, and his Rings—if he hadn't put Feya's life first.

"It occurred to me," he conceded urbanely.

He'd thought about leaving her. Of course he had. Nevertheless, his admission hurt. If Feya hadn't been injured, if not for Djetth's alien compassion and unDjinn-like decency, he'd have gone.

He'd forgotten . . . what Feya had interrupted.

Even knowing this, she wanted him.

Besides, he had not gone. There was still hope.

"I thought about it for about a second." Djetth's voice

deepened. He turned his head and smiled teasingly. "Then I realized . . ."

Marsh, I love you! She held her breath, her senses twirled, anticipating what his next words must be.

". . . the cost. If I took Tarrant-Arragon's place, I'd have had to kill you."

Djetth butted her bare shoulder with his. His skin was firm, slightly sticky, salty. His armpit smelled of male strength . . . and sex.

"You can't keep a secret, Marsh," he said in an intense, husky voice, as if he'd seen the heartbreak on her face and guessed too late what she'd hoped he'd say.

There was no point in arguing. It had been a foolish, unreasonable hope. No one had ever said "I love you" to her, not even during sex.

Still, I would like to hear the words, just once, even if he doesn't mean it!

Dampness from the sea-saturated sand was creeping up her unforgettably stained T-shirt, making it cling to her hips, turning it transparent, reminding anyone who cared to look that she hadn't worn knickers since Feya's arrival.

Her abandoned knickers would have gone up in flames last night, with everything else.

At that moment, a cold wavelet tickled along the side of her calf and wriggled an icy finger of wetness into the warm hollows under her knees. The shock of it pinched her nipples and made her shudder.

The tide had turned. Here was an excuse to beat an honorable retreat.

Before she could move, Djetth's large Ring hand closed over the sensitive inside of her elbow, holding her down. As she angled a glance down, she saw what he was staring at. Her hardened nipples stood out like twin *thimbleberries.*

She wasn't wearing her corset.

"Alone at last!"

Djetth's strangled drawl echoed her own earlier thought. He'd rolled onto his side for a better view. He loomed over her. His shadow slid across her belly. "Marsh, we have unfinished business. Shall we?"

Djetth wanted sex? But, now? Where?

Their shelter would have burnt to the ground, and the hammock, too. The possibility of a gold-foil tent had gone with Feya. There was no privacy at all.

"Someone could be watching," she warned. Her voice quivered.

Once, long ago, she'd tried to trap a lover by not telling him they were being watched. Never again.

"Let them watch!" he said savagely. The hairy back of Djetth's hard, heavy-muscled left thigh rode over the smooth top of her thighs. His knee nudged hers apart, and pressed down between her legs. His free left hand splayed over her right breast, and he squeezed rhythmically, like an Imperial pet tiger with his eyes half closed from the pleasure of kneading and daydreaming of suckling.

"I don't care." His words became a muffled purr that vibrated from her nipples to her groin, as he dipped his head and held her thoroughly kneaded breast to his open mouth.

In a flash of insight, Martia-Djulia understood why he'd turned exhibitionist after being so careful not to be seen consummating a Mating he'd never wanted.

Flagrant defiance now was the whole point.

Djetth was a god, one of the greatest of the Great Djinn. He'd let his deadly rival, Tarrant-Arragon, live. He'd been too noble, and his alpha-male machismo now demanded that he prove to himself and to anyone watching that he hadn't gone soft.

Openly taking Tarrant-Arragon's sister, by force if necessary, would go some way to restore his bad self-image.

Force would not be necessary.

The sea was between her legs, and so was he. One cold. One hot. Both inexorable in their advances. Eyes closed, Martia-Djulia felt her knees go limp with pleasure and fall apart.

She wanted this. Even if he didn't love her, this was better than anything she had ever known.

Perhaps, if he ever gave up all hope of retaking his scent-love—who did not want him—he would settle for a willing second-best, even if he could never love her.

"Oh, Djetth. Djetth!" she breathed.

"Mmmmm!" he responded. Through flimsy T-shirt fabric, he sucked, and licked, and sucked again, as if he would draw all the remaining circles of sweet berry juice into his mouth.

She reached up to cup his lean cheek with her palm, and her fingers touched his new-grown hair. It felt prickly-soft, like the plush fur of Tigron's hot-crater-living predators. Would Djetth mate like a predator?

"Please, Djetth. Fuck with me." She chose his word for sex. Under the circumstances, it would be bad form to ask him to make love to her.

His throaty chuckle startled her. Her eyes flew open. His passion-dark eyes met hers, and his stained lips pouted into the sexiest grin she'd ever seen.

"Sweetheart, I never thought I'd have to teach you to decline 'to fuck,' but one day, I will!"

Decline to fuck? His words made no sense. Did he want her to struggle and fight him? The tender depth of his voice said otherwise. His hand, which had worked its way up under the hem of her T-shirt, was expertly stroking her . . . it said otherwise, too.

Suddenly, the cold-tongued sea licked higher, lapping between her legs, stealing the heavy warmth his fingers had drawn from her crotch.

With an involuntary gasp her body clenched.

At the same instant, she felt his fingers.

"Whooo-Haaah! A snapper—"

It really didn't matter that she did not understand his alien terms of sexual reference. His fingers pushed deeper inside her. His thumb had found somewhere very right to press.

". . . Do that when I'm inside you."

A fresh wave came tingling in the small of her back, and at the base of her spine.

"Djetth, we should move. The tide is coming in."

"So am I," he murmured, watching his own wrist as he pumped harder and faster with his fingers. "You're not afraid, are you?"

"Yes!" she whispered.

"Not of me?"

"Of the sea."

"Of course. I knew that!" he said, breathing heavily. "But with all this surf . . . and sand in the water . . . if we don't thrash around too much . . . if I stay on top of you . . . they won't know for sure if we're just fooling around . . . or if We get our rocks off."

Martia-Djulia trembled at the sexy ferocity of his words. She assumed she knew what his "rocks" were, and that in his passion he'd defaulted to using the Imperial Pronoun.

"Spread your legs," he rasped. "I'm going to dock with you."

Another wave broke and foamed over his hips as he positioned himself. She flinched at the coldness gushing over her sensitized labia.

"The water's cold," she murmured apologetically.

"This isn't." His hand moved again between their bodies, and she felt his fist guide his positor into the opening of her bay.

She cried out in surprise at the blunt, pulsing heat.

"How's that?" he exulted.

"Oh, Djetth, that's good."

"It's better than good. Try it for size." He pushed in, and went on pushing. "Mmmmm. We're a good fit!"

"Perfect," she sighed.

She clamped down to take all the heat from him. The heat went on and on. Pleasurable sensations sparkled at the base of her spine, and in the backs of her knees.

He'd hardly started, and she was panting. Her tongue tip caressed her teeth. He was hard and silken-smooth, and as he began to thrust inside her, his tattoed underside tickled and fizzed against her insides in ripples. Dimly, she remembered a feeling like this long ago.

He plunged. When a wave slapped his buttocks, he thrust deeply into her, and withdrew slowly, slowly, dragging out his throbbing retreat so he never completely left her before the next surge overtook them.

Both his hands cradled the back of her head, keeping her face out of the water, holding her still for his kisses, as he pounded into her in time with the surf.

"Djetth!" she cried out when the flutters became great wingbeats. "I can't go on. I'm overtaken. Oh, Djetth. Djetth!"

She clamped around him, and her senses soared. Perhaps he said something, perhaps he didn't. Perhaps he roared and flooded her bay with wave upon wave of his seed. Perhaps she left him behind.

"What would you like?" she asked, when her senses reformed, she was able to think of him, and realized they were still joined and he was ready for more.

Djetth chuckled.

"A rain check, I guess. We're about to have company."

Glaring over his shoulder up into the sky, she saw two approaching shapes, but no ominous clouds.

"I hope they're going to recover our Thorcraft from the seabed," he said. "I'd like to take you to the Pleasure Moon of Eurydyce. I want to find out who tried to kill us, and why. Also, there's something I want to ask your mother to her face."

"My mother?"

"Call me old-fashioned," Djetth murmured cryptically.

CHAPTER TWENTY-FOUR

ARK IMPERIAL, Imperial Suite
A week after the battles

"The invitation came," Tarrant-Arragon said, taking off his robes and joining Djinni in the murk-bath. "It was from my mother."

"Are you going, even though it might be a trap?" Djinni knew that he would have to go if his mother needed him, but she asked anyway.

"I think so. Djetth and Martia-Djulia were invited, too, but they'd already gone on ahead. Feya was invited, which I take to mean that, if there is a trap, it's not for me. At any rate, the *Ark Imperial* is invisibly approaching orbit in the star roads off the Pleasure Moon of Eurydyce."

Djinni nodded: He'd told her about rescuing Feya, and the chilling moment when he'd seen Djetth's Rings and thought he'd lost everything.

"Borrow this." Her fingers weren't too badly swollen now she was spending more time in the murk-bath. She twisted the Death Ring off her finger and gave it to

Tarrant-Arragon. "If it's an invitation you feel you can't refuse, at least don't be predictable. Go in force. Go late. Keep an element of surprise. Don't show your hand."

"Literally?" he quipped, sliding the Ring that signified his absolute Right to kill back onto his little finger.

"Literally!" she agreed, and snuggled into the hollow of his arm. "There's something else I want you to consider. I think you should give the entire planet of An'Koor to Djetth, free and clear, no strings attached."

"Why would I do that?" Tarrant-Arragon murmured.

"You want him there. He can do a lot of good, but not a lot of harm. He should have a world of his own. From what you told me, he could have taken your life, and all your worlds. He didn't. Secondly—"

"There's a 'secondly'?" he teased.

"You should release Djetth from his promise to Mate with Martia-Djulia." She placed her fingers over his parted lips. "Hear me out. After what you've put them through, either they already love each other, or they hate each other. Either way, Djetth is probably determined not to submit to your high-handed tactics. If you tell Djetth he doesn't *have* to marry her, he probably will."

"Ah!" said Tarrant-Arragon. "My sister is the same way. I'll tell her that she doesn't have to marry him if she doesn't want to."

ARK IMPERIAL, sick bay

Grievous took the next-best thing to flowers to the *Ark Imperial*'s sick bay: a flagon of fruity wine and two glasses.

"Hello, lover," he greeted Feya hopefully. "I bet you don't remember me, do you?"

"I don't remember anything." She stared blankly at him with her beautiful, golden, alien eyes.

"Massive blood loss will do that to a girl," Grievous replied knowledgeably. "We were worried about you."

He turned in a tight circle to give himself a moment to hide his emotions.

"Okay if I sit down?" He sat on the foot of her bed. "I dare say you do remember how to eat, drink, and what-not?"

"I don't remember what-not."

"Not to worry, love. No bad thing, that. You can look forward to a fresh start. I had a word with your doctor. He said you could have a sip of wine if you fancied it."

"Who are you?" the poor girl asked.

"I'm known as Grievous. I'm from Earth. I used to be a professional soldier until I disgraced myself over a woman, but that's another story." He opened the flagon and poured Feya a small glass as approved by the head of surgery.

"Between one-off jobs I was a chauffeur and private tour guide, until Prince Tarrant-Arragon took a shine to me in the course of an alien abduction that he was perpetrating. He made me an offer I couldn't refuse. May I?"

He indicated his glass, and took her confused shrug for permission to join her in a nice, festive drink.

"Now that he's happily married to his abducted Earth-girl, and not contemplating more invasions of Earth any-time soon, I 'mind' prisoners if they speak English."

"Am I a prisoner?"

"Nah, love. You're a patient."

"Do I speak English? Why do I understand you?"

This was a tricky question. He wanted to be as honest as possible, without reminding Feya of her former profession.

"You used to hang out on an An'Koori war-star. Your old friends watched pirated TV shows from Earth. The humor's similar. I'd say that's how you picked up some English."

He checked out her blankly polite expression.

"You used to see a lot of a tall chap called Commander Jason. He's dead. They're all gone—the war-stars, your friends. See, the An'Koori military was overrun by enemy infiltrators, and disloyal mercenaries. One of them was Commander Jason, who, as I said, is dead."

His orders were to make sure she believed that.

"Are you an old boyfriend?" Feya asked innocently.

"I'd like to be a regular boyfriend, love, but I didn't come here today about that." He sat forward in his chair, his forearms on his thighs and hands clasped. "Do you remember Madam Tarra, love?"

"I don't know." Feya sighed.

"Not to worry. She sent you an invitation, but you're not well enough to go. I'm telling you, anyway, because there's a very bad villain. He's responsible for the injury you suffered, the horrible death of one of your friends, and a lot more deaths and destruction, as well."

Feya looked as if she might weep.

"Nah, don't distress yourself, darling. Madam Tarra is having what you might call a Closure party. Well, you might call it that if you spoke psycho-babble. I dare say the bad guy's victims are going to plot his comeuppance, or witness his shame and ruin. The point is, everyone this villain wronged, or their representatives, are to go. You were invited, also Tarrant-Arragon, and—"

"I can't go with Tarrant-Arragon."

"You remember who he is, do you? Scary fellow, isn't he? Gives hardy fighting men the trots when he is in one of his bad moods. Not so much these days, though."

"What are trots?"

"Montezuma's revenge, love. The squirts. Loose bowels. The runs. Trotting is just a slower, more vertically jerky method of running. I'd say that a man might elect to trot if he wanted to clench his buttocks while moving briskly in the direction of a toilet."

Grievous considered a demonstration trot around the room, but decided against. It wasn't the image a suitor wanted to impress his future ladylove with.

"No, love. Even if you were back on your feet, and

able to share a story of what the villain did to you, you can't go to a party with Tarrant-Arragon."

Grievous shook his head decisively and tossed the rest of his wine down his throat. "It wouldn't be proper. He's a happily married Djinn, the Great Tiger Crown Prince, and the heir to the Imperial crown, amongst other things."

"How did this villain wrong Tarrant-Arragon?" Feya asked in a wondering voice.

"Now, there's a good question. Of course, the villain did trick the Volnoths into attacking the Saurians, and he incited the Scythians to invade An'Koor, seize the seat of government and so on. A good many of the Imperial armed forces made heavy sacrifices to squash the invasion.

"As Commander of the Star Forces, Tarrant-Arragon is probably representing those who fell, but he might be there for some other symbolic purpose."

Feya hauled herself up on her pillows. "If I'm owed revenge, I want it."

"That's my girl! What I was thinking is this. If you like, I could go as your representative, or proxy. Then I'd come back and tell you all about it."

"I don't remember you. There's someone I'd rather send. I can't remember his name. There's also the lady who gave me that corset, and saved my life. . . ."

"That's okay, love. You're thinking of Prince Djetthro-Jason and The Princess Imperial, Martia-Djulia. They're going to the party on their own accounts. The bad guy was trying to have them killed. You were collateral damage."

"If they are going—"

"They can't represent you as well as themselves. Think of it as being like a movie funeral. Lots of movies start or end with a funeral. Everyone wears black and puts a flower or a scoop of dirt on the coffin. Nobody gets to toss two scoops. See, it's not the quantity of roses or dirt that is symbolic, it's the number of people who participate."

Grievous started to scratch the back of his head, then remembered his thinning patch, and decided he'd better scratch hairs off his thigh instead.

"You need to send a commoner, love."

Feya cocked her head. She really was a pretty little thing. Like a bluetit.

"The symbolic of the bad guy having little persons stand up and throw dirt against him is important?" Her English was not perfect, but by George! She got it! "Are you common, Grievous?"

"Ask anyone, love."

"Then, please go and get my revenge for me."

Hologram from the Asgaard, The Pleasure Moon of Eurydyce

"Dragon, where have you been?"

Tarra couldn't see the expression on Ala'Aster-Djalet's face owing to the full headmask he always wore during holographic transmissions.

"Fighting," he replied in his pleasantly modulated, deep voice.

"Did you win?"

"I had help from an unexpected quarter." The Saurian Dragon held out his arms in a gesture that might have been slightly mocking. Strapped to his side was a ceremonial Saurian Sword, which was revealed when his red outer robe fell open. "Otherwise, I'd be dead."

Wry, elusive, laconic, this was the Ala'Aster-Djalet of old, the technically illegitimate Djinn Prince who was ever ready to fight to the death, stand up for his beliefs, and mate with any female who took his fancy, regardless of his current marital state.

Thrice widowed, he'd fathered a child each by two of

his three mates, adopted his own twin brother's twin sons, and his elder half-brother's son.

Tarra sighed. It was time Ala'Aster-Djalet gave up power politics and settled down for good. She doubted he would.

"Who were you fighting?" she asked, worried.

"Volnoths, mostly," he said. The time lag was short on the hologram. He could not be very far away.

"Volnoths?" Tarra's heart thunked. Was it possible that Django-Ra was innocent after all, and that she and Helispeta were about to perpetrate a massive injustice and make complete and utter fools of themselves?

The thought made her feel sick. Moreover, her eldest daughter, Electra-Djerroldina was married to the Volnoth leader. Would her children forever be at war?

Tarra tasted bitterness rising in her throat, and felt its burn behind her breastbone.

"Mostly?" she asked in a faint voice.

"I responded to a distress call on the Rim. Not personally." There was a rueful smile in his voice. "My rescue vessels were attacked. Then, the *Asgaard* came under fire from multiple non-aligned war-stars disguised as Imperial Forces."

Tarra shuddered at the thought.

"You saw through the disguise?"

"It was thin, and I know my children. Djarrhett and Djinni-vera seem to trust Tarrant-Arragon. I am beginning to know Tarrant-Arragon. I met him at Martia-Djulia's non-event of a Mating Ceremony. He's an impressive male. A bad enemy to have, but not a bad friend."

"You must be very sure." Tarra spoke in her unaccented Seer's voice. Her words could have been a question or advice.

"I was sure when help came just in time from a real Imperial war-fleet." He smiled. "My enemies' enemy is my friend. When the newly arrived Imperial vessels started blasting the vessels that were blasting me, I ceased to blast any of them."

"And before that," Tarra insisted. "I didn't understand the reference to your being at Martia-Djulia's botched Mating."

"Ahhh," purred the Dragon. "I attended, uninvited and in disguise. Only Djarrhett recognized me—as far as I know. The traitor in the Palace obviously did not recognize me. He didn't know that Djinni-vera had drafted a peace treaty, which Tarrant-Arragon signed, sealed, and gave to Djarrhett. Djarrhett put it into my hands that extraordinary day.

"Tarrant-Arragon is not a Djinn to offer peace with one hand and attack with the other. Therefore, when I was attacked by a coalition purporting to be Imperial Forces, I spoke to the *Ark Imperial.* Funnily enough, they were expecting me to make contact. Djinni-vera's doing."

"What of the Volnoths?" Tarra asked, anxious on behalf of Electra-Djerroldina. "Will they now go to war against the Empire?"

"There were no survivors to contradict the official version, which has yet to be published. Tarrant-Arragon's people and mine are working on a statement. What really happened hasn't yet been discovered. Why did you call? Do you want me for something?" His deep voice took on a flirtatious tone.

"Your enemy could be my enemy, Dragon. After all these years, I am moving against him. Helispeta is here, of course. Djetthro-Jason and Martia-Djulia are on their way." She smiled, imagining that behind his headmask a mobile eyebrow had shot up. "I want you to come and be a witness. How soon can you be here?"

"How soon do you want me?"

What a typical male Djinn answer. Tarra smiled.

Chapter Twenty-five

The Pleasure Moon of Eurydyce
A week later

"Django wouldn't recognize you," Marsh protested as she watched Djetth dressing—quite literally—for a visit to the casino with his Grandmama Helispeta.

"That's the general idea."

"I meant, he wouldn't recognize you if you went in male clothing, now you're clean-shaven," she persisted.

"We don't want him to think I'm Tarrant-Arragon, either. Django must believe he's invincible for the sting to work."

"I don't understand this 'Sting' at all. It's too convoluted. I don't like it."

Djetth curled a hand in front of his mouth and blew on his newly painted fingernails. He grinned.

"You don't like that you can't be part of it!"

Djetth hadn't asked what she wanted during, or after, sex in the surf or at any time since. If he had asked, her answer would *not* have been to hide in a brothel with her disreputable mother, while Djetth acted as pusher of a chair-on-wheels—which Helispeta didn't need—and went to a high-stakes bridge tournament to provoke a killer.

"If you can dress up as an elderly female, I think—"

"No!" Djetth's voice lost its teasing note. "Django knows you a lot better than he does me. He'd notice you. And he'd read your mind."

Marsh could have asked why everyone seemed to think that Django could read her mind, or her mother's mind, but not Helispeta's or Djetth's, but further argument wouldn't change Djetth's decision.

And she did love his masterful streak when he showed it. So, she smiled sweetly, and looked around the room. Her mother's brothel was nothing like she'd expected. Nothing was what she'd expected.

Who ever would have imagined a bed in a white-and gold-framed, elegantly curtained alcove? It was a very restful-looking bed. Everyone assumed she and Djetth would share it. A lot of people took a lot for granted, including Djetth.

Sitting primly on their bed, Marsh watched him admire his newly smooth-shaven arms and chest in front of a long mirror in which she could see her own seated reflection. She was wearing a secondhand, black dress, borrowed, with Tarrant-Arragon's permission, from Djinni-vera, who was too pregnant to wear it.

Black didn't suit her.

Marsh tried very hard not to think of Djinni-vera's hand-downs and cast-offs. She threw out her chin and steeled herself not to weep at her shorn explosion of white hair, and how much she looked like the handsome youth Django-Ra must once have been.

"What are you thinking?" Djetth asked huskily.

"That you are right. That Django would recognize me," she lied. "Most of all"—she stood and pinched up her long skirts in a parody of a curtsey—"that I've his eyes, his legs, his hair. I have his power to zap those who annoy me."

She held in her stomach, held out her arms, letting her skirts fly out, and twirled. "But despite that, I'm not at all bad-looking. I love being 'Marsh.' "

Djetth caught her around the waist in both arms, crushed her to his perfumed, padded chest and swung her in circles until her feet flew out behind her.

"You are beautiful, my Marsh. Also brave, and smart, and clever, and funny. I'd be honored, proud, and immensely happy to have you as my Mate."

Was that a Mating proposal? It didn't sound like he was asking but . . . ah, well, if he took *that* for granted . . . it was absolutely fine with her.

Marsh linked her arms around his neck. "I never want to go back to Tigron. Can you promise me that?"

Djetth said nothing. He seemed to be staring over the top of her head into the distance.

"I'm not comfortable here, in the perma-dark, either. Sometimes I think I'll never fit in anywhere!" She spoke in a rush to cover her embarrassment and dismay at his silence.

She turned her head, and saw what had caught Djetth's attention. From the doorway, a silent figure in a wheelchair was watching. Marsh glanced again, then quickly looked away.

"Hey, Mother," Djetth called. "Come on in. You've seen me dressed worse! I'm relatively decent for this caper."

Marsh had been told that everyone called "Madam Tarra" "Mother." Apparently, it was the correct protocol for addressing a psychic.

She didn't understand her inner resentment that everyone except her called her mother "Mother." She didn't understand why it hurt so much that her own mother hadn't been a mother to her, but was a mother to prostitutes, spies, fugitives, and sexual deviants.

"I once—" Djetth suddenly seemed to think better of whatever he'd been about to say, and started to pluck at his blue-rinsed wig. "I say, is this wig on straight?"

"You once what?"

"He once dressed up like a dominatrix," Madam Tarra interjected from the doorway. "Complete with a black leather corset, hooded cape, and a utility belt from which he hung outrageous sex toys."

Her severe expression challenged Marsh on many levels, and Marsh had no idea how to respond appropriately.

She wanted to look at Djetth and visualize him with "sex toys," but she was afraid that it would be rude to look away when her hostess was speaking.

It would be equally impolite to stare. She wanted to study this runaway mother of hers, to see whether they looked alike, whether her mother had the pale blue eyes, wild hair, and long, slender legs that Marsh secretly dreaded she'd inherited from Django-Ra.

Of course, she couldn't look at her mother's legs.

Marsh had never met anyone who couldn't walk before, except for Feya, who didn't count because her disability was temporary.

It was disorienting to meet senior Royal females whom she'd been told were dead. For forty-six gestates she'd believed that she had no living female relatives apart from her sister, Electra-Djerroldina.

Then, less than a gestate ago, Marsh had learned that she'd been lied to all her life. First Tarrant-Arragon brought home a distant cousin, Djinni-vera. Now, it seemed that the Palace had lied not only about her mother's death, but also about that of her grandfather Djohn-Kronos's second Empress, Helispeta. Not that Helispeta mattered, except as living proof of another anomaly on the Imperial Genealogical Diagram*. How inaccurate was the official lineage?

"Manners, Marsh," Djetth growled, and jerked his head slightly in the direction of the doorway.

"Oh!" Marsh turned to the seated figure. "Oh, yes, do, please, come and join us."

Something more seemed to be expected. But what? Surely she wasn't expected to bow to her mother, the brothel-keeper? Marsh felt awkward, and at a disadvantage.

"Do you need . . . ? I mean, would you like some help with your chair?" she asked hesitantly.

"Yes, please. Thank you for offering," her mother said in a pleasant, aristocratic voice. "I manage very well most of the time, but this is not one of the rooms that I ever thought to have adapted for my needs."

What had I expected? Horrible, vulgar diction? Cursing? A speech impediment? People with injured legs don't necessarily drool, tremble, suffer incontinence, or think any less clearly than people with undamaged legs.

Marsh crossed the room. It felt like one of the longest walks of her life.

"Never be afraid to ask a person with a disability what happened," said Mother as if she understood completely. "Usually, people like to be asked, as long as you speak to the person in the chair, not whoever is accompanying them."

Marsh didn't know what to say. It seemed only polite, since her mother was speaking, to bend down so their faces were on a level.

"You see, Martia-Djulia, whatever you ask, I have the power to refuse to answer. As it happens, I do refuse to discuss my injuries, and I do not explain why I favor this antiquated chair instead of—for instance—bionic legs."

Mother smiled. Marsh smiled back.

"I've refused to give the answers certain males expect,

too," Marsh said with a wry smile, and a meaningful glance at Djetth.

"So I have heard. I hope you will tell me all about it, later. My dear, I heard Djetthro-Jason call you 'Marsh.' It seems an unusual name. Do you like it?"

Marsh nodded. *I think of myself as Marsh, now. Every time Djetth calls me Marsh, we both think of him sinking into me.*

"May I call you Marsh? Or is it a private name? Oh, what is Djetthro-Jason doing? Shall we intervene before he makes himself look inappropriate? Push me slowly, please."

The resident "girls" had given Djetth their own makeup, and he'd applied flesh-colored paste to his cheeks, gold powder to his eyelids, and had started to smear exotic black eyeliner under his lashes.

Marsh snatched it away from him.

"As I understand the plot, Djetth, you're supposed to look like a large, but otherwise unremarkable elderly lady of great sensibility and stupidity. You are not supposed to draw attention to yourself. Your task is to make Django-Ra curious about one particular hand of cards."

"Martia-Djulia is right," Mother said unexpectedly. "Djetthro-Jason, let me ask you something. I am thinking of having my lips tattooed. What do you think of the idea?"

Djetth's hastily assembled evening dress billowed as he squatted down in front of Mother's wheelchair.

"May I touch?" he murmured. "Or will you zap me with a static shock for invading your space?"

"You may," she said.

Djetth rested his bent arms on the armrests on either side of Mother's arms, and stared at her mouth.

"For you, it's a terrible idea. You'd be sorry before the swelling went down. Do you realize that you'd have the same color all the time? Even if you just had the outline done, nine days out of ten the outline wouldn't match."

How well Djetth knew her mother. How kind he was to her. Marsh found that she was not dreading the night ahead, getting to know her Mother, while Helispeta and Djetth went off to the Casino Imperial to carry out their "Sting."

Chapter Twenty-six

Casino Imperial, The Pleasure Moon of Eurydyce

Prince Django-Ra resented being "Dummy." Later, if he had nothing more interesting to do, he might just kill his slack-wit partner for her presumption in overbidding.

"Six Spades was there," he commented sourly as he laid down his cards.

"Thank you, partner," his partner said, as if he had bid perfectly and there were no surprises in his hand.

"Aaaargh!" someone gurgled.

Spectators were not permitted to comment. Django-Ra glanced up in annoyance at the broad-shouldered giantess behind his partner's strange, wheeled chair.

"It's a Sign!" the blue-haired monstrosity croaked, holding her large hands to her spackled cheeks.

"Hush, my dear," his partner admonished her servant and placed her own fan of cards face down. "I beg your pardon, partner. One would have to be very superstitious to believe that your cards indicate anything sinister."

"Indeed?" Django-Ra frowned slightly.

"He's marked for Death!" the irrepressible giantess

breathed, too quietly for the tournament adjudicators to hear. Only Great Djinn ears could have heard her.

Narrowing his eyes, Django-Ra tried to probe her mind. Incredibly, she was mentally dying her pudenda blue, one crinkly hair at a time!

It would have been quicker to read his partner's mind, but he had already tried that without success during an earlier hand.

"What does the twittering fool see? Do you know?"

"Yes, I know. There's nothing in it." His partner was still exercising Declarer's right to examine the Dummy hand. Her restraint was too provoking.

"Tell me," he hissed.

"Well, my dear," she began reluctantly. "The Ace of Spades is the card maker's signature card. The fact that it is also considered the Death card is neither here nor there."

"Is that all?" Django-Ra purred, relieved.

"Not quite," she said. "You do have the Suicide King. You see? The King of Hearts. He appears to be thrusting his own sword into his ear. It's quite ridiculous. Moreover, the Suicide King is never read as suicidal."

Django-Ra raised a questioning eyebrow.

"Also, you have the King of Spades—the treacherous and powerful male, sometimes thought of as a warrior, sometimes as an intellectual. So much depends on whether or not one is disposed to like lawyers."

"I don't." Django-Ra thought of Tarrant-Arragon, who was a spoilsport. "Is there more?"

"Some fanciful reader might say it is a pity you have the Jack of Spades. He is generally considered . . . oh, what is the term . . . a hit man; a mercenary; a hired killer. It is all in fun, of course. Strictly entertainment."

The white hairs rose on his wrists, at the back of his neck, and no doubt on his balls, too. This nicely aged female might be dangerous, though she did not know it.

"I am vastly diverted. Dare I ask . . . ?"

"You strike me as too intelligent a male to worry about the Queen of Hearts." She tapped the next card in his long suit. "Now, the ten of Spades *is* an unlucky card. Nobody has a good thing to say about it. It means violent death. Oh, not necessarily your own, dear."

She smiled condescendingly at him. "In a hand of bridge every fourth hand is dealt the ten of Spades. I have yet to see a duplicate bridge player either be literally stabbed in the back at the table or be led away from it in chains. Metaphorically . . . well, that would be another story."

"Really?" While he had never yet stabbed an incompetent bridge partner in the back, a few unworthy players had suffered a Djinncraft-induced vital organ attack.

He could always kill this too-perceptive female . . . but he did so like trophies, and they were doing rather well. He'd been lucky in the random draw for partners, but if his partner were to die before the tournament ended he could not take home the bridge trophy.

After he'd won, he'd find out where she lived, and he'd take his pussy scalping knife.

"Of course," his partner was saying, "you do have the nine of Spades. Also the four."

"That is bad?" *That is why I bid Spades!*

"It all depends if Spades are trumps, doesn't it? Some readers find the nine of Spades rather ominous, and since you also have the nine of Clubs—two of a kind, and both black—the nine of Spades' malign potency might be doubled."

"I had two Kings," Django-Ra pointed out.

Enjoying the thought of his own malign potency, he reached into the deep sleeve of his robes and stroked his souvenir, which had the striking addition of four soft tufts of Petri-Shah's black pussy-feathers.

"Yes, dear. I wasn't going to tell you that. The second King magnifies the nastiness of the first."

"Hmmm. I have two eights. Also two fives."

"So you do, dear, but you shouldn't worry about the eights. Eights and Aces are considered a Dead Man's Hand. I drew such a hand recently. Two Aces. Three eights. Much more deathly than your hand. As you see, I live."

Ahhh, but for how much longer?

"Deathly?" he questioned. "An interesting adjective. Was there some reason you chose that word?"

"You expected me to say 'deadly,' no doubt?"

"Why, yes, I did." Django-Ra smiled, and smiled, but there was something about her diction. . . . She'd thrown him off the scent by using contractions, sprinkling her sentences with genial and low-class "Well-my-dears" and "Why-this-or-thats," and dropping the Imperial Pronoun.

Her Island School accent betrayed her to him. After so many, many gestates this exiled Princess in the wheeled chair had learned to mind-shield, and she had grown careless.

Had she had the temerity to forget Django-Ra? He would take great pleasure in reminding her.

"Oh, no, my dear," she was saying, blithely unaware that he had seen through her disguise. "Your cards say that you are definitely a great deal more deadly than I am. You see, dear, your hand is The Murderer's Hand."

Django-Ra smiled at the irony. *Ahhh, Tarragonia-Marietta. You do not know how right you are!*

Chapter Twenty-seven

Pleasure Palace, Pleasure Moon of Eurydyce

"Djetthro-Jason, I am about to risk my life to uncover a secret. If my suspicions are correct, Django-Ra will try to silence me."

This was not a conversation Djetth wanted to have, so he responded flippantly. "And, if you're dead, Grand-mama Helispeta, you'll have left it too late to tell me what you correctly suspected."

"I do not find it an amusing dilemma, Djetthro-Jason. If I am mistaken, I shall have done you a great wrong by raising hopes you have no right to cherish."

"Sorry, Grandmama. I'm confused. I thought you'd asked the entire family here to watch you prove that Django-Ra is a murderer, and establish why he sent assassins to kill Marsh," Djetth said penitently.

Helispeta sat bolt upright on the edge of her low, made-up, futon-style bed.

"I see you are wearing the Rings, Djetthro-Jason."

Djetth stretched out the beRinged fingers of his right

hand, and studied them. "Is your secret about whether or not I have a Right to wear them, Grandmama?"

Helispeta glanced sharply at him.

"I shall tell you a story, Djetthro-Jason. You will please remember that it is pure extrapolation, and may not be the truth—"

"Unless Django tries to kill you," Djetth interrupted. He wasn't joking anymore. His right hand curled into a fist. "Tries! Trust me, he won't succeed, Grandmama."

Helispeta arched a thin eyebrow. "You may hit him, but I forbid you to use your laser Ring in this House. The sight, the smell, would be too much for Tarragonia-Marietta. This entire business has made her . . . nervous."

That's an understatement! Djetth thought. 'Rhett, who'd acquitted himself pretty responsibly since discovering what the old ladies were up to, had confided that Tarra's hands had been trembling ever since she'd heard that Django-Ra was on the planet for the bridge tournament. There was no way she could carry off a Reading.

"Moreover," Helispeta was saying, "Django-Ra would not keep his fiery death tidily to himself. He would spread the flames." She gave him a thin smile. "Tarra keeps a blaster clamped to the underside of her fortune-telling table. I am quite capable of pulling a trigger in my own defense."

"Fire away, then, Grandmama!" Grinning at his pun, Djetth lowered himself to the floor and leaned against the futon's mattress.

"Once upon a time, my dear, there was an Emperor. This Emperor, for reasons unknown to anyone, perhaps not even to himself, could not control his sexual appetite."

"Your ex, Djohn-Kronos!" Djetth guessed.

"No, not Djohn-Kronos. The villain was the father of Djohn-Kronos, Deveron-Vitan and Django-Ra—your great-grandfather Djerrold-Ramses.* One dark and evil day, he caught the first fertile scent of a young Princess, who should have been sequestered on the Island School for Princesses, but who was not. Then, home came mature and hot-tempered Tiger Prince, Djohn-Kronos—"

"And Djohn-Kronos killed his father, and had the rut-rage with her, too." Djetth had heard this tragic and disgusting story many times. Now that he'd experienced the rut-rage himself, he could empathize with Djohn-Kronos's villainy.

"I do not think Djohn-Kronos touched her, dear. The rut-rage would have been brief, as it was the first time she came into season. Djohn-Kronos crowned himself, took the pregnant Princess as his Mate, and allowed All the Worlds to assume that his bastard half-brothers, Djerrold-Vulcan and Djethren-Djove, were his own sons."

"But they were not his? That's damned heroic." Djetth wanted to know more about this new side to his grandfather. The constitutional implications could wait.

"About the rut-rage?" He turned as he asked, "Surely Djohn-Kronos *could* have had it twice. Either Djerrold-Ramses had it with multiple partners, or Djohn-Kronos did."

For reasons Djetth didn't understand, he wanted it to be Djohn-Kronos who'd had the rut-rage with different Princesses.

"*This* is sheer, irresponsible speculation," Grandmama cautioned, "but, have you seen the statue of Djerrold-Ramses in the Imperial Portrait Gallery? His face was always shown damaged. Possibly when his original wound healed, he grew more saturniid glands than normal."

"Like frogs with seven legs?" Djetth pinched the bridge of his nose, and wondered how deep his old, deep whip scar had been before Tarrant-Arragon's surgeons erased it.

Why not?

"What I don't see is how Django-Ra plays into all this, Grandmama. Of course, if Django knew, I'll bet he was wild that his illegitimate half-brother Djerrold-Vulcan should take precedence over himself. Django was older, and legitimate, so he should have been Emperor when Djohn-Kronos died!"

"Not necessarily," Grandmama said with an enigmatic smile. "However, *if* he knew, Django-Ra may have felt he was entitled to everything that Djerrold-Vulcan had. It would shed new light on why Django-Ra attacked Djerrold-Vulcan's Empress, Tarragonia-Marietta. Why he did something so vicious, foolhardy, and self-destructive is hard to explain otherwise. Martia-Djulia was the result—"

Is this about Marsh? Djetth's emotions did a cartwheel. *If Grandmama's building up to the liability-wife scenario, she's wasting her breath.*

"Marsh has guessed that she's Django's daughter. It makes no difference," Djetth said shortly.

"We are not here to discuss Martia-Djulia today," Grandmama agreed. "We have digressed, Djetthro-Jason. There is only one secret which I am not prepared to die without divulging. You have always known that Djohn-Kronos impregnated me before I left him. Your father was Djohn-Kronos's son. You are the Emperor Djohn-Kronos's grandson."

"I know that."

"What you do not realize is that you may be Djohn-Kronos's *only* grandson . . . the only son of his *only* son. If this is the case, you, Djetthro-Jason would be the rightful Emperor."

"I see," Djetth murmured. "At least, I think I do. And you are telling me this now because . . . ?"

"Firstly, because I feel it my duty to inform you that you may be the rightful Emperor." Helispeta spoke as if goaded by his slow-wittedness.

"Secondly, because I may not have another opportunity to tell you so, if it turns out to be the truth.

"Thirdly, because I want you to watch Django-Ra

very carefully, and judge for yourself whether or not he confirms that you are the rightful Emperor. . . .

"And finally because, if you want your birthright, you should be prepared to act quickly."

Djetth stared at Helispeta.

"Grandmama, why should I act quickly? The Communicating Worlds have been deceived for seventy years."

"It is a matter of timing, my dear. There may never again be such a convenient opportunity for a bloodless coup, if you want one. Tarrant-Arragon will be here, suspecting nothing. He will be outnumbered by you, the Saurian Dragon, also your cousins and half-brothers. I imagine five Great Djinn can overpower one."

"So, it's to be a double sting, Grandmama? Django-Ra is to spill his guts, and Tarrant-Arragon will be at my mercy . . . regardless of what Django reveals?"

"It is a decision only you can make," Grandmama said grandly. "I do not intend to influence you either way."

Chapter Twenty-eight

Tarra's Pleasure Palace, Pleasure Moon of Eurydyce
Two days later

"Are you here to learn your fortune in love, my son?"

Marsh heard Helispeta give Madam Tarra's invariable greeting to an unknown client, and knew that Django-Ra had walked into the trap.

"One always asks that . . ." Helispeta added apologetically. "And One also asks armed querants to disarm."

Django swore.

Nervous, surprised, and wildly excited that he'd come, Marsh looked around to be sure that the secret "Jury" was in place and well hidden behind hollow half-statues of strange gods, false walls, see-through portraits and mirrors, and deeply folded, staggered curtains that looked continuous, but weren't.

Djetth stood nearby, as did 'Rhett. Unseen, and covering the other side were their twin cousins, Devoron and Deverill. Tarrant-Arragon's man, Grievous, lurked by the entrance, watching through the cut-out eyes of a sarcophagus-like bas relief whose erect phallus housed a metal detector.

"We have metal detectors," Helispeta hinted calmly. She could see Django-Ra through hidden lenses and decorative fish-eye mirrors. "Such an unfortunate necessity."

Presumably, Django concluded that he could not enter without disarming. He could be heard swearing as he slammed his weapons into convenient slots.

"A sword stick, two throwing stars, a bladed bolus . . ." 'Rhett—watching a scanner—took whispered inventory. ". . . A Scythian scalping knife! The bloody bastard!"

Marsh heard Tarra draw in a shuddering breath, and saw that Tarra had turned the color of sea-bleached driftwood, and was twisting a softly scented cloth around her trembling fingers.

"One of my girls, Petri-Shah, was tortured and killed by a Scythian," Tarra gasped.

Marsh assumed there was more to it. Everyone agreed that Django would be most likely to say something damaging if he wrongly supposed himself alone with a victim, but the real Tarra could never have carried off either the "Sting" or the "Inquiries."

At last, Marsh understood why Helispeta had taken Tarra's place at the Casino and as the fortune-teller in a wheelchair behind the velvet-draped, candle-lit table.

"Ironic, isn't it?" Djetth whispered, "Django comes looking for love, armed to the teeth."

"Is that why he thinks he's here?" Marsh retorted.

In the deceptively cozy inner room, Helispeta waved a languid, welcoming hand to a worn, green velvet chair—spiked with the truth drug, Loquacity—and Django-Ra flung himself into an insolent, sprawling pose.

As she reached for the pre-selected Tarot deck, she felt safe knowing that at least four Great Djinn males were hidden close by, and also that Django-Ra's shark-like Djinn senses must be confused.

Her own senses were at once oppressed, overloaded, and exhilarated by the sights—such as the displays of sex-play paraphernalia and love charms—by the whisper-masking sounds, and especially by the aromas from scented candles, and drying bundles of aphrodisiacal herbs.

"You are troubled, my son?" She made the time-honored preamble sound like an observation.

"Am I?" Django-Ra smirked.

"Very!" With the backs of her fingers, Helispeta pushed the oversized deck towards him. "Be warned, the Tarot does not give direct answers or predict specific events, such as death, or paternity. As you shuffle, ask what is on your mind and the Tarot will point your way."

"Perhaps," Django-Ra purred, "I shall ask what lies in the near future for Tarragonia-Marietta and myself."

"That seems a strange question."

"Not really." With an inscrutable smile, Django picked up the deck. His long, thin fingers were supple and strong. He shuffled expertly.

"When you are ready, you may spread the cards face down in a fan shape on the table," she said.

Django-Ra put them down in the manner of a flamboyant, stand-up piano player rippling the keyboard. Candles' flames bent and tossed. One went out. The parlor got darker.

Someone should have spanked you, Django-Ra.

Fleetingly, Helispeta wondered what Palace life might have been like for Django-Ra as a boy at the dubious mercy of his sexually sophisticated, older half-brothers.

"Without letting me see them, choose any ten cards, and stack them."

He complied, sneering.

"Thank you." She reached across the table and picked up his stack of ten cards. "I shall now lay out your

Spread. The first card you choose is the most important. It is sometimes called the Covering card."

Dealing from the bottom, she put the first card that he had selected into the center of the table.

"Covering . . . ?" He raised an eyebrow.

"The Covering card gets Crossed." Ignoring his stud-farm sense of humor, she laid the second card across the first.

"Crossed as in 'thwarted'?" Django-Ra asked.

"Crossed as in another card lies on top of it."

"I prefer to be on top," he remarked.

"Really?" Helispeta drawled.

"How could you forget, my dear *Tarra?*"

Marsh took one of her mother's trembling hands in both her own.

"Did he just imply that you and he . . . ?" Marsh didn't know how to finish her question. It raised too many others. *How? When? Was this before—or after—your legs were damaged? Is Django the reason that you read brothel patrons' fortunes before letting them near the "girls"?*

Tarra gave a slight nod, and a warning hand squeeze.

"Watch. Hell will place the next four cards in a cross around the two crossed cards," Tarra said in the hushed tones of a commentator. "Then, to her own right, she will deal a vertical 'Tower' of the remaining four cards."

Marsh glanced at Django, watching Helispeta.

"If Django-Ra has not had his Tarot read before, he may not know how much depends on the order in which he chooses and stacks the cards," Tarra continued.

"Let's see what my Covering card is!" Django snatched up the card, turned it over, glanced at it, then threw it down on the table in disgust. "A pregnant female?"

"He's made a mistake!" Tarra whispered. "He turned his Covering card around. It was Reversed. Now it isn't."

"Does that matter?" Marsh mouthed back.

"Yes, indeed. Every card has opposite meanings. A bright side and a dark side . . ."

"The Imperatrix. . . . Right way up. How strange!"

"Did Grandmama just imply something about Django's sexuality?" Marsh heard Djetth mutter to 'Rhett.

"She implied at least three very different things. Watch his face," 'Rhett rasped. "She'll imply everything to see what gets a reaction."

"It does not mean what you seem to infer, dear. The Imperatrix does not represent your physical self. The Covering card represents where you are now."

"Hah! In the presence of an Empress," Django said. "But I doubt you'd stand up to defend me if I were ever brought to trial for having my way with you . . ."

How offensive! Marsh's blood seethed with indignation.

". . . would you, Tarragonia-Marietta?"

Was that thrust deep enough to hurt, my dear?

Smiling to have shocked her, Django-Ra reached into his sleeve pocket and put his trophy on the table.

"What makes you think that I am she?" Her voice shook.

If not for the distracting sizzle of incense burners, the splash of water somewhere, the rustle of her garments as she trembled, he'd have heard her heartbeat. Though the scent was faint, he could smell female fear.

"Making the connection was hardly a challenge," Django-Ra drawled. "Madam Tarra is Tarragonia-Marietta? The alias does not greatly stretch the imagination. That you run a houseful of whores . . . that I do find interesting."

"If you think I might have once been Tarragonia-Marietta, why did you come here?" Her voice was less faint. She'd recovered her composure, for now. This game was highly arousing.

"Curiosity." He shrugged. "To see if you are as good as everyone says. For old times' sake."

Helispeta kept up her mind-shields.

She had expected that Django-Ra would mistake her for Madam Tarra, the only female on the Pleasure Moon in a wheelchair, especially after the "impromptu" card reading at the bridge tournament. She had not foreseen that he would be so quick to identify "Tarra" as "Tarragonia-Marietta."

"Soooo," Django-Ra purred. "What does my most important card, my thoroughly impregnated Empress, mean to me?"

Helispeta shrugged. "The Imperatrix is good," she said truthfully. "Her positive side brings fertility and love."

"But wasn't it originally Reversed?" Marsh whispered to her mother. "She should be telling him what the negative side brings."

"If he is misled, he brought it on himself," Tarra retorted. "Look. Hell is about to read his Crossing card."

"The Moon! How interesting. Here, together, we have two of the three cards in the maiden-mother-crone triad. That in itself—"

"Mmmmm! I'm positively surrounded by females."

"That does *not* mean they like you!"

Marsh was immensely pleased by Helispeta's retort.

"How delightfully stimulating," Django-Ra drawled.

"Bastard!" growled Djetth, who could name more than one female whom Django had raped. No doubt if Tarrant-Arragon and Ala'Aster-Djalet had bothered to turn up, they'd have known of other victims, too.

Djetth glanced at the beaded entry. There was no sign of either of the Worlds' Leaders. It was a pity. The presence of either The Terror of the Dodecahedrons or of The Saurian Dragon would give legitimacy to their scheme.

On the other hand, if Tarrant-Arragon didn't turn up, the possibility of a coup became a moot point.

"Your Crossing card indicates a situation that leads to conflict," Grandmama Helispeta was saying. "An older woman may be trouble for you . . ."

"You won't give me trouble, will you, my dear?" Django jeered, cocking his head like an albino crow trying to decide which eye to peck out first.

". . . Or you might be entering a time of uncertainty, or change which you may not like."

"He's frowning. It looks like we guessed correctly. Django does not like change," 'Rhett observed quietly. "Still, not liking change isn't a motive for murder. Grandmama has to find a link to something that changed recently."

A hell of a lot has changed!

Djetth rubbed his left forefinger across the three Rings of Imperial Authority on his right hand. In theory, he'd as much Right to kill Django as Tarrant-Arragon did. More.

'Rhett was watching him. Djetth pretended it was his knuckles he was planning to use.

"He won't like the change I've got in mind," he said.

"What mystifies me," Helispeta continued, "is the fact that these two particular cards have come together."

"It doesn't particularly mystify me," Django-Ra taunted her. He smiled, and buried his nose in the thistle-shaped cat's paw, or whatever his lucky charm might be.

"The Empress crossed by The Moon means quite literarily a birth obscured by secrets."

Django-Ra leered knowingly.

"Do you understand that?" she asked.

"Don't you?"

"I am not sure that I do," Helispeta replied frankly. She made a shrugging gesture with her hands. "I sense this is . . . darker than an illegitimate child."

Django's grin collapsed. "Even if the illegitimate child is a Princess?" He sounded anxious, if not defensive.

Helispeta took a chance. "This is an older issue than Martia-Djulia."

You're dead, his cold look implied.

Helispeta hoped that the Jury of Swords had seen the murderous look Django-Ra gave her. There must indeed be an older, darker secret. He would not so easily have conceded that he knew he was Martia-Djulia's sire if he hadn't been focused on withholding a more scandalous secret.

"I might be wrong." Helispeta pretended to be confused. "Only males inherit . . . Even if Djerrold Vulcan were to find out that Martia-Djulia is not his get, I cannot imagine her paternity could be significant. No, she is not the genealogical secret."

Django-Ra said nothing. Helispeta decided not to push her luck just yet.

"Does that mean Django is my father?" Marsh whispered.

Tarra lowered her eyes and pressed her spice-fragrant cloth to her trembling lips.

How could he mistake Helispeta for Tarra?

Yes, they were aunt and niece. They shared tricks of expression. Their bone structure was similar, and thanks to a life in Earth's lesser gravity, Helispeta's skin tone was better than Tarra's, though Tarra must be forty gestates younger.

Either Django had raped Tarra but never noticed that her eyes were a cold-sea gray, or perhaps his pale blue eyes were poor-sighted . . . like his daughter's.

". . . To your Crowning card," Helispeta said.

Django's indrawn breath hissed over his bared teeth.

"Crowning hit a nerve," Djetth commented.

"Not an Imperial crown, dear. 'Crowning' refers to the card's position, to the aura surrounding you, or what is hanging over your head. And, how interesting! Look, you chose the Page of Cups."

"It's the love messenger," Tarra explained in a low, emotional undertone. "Usually shown as a boyish girl or a girlish boy carrying a loving cup. Here's her chance to ask about Petri-Shah."

"Have you any idea why a love messenger might be over your head?" Helispeta sounded politely incredulous.

"Presumably there is a prostitute in a room above us?" Django's voice oozed contempt.

"Ah, well. Not every card will be subtle." Helispeta's laugh sounded forced. "The fourth card, now . . ."

"Is something the matter?" Marsh asked, noticing Tarra's pursed lips.

"She didn't tell him that the Page of Cups also refers to quicksands, quagmires, marshes, traps, and misleading appearances. Also untimely death."

". . . the fourth *position* pertains to your drive—"

"My sex drive?" Django-Ra crowed.

"Not usually. More likely your unconscious motivation, your ambition. And . . . how ironic. The card is Justice, Reversed. Something out of balance is about to be restor—"

"Hah! My Justice card is upside down." Django interrupted Helispeta with a shout of laughter. "Might it mean that my goal in life is to pervert Justice?"

"His joke is hardly damning," Djetth growled.

"Au contraire," 'Rhett said. "Our duty as Jury is also to look for remorse, for reasonable doubt, for any sign that Django shouldn't be held accountable for the evil he's done. Django's obvious amusement shows he's unrepentant. He thinks he'll always get away with anything."

"Then, haven't we heard enough?" Djetth growled.

"Not yet. She's got six more cards. Give Grandmama a chance to get to the truth."

"My dear, do you feel very strongly that you have been cheated?"

This is it! Djetth's stomach took a dive. Grandmama had warned him she'd find a way to ask Django about this. This was the part of the interrogation that could change his life.

"Cheated of what?" Django drew out each word.

Fists clenched, Djetth watched Grandmama Helispeta splay her fingers on Justice With Leashed, Blindfolded, And Aroused Dragons, and close her eyes.

"Justice Reversed tells me—this is very unusual—the cards suggest that you feel you should be Emperor."

"How could that be?" Django replied with convincing calm, giving nothing away.

"A more interesting question would be, did you know it? And if you did, why did you never claim the throne?"

"Hmmm," 'Rhett whispered to Djetth. "Grandmama is really fishing."

"That is an interesting question," Django conceded. "I cannot answer it, of course."

"Of course not." Helispeta shook her head as if to clear it of wraiths. "What a strange notion."

What a fart in a bottle! Djetth thought, then wondered why he felt frustrated and furious.

"That was revealing," 'Rhett whispered, leaning close. "A bombshell! I wonder what she'll ask next!"

Djetth threw him a look.

"I'm serious. Djetth, if someone told you out of the blue that you should be Emperor, would you say, 'No comment'?"

Marsh sensed an undercurrent—a tension—between Djetth and 'Rhett. She'd noticed the way 'Rhett watched Djetth, eyed his Rings, and commented on questions raised by Helispeta that didn't seem to have anything to do with whether or not it was Django who had sent assassins to kill Djetth on Freighter Island.

What had long-ago pregnancies and illegitimate births to do with anything? Why was her paternity an issue? Unless . . . as a bastard—Django's bastard—she was unfit to be Djetth's Mate. Was that the real reason she hadn't been included in anything important?

Two dayless nights ago, Djetth had almost made a commitment, but she'd set a condition. She hadn't meant to. But perhaps she'd made him feel that he had to choose between her and Tigron.

Miserably she registered that Helispeta was quizzing Django about his powers—his fifth card was something to do with Strength. Everyone else seemed fascinated.

She thought there was a bulge in the drapes near the door that had not been there before, but it could have been a draft.

"Beware of a threat to your future from someone who has been denying, or not using, a certain gift," Helispeta was saying.

Peripherally, Marsh saw Djetth smiling at her. 'Rhett was looking at Djetth's Rings again.

"I believe that threat has been eliminated," Django drawled, and grinned.

"He thinks you're dead," 'Rhett whispered to Djetth. "That might be his most incriminating remark yet."

"Did Helispeta exchange his cards for these?" Marsh couldn't contain her astonishment.

"Hell rigged the playing cards for The Murderer's Hand. One does not manipulate the Tarot," Tarra chided, sounding shocked. "One must be fair! Django-Ra is on trial for his life, though he doesn't know it."

"Seventh," Helispeta touched the innocuous backside of the card closest to her, at the bottom of the "Tower" of the remaining four cards. "Where you will soon find yourself."

With a flourish, she turned it over.

"Oh, my dear! The Tower itself!" Helispeta allowed herself to laugh. "I apologize. I was thinking of The Tower of London. Indeed, this is a white tower. The White Tower was where all Royals were imprisoned prior to execution for treason."

The Saurian Tarot Tower was a pornographic joke. The tower was what in some parts of Earth would be known as the Royal Lingam.

Its white shaft rose and buried its head in what could have been clouds, or hairy buttocks, or badly plucked pudenda. Lightning flashed around it and in front of it.

Django-Ra stared at it, white-faced. "What does it mean?" he croaked.

"To quote an expression my grandson uses too often," Helispeta said in her crisp, perfect, Court-formal elocution, " 'You are fucked.' "

She turned over the eighth card. "This relates to what others think of you. You have dangerous friends. Ah, yes, the Knight of Swords, and Reversed."

"I have a dangerous family," Django said sulkily.

Despite everything, Helispeta felt a pang of sympathy. "Indeed you do. It must have been hard to survive."

He looked bleakly at her. "It was." His gaze dropped to the Knight of Swords. "So, what does that card mean?"

"Sometimes rapid and violent change. Reversed, it could indicate someone devoted to lies and confusion and deception. Do you keep company with assassins, by any chance? If so, beware. Mercenaries do not make the most loyal of friends. I suppose you would not like to hand them over to the proper authorities before they turn on you?"

* * *

Djetth was shocked. First, to hear his beautifully spoken Grandmama quote him. Secondly, to hear her equate mercenaries with assassins. He'd been a mercenary.

"It's fairly standard to offer a plea bargain," 'Rhett murmured.

"Now we turn to your hopes and fears." Helispeta turned the ninth card. "You fear change!"

"What makes you so sure?" Django snarled.

"You chose the ten of Wands. All Wands portend change . . . violent change, especially the ten. The ten of Wands tells me that you have taken on too much. You have too many enemies."

"Murder is a pretty violent way of bringing about change, wouldn't you say?" 'Rhett quipped. "But after this card, there's only one left, and I'm not sure she's proven anything."

All Wands . . . violent change . . . too many enemies.

Djetth clenched his fists. He'd had his own cards read by Tarra on his many visits to this establishment, as Commander Jason. Tarra had always called him "The King of All Wands." He'd assumed the tag had a bit to do with his love of farming, and a lot to do with his flashy, tattooed "lightning rod."

I have a choice.

The shadows in the inner room seemed darker and more numerous. The flickering scented candles had burned lower. Helispeta turned the last card.

"And, finally, in your Outcome position. . . ."

The back of her hand blocked his view. He could not see what the card was. Slowly, Grandmama Helispeta rested her forearms on the table, and steepled her fingers.

"I'm so sorry, Django-Ra" she said, and she sounded genuine. "I never like to see Wands in the Outcome. All Wands portend fire, and change. It's never good. Wands are potentially inflammatory and dangerous . . ."

Not this Wand! Djetth resolved.

* * *

"You are not Tarragonia-Marietta!" Django snarled.

Marsh wondered how she'd missed Helispeta's mistake. Tarra had grandsons . . . but Henquist and Thorquentin probably did not go around the Palace using Earthisms to inform their victims that they'd been sexually violated.

Was it something in the way Helispeta pronounced Django-Ra's name?

"You!" Django spat the words. "Helispeta!"

Beside Marsh, Tarra began to gag. Tears streamed down her face. Djetth crouched by her chair to help her.

Marsh felt Django's fury flow past her, somehow affecting Tarra. Marsh was on the turbulent edge. Not in his direct line. She hated him so much, she wanted to deflect his evil right back at him.

"She's fine."

"She's not."

"She hasn't finished with the last card. Wait for it."

"He's losing it."

"Look at her hands. She's all right."

Whispers surrounded Marsh. She defaulted to reading the only lips that mattered at this chaotic, frozen moment. Django's.

She is not all right!

Helispeta's steepled fingers seemed fused. She could not move them; could not reach under the table for the blaster. Her mind worked. Her body could not. She had been struck by Djinncraft.

She had never felt anything like it.

She had not planned for this. . . .

Django-Ra had shot to his feet, pale eyes blazing. The raw hatred that he projected was unexpected. Stunning. Quite remarkable, and absolutely terrifying. One was so shocked that One was literally frozen.

With his thin legs wide apart, his hands braced on the table, Django leaned forward close enough to kiss her.

She quite thought he might. If he wanted to do so, she was powerless to stop him. Even if she could Will the blaster under the table to fire, the projectile would fly harmlessly between his legs.

"Only you and I survived," he breathed. Helispeta was not sure that he spoke at all. "Djerrold Vulcan does not count. He never counted."

He shifted his weight subtly to the right. His left hand moved slowly, inexorably towards her throat. His thumb stroked her windpipe, his little finger tickled the nape of her neck.

"You are too good to live. You were right on every count. There's more . . ." he said quite distinctly.

He thought the unthinkable. His thoughts were explicit and he deliberately put them in her mind.

Once upon a time, Helispeta had boasted that she was too old to be shocked. Django-Ra's thoughts showed her how wrong she had been.

The irony was, while he slowly bedjinned her to death, those who should come to help her would be reassured by her outward calm; they would be holding their breaths, eager to hear "more. . . ."

You weren't supposed to be rut-rageous when you came to the Palace for your Mating Ceremony. You only thought of your effect on my big brother. It never occurred to you to think what you'd do to me.

Django-Ra breathed heavily. His hand moved slowly up and down the white column of her neck. It was obscene, and if it had been almost anyone other than Django-Ra it might even have felt erotic.

You cost me my one chance at the rut-rage. All my life, I tried to have it with others. It never worked. I wanted you, and I never had you. For ninety-three gestates I've yearned to have you helpless and in my power.

He used his voice again. "With you dead, I will have survived all my enemies."

His grip tightened.

"I can take you back to Tigron and claim the outstanding reward." His fingers moved agonizingly slowly. Everything was happening slowly. His words sounded distant and drawn out, his small movements seemed exaggerated. Tai Chi shadows stretched . . . drifted.

"I want you to know this, before you pass out. Can you hear me? Is your blood pounding in your ears?" He raised his voice slightly. "I'm not going to risk taking you alive. I shall dishonor you—aaaah."

Hwoooooyyyy! Hah!

What an extraordinary sound . . . Helispeta thought. What an expression on Django-Ra's fa—

Marsh!

Tarra's gagging stopped abruptly.

Djetth looked up, and saw Django hurtling backwards through the air, eyes bulging, sparks fizzing in his shocked white crest of hair, with a large beRinged hand finishing off a classic "Clothesline" at his throat.

Tarrant-Arragon had arrived.

Although he'd heard Marsh's battle cry, it looked as if it had been Tarrant-Arragon who had grabbed Django by the throat, jerked him away from Helispeta, and thrown him bodily across the room.

As that thought penetrated, Django crashed into an upwardly projecting portion of one of the twin stone god statues that symbolically guarded the door, and collapsed out of sight with a muffled triple thump.

Tarrant-Arragon and another tall—but hooded—figure threw themselves upon Django, as if he required further subduing.

"Enough to convict, I think," Tarrant-Arragon's icy voice remarked urbanely.

"Sufficient to convict, pass sentence, and execute summarily," Ala'Aster-Djalet's voice agreed in tones of outrage and disgust. "Djarrhett, your grandmother."

As far as Djetth could see, the order was unnecessary.

'Rhett already was squatting beside Helispeta, his dark head pressing her regal gray wig askew, offering her a glass of something restorative.

Marsh was a step ahead of him, and trembling violently. Djetth moved closer, stood behind her, and folded his arms across her thudding chest.

Tarrant-Arragon and The Saurian Dragon. Djetth took in the spectacle at the unlit end of the room. Perhaps they were not exactly sitting side by side on Django, but they were like two grim-robed Justices on a bench.

The day was not going according to Helispeta's plan.

'Rhett could imagine that Grandmama Helispeta was silently berating herself for getting too caught up in her hunt, and forgetting to keep her hands off the table!

He was quite sure that—whatever she said about the difference between justice and vengeance—she'd intended to shoot Django-Ra in justifiable self-defense, sparing her grandchildren the unpleasant uncertainty of execution squad duty.

"Is Django-Ra dead?" Helispeta croaked.

"Ahhh . . . do you want him to be dead?" Tarrant-Arragon drawled. "I could very easily arrange it."

"Grandmama, permit me to introduce Tarrant-Arragon," 'Rhett murmured. "Tarrant-Arragon, may I make known to you The Empress Helispeta?"

"Your Imperial Majesty," Tarrant-Arragon said, inclining his head in greeting. "I have my knee on Django-Ra's neck. You must pardon my discourtesy in not rising."

"Thank you, Tarrant-Arragon," Helispeta said. "I am too profoundly . . . moved." Her voice broke.

Tarrant-Arragon probably didn't know it, but when he said "*Ahhh*" it was a preface to a lie, or at least to some economy with the truth.

Django-Ra was almost certainly dead already.

There was nothing at all wrong with 'Rhett's eyesight. He'd seen Ala'Aster-Djalet check Django-Ra's wrist for a pulse, and the meaningful exchange of glances between Ala'Aster-Djalet and Tarrant-Arragon.

The only question in 'Rhett's mind was whether Martia-Djulia or Tarrant-Arragon had done it.

Of course, it would be politically incorrect for Martia-Djulia to be allowed to think she'd killed a senior Tiger Prince. She was altogether too scandalous as it was.

Grandmama Helispeta cleared her throat. "There are nine of us. We should all have a stab at the bastard. No one should know who dealt the death blow."

One had to admire the game old bird.

"You think so, Your Majesty? Nine?" Tarrant-Arragon's supercilious voice queried. "Is that not a touch, ahh, excessive?"

'Rhett could appreciate Tarrant-Arragon's dilemma. If nine witnesses approached, they'd see that Django-Ra's head was caved in where it had hit the statue's upright member, and his neck was twisted, broken, and crushed for good measure.

"It would be simpler and safer if I do it, you know. I have the clear Right, and unlike some of you, no conflicts of interest." Tarrant-Arragon spoke like a master negotiator, looking to offer a compromise.

"However, I think three of us can stab him quite sufficiently. I represent the Empire. The Saurian Dragon represents the Free Worlds. And Djetth, would you mind . . . ?"

'Rhett noticed His High and Mightiness's slight smile as his gaze fell on Djetth and Martia-Djulia, who were standing together like lovers.

Tarrant-Arragon used his right hand to gesture, showing anyone who was looking that all three Rings were on His Imperial Highness's hand.

"Djetth has Rings, so technically has an equal right to dispatch Django-Ra if he feels like it. Moreover, Djetth may have local jurisdiction very soon."

'Rhett sensed the tension, heard hearts beat harder, and air being sucked in through gritted teeth.

"Grievous," Tarrant-Arragon continued. "Kindly collect Django-Ra's weapons from the foyer, and while you're out there, inform Storm Master Xirxex outside that We will want a few volunteers from his division to remove a body."

Thus letting us know there's at least one Imperial division surrounding the building, and neatly nipping off any thoughts of a bloodless coup! 'Rhett grinned. *Better the devil one knows . . . Especially when he is such a clever devil.*

Marsh stood by as politics took Djetth from her side.

"What's that about 'local jurisdiction'? Eurydyce's neutral," Djetth said as he joined Tarrant-Arragon and The Saurian Dragon, and they each took a proffered weapon from Grievous and used it.

"So is An'Koor. For now," Tarrant-Arragon retorted. "But I'd rather not blockade it forever. Djinni tells me you should have all An'Koor, free and clear, with no strings. You don't even have to marry Martia-Djulia."

Marsh closed her eyes in anguish. Her brother's casual, public brutality took her breath away.

"I want Martia-Djulia!" Djetth stated.

Her eyes flew open. He was smiling at her. His raw, masculine words meant more to her than any number of I-Love-Yous panted during explosive sex.

"Oh, Djetth!" Her happiness was complete.

Djetth stood grinning at Marsh. From across the scented room he could smell how happy he'd just made her. It was a heady feeling to be responsible for such feminine joy.

Really, he should make an effort to get his tongue around romantic declarations more often. He would!

"Let's adjourn." Tarrant-Arragon stood up and approached the card table. No one looked back as silently efficient warriors removed the body. "As a matter of interest, what was the final card?"

Princely tact, Djetth supposed.

Grandmama Helispeta seemed to have a similar idea; she snagged 'Rhett's arm and drew him aside. "Djarrhett, dear, what on Earth was in that drink you gave me? I feel quite unsteady."

Djetth hung back as his uncle, The Saurian Dragon, and his cousin, The Terror of the Dodecahedrons, moved to the table to stare down at a fortune-teller's card.

Neither Ala'Aster-Djalet nor Tarrant-Arragon ought to be where they were, if virtue, the assumptions of primogeniture, and democracy reigned supreme. But they were both were very, very good at what they did. He, Djetth, was more interested in life, liberty, and the pursuit of happiness—with great emphasis on the pursuit of happiness.

Djetth collected Marsh, and, with his hand on the small of her back, guided her into the family circle.

"It's the five of Wands," Tarra said with only the slightest tremor in her voice. "The number five is the universal lever of change or the sign of disruption to come."

"I thought Wands were a sign of change?" Helispeta murmured from the shadows, where 'Rhett had apparently persuaded her that the hair of the dog was good for unsteadiness.

"They are, Hell. Change and fire. That is why the five of Wands is so very disruptive and dangerous."

"If you don't have other plans for these cards, Mother," Tarrant-Arragon said, "I'd like to frame this spread, and hang it in the Palace for Django-Ra's epitaph and as a warning to others."

Djetth bent his head close to Marsh's ear.

"Look at that card, Marsh. What does it remind you of?"

A bare-chested male battled a huge, fertile-green, fire-breathing dragon with wings like Scythian parachutes. He aimed three long staves up at the beast. At his side was a beautiful, long-legged female in a smutty tabard which did nothing much to hide a splendid, low-slung bosom that a male could bury his face in. She threatened their attacker with one flaming stave in each of her hands.

"It reminds me of us, fighting off Django-Ra's assassins," Marsh answered.

"Yes, my darling. That's us, fighting our personal dragons together. If any more come up, we can fight them, too."

He nuzzled his forehead against hers.

"And by the way, Marsh? There's something I've been meaning to tell you. Read my lips."

She blinked up at him.

And he whispered so quietly that not even a Djinn could hear, "I love you."

Epilogue
The Farmer-EMPEROR of An'Koor

EARTH DATE EQUIVALENT: FEBRUARY 1995

Vice-Imperial Palace, An'Koor

Djinni-vera was Jasmine. Marsh is Dogwood. That was an oversimplification, but in a nutshell, that was it. His first scent-love had been stolen from him, never to be returned.

It no longer mattered.

For Dogwood he tried a little harder, and had a lot more fun. The jasmine scent had been faint, and second-hand. Those who'd seen the film of Jason and Martia-Djulia had said his performance had been boring, self-centered. He was much happier, and freer—even when tied to a bed—with Dogwood.

Djetth leaned on the wraparound balustrade of their palace, overlooking the safety-netted, shellfish beds and the terraced vineyards and orchards.

Marsh was down there with the fish-farmers, up to her smooth knees in water, learning about oysters and pearls, and wearing a stylish but practical garment of her own design. Underneath, next to her skin, she wore a newly—and slightly more discreetly—tie-dyed T-shirt.

She'd found her niche. As An'Koor's Empress, her special interests were oysters, pearls, and contraception. Her rebellious streak had found a profitable and socially responsible outlet.

Marsh was a laughing, sparkling beauty.

Gone were the careful coifs and gravity-defying braids of her old, Imperial Palace life. She hadn't even tried to grow them back. Marsh was too busy for prolonged hairstyling, and too energetic to keep an elaborate do in place.

Where once her hair had been artfully arranged to balance a slightly full face, now her wind-blown crest of pale hair tumbled free about her shoulders. The wind and the water had put a curl into it.

Her alien diet had made her snow-shadow eyes a little brighter, a little more blue, and chased out the fleeting grayness. She saw better . . . when she wanted to.

Her glorious, matronly figure had melted away in An'Koor's lower gravity, and she took a wanton delight in the way she looked and felt. She was a perfect breeding weight. Djetth couldn't wait to find out if she was pregnant with twin daughters, which was what they'd been trying for.

A shadow slid over the balcony. Djetth turned and smiled a welcome, and Grandmama Helispeta joined him at the rail. Hell and Tarra had come to stay. Marsh loved suddenly having a mother and a grandmother. Djetth tolerated their unsolicited advice on how to be an

Emperor, and went among his subjects unarmed and bare-chested.

"There's something else you have to tell me, isn't there?" Emperor Djetthro-Jason I of An'Koor prompted, seeing her serious expression.

"I believe I should," Grandmama said.

"We're very happy," Djetth murmured a gentle warning. "You're not going to cast a cloud, are you?"

"Perhaps a very little one, dear. I never finished the story I began some days before Django-Ra's death. Martia-Djulia's conception was not the end of Django-Ra's wicked violations of what we consider natural law."

Djetth ran his forefinger up and down the crease between his eyebrows. "You are putting two and two together, aren't you, Grandmama?"

"Yes, dear," Grandmama agreed. "And this old lady may have her simple arithmetic badly wrong. My age . . ."

When you fall back on your age, Grandmama, you know and I know it's to deflect responsibility for whatever you wish to allege.

". . . There's talk about the paternity of Martia-Djulia's elder son, who is older than he ought to be. Either her first Mate, the War-star Leader, did not wait as he should have, or she was Mated to the War-star Leader to cover up a scandal."

"My one tyrannical indulgence is that I don't allow a free press on An'Koor," Djetth growled. "Talk doesn't bother us."

"It might bother Martia-Djulia's sons one day. Do you plan to let them run wild with their grandfather? If Henquist and Thor-quentin make Django-Ra's terrible, tragic mistakes, comparisons will eventually be seen."

Fair point, Grandmama.

"Djetthro-Jason, is it possible that Django-Ra could have attacked Martia-Djulia at The Island School for Princesses?"

Djetth thought of Marsh's terror of water and her inability to account for it, her scar, her dread of being bedjinned and the gaps in her memory. Something traumatic could have happened. It was no one's affair.

"Is this story coming to a conclusion, Grandmama?" he asked instead of encouraging speculation.

"Yes, my dear. We never did explain why, after so many years, Django-Ra decided that Martia-Djulia was such a danger to him that she had to die."

Djetth nodded. "I should like to know that."

"After Martia-Djulia became a widow, she found a way to go into reproductive hibernation. Life went on smoothly until Tarrant-Arragon became determined that she should Mate with Prince Djetthro-Jason.

"Django-Ra may have worried that you were not only the rightful Emperor but a real Djinn. Then, at your Mating, Martia-Djulia demonstrated publicly, and for the first time, that she had Django-Ra's distinctive gift. When she hurled you across the Throne Room, she ignited a firestorm of curiosity and speculation."

"Grandmama, you didn't say 'not only the rightful Emperor but a real Djinn' that way around by accident, did you?"

She smiled. She always said exactly what she intended.

"A Djinn can undo a bedjinning, dear. Hypothetically, if Martia-Djulia had been bedjinned, possibly to make her forget something inconveniently scandalous, a Djinn Mate could retrieve her memory."

Djetth narrowed his eyes at Helispeta. *I've been warned, haven't I? Some past events are better left forgotten, some lost memories are better not retrieved.*

No, I won't ask Marsh to remember. Her past doesn't matter. Nor does mine. She's never questioned my tattoo, and I certainly didn't need to invoke her memory of Jason to get her into bed.

"Someone paranoid about the status quo," she continued chattily, "might worry that, together, Djetthro-Jason and Martia-Djulia would piece together their history and lineage, and seek revenge. Or seek the throne. Either way, Django-Ra would not have a comfortable place in the new regime."

"So, we assume that Django-Ra was prepared to kill in order to make sure that nothing changed?" Djetth summarized. It made sense. As far back as his original Mating Day, Django had advised Tarrant-Arragon to kill him.

"Yes, dear, all things considered, I think the theory that Django-Ra did not want a regime change is much more appropriate than any other theory."

If a flower, fruit or vegetable looks like genitalia, it probably is an aphrodisiac . . . or so Tarra said.

Marsh stopped at the pea trellises to wonder what her mother would make of An'Koor's most popular export—a strange little hybrid legume that looked like a perky green bean growing out of a double pod containing two large peas.

She saw Djetth strolling towards her, tanned, bare-chested, head and shoulders taller than his adoring subjects, and grinning. She waved.

"Having fun?" he greeted her.

"How could I not be?" she laughed, gesturing at the green abundance around her.

"Those things remind me of something . . ." Djetth teased. "While we're on the subject of little pricks, do you think your sons might be bored at the Palace?"

Marsh had never considered that.

"I used to be a bit of a troublemaker," Djetth said seriously. "Boredom will do that. Then, Grandmama Helispeta sent me on an Outward Bound course, which is where groups of wild young human males, and some timid ones, are sent out into the Earth's wildernesses and taught to survive."

"So that's how you knew what to do on Freighter Island," she exclaimed. All of a sudden, so much that had been a mystery fell into place and made perfect sense.

"Yes. Ironic, isn't it? Do you think Henquist and Thor-quentin would like to go camping with me?"

"No." Marsh wasn't ready to talk about her delinquent sons, but at the same time her heart swelled with gratitude because Djetth was taking an interest. "If you gave Henquist or Thor-quentin a knife, they'd be likely to plant it between your shoulder blades," she said as if she were joking, because it was too embarrassing to be said any other way.

"Can they read?"

She nodded.

"Then, when Freighter Island is green again, we'll dump them there, with a variety of survival manuals and let them figure it out for themselves."

"You're hard!" She laughed, because he was wickedly funny and because she loved him with all her heart.

His answer was a true Djinn innuendo.

"Always!"

Prince Devoron-Vitan
(1900–1962)
mistress Helispeta
(1905–)

Ala'Aster-Djalet (1932–)
The Saurian Dragon from 1962–
wife #1 Freya (1937–1966)
wife #2 Djavena (1932–1975)
wife #3 Virginia (1933–1976)

Djarrhett ('Rhett)
(1967–)

Djinni-vera
(1976–)

Emperor Djohn-Kronos
(1900–1950)
wife #1 Djustine-Saturna (1915–1927)
wife #2 Helispeta (1905–)

Djason-Merkur
(1928–1961)
wife Djavena
(1932–1975)

Emperor Djerrold Vulcan V
(1927–)
wife Tarragonia-Marietta
(1936–)

Djetthro-Jason
(1960–)

Martia-Djulia
(1959–)

Tarrant-Arragon
(1956–)

Henquist

Thor-Quentin

— Child
\+ Other Children